Praise for Tale of the Dreamer's Son

"*Tale of the Dreamer's Son* is a riveting, painful, funny read from the author of the powerful *Evening Is the Whole Day*. I'd been waiting for this book. Nobody writes like Preeta Samarasan. Through astute characterization, sheer drama, evocative settings, superb prose, and blended language, Samarasan draws me into all the deep questions that rattle the foundations of her beloved Malaysia. I love this book in many ways, for the storytelling, for the music in her writing, for the images, but also for how it reminds me of how issues in Malaysia continue to mirror ours in Nigeria and many other parts of the world. What a fantastic, fantastic book!"
UWEM AKPAN, author of *Say You're One of Them* and *New York, My Village*

"Politics, religion, culture and love collide on every page of Preeta Samarasan's new novel. At once furious and funny, majestic and intimate, *Tale of the Dreamer's Son* is an ode to the glorious and complex mess that is Malaysia."
TASH AW

"Samarasan continues to be a wonder, a wryly vibrant, passionately astute chronicler of recent Malaysian history."
PETER HO DAVIES

•

Praise for Evening Is the Whole Day

"An impressive debut. The language bursts with energy, and Samarasan has a sure hand juggling so many distinct characters."
Publishers Weekly

Tale of the Dreamer's Son

Preeta Samarasan

Tale of the Dreamer's Son

WORLD EDITIONS
New York, London, Amsterdam

Published in the USA in 2022 by World Editions LLC, New York
Published in the UK in 2022 by World Editions Ltd., London

World Editions
New York/London/Amsterdam

© Preeta Samarasan
Published by arrangement with Agence littéraire Astier-Pécher
All rights reserved
Cover Image by Rockman, Alexis: *Host and Vector.* 1996. Oil on plywood.
© 2022. Digital image Whitney Museum of American Art / Licensed
by Scala
Author portrait © Guillaume Comte

Printed by Lake Book, USA

World Editions is committed to a sustainable future. Papers used by
World Editions meet the FSC standards of certification.

Library of Congress Cataloging in Publication Data is available

ISBN 978-1-64286-120-4

Twitter: @WorldEdBooks
Facebook: @WorldEditionsInternationalPublishing
Instagram: @WorldEdBooks
YouTube: World Editions
www.worldeditions.org

FOR R, R, & J
who are my favourite sceptics

"... and this made me also ambitious to leave some monument of myself behind me, that I might not be the only man exempted from this liberty of lying: and because I had no matter of verity to employ my pen in (for nothing hath befallen me worth the writing), I turned my style to publish untruths, but with an honester mind than others have done: for this one thing I confidently pronounce for a truth, that I lie: and this, I hope, may be an excuse for all the rest, when I confess what I am faulty in: for I write of matters which I neither saw nor suffered, nor heard by report from others, which are in no being, nor possible ever to have a beginning. Let no man therefore in any case give any credit to them."

– Lucian of Samosata, *Lucian's True History*, transl. Francis Hickes

"Begin all over again? It would be no good. It would all turn out the same—all happen again just as it has happened. For certain people are bound to go astray because for them no such thing as a right way exists."

– Thomas Mann, *Death in Venice*, transl. David Luke

"It is hardly my fault if his lordship's life and work have turned out today to look, at best, a sad waste—and it is quite illogical that I should feel any regret or shame on my own account."

– Kazuo Ishiguro, *The Remains of the Day*

CONTENTS

PART 3

PART 4

Annunciation

In the beginning was the word.

My father was twenty-nine years old when God said to him: *Rise, Cyril, and lead the way.* Like the Queen knighting somebody like that. Like a voice-over in a superhero movie.

Later my father would say, "I knew it was God because it was not one of my migraines. It was completely different." He would smile as he remembered it and that smile would remove him even further away from us. "I could feel God that day," he would explain. "Just like any of you can feel it when someone enters the room."

Dutifully we would picture it: God's breath rough and dry like a cat's tongue on the back of his neck. A smell of burnt earth and coal fires. But only many years later would I look back and wonder if he might have meant that day only. *On other days I looked for Him but where was He?*

What my father was said to have experienced was exactly what you imagine: a flash of light and the air shimmering like on a hot day above an endless road. Some said that it was more than a flash, that it had a human form of some kind, except that it came and went so quickly Papa was left standing in the upstairs front room of his father Ambrose's house on Old Klang Road with nothing but the memory of two eyes like eternal suns.

Every single day of his life from approximately age four my father had been going to the sundry shop across the street. He went there to buy their coconut biscuits: two each day, you know the type I am talking about, the colour of sawdust and sometimes you will find real sand and stones and bits of gunny-sack threads in them. He was a creature of habit with all the obstinacy that this implies but also all the loyalty: though he could not cross the street to buy his biscuits on May 13th, 1969, he could think of nothing else but the shop man and his family. All he could do was tremble and peer at the Malay Regiment boys marching down the street towards Mr Lim Loke Kee's premises.

A salient fact: when Cyril's mother Dorothy was eight months pregnant with him she witnessed the summary decapitation of a poor Chinese bugger who had failed to bow deeply enough to a Japanese soldier. Chop-chop and then the Chinese fler's head impaled on a stick for all to see. An excess of empathy swept through Dorothy, hotting up the waters in which her frog-limbed boy bobbed, throwing her on the spot into premature labour. Poor Dorothy didn't make it, but like Obelix with the magic potion, Cyril was infused with enough sorry-feeling and guilt to last him the rest of his life.

He pictured the Lims hidden sardine-packed in some storeroom sweating and being eaten alive by mosquitoes, holding kitchen knives and cangkuls and whatever they had managed to find. My father's heart went dup dup dup dup dup dup together with those eight hearts across the street, each beat of his matching each beat of theirs. When their hearts skipped a beat his did too.

Not that he and Loke Kee were best friends or anything of the sort. He did not even know Loke Kee that well: if you had asked him, which does Loke Kee like better, Milo or Horlicks? or, which of Loke Kee's five children is his favourite? he would not have been able to answer. My father was that type, that's all. The soft type, as some call it: he was the type to feel for whichever person or animal was suffering the most, to walk a mile in another man's shoes without being asked, to give a beggar fifty cents and keep only ten for himself. Even in his looks he was soft: curly brownish hair, fine bones like a bird, fair like custard. Could not take the cold, even on a rainy morning in Kuala Lumpur; at once he would pull out his grey monkey cap and cardigan. Leave him to his routine: oats for breakfast at seven o'clock, after lunch the newspaper, coconut biscuits for teatime, a half-hour stroll before the streetlights were switched on, Nat King Cole or The Platters after dinner. Weekday afternoons he gave individual English tuition at home.

Think of the conviction and passion required to uproot a creature like that and deposit him in the damp mists of Cameron Highlands. It is an uprooting worth witnessing if only for the drama of it, whether or not you believe in the big man upstairs. I myself do not believe, now itself I can tell you. But still I think back to that day, to my father crouching at the front window, to God's slash-and-burn smell, and I get a kind of chill at the nape of my neck. A good story is a good story.

There had been talk of trouble after the opposition gained so much ground in the general election, rumours flying here there everywhere. My father had been feeling uneasy for days but all the same it was the sight of it—the army boys clomping down the street in their black boots and their kneesocks and their Brylcreemed hair like a scene left over from the Japanese Occupation—that shocked him into realizing that his country would never be the same again. Behind those boys in uniform, the mob followed set-ting fire to anything they could get their hands on: cars motorcycles bicycles dustbins.

Look at my father gripping the windowsill, his long thin nose pressed to the crack between the shutters. His head throbs from the smoke. His lungs crackle and burn inside his chest. *It's coming it's coming it's coming*, he thinks. *I'm going to faint.* Then all of a sudden a sight so shocking his body can't even gather the wits to pass out: Loke Kee's fifteen-year-old son bursts out onto the street swinging his mother's meat cleaver. *The boy has gone amok berserk chee sin paithium*, whatever you want to call it in whatever language you like to call it in; the fact of his madness is the same in any language or none.

You could blame it on evil spirits or you could say it was panic. Or you could say that mental imbalance ran in the family. But the why matters not. Only the what and the when have any bearing on this narrative. Like a five-year-old boy playing "Kung Fu Fighting" the boy swings and swings that cleaver and then he starts to scream: "Balik kampung! Balik kampung! Balik kampung!"

Because that was how to hurt the Malays at that time and even now, i.e. to brand them all country bumpkins out of place in Kuala Lumpur. You see, the longer different peoples have lived together, the more expertly they can hurt each other. Which means that here in Malaysia we knew all the most wounding words to say to one another and we knew just how to say them. Flamboyantly enough to splash ourselves across front pages; in impassive monotones in playgrounds and offices; hissed under the breath in market-stall queues.

And screamed out in the hot streets in the middle of a riot. Loke Kee's son presses that button without knowing what he is doing and it works like magic: two of the soldiers—they also holding their guns with too-small shaking hands like children playing police and thief—zip round and shoot him. Bang-bang. The two bangs so close together that even my father who has not blinked for over ten minutes cannot tell which bullet killed the boy. He stares and stares at that boy in his spreading blood puddle until his mind begins to play tricks on him and he sees— oh, what-what he sees, you will think we also are another family of lunatics to hear it! Flashing purple lights in the sky. A tree bursting into bloom. The spirit of the dead boy soaring up like Ultraman.

Tricks, tricks, the mind is full of tricks, you can never

trust it. How to separate the tricks from the truth? I want—wanted—so much to believe. Consider Julian of Norwich and Margery Kempe and Joan of Arc. Consider also my father's medical history and theirs. I can only pass his story on to you and let you be the judge.

No sooner has the dead boy's ghost taken off into the bruised sky than my father sees two-three Malay Regiment boys drag Loke Kee and the rest of his family out into the street. He cannot make sense of the exact words but he grasps the gist of the soldiers' purposely pasar-fied Chinki-fied Malay: the *r*s crushed into *l*s and spat into their stunned faces; the choice of *lu* over *kamu* or *awak* or any of the half-dozen other ways our peoples have to denote the second person.

My father sees Loke Kee on his knees shaking his long head. He sees terror cloud the humiliation in all those familiar faces. He sees the soldiers' hands holding two or three by the scruff of the neck so that they cannot even shake their heads to beg.

As though to mirror Loke Kee in some empathy-building exercise gone too far my father falls to his knees. He closes his eyes tight-tight he tries to block his ears he shakes and cries, cries and shakes. And it is at that moment that God appears to him to urge, *Rise, Cyril, and lead the way. Only you can see the true path. Unite your people. Bring them together under Me. I am one but my names are many.*

Then and there Cyril collapses like Saul in the Bible. He falls backwards his head knocking down an antique brass pen holder, his shoulders one after the other banging the corner of his desk and then the wooden floor and his long legs toppling the chair. Boom dappa dappa dappa boom thud. Downstairs his three elderly spinster aunts are wondering what is going on asthma attack or seizure or what, but they themselves are shitting bricks, they will not go running up and down on those creaky floors attracting the attention of the mob and risking their own lives to save their nuisance nephew's. All his life they've been united in their resentment of the feckless and frivolous Dorothy ("forever pretending to be sick some more!") for saddling them with her offspring. So what if it wasn't his fault? It was even less theirs.

Only the servant girl for one brief moment considers slipping up the stairs to investigate. She thinks of motherless sensitive short-sighted Master Cyril. His blazing migraines, his heart thing, what was that English word, flutter or murmur or maybe it was both. She knows she ought to go and check—even if only to confirm her worst fears—but she has lived so long under the terrifying collective thumb of the aunts that she is paralysed: if she asked them wouldn't they snap *you keep quiet and mind your own business?* Her thin thighs are shaking inside her sarong her overfull bladder is throbbing to the erratic rhythms of the shouts and shots from outside she can't make it up the stairs she just can't. And my grandfather? Completely deaf the old man is. Sleeps through the whole thing lucky for him. The only one on that street who never hears the hullabaloo. In great bafflement he will read about it in the newspapers when it is all over.

When my father regains consciousness all is quiet. In the five-foot entryway of Loke Kee's shop there are three bodies: 1) Loke Kee 2) his son and 3) his old father. Three generations just like that. What happened to the women and children my father will never know. His story of that day ends just like it begins, with small details: the father's face as black as a dried buah kana in the evening light. The legs of his blue shorts as wide as two tunnels at the end of which Cyril can see the underpants yellowed with age.

Striped cotton underpants. That home-sewn type that they don't make anymore.

God whispers to him again: *Let it not have been in vain, Cyril. Let all these lives not have been wasted.* A thin hum rises in the distance like as though a failed generator has come back on. In the street someone is shovelling or scraping something with a metal utensil. Cyril does not want to know who or what exactly. He shuts his eyes again and turns from the window. *They have gone astray!* whispers God. *Show them. Show them my singular nature.*

My father brushes the salt crystals from his lower lashes. His spit still thinned with tears. He knows he should rise and in the name of the Lord declare ... what? *Speak, Cyril speak! In my eyes all men are equal.* Cyril Tertullian Dragon, twenty-seven years old, reluctant saviour, asthmatic prophet. *Okay okay Lord,* he sighs inside himself. *I am your servant.*

"Come off it," his aunts will say. "Cut it out. Of all your nonsenses this is the best/worst one yet. Please. Enough of it or you are going to land all of us in the lockup. This has nothing to do with our people! It is between the Chinese and the Malays. Leave them to settle it between themselves."

"Our people?" Cyril says. "They are all our people."

"Now is not the time to talk like a book or a film," they warn him. "It's all very nice and beautiful until somebody comes lunging at you with a parang."

"It's beautiful even then," he replies. "We all feel the same terror we all bleed the same blood we all die the same death. It's the most beautiful thing. It's the *only* beautiful thing. It's the only thing that can save this country."

The aunts bury their faces in their hands. So he is going to save the country. This insect-limbed son of his useless mother. This boy who had to be kept back from school for two years because of dead-mother dreams and hockey-field bullies. This boy who cannot swim or ride a bicycle or get a real job in the outside world.

My future father is not the only one who believes the May 13th riots have revealed a great truth to him: unbeknownst to him a man not quite twice his age is laying out the Dilemma of his people and his own master plan for saving the nation. His solution is the exact opposite of my father's: some people are *our people* and other people are their rivals. Simple as that. Distinct categories. Clarify and label, sift and sort and seal off, cancel out Darwinian realities with government policy. The Father of Modern Malaysia and my own father will never meet in real life but their dreams will circle each other in slow motion for seventeen years until one dream snuffs the other out so deftly so neatly so elegantly.

"Go right ahead then," Cyril's aunts say with a shrug and a cackle in 1969. "Go tell it on the mountain. Let's see who comes flocking to hear your good news."

And so he does and they do. It is a flock of only nine-plus-baby (and should baby Kiranjit count at all? Those who follow on their own adult legs and those who are dragged along: the difference between them is after all the subject of my tale). But they are a flock nevertheless. Some feel they have already lost everything they had to lose; some feel they have never had anything to lose to begin with. That what people think they have to lose is in truth nothing but illusion after illusion. They are survivors of cancer and bankruptcy, abuse and loneliness. They are predeceased by husbands or children or babies. They are concubines and cuckolds and disowned offspring.

"Yet only dare to imagine what could be!" Cyril Dragon tells them. "Imagine if we each of us saw the Divine in our fellow man. Imagine if we could all close our eyes and feel that Divine breath moving through all of us as though we were nothing but cells of one infinite eternal body."

Obediently they imagine and they see what he means: it is the only beautiful thing.

Presentation of the Narrator

Which is to say, of the tale made flesh: the incarnation of the Word. Do I exist without my story? Doubtful. Debatable. I tell, therefore I am.

My name—for now that you know my parents' and brother's names it is time you made the acquaintance of the family's lowest rung—is Clarence Kannan Cheng-Ho Muhammad Yusuf Dragon. To those who know me well I am Kannu which in Tamil means not only beloved but also eye. Thus I am the Eye of the Dragon.

Of course the registration clerk in Tanah Rata never approved my name. The man tapped his pen on the form like a woodpecker like that and said to my father, "You cannot have twenty-five names. You cannot be Christian and Hindu and Buddhist and Muslim at the same time. This is against the law."

"Who says? What law?" said my father.

The clerk dug his nose a bit and thinking-thinking he inhaled deeply and exhaled slowly. He was clearly looking for excuses and ways to find fault, in short anything that would allow him to teach this arrogant Don't-Know-What-Race bugger a lesson. Leafing through the documents my father had brought he found his next move.

"First of all I cannot put your name as the father if you don't show me your marriage certificate," he said. "Don't have certificate means—"

"Okay then," my father said. "Just leave that part blank."

"Leave it blank! Leave it blank! So you mean your son will have no father?"

"If he is my son, as you say yourself, then I am his father isn't it?"

The clerk shifted his weight from his left buttock to his right. "Secondly," he said, "you cannot give your son this Muslim name, Muhammad Yusuf. Only Muslim can have Muslim name. And you not Muslim. Am I right? Thirdly—"

"There is only one God for all of us," my father said. He flashed the clerk a bright and saintly beam that lifted his eyebrows. He went on, "The same God with different names. We are all Muslim. We are all Christian and Hindu and Buddhist also. I want to give my child one name from every Malaysian religion, that is all."

"*Thirdly*, you are already in the wrong. Yes or not, *in the wrong*? Because here I see your wife's name Muslim, but you not Muslim. Where is your Muslim name? Please?"

Still smiling my father bowed slightly and announced like Raj Kapoor like that, style only, "My heart is Muslim."

The clerk took off his spectacles and rubbed his eyes with his pointer finger and thumb.

To this day I do not know why then and there he did not call up some big boss or other to come and question my father some more. I got only one guess which is that he had taken too much sambal with his breakfast nasi lemak and needed to run for the jamban. In his head he was already picturing the peeling white-painted door to the amenities with that glorious red word on it: *TANDAS*. Oh you can laugh and say my mind is literally in the shithouse, but I have spent the greater part of my life studying the Lesser Malaysian Government-Department Desk Clerk, Kingdom Phylum Class Order Family Genus Species. With all the teabreaking and coffeebreaking that thesemilkfed UMNO bureaucrats do and with the vast amounts of oily goreng pisang and ubi and cempedak that they consume daily, is it any surprise if they were plagued by irregular bowels? Our clerk winced and decided that sooner or later somebody else would find out about this fool and his heretic wife anyway, why should he be the one to stick his neck out?

"Okayfine mister," he said. "Why don't you just choose a Hindu name and a Christian name and stop there? Hindu and Christian is okay. Biasa aje, yes or not? Nobody will look at you macam you dah gila."

"Why should I care how people look at me?" my father said. "The only thing that matters is that I am doing what is right. If you—"

"Mister ... Mister ... what is your name now?" The clerk put back his spectacles and brought my father's identity card up to his nose.

My father kept going. "If you do things differently people will always look at you one kind isn't it? But where would we be today if nobody ever decided do things differently?"

"Mister Dragon! Even your own name also very funny lah! Ada ke orang with a name Dragon? Anyway"—he gave my father that type of nice big smile full of special patience for the hopeless case—"the other problem is also this Cheng-Ho Beng-Ho! Basket! You cannot simply find your child's name from the history textbook!"

"No, no Laksamana please, no title necessary, just Cheng-Ho. It is because we admire the Admiral, haha, admire-als are for admiring after all isn't it? But no, seriously, encik, if you know anything about Admiral Cheng-Ho, then—"

"You ingat kita orang takde kerja lain ke?" the clerk said. And although Cyril knew it was a rhetorical question, a part of him wanted to say, *Yes yes of course you have other work but* this *my good man this is exactly what you should learn for your work. Learn this history and your pen-pushing and box-ticking will be transformed.* But it was the sudden change in the clerk that held him back: the man's voice was tired now. His lips thick and flabby and slow like as though he had suffered a stroke while my father was talking. Gone was the mean, bullying attitude.

With renewed benevolence my father offered, "Do you know, Admiral Cheng-Ho was born a Muslim? In fact his father and grandfather were hajjis. And he himself made the pilgrimage to Mecca, but he also built a great monument in Ceylon, a monument to Buddha and Shiva and Allah—"

"Got thirty people behind you already, mister," the clerk muttered. "No need to waste your breath."

While his left hand rubbed the back of his thick neck his right hand was already crossing out this and that and scribbling here and there on the form my father had given him. Tup-tup-tup just like that he pushed the form across his desk to my father, toppled his chair as he jumped to his feet, and disappeared through a door in the back. In those few seconds the door was open, my father glimpsed the insides of the government. He saw a dim, narrow corridor made even narrower by the filing cabinets on both sides; he saw chests of drawers so full they could no longer be closed; he saw clerks eating goreng pisang that surely would leave oil stains on the papers piled up on their desks, clerks drinking cincau with straws out of dripping plastic bags, and clerks redoing their lipstick after eating goreng pisang and drinking cincau. And seeing all this, he picked up the edited form and confirmed that as he expected the clerk had censored my name to Clarence Kannan. He snaked his long arm through the opening in the window, took the clerk's still-uncapped pen, and added: *Cheng-Ho Muhammad Yusuf Dragon*. Could even write it nice and neat, no need to squeeze up his handwriting, because the blanks were made to fit five-syllable-son-of-six-syllable Tamil names and the quadruple-barrelled names of Chinese Christians. Nevertheless in his eagerness to make a hasty exit he did not attempt to tamper with the clerk's carbon copy.

So I suppose my name is debatable depending on

whether you prefer official or unofficial stories but at least now you have the choice.

As you cannot even fart in this country without giving your name–age–race–religion–ic number–length of your dicky bird–colour of your morning stool, one gets into the habit of it. Therefore please find enclosed herewith my remaining biodata very quickly please just hold your noses and swallow.

PLACE OF BIRTH: Muhibbah Centre for World Peace, somewhere between Brinchang and Tringkap, Cameron Highlands, Malaysia.

PLACE OF DEATH: Up there in the hills I was born and down here in the valley I will die. Right here in fact. In this no-name no-face apartment in the choked chrome-glittering boiling city of Kuala Lumpur. It is an apartment like millions of others in this city and its satellites: brand new, shiny white floors like a bloody hospital, balcony for drying clothes, convenient to shopping centres. Good enough. My body is not old but I have nowhere else to go and nothing else to do. I'm over. Finished. Just biding my decades until body and soul can come to an agreement on closing shop.

AGE: Younger than I act but older than I look.

SEX: Here is the time and place for one of those uncle jokes. *Not as often as I'd like. Yes please! Whenever I can get it.* Oh all right. I am a man pure and simple. Not one of those poor neither-here-nor-there creatures that elicits such revulsion in the hearts of the club-wielding defenders of our morals. One penis. Two testicles. Chest hair and a shave every morning. Satisfied?

OCCUPATION: Tuition teacher–Liar–Sadman–Poorman.

ADDRESS: Apartment Anything-Also-Can, Jalan Three-Hours-to-Get-Anywhere, City of Malls.

RACE (ah, I know you were waiting for this, my friends, for without the *f-a-c-t-s* how can you know where to place me what to think how to judge me?): One part bona fide soogee-cake-eating Eurasian one part Anglo-Indian well and truly stirred together on father's side, two parts mostly Malay on mother's side, good unfiltered Malay stock—and though unfiltered stock is cloudy as those of you with any kitchen experience will know, who really cares about the cloudy bits in this country when you have the correct name and face and faith? Of the impurities in Malay stock we must never speak lest we blur the distinction between ourselves and Those Who Came Later. Therefore let the record show that I never mentioned the dash of Arab trader here, the splash of white missionary there, the pinch of Chinese thanks to some saucy sailor who put his anchor down in the personal port of one of my great-great-great-grandmothers. I was 1Malaysia in the flesh before our man Najib ever came up with the catchy concept to distract us while he emptied our coffers and killed off those who threatened to sniff him out. I mean to say: what could be a better symbol of National Unity than the product of nations that have cleaved unto each other and become One? The living proof of harmonious interethnic relations: that's what I am. As though God in His heaven declared preemptively to our future Prime Minister: you want Unity, I will give you the ultimate Union, ho ho ho! How do you like them apples?

Turns out those in power don't like these particular apples all that much, do they? From which one could conclude that 1) some people are never happy; and 2) the matter of Harmony and Unity is slightly more complicated than what meets the eye on a shiny billboard. Because smooth and productive relations between the Races don't count for anything in our nation if the end result isn't (which brings us to the next item on my form) an increase in numbers for the correct—

RELIGION: Officially I do after all increase said numbers. But what I feed the official records of the System is one thing. What I tell well-meaning guardians of my purported faith is, well, the same thing. But for you dear reader I have a one-time-only while-stocks-last special offer of the truth: I do not believe. My father believed in all gods and to compensate for his folly I believe in none.

EYE COLOUR: Brown mud.

HAIR COLOUR: Grey mud.

BLOOD COLOUR: Red plus a bit of blue equals purple (like every other bugger's mostly Malay bloodline mine has royal aspirations).

HEART COLOUR: Ha! Let us say indeterminate. You will have to decide for yourself at the end of my tale.

Of Namesakes and Lineages

Let us call him by his old name. The name by which we knew him before the Malays became Arabs and the Chinese became Mandarins. In those days Kong Hee Fatt Choy had not yet lost out to Gong Xi Fa Cai and Cheng-Ho was not yet Zheng-He.

By today's standards Laksamana Cheng-Ho's story is riddled from beginning to end with sins and ugly notions. The mixing and equating of diverse faiths; the meddlings of foreign intruders; porous racial and religious and geographic boundaries; the supposed irrelevance of God's will as manifested in the bodies He creates for each and every one of us. For Cheng-Ho was born a boy but with two slices of a sharp infidel blade he ceased to be one.

You'll be glad to know that unlike Cheng-Ho I draw the line at castration without consent but as to the rest: what passes for progress when you look at GDP and all its visual markers (number of malls skyscrapers luxury hotels gated communities) suddenly smells like the decline and fall of civilization when you compare the Laksamana's world to ours. At the peak of his career the Laksamana built a great shrine to all faiths. This before we had the word interfaith with all its nasty Orwellian undertones and despite the fact that he had inherited three generations of Islam at birth: his father and grandfather were hajjis. Yet wherever Cheng-Ho went he demanded that equal offerings be made to the Buddhist and the Hindu and the Muslim shrines because God is One and we are all brothers. What the poor Laksamana would say if he could see us using all our resources to build walls instead of bridges! Protecting our hoards with higher and higher gates and erecting monuments to our own hubris to one-up the other fler. The Admiral would rise from his ashes to set us right.

For my father he was a natural model: a skilled diplomat; a formidable warrior (oho yes my father may have been a different kind of warrior but a warrior he was); a man in whom eclectic influences had produced all-embracing impulses. My father undoubtedly drew inspiration from his varied reading material but rewind his story a few more years and you will see that heterogeneity ran in his very blood. He was only the latest descendant of a variously proud and variously upright Indo-Anglian family that could supposedly trace its ancestry all the way back to one Francis Drake whose ship the Golden Hind was almost smashed on a reef in the Moluccas in 1579. In other words: as mixified as we come even by the standards of this peninsula and its surrounding islands.

Francis himself was known to the Spanish as El Draque, or The Dragon (even though when you look at him in his tights and bloomers and goatee he looks like a bloody pondan). The bastard son who sired our line, James, could not call himself Drake so he took the nickname and wore it proudly—and why not? Dragons are fiery and proud and not to be trifled with whereas a Drake is nothing but a male duck.

By the eighteenth century our family was English Portuguese Indian Dutch Chinese. What remained was only to add a drop of Malay, stir stir mix mix and we would be the whole history of Malaysia in microcosm. The perfect advertisement for the forthcoming 1Malaysia phantasm if they could have imagined such a thing. Except back then they had no slogans and no advertisements. They were exactly the opposite of us: all action no talk. When James Dragon lands up in the new colony of George Town in 1792 he finds that the great Captain Light himself, finder-keeper of the island, has a dusky-skinned mistress and, like a man truly ahead of his time, is busy 1-ing up Malaysia before the country even has a name.

For the next two hundred years we Dragons do not budge from the Malay peninsula and Singapore. Oh, we go this way and that way and that way and this way but there we are for two hundred years growing roots so tough and fat that you cannot walk around any city there without tripping on them.

Well. That was our prehistory. There was a time when the word *prehistory* could not even have crossed my lips because in this country we like to pretend nothing existed before us. By which I mean that *they*— our lords and masters— liked to pretend their princes and sultans sprang from the forehead of Allah in a land without form, and void, or at any rate uncontaminated by lesser faiths; and darkness was upon the face of the deep. And the spirit of UMNO moved upon the face of the waters. And UMNO said, Let there be civilization, let there be plantations and mines and mosques and schools, let there be villages and ports and markets and schools: and there was civilization. That is the official narrative of the august standard-bearers of the United Malays National Organisation. That is our creation myth accepted and perpetuated by all the good vassals of the Party.

They have their myths, I have mine. Here's the thing: even when you were there and you think you have proof, the truth is that there is only your story versus my story. There are a billion stories and until you have heard them all you got no special claim to The Story so you know what? You may as well shaddup and listen to mine.

Operation Lalang

being the name given to that National Weeding Program in which one hundred and six people (among them my father and his followers) were arrested under the Internal Security Act. Having told you about our beginnings in my father's visitation from God it is only fair I tell you about our endings. All the cards on the table and everything out of the way: I am like that only.

Here is the thing about lalang (Latin: *Imperata cylindrica*): you cannot afford to close one eye and let the insidious stuff grow. It is a ferocious and redoubtable foe. Its roots go deeper than you can imagine. If you try to kill it with fire you will end up burning all the surrounding trees while the lalang itself will come back stronger than ever. If you grab it with bare hands it will cut you: along its fine-toothed edges are embedded invisible shards of glass. For too long the rightful owners of this country had let all these buggers take advantage of their tolerance: the opposition rabble-rousers the so-called journalists the missionaries the activists the bigmouth too-big-for-their-boots Chinamen. All the scum elements who had forgotten how to be grateful for what they had. What they had was peace and prosperity and the right to live off the fat of a land that was not theirs by blood. What they wanted was more more more because (China)man is by nature greedy.

These are the crimes of which they stood implicitly accused: Fomenting unrest inciting racial hatred stirring up sensitive issues. You know I know lah. No need to charge them with anything also let alone put them on trial.

Sensitive means sensitive isn't it? For a country like Malaysia to survive those with any decent sense of patriotism loyalty love-for-country had to not-talk about nasty matters. The main problem was not the nastinesses (real or imagined) themselves; the question was how to discourage the masses from making a big hoo-ha about every little thing and train them instead in the art of not-talking. That these greedy Chinamen and rowdy Indians were up in arms because the National Language was supposedly being forced upon them in their university departments and their special vernacular schools: was it not enough that they had university departments devoted to their non-National languages, that they had vernacular schools? The beauty of the National Language was it already had a graceful description of such people. *Give them your calf and they'll want your thigh.* But give them your thigh and then what? They would swallow you whole. They were pendatang but they didn't want you to call them pendatang: what kind of a demand was that? The word was made to be used but if you used it they held you hostage with their tantrums.

And then all this nonsense about so-called forced conversion. One had to look at the thing from all angles: people had minds of their own did they not? If they wanted to convert to Islam because they understood the benefits of it why should that be considered forcing? Anyone who had had a chance to read the scriptures and think about Truth with an open mind would want to convert to the right religion: how was that the government's fault? On one side you had the spiritual benefits and on the other side (not that anything was as important as the hereafter) you had the many benefits of assimilating. It had always been this way: your blood could be Indian or Chinese or Thai or Turkish and as long as you were Muslim you would be accepted into the Malay fold. To see this as *forcing* rather than evidence of the open-armed deeply accepting welcoming nature of the

Malay people was sheer bad faith no two ways about it. Anyone who wanted to become Malay should be able to become Malay and why should there not be rewards for this?

When you had all this plus the indisputable evidence (read the holy books just read and you'll see) that Islam was the way of life God wanted for his people then you could not deny that the loyalties of those who still refused to assimilate must lie elsewhere. Always they were plotting and scheming always this fifth column threatening the country's very soil choking weakening causing visible and invisible damage: if you wanted to talk about forced conversion then look at what the non-Muslims especially the Christians were doing. Preaching and proselytizing passing out their Bibles in every language and collecting for their so-called charities which when you looked closely were nothing but missionary operations. It was no great secret that they had enticed a few Malays away from Islam. In fact rumour had it that one apostate had gone so far as to become a pastor at a Baptist church in Petaling Jaya.

Now the Chinese were planning boycotts and strikes and whatnot all because they suspected the government of trying to unChinese their Chinese schools. Like as though they had forgotten that this was Tanah Melayu not China. Which people on earth would not be feeling a bit uneasy seeing this kind of insurrection? Who could blame the Malays for marching in the streets? All that kissing of the keris and threatening to soak it in Chinese blood was just a bit of theatre really an unfortunately necessary reminder that history must not repeat itself that May 13th 1969 must not happen again etc. etc. but perhaps it was excessive or ill-timed. Paranoia was rampant. Nerves were frayed. And then finally one random fler choosing this moment to run amok out of all the moments he could have chosen and out of all the areas he could have chosen he chose Chow Kit which sat nicely between a Malay area and a Chinese area both simmering seething spitting sparks ...

Time for our good Prime Minster Dr M to swing into action and no doubt about it: it had to be quick and drastic. Pull out the lalang by the roots with thick-gloved hands; douse the earth in weed killer. The only possible solution. No one could get the situation under control but the big man himself. On the 27th of October the redoubtable Dr issued his orders. Who whispered names into his ear who helped him draw up the list who made sure my father's name was included we will never know. But the black vans setting out to bring back their quarries were only the beginning. One by one Dr M-for-Maestro silenced all the cacophonous sections of that renegade orchestra once and for all. Banned the rallies. Shut down all the treasonous newspapers. Blacklisted the potstirring organizations. Defrocked the stubborn judges. And as a spectacular grand finale—before an audience holding their breath at the edge of their seats—sacked the Lord President. Time for a fresh start. A clean-slate country.

You see, Dr M and my father were both visionaries, but the former had understood what the latter had failed to: that to build a new world it is not enough to sow seeds quietly in your own little patch. To build something new you have to strip away the old. Melt it down. Dissolve its bones in acid if necessary. Before the rest of the world had time to turn its slow heavy head away from all the more pressing matters (wars and famines and the imminent fall of the iron curtain) our mad doctor's power would be impossible to challenge. Sikit-sikit lama-lama menjadi bukit. The whole mountain erected in that smooth Malaysian way that relied upon the key elements of our national character: politeness and apathy. Or call it pragmatism if you must. Cari makan. Which is more important: abstract principles or food in the belly?

So it was, that in October 1987 when I was ten years old my life as I knew it ended. The old me began his slow death while the new one waited to be born.

And now all these many years later I am here to stand up and be counted one hundred and six times. But beyond the counting you will reach my limits. For what do I know of those other stories? As I have said: I can only tell my own but if you ask me it's as good as anyone else's. The tale of a single sad lalang shoot. My father and mother and brother (whose claim to this story is perhaps strongest) are not able to speak for themselves at the present time for one reason or another. And so the task falls to me to make my story theirs too. I must close my eyes and open my mouth. Let them take possession of my memory and my tongue. Tell it like they lived it.

PART 1

Cinta Pandangan Pertama

(Love at First Sight)

My mother and my brother washed up at the Muhibbah
Centre for World Peace on a fine and sweet May morning
two years before I was born. Nowadays in this godforsaken
country every morning all year long is hot and stinking
and, often as not, clouded with dubious Indonesian haze.
But in those days every morning was fine and sweet regardless of the month. One took it all for granted.

Reza was six and my mother twenty-eight. Straight out
of school she'd gone to work for the newspaper and now she
had nine years under her belt. Nine years of smoky inky
newsrooms; nine years of ballcarrying and arselicking at
the Press Club; nine years of ministers' and towkays' hands
lingering too long on a friendly knee pat; nine years of
I-scratch-your-back-you-scratch-mine arrangements with
policemen and lawyers and judges. Tired of the game and
unlucky (yet again) in love she had begun to wonder if
there could be more to life.

It was 1975. Smack in the middle of those funny in-
between years after the May 13th riots but before Mahathir's Machiavellian race-baiting dictatorship. A few mutterings of discontent about the New Economic Policy
peppered the atmosphere but who could really see the
magnitude of our transformation-in-progress? It was less
than ten years since P. Ramlee had romanced Chandra
Shanmugam to the tune of "Oh My Darling, Clementine."
(Malay boy darling-darlinging an Indian girl on the big
screen!) The village tok dalang could use his wayang kulit

puppets to tell stories straight out of the Hindu epics and no Islamists popped up to denounce them and blacklist their art. A Malay in those days was not yet a glorified flat-faced Arab. The beckon and tease of a lady's kebaya was a joy to be savoured. If you had told them the sack silhouette of the tudung labuh would one day replace it they would've laughed in your face. Muslim or non-Muslim a little bit of Sex Appeal was nothing to be ashamed of in those days.

Mama was an unadulterated product (asli-tulen-sejati!) of that breezy post-war country. Now twilight was falling upon it but not a happy glowing twilight. In her kitten heels Mama stepped straight down a side exit—and into my father's Utopia—dragging Reza by the hand. She knew she was doing something risqué, something guaranteed to earn the disapproval of those who sit in judgement. The knowledge delighted her greatly.

She had hired a taxi for the drive up to the hills. At first the weather-beaten taxi driver had shaken his bristly head. He'd been hearing stories about that place for five years. Of course the house was already infamous before that. How long had it sat empty after the Scottish tea planter who had built it had abandoned it? He'd built it for his wife and when she'd run off with some playboy he'd left it for the jungle to eat. People said his ghost lingered there and some-times all the local favourites too, pontianak and hantu this and hantu that. Pontianak lah, drug addicts lah, you name it it haunted that ruined house but at least the locals had had the good sense to stay away. What to do though, the place was built by one gila fler so naturally another gila fler would come from somewhere to take his place.

The taxi driver knew that Cyril Dragon and all his crack-pot followers by sight. Their rickety van and their earnest mousy faces. The way they would come and kacau you with their bunkum leaflets first thing in the morning when you were quietly enjoying your soft-boiled egg and kaya toast in the kopitiam. "Tau mo lo," he said. "Itu lumah saya talak pigi."

But my mother begged. For this she put on her best schoolgirl manners. "Sopan santun lemah lembut," she said. "Please lah Uncle. Look"—she gestured at my angel-faced brother whose feet did not reach the taxi floor—"my son so small, how can we climb all the way up, Uncle?"

The taxi man sighed and rubbed a hand down his leathery tea-coloured face. In the rearview mirror he considered her doe eyes and her soft guileless mouth. He felt a yielding in his chest. A crumbling and a slow trickle. "Okay," he said. "Okay, you give me a bit extra, I take you."

White and yellow butterflies were flitting among the hydrangeas and roses. As the taxi drew up to the front entrance of the house faint cloud shadows drifted across its stone walls so that the house appeared to be gathering and regathering the weathered skin of its face. Now a frown. Now a pout. Now a lifting of its brow in wonderment. Every tree quivered its tender green leaves. The sap-spiked air trembled with birdsong.

All her life Salmah had been searching for something. All her life it had been just around the next corner. All through the pleasant-enough Kuala Kangsar childhood the good-enough exam marks the decent-but-not-enthralling steady job, the Thing had been imminent. At times she had associated the Thing with the sensation of falling in love and those early days of romance. But invariably after three months six months a year the feeling would fizzle and dull. Perhaps nothing great was ever going to happen to her after all; perhaps her lifelong certainty that the meaning of life would be blazingly revealed to her was a delusion. And then at the lowest the most despairing point of her life a chance conversation at a Deepavali open house had introduced her to the astonishing ideas of one Cyril Dragon. "You simply must go and see him for yourself," one Mrs Subramaniam had said. "Such incredible peace you'll feel immediately. Such bliss." Salmah had looked at Mrs Subramaniam shovelling mutton biryani into her mouth and thought what a joke she was what a cliché to blather on about bliss when it had changed nothing about her own life—but Salmah would be different. Already she felt a tingling at the nape of her neck.

By the time the taxi was snaking its way up that hillside, it had turned into a full-body tingling. And when it coughed her up in front of the porch she could barely hold her weight on her legs barely breathe to say, "Come boy come Reza here we are."

Never before had any of her searching turned up anything like that dim humming house in the hills. The woody smell of it. The soft cool shadows in the stairwell. The contented faces of all of them all these lucky people and then at last *his* face. The man she had heard so much about. Cyril Dragon with his skin out of an old Dutch painting like as though he was bathed in a light all his own. His grave gentle eyes and my god the colour of them: what to even call it? A light gold. The colour of sunlight or honey. The heaviness under them still new; the lines at the corners still barely perceptible. His slender yet solid hands with their square nails. He had a beautiful sadness about him. He wore it with dignity like the cape of a cardinal.

What my father and his ten followers saw first: those thickly lined eyes. Then that sheer lace kebaya. And that magazine hair. A proper bouffant with a perfect curl on each cheek.

Add to this aura of glamour the remarkable coincidence of her name and you will understand the excitement and incredulity following her arrival at the Centre. It was as though my father's followers had been jolted out of their exalted mission to fall headfirst into somebody's school-play version of a P. Ramlee film. The prettiest girl had been picked to play the lead as usual; as in every convent-school production the male lead would be played by a stout girl with a pancake face and the singing would be a fraction out of tune. But here Mrs Arasu—the Ceylonese maami of the community—stepped forward to consider the details. She was a woman comprised entirely of spheres and circles: the sphere of her body that far from being flabby was firm and neat as a well-made plum pudding; the perfect sphere of her tight little hair bun; the sharp circle of the giant pottu on her forehead; the smudged circles of her specs and behind them the enormous blurry circles of her eyes. When she had been widowed five years ago at the age of fifty-six she had found that relief was her primary reaction. Among her late husband's innovations: limiting the use of the electric fans to an hour per week; rationing the number of ikan bilis allowed to each family member when she prepared nasi lemak; buying heavily discounted rotten vegetables from the market at the end of the day; stealing the children's marker pens to black his shoes because polish was too costly. With him finally dead and her children settled in London and Perth she was free at last to devote herself to loftier causes. Yet notwithstanding her five years of nourishing the Mind and the Spirit her eyes had remained matchmaker-sharp:

"This Salmah like a lidi stick next to the famous one," she said. "You turn her sideways she'll disappear. Whereas P. Ramlee's woman ..." With her two hands she illustrated the twin cones of Mama's famous namesake's breasts.

Out of the chorus of tittering arose an urgent whisper.

"She's definitely Malay isn't it?"

"Sure Malay lah. The son looks mixed but not the mother."

The brief silence that followed was broken by Hilda Boey, a mournful city pigeon of a woman with wide-set eyes and a downturned mouth. Her scalp showed through her brittle post-chemotherapy perm. Her receding chin receded even further as she haltingly spelt out their collective fears.

"I only hope people don't find out and think we're trying to convert other people from their religion." Then she pigeonstepped backwards as though she might already have said too much. But when news of these concerns reached my future father he said only: "All are welcome here. All means all. If we start to make exceptions then we have defeated our own purpose."

It was not what you—reading this with the benefit of hindsight not to mention lashings of judge-judge-wink-wink superiority—might think. What Cyril Dragon wanted in the beginning was simply to do the right thing. Moral consistency. Upholding his principles. Oh yes I believe that I really do. Perhaps Mrs Arasu with her one-track maami mind was already telling herself: *In the end all men are the same. Even holy men think with their down-there instead of their up-here.* But Cyril saw the sparse facts of the case: a woman not yet thirty alone with child-plus-suitcase. And that boy—hazel eyes and cherry lips and curls that shone red in the sun. But look more closely at his angel face and what looked back at you was the type of wisdom a child that age should not have.

And after all wasn't this what they had been awaiting for five years? How could they claim to be building a new society out of the ruins of 1969 if no Malays were involved? There could be no reconciliation between the two sides if one side was simply absent.

On Salmah's very first evening at the Centre, Cyril invites her to lead the Bismillah at Evening Devotional. The way her cheeks and chin dimple in surprised acquiescence! The bowing of that long thin neck to avoid those fourteen pairs of hostile eyes! For a brief moment Cyril thinks he will not be able to bear it. She is shivering very slightly—no one can see it but him—and he wants to tell her, *Never mind, let's find you a shawl and a cup of hot Milo.* But she has already begun.

"Bismillah ir-rahman ir-rahim ..."

Beside her Reza stiffens his shoulders into a beetle shell. He is embarrassed for Mama and by Mama: all those people staring at her and that too-sincere way she has of closing her eyes. He looks at Cyril and thinks: *Action-action only*

that man. Talking like the lord and master of the whole universe.
The way he moves his mouth and eyebrows. Just that alone
could make you sick. Reza had not wanted to come here.
He'd not wanted to leave the house in KL for some *adventure*
as Mama put it when trying to trick him into enthusiasm.
Why must Mama always be searching searching searching
for one thing or another? He is tired of quests and he does
not like this place: the rotty wood smell and everybody putting on saintly faces and sitting on the hard cold floor. The
mumbo-jumbo talk. The pompous sissy man in front. Only
action-action. Why do adults—teachers mothers fathers—
always like this type of puffed-up fool? Why can't they see
through the airs people put on to impress them? Unable to
take another moment of the spectacle Reza reaches out a
finger to draw in the windowsill dust. The sill is damp with
the promise of an imminent drizzle but when he puts his
finger to his nose the smell is like something burning.

Batchmates

It was nearly impossible for people to see anything else if Reza was in the room. One could try to explain this phenomenon away by pointing to his exotic hybrid features and complexion but the truth is that these were only one small element of his overall charisma. He had a donnowhattocallit, an aura, a fierce inner light by which I do not mean a light of kindness or wisdom as it is usually understood but a light of pure being. You wanted to be close to it without being seen; you wanted to hide in the bushes and look and look and look at him and have your fill of the spectacle.

"How old?" people take turns to ask Mama. "Your son how old?"

She turns to Reza and ruffles his hair. "How old are you boy?" she says and then immediately: "These aunties and uncles are asking how old are you."

He sees that she thinks they are both being evaluated in some way. He sees that whether or not he trusts these people—and he does not—she needs them to like her.

"Five," he says to his swinging feet.

She smiles. "Five and a half. Six years old this year."

The attention in the room shifts like as though the hand turning the radio dial has finally settled on a station.

"Another one!" Mrs Arasu cries. Her round eyes gleam behind their owl spectacles. Her beaming grin is full of too-straight teeth. "Got a lot of 1969 babies here. Leo for example. The cook's son. That boy there." She points with her chin.

"Oh!" Salmah says. "He looks so small, I thought he was at the most four!"

"His mother," Mrs Arasu says with a thrust of the chin at the woman serving the food, "that Neela there, she's the one who cooks for us, well, she landed up here just like you. Not too long after the rest of us. But she came in the night. Walked all the way up the hill in her Japanese slippers with a baby and all, hoo wah, no joke I tell you."

The *no joke* gives Salmah pause for thought: is it supposed to imply that her own commitment paled next to the mother of this boy? What was her cushy taxi ride compared to the other woman's long trudge in the black night? She looks at the woman bustling in and out of the room clearing plates bringing in dishes wiping spills and doing all of this with a perfectly closed face. With no effort at all she pictures this woman in her batik sarong and her cheap cotton blouse marching up the hill with her baby clutched to one hip. The dogged sound of her Japanese slippers on the soles of her feet: thup thup thup thup at first a quick rhythm and then slowing as the climb grew steeper and she grew more tired. The baby grizzling as she shifted him from one side to the other in the dark. One hand slapping at mosquitoes on his legs and pulling a grimy blanket around him.

Salmah looks around her at all the faces smiling expectantly as though waiting for her reaction to Mrs Arasu's implied comparison between her and the cook. But her vague unease won't be put into words.

"You said a lot of 1969 babies," she offers instead. "So who else? Where are the others?"

Mrs Arasu counts them off on her fingers though there are only two more. "One is Harbans and Gurmeet's daughter. Kiranjit. The other is Annabelle Foo, there. All same batch only."

Salmah turns to look at the child Mrs Arasu is indicating to with her chin.

"That girl?" she says. "So tall! She looks at least ten years old!"

Estelle Foo considers her daughter with the distracted but not unkindly interest of a stranger on a train.

"Hmm," she says. "Yes, quite tall for her age." Estelle is a woman so thin and pale she is hardly there at all. Her bland face fades from your memory as soon as you turn away. But look at her husband—indeed how can you stop looking? That glossy hair, that perfect leonine head, those straight white teeth. Salmah looks from him to his wife and back and wonders what he sees in her.

"Anyway," Mrs Arasu insists, "I must say it is *quite* a coincidence to have four 1969 babies in *such* a small group of children!"

Salmah simpers politely. "And all only children too? Must be after we saw what was happening to this country we simply could not bring ourselves to—"

"Ah," Mrs Arasu says and twitches her small solid shoulders. "Ah, well—"

"We had another daughter," Selwyn says.

Annabelle finally turns her face towards them. Salmah's heart lurches as she considers this face: its cool slow blinks its bright lips pressed tightly together its pointed chin so delicate it should move Salmah to pity. But she can't decide what she feels or why a child's face should make her slightly nervous.

"My older girl died," Estelle says. "In 1969."

"I'm sorry to hear that," Salmah says. "What a terrible thing. I'm very sorry." Of course she has her answer now: grief is the centripetal force binding this featureless woman and this filmstar-faced man.

But it is the heat of Annabelle's neediness she feels most: as palpable as the hands of a small child grabbing her mother's face to turn it towards herself. But Annabelle is past the stage of trusting in such simple manipulations. By now she knows a hopeless cause when she sees it. Her dead sister swims in her parents' eyes, leaving room for nothing else, and if you look closely you can see the whole story there playing and replaying in an infinite loop: the empty car that secretly holds a little girl hiding from the mob, the father running back but not fast enough, the petrol-fed flames, the father's screams and the answering cries of the mob when they realize what they have done. There she is still: little Angeline, curled in a blackened ball. A tiny cicak fallen out of its smashed eggshell. Forever frozen in time.

Annabelle learned very young that however fair her skin however lovely her mouth and eyes she could not compete with burned-up Angeline. But she learned just as quickly that there are other sources of attention in this world. She looks now from Salmah to Reza with an appraising smirk.

The Sad Tale of Salmah Majid

She tells him her story on the very evening of her arrival. She has answered other people's questions politely enough but with nowhere near the eagerness the soft earnest gush the delicate forthcoming she has reserved for Cyril Dragon.

In the story Reza's omputeh father quietly packs a suitcase one morning while Salmah sleeps. He leaves a note on the kitchen table with money for one week's provisions. It would have been better—my mother says—just to leave isn't it? Just to bugger off without pretending to compensate her as if she were nothing more than a glorified prostitute.

In the story the car engine makes a farce of Salmah's breaking heart by starting and stalling and starting and stalling again until finally it marshals its resources and bears the whiteman away.

In the story Salmah lies in bed crying until Reza comes in with two slices of toast and a cup of Milo—always that cup of Milo!—on a shaking-rattling tray.

When Cyril pictures this woman crushed by another man's callousness he has to press down on his chest with the splayed fingers of one hand. But it is hopeless. Like a water balloon his heart fills until indeed it bursts. He cannot lift his hand. He cannot speak. He cannot breathe. His office clock ticks the seconds away. The wooden floors creak.

Oh that Mama of mine! She could have been a tok dalang she could have been a penglipur lara she could have been a tukang karut but she was born a woman so her talents were shunted into lesser channels than professional storytelling.

I am not saying the story was a wholesale fabrication. But a good storyteller knows what to leave out and what to inflate as a glassblower would into marvels of form and colour. An even better storyteller can do all this without the audience ever noticing her sleights of hand. When such a storyteller tells her story we listen as though there were only a single story. As though absolute truth were not only possible but inevitable.

As Salmah puts the finishing touches on her tale the Centre's goats—tireless lawn mowers and generous providers of fertilizer for the vegetable garden—bleat companionably far below the attic office. A cool breeze moves down the terraced hill like a hand stroking a cat. Up and down the stairs footsteps creak thump slap shuffle. Cyril may not be the only member of Salmah's audience.

Cyril was no fool. He was not as others have made him out to be a booksmart simpleton ripe for the picking. Booksmart he certainly was. But if you think that to spend your life with great books is to know nothing about the Real World then you do not understand books. Everything a boy can learn about human nature from books—which is a great deal indeed—Cyril Dragon had learned by the age of twelve. He knew about jealousy and desperation and madness. He knew the meandering and tricksy pathways of the mind. He understood that the centre of the heart can be both molten and flinty. And most important of all he knew how clever we are at hiding the truth from everyone including ourselves and this you see is a thing that can be learned nowhere but from books. Out there on the gritty streets of the real world you cannot learn about all the hidden things; they unsheathe themselves only between the pages of Victorian novels. What a thin and trusting idea of the world a man forms without such textbooks!

Not so Cyril Dragon as he sits listening to Salmah in his office. What she leaves unsaid he fills in with crushing detail. The opprobrium a nice Malay girl would have had to face from relatives and friends for marrying a mat salleh. The isolation ensuing from being turned away by her own people yet only superficially accepted as one of the white expat crowd and certainly not when it truly counted. The loneliness at get-togethers and parties when she found herself surrounded by in-jokes and shared backgrounds. The long nights alone with a small child whose father was—of course—carrying on with other women otherwise why would he have left like that?

In Salmah's face Cyril sees not just the boldness of the storyteller swept up in her drama but also—embedded in that audacity as clearly as a vein of copper in a lump of rock—this other glimmer. An element of exhaustion and loneliness and emptiness. Of lostness and searchingness. That little-bit-mad yet languid desperation that he has seen in the eyes of widowers and jilted women and unwashed hippies from places like Liverpool and Sheffield. For after all just beneath the eyeshadow and the lipstick her face is unmistakably travel-weary; her elegant coiffure, wind-loosened, droops a little.

"Why have you come here?" he asks her.

"Oh!" she says lightly. With a shrug and a faraway smile. "I thought of it a long time ago. I always had it in mind. Years ago somebody told me about this place. I thought, if I can find that kind of peace, how wonderful! My whole life I've been looking for it. Not money, not a rich husband and a big house and a nice car. People always thought I wanted all that but actually I didn't. I wanted ... I don't know how to call it also!"

She gestures around the room with one hand and those wide eyes. This, the gesture says, this is what I wanted but I didn't even have the words. Tell me. Show me. Help me. She puts her hands neatly together in her lap and looks up at him. Ready and waiting. Do with me as you will.

"But ..." Cyril begins and then stops. A half smile on his face. He shakes his head and takes another breath and, still smiling, starts again. "You are not supposed to come to places like this. I am not ... *we* are not the ones who say so. We say our teachings are for everyone. But your people would not approve. Am I right? You are not supposed to follow teachers who do not call themselves Muslim."

Salmah looks down at her hands. Her eyelids so thin and delicate Cyril can almost see her eyes through them. The lashes like so many blackbird feathers laid side by side.

Up to this point it is still possible for some ghost of the future to turn their faces away from each other and say, "Stop, stop now while you have the chance! Can you not see how complicated this is? A Malay woman and a mixed-up rojak man. A Muslim and a who-knows-what bleeding-heart hocus-pocus God-is-love hippy born in the right century but the wrong country—and look the woman has a son on top of that. Not one single thing about this is going to be easy. You will destroy yourselves. You will destroy each other. You will destroy everything you love and not even realize you are doing it."

But when Salmah looks up her eyes are narrowed and one corner of her mouth is lifted. Something about this expression—at once cowboy and Hindi film actress, at once sage and small girl—stops Cyril's breath. All the ways we have of taming these ineffable moments, forcing them into jerry-built frames—*somebody did something she put a charm on him she used jampi*—are in the end inadequate attempts to describe what the Real Thing itself feels like. Cyril's stomach drops. His heart burns through the skin of his chest.

"Oh!" Salmah says again. "We all do things we're not supposed to do isn't it?"

In the front hall the grandfather clock strikes the hour.

Cyril clears his throat and pushes his spectacles back up

the bridge of his nose. He shoots a full two-dimple smile at Salmah. What to make of this smile? It is shy about its feelings yet confident in its intentions. It humbles itself it pledges its service but look closer and you will see that its humility is that of the elected statesman: there in the irises and here in the symmetrical dimples is a kind of gentle arrogance.

The boom of the grandfather clock bullies all the smaller clocks into delivering their many unsynchronized chimes: the Big Ben clock on the staircase; the cuckoo clock far below in the dining room; the Recreation Lounge clock; the prayer room clock upstairs; the front hall clock; and finally the clock in my father's office. In seventeen years nobody has been able to align the measurements of the house's seven clocks. A few times Selwyn Foo tried to handle the problem and, once, the young George Cubinar armed with a whole pouch of keys made a brave effort to no avail.

One by one they resume their ticking. Gradually Cyril's heart steadies itself. It matches the ticking of his office clock exactly: a beat for every tick a beat for every tock.

Salmah looks at him and thinks *How decent he is! How kind how patient how different from all the others. This one would never stumble in smelling of someone else's perfume. This one would never give me a black eye and then swagger off to smoke and drink at the club. And so what if he is a bit smooth and pale and his hands a bit soft—so different from her usual bad-boy type—well that is not to say that he is not handsome in his own way. That refined face with its not-Malay not-Chinese not-Indian features.*

And Cyril? For the moment he is only feeling not thinking. He is no Don Juan who pictures himself ripping off Salmah's lacy kebaya under a mosquito-net canopy as she sits in front of him in his office; on the contrary he maintains a vice grip on the reins of his imagination. To think embarrassing thoughts now would be to spoil the purity of this moment. This blissful connection he feels with this lovely woman in his office as though they might have known each other in a previous life. What he sees in her he has never seen in anyone else; what he feels for her is so different from the shameful and inconvenient urges of his youth that he cannot—he must not—even compare them. In Salmah's exquisite presence he must he simply must keep his twenty-year-old self at bay. He must exist only in the here and now. The pearl pink of her fingernails the rose pink of her lips the deep brown of her eyes.

It will be weeks before he dares even to kiss her. But make no mistake: it is too late for that ghost of the future to stop them now.

Forecast

Late into the evening following Salmah's arrival Cyril spins his thoughts out in the privacy of his office. Remember that he is a revolutionary at heart or he would not be here in the Scottish tea planter's house in the hills with this collection of outcasts and misfits and dreamers. For dreamers were what they had all once been; dreamers were what they had to be to follow my father out of the city to this godforsaken place. Once upon a time they had rescued this ruined house to fill it with their dream. They had ripped roots from the cracks with their bare hands torn away moss with their fingernails scrubbed the floors on their hands and knees. But now human nature in its various forms is reclaiming them: petty squabbles and mundane fears and a disregard for the spirit of the law. What if the authorities find out? What will people say ...

Here was an opportunity to restore his ideals to their original glory. What could be a stronger stand than taking a Malay wife? What could be a more powerful symbol of one race one religion than the two of them living together under this roof worshipping God by all his many names? Because of course it is easy to pontificate when only Indians, Chinese, and Others are involved but that was not what his dream was in the beginning. It was not about doing what would be easy. But of course the living out of his message would merely be the bonus. The main prize would be Salmah herself. A delicate and precious prize: a baby-pink blossom between two cupped palms.

You may well accuse me of putting these words in Cyril's mouth. You may think I am simply minting metaphors in his absence. But I am certain that my historical reconstruction captures the spirit of the original event. My father had the soul of a poet. He had grown up in a home where the adults had no use for him. Spun tight into the cocoon of his sorrow his father Ambrose could hardly bear to look at Cyril so much did he resemble the mother who had died giving birth to him. And so Cyril had spent all the afternoons of his boyhood in his father's library reading the Romantics and the Modernists at the expense of real life. If I take liberties in the telling of his story they are informed liberties: a fire was in his head and Salmah was his glimmering girl.

They would be bound—Cyril decides—not by manmade laws but by love. They would not seek the blessings of the state and its appointed clerics. He believed in God by any name. The fact that Salmah had come to this house meant that she too must believe in God by all His names. Now for the first time Cyril truly grasps the meaning of what he has preached for more than five years: God is Love.

He would treat her like a queen. He would read her Donne and bring her flowers from the forest. He pictures their children in white nightclothes. Their Victorian fairy-tale heads bent low over their armfuls of hydrangeas and roses. In his waking dream he tries to lift their chins with his thumbs but finds himself unable to. It is as if their heads have grown strangely heavy or his thumbs suddenly useless. He is left wondering: Will they look like him? Will they have Reza's curly lashes and Cupid's bow? Will the girls have their mother's narrow wrists and ankles? And now that the crux of the fantasy has eluded him the rest of it begins to slip from his grasp. Here he is alone in his office. He leans back and closes his eyes, he summons Salmah's airy voice into his head, but none of it is any good. Here is his scratched-up second-hand desk and here is his grey rag rug. Here is the chipped patch on the wall and here is the black telephone. He would have a son who would call him Papa. A boy who would be born here in this house and who would never know anything else but a world without warring tribes and creeds. Then why instead of soaring does his heart feel as though someone has very gently rolled a stone onto it? He did not see the stone coming but here it is. Here is the stone that crushes his ribs. Here are the hands and feet that must belong to him. Here he is struggling for air.

Toilets

JUNE 1971

It's always been toilets for Neela hasn't it? It was toilets in the old place where she had been *lucky to get a job* until she was thrown out and it's toilets here too. Cyril doesn't like it when people call her *the cook* but sometimes she feels like telling him, you should count yourself lucky they don't call me what I really am. *Cook* would be a promotion. Oh of course they always tell you at first that it is marketing and cooking and all that sort of thing. Then if you are cooking it is understood that your job includes keeping the kitchen clean. Then they will say a little light housekeeping: sweeping as needed dusting once in a while no need to mop too often. If anything it was more honest in the old place: the whole thing a speedy progression from cooking to toilet scrubbing. Whereas here she knew they were waiting with bated breath to be able to saddle her with the shithouses. "After all the cooking only takes a few hours a day," she heard that Mrs Arasu remark to Hilda Boey but they couldn't just come out with it and issue orders could they? *There are no leaders there are no followers* oh the bullshit they tell themselves. In degree of falsehood this was second only to *there are no masters and no servants* which only Cyril Dragon tries to believe and even then not very successfully.

Still. The suggestions and instructions never came from him. It was because they did not want him to see what they were doing that they had to hide them. *Oh Neela if you wouldn't mind just* ... but only when he was out of earshot.

So what. She can do toilets if it means her son gets to

grow up in a house full of books under the watchful eye of someone who does believe he deserves a real education. No danger of the temptations the boy would be facing out there. Out there if she nudged him towards higher ambitions he'd be a keling too big for the rubber estate boots he should've been wearing. He'd be mocked and bullied for tucking in his shirt and doing his homework. By age twelve he'd be in a gang. If the price for this is swallowing her memories and her pride and scrubbing toilets so be it.

The funny thing is she has to deal with both categories of toilet customs here: the wiping and the washing. Biggest feud in the country—You Chinese who don't wash your bottoms! You Indians and Malays who wash your shitty backsides with your hands and then eat with them!—but of course here the fight has to be buried like everything else. It falls to her to mop up the splashes from the secret cebuk the washers smuggle into the stalls (and why the smuggling? In this place nobody is supposed to be ashamed of anything anymore isn't it?) and also to replenish the toilet roll so that the wipers are not reduced to hoarding old newspapers. Oh she knows all their secrets all right being in charge of both input and output. Whose stomach can't handle what. Which of the men has the worst aim.

Scrubbing feels almost good for her soul. At least she can take her anger out on a shit-streaked toilet bowl. She is not yet thirty and her hands are the hands of an old woman but someday her son will hold his head high. That is what she tells herself at the end of each day when she massages her hands with their pruney chapped skin and their bulging veins.

The Bee in the Bonnet

2023

"Not long now," Mama says. "God is sending me signs. Soon I will see my son."

When she starts talking like this Ani and I look at each other. A servant must never presume to roll her eyes of course but we recognize each other's internal eye rolls. It is these tiny moments of solidarity in my lonely days that keep me going.

The truth is I don't even hate Mama for saying "my son" anymore. Look at her sitting there watching the Asian Food Channel: with the aid of a minor trick of the light I can almost convince myself she's a sweet old biddy who never did anyone any harm. A tiny shrivelled bony thing slumped in its chair. Her hair shines more silver than black under the lamp and her teeth are yellow from all those years of ciggies at the pubs and bars and clubs of Kuala Lumpur and then finally in the johns of the Muhibbah Centre.

All these many years since we left the Centre her life would have been happier if I could have been enough for her. It's herself she has deprived. What is there to hate in that?

"Is that right, Mama sayang?" I say. "Where are you meeting him?"

Mama sayang. She likes it when I call her that. Once I was much more honest than kind so nowadays I make up for it by being much more kind than honest. The *Mama* part is true; the *sayang* is not. Beloved is too simple and pure a word for what I feel. But you see: I am the son of doing-what-you-need-to-do-to-get-by. I may be the son of my father's ruination but I am also the son of my mother's fast learning. Only teach us a game and we'll beat you at it.

"Oh!" she says now. "When I see him again his body will be whole. I won't have to think of him like that anymore. The eyes all gone soft like overripe fruits. The ears eaten away like lace. The fingers and toes all bloated ..."

In the background Ani pauses in her bustling to shudder and raise her eyebrows.

"Oh, Mama," I say. "For heaven's sake."

It's no use telling her it's all nonsense you see. I've tried that. I've looked her square in the eye and said: "Your son did not drown." But it's as though she needs that nightmare. Feeds on it somehow. I can only try to minimize the least savoury elements of these pleasures.

"It was not like that, Mama. You're getting carried away again."

"I'm preparing myself for the next stage, Yusuf. I'm not frightened, you know? All these years I've been waiting and now finally, *finally*, I'll get to hold him and tell him everything I want to tell him."

These days Mama sometimes favours one of those knitted bonnets normally worn under a tudung. It's a costume: wearing it she slips into the character of someone very subtly different from the normal Mama sayang. She speaks with a more kampung accent. Her voice is higher and more quivery. On those days it is impossible to believe that the nenek in the chair is the woman at whose feet half of Kuala Lumpur once swooned, with her thickly lined cat eyes and her pointy cone-bra under her glove-fitting lace kebaya. That other woman is as dead as her glamorous namesake Saloma; I look at this bonneted biddy with her loose screws and her rambling tongue and feel only pity like a toothache.

Twenty years ago I might have wondered, *What? What are the things she wants to tell Reza that she cannot tell me?* But it's no use pining for what cannot be yours.

"Aaaaah," I say. "That's all ancient history now."

For a moment all I can see in her eyes is confusion. Then the clouds part and the sun blazes in a clear blue sky. She can barely speak through her grin but she forces herself to say:

"It's a blessing you know. It's a blessing to be able to say sorry. I'm looking forward to it. To be able to say, 'I failed you, I didn't teach you any better, you were just a boy, the sin was all mine'—ah, what a blessing!"

When people begin to spout rubbish like this it's best to leave them to it. I glide out of the room like a ghost.

But after weeks of telling me with her blissful little smile that she is preparing to see her son soon oh so soon in the happy hereafter suddenly one morning as I'm reading my newspaper she looks at me like a child waking up teary from a nightmare and says, "Can't you contact your brother, Yusuf?"

No bonnet in sight on that day. She's had Ani neaten her up. Hair washed dried and coiled into a bun. Freshly ironed baju kurung.

Like generations of the best men before me I take refuge behind my newspaper.

"I don't have much time left here," she insists. "My time is coming. My mind is already going. You yourself know. Many days I can't think clearly anymore. There is only one thing I want. Here or there, before or after, I have to see him."

Which will it be? I should ask her. In the beforedeath or in the afterlife?

"Can't you all help me?" she says. Looking around the room as though we might be a crowd of fifty ignoring her needs. "Can't you find my son and ask him to come?"

Her eyes grow larger and larger until it seems possible they might simply slip out of their sockets.

"But *why*?" she whimpers. "Was I really so much worse

than all the other mothers? At least I tried to give us an interesting life. And if I made mistakes—well I just want to say sorry now. I just want to say sorry. Shouldn't I have a chance to say sorry?" Pleading now as though I am the judge presiding over her case. Well, if she forces me into the position of judge then she must hear my verdict.

"He doesn't want your sorry. Even if he's alive, he doesn't need it. He's doing perfectly well without it. All this self-flagellation is a waste of time, Mama."

She blinks at me in surprise. "A waste of time!" she says. "No, it's the most useful thing I can do at this stage. Reflect on my past. Seek forgiveness."

If it's forgiveness she wants to seek am I not right here at her service? But no. It's Reza she wants, and over the weeks that follow the badgering grows more frequent. Tell him this tell him that. Just ask him if he's okay. As long as he's happy I'm happy. No need to come and see Mama just tell him to send one sentence to say he's okay.

No fear never not once do I have the slightest intention of going after him. Dead or alive in real life it doesn't matter: we're the ones who are dead to him. That time itself, he made it clear that he wanted nothing more to do with us. What more is there to say? If you are dirt on the bottom of a shoe to someone then you must not pine for them. It goes against all cosmic laws of justice.

Home Life

2023

I am a lonely man. Shameless of me to admit it I know. Did I once dream as other boys do of finding love? Or did my earliest childhood teach me this defining lesson: I was not worthy of the sweet & tender looks the secret smiles the hand on the knee the wink across the room ...?

There was that. But also, what did I really know of sweet & tender looks and secret smiles? What did I see around me but dark secrets all of which came to disastrous ends? And then of course I had a part in those disastrous ends. I cannot deny that. And if I destroyed other people's chances at happiness then shouldn't I pay for it in the form of guilt and lifelong misery?

At the age of twenty I thought to myself if I cannot have that incomprehensible package deal—the I-love-you the kiss the happily-ever-after—then let me be selfless. Let me give myself to the multitudes. After all, my father did it. He might have been (un)lucky enough to stumble into love despite his chosen path but that did not mean I could not model my own life upon his. I could not be the messenger of a God I did not believe in but I could still be a teacher. And so I found my way into government service and a classroom of thirty blank stares. In bygone times people used to say "Nothing like a government job," because they'll never sack you and then you get your pension.

Well I am that rare phenomenon: a government servant who was sacked. All sorts of fiddlers and fondlers embezzlers and abusers were simply transferred to different schools but for teaching the impermissible I got the axe.

Mama said, "Just give tuition lah then."

The lesser calling. At least then you can admit you are in it just for the money.

At one time Mama loved nothing better than to plan my life out for me. It was she who announced that we find ourselves a maid. Said to me, "I'm not getting any younger and you are even busier than when you were teaching in government school. Cannot simply close your eyes and teach yes or not? Slightest thing, the tuition centre can find somebody else to take your place so you better put all your energy into your job and get someone else for the sweeping and mopping."

I'd hardly had time to think about the idea before Mama had rung up an agency. Told them she needed a strong young girl—orang Islam please we cannot be having anyone who will curi-curi tapau pork into the house—because she was old and feeble and needed help getting in and out of bed walking up and down the stairs taking her bath combing her hair. Seeing my surprise she put a finger to her lips whispered with a placid grin, "If it's not true yet it'll be true soon enough."

Oh the suggestive and encouraging smiles Mama gave me when Ani first arrived! A simple honest woman she said. You know boy they all want to stay here if they can. If they haven't left behind a husband and children. And Ani had no such leftbehinders so: nothing wrong with a mutually beneficial agreement Mama said. Ani gets a blue IC and you get a wife. She'll have no cause for complaint, you are able-bodied you are earning a decent living you are not even bad-looking.

But if I had ruled out true love it did not mean that I was willing to accept imitations and substitutes. Ani was herself able-bodied and not bad-looking but what did I feel when I looked at the not-badness of her? What do I feel even now? Nothing at all.

Am I a man or a stone? Once I was capable of feeling. I cannot relive the feelings themselves—I cannot call them up from their graves—but I remember them as surely as one remembers a journey to a foreign land. And if I once felt, then in theory it is still possible for me to feel. But we need not hold our collective breath. It would be unfair of me to trap Ani into a serviceable marriage with a man who provides but does not love. A man who is capable only of duty and nothing more.

We may not be lovers but at least we are allies. We know what needs to be done and together we do it with no need for discussion. We tell Mama there is no more ais potong in the fridge to curtail her binges. We tell her the TV is broken when the binge-watched B-grade hantu movies start to addle her brain. We fail to relay telephone messages from friends who may as well be enemies: the ones who call to boast about the promotions and Datukships of their sons and *Oh how is Yusuf doing? Still giving tuition at home?* Quietly Ani will tell me: "Puan Rokiah called." Then she will press her lips together and get on with her work. She's the practical type. No airs and graces and no time for frivolities. Knee-length pasar malam leggings and half a dozen T-shirts that all seem to have come free with things. Solid calves strong hands and a face like a biscuit tin under hair that is double-secured: first the tight three-inch ponytail then the wide plastic headband. Pleasegod let her not be sidetracked in her labours by one single hair in her face.

But no doubt about it: in Ani I have nearly all the benefits of a good wife and none of the burdens or distractions. Do I still think about True Love? Well. I am a man after all and not even an old one yet. I am only forty-three. Certainly the sight of a certain shape of rump under a silky skirt or a particular way long hair will fall over a lady's face might turn me momentarily wistful. But not enough to spur me to risk my safe and comfortable existence. My peculiar childhood cured me of all need for excitement.

PART 2

Wise Men Say

In the beginning—when she first begins to spend hours at a time in his office, when first he takes to draping his cardigan across the back of the dining chair next to his to chope a seat for her—they notice how he looks at her: his beating heart like a bird on a string and the end of the string in her hand. Right in front of them he is turning into steam. He clouds the windowpanes and trickles down onto the sills. And she? She gathers up the droplets and drinks them. Like a prize rose she glows. How not to be envious?

If some of them have believed him to be so devoted to the cause as to have no time for All That—wasn't it their mistake rather than his? Cyril never claimed to be a holy man. Quite the contrary; from the beginning he insisted he was just one of them. What they were building they were building together as equals, so what right does any of them have to feel betrayed now?

"Look," Rupert Boey consoles them, "even Nelson Mandela has a wife." Over the decades of their own marriage Rupert and Hilda have developed an uncanny resemblance to each other: the same wide-set eyes the same downturned mouth above the same weak chin. "Even Martin Luther King had a wife. And Mahatma Gandhi—"

"Gandhi had no time for his wife!" says Mrs Arasu sourly. "He was too busy changing the world."

Rupert Boey pulls his head into his neck and hunches his shoulders. "Those who change the world are still human," he says. "Why should we begrudge them their happiness?"

"But ... but it's not that we *begrudge* them anything," George Cubinar says, and look what happens the minute he speaks: all the heads swivel cartoonishly to face him. Something in his voice perhaps or just the fact that George oh dearold smallboy George surely cannot have something meaningful to say on the subject of Men and Women. He is after all the youngest of the bunch. So young he barely needs to shave. His chest is hairless. His arms girlish. He wears spectacles with thick black frames. With one delicate finger he keeps pushing them back up his long nose. His lashes are thicker than his kutty shadow-moustache. "It's not that we begrudge them anything," he repeats. "It's just ... it's just it makes us uncomfortable, isn't it? To think—I mean—in our culture ... well, whatever the case ... certain things make us uncomfortable and when you think of a man as above *All That* ... although of course it is like something from a Hollywood movie isn't it?"

And so, it is George Cubinar—innocent smallboy though he may be—who forces them to face their envy. Take a random sample of humanity and few will be fortunate enough to have experienced what my father did in those early days. I shall not call it "true love" because bullshit by however grandiose a name is still bullshit. It is a fleeting and insubstantial thing; only the innocent and the unreasonable (of which my father was both) ever expect it to last. But while it lasts it must be a marvel. A dizzying riotous marvel that hollows you out and gives you wings clips your tongue and sets you on fire like all the world's marvels. Mrs Arasu tries to console herself with a knowing cynicism but her sharp salty satisfaction is brief. When she looks at Cyril Dragon looking at Salmah she cannot help but think *How come I never had that?* No one told her that was what you were supposed to look for or that you could approach the end of your life before you realized you'd missed your chance. Assiduously she kneads her feelings into some semblance of wistful sadness befitting a woman of her age but no luck: as soon as she lets down her guard and stops kneading they spring back into that familiar shape she recognizes as anger. But where should she direct this anger? Not at Cyril and Salmah who did nothing to engineer their great luck. Not at the people who never told her what she could demand of life, because they themselves were not aware. It is anger without a target. Anger she has to carry around with her and never fling into any receptacle. Her shameful secret which must be hidden from everyone now that George Cubinar has nudged them all into fits of swooning and sighing at the spectacle of the happy couple.

Salmah is the one and only thing about which Cyril Dragon has ever been certain. This is his secret: for all his radical ideas he has so often thought himself an imposter. What does he know about changing the world? He was twenty-six years old when he fled that world and no one was more surprised than him by the following he gained almost overnight. He had been in the right (or wrong) place at the right (or wrong) time and that was all there was to it. People come to him and ask him to pray for them and then claim to have been cured of asthma or cancer; they claim their husbands have come crying back to them or their wayward daughters have seen the light. He tells them himself: I am not praying for you I am praying with you. You could do the praying yourself.

If they refuse to believe him it is because this is a nation hungry for miracles and holy men. A nation itching to abandon the laws of logic at the slightest excuse. No one has ever been more surprised than my father himself at people's readiness to follow him into the hills. When he looks in the mirror he does not see a man capable of such feats of charisma but a self-effacing and even unprepossessing fellow.

But you know how our people are: they cannot resist a half-white face. That English custard colouring those red hints to his hair that fine beaky nose had hypnotized them. That and his habit of quoting Donne and Trollope and Yeats and Auden so nicely and naturally as though he were merely reciting a shopping list. Who among that generation will not go weak at the knees when a fellow spouts English poetry like tying his shoelaces like that? They heard his voice and thought *Put this chap in charge!*

My father has always seen that their trust is built upon fairy tales and fantasies. In the past this knowledge frightened him. Kept him awake in his clammy bed listening to the tea planter's house shift around him. Deep inside the stone walls water seeped and trickled from ceiling to floor. He would pull his monkey cap down low over his ears and hold himself stiff as a corpse in order not to touch the unwarmed portions of the sheets. *Dear God* he would beg *Dear God send me a sign just one small sign, anything at all.*

Into his echoing head my mother has blown like a hot desert wind. Her cat eyes her soft full lips her thin neck her halting way of speaking her narrow feet and hands the brightness oh the starry childlike brightness of her, the way she claps her hands when delighted, the way she knits her brow and nods to herself when absorbing new ideas, the way she serves herself more than she can possibly finish and eats with an undisguised appetite for a few minutes but then pushes her plate forcefully away as soon as her belly is full, the way she bends her head to spit the seeds of an orange into her cupped hand.

He feels all their eyes on her. The two of them cannot leave the house for a ten-minute walk without all those eyes tracking their movements. They are waiting for her to fail the test but what is the test? She cannot be after money or prestige because he has none. If she came out of desperation she has stayed because of him. Never in his life has he talked to anyone else the way he has talked to her.

In her few weeks on the hill she has learned:

– That his dead mother Dorothy would sometimes appear to him in his boyhood bed wearing a daffodil-yellow dress and smelling of a tailor shop.

– That on top of the piano in his father's house on Old Klang Road perched a silver-framed picture of Dorothy in a hat with a lace veil.

– That the books he loved best as a child were *The Old Curiosity Shop* and *Heidi* and *Little Women* although he gave *Swallows and Amazons* and *Swiss Family Robinson* and *Tom Brown's Schooldays* a fair chance.

– That by the time he was twelve he had declared himself a vegetarian.

– That his Aunt Dolly served coronation chicken for a whole month following the coronation of Queen Elizabeth but did not succeed in wearing him down. For a month he ate bread and butter.

"I was a stubborn boy and now I am a stubborn man," he tells her. "But I am not a hero or a saint."

"Ah, hero, saint, what does that all that mean anyway?" she says. "You are an old soul. Every age has got its advanced souls. When people see them they can recognize immediately."

"But I struggle with everything," he says. "I argue with God. I am full of doubt."

"Of course!" she says and her face is so kind he wants to sink down onto his knees and lay his head in her lap. "You've read all the books so you yourself should know. No matter what their faith the greatest souls have always been full of doubt. The prophets and the mystics and the monks. Even Jesus. Even Krishna. Even Muhammad wanted to throw himself from the mountains! Without doubt faith is meaningless isn't it?"

"Jesus!" he cries. "Krishna! Muhammad!"

He wants to run from the room to escape the heat of her admiration. But he only grips the windowsill and says, "Why even speak my name in the same breath as the names of God's greatest messengers? I am just an ordinary man."

"You are a man," she says, "but you are far from ordinary. Ordinary is ... is ..." She gestures towards the window of his study with its view of the long road down the hill. "Ordinary is all the men who get up and go to their stupid jobs every morning and get married and buy a house and buy a car and their whole life they never once stop to think about any of it. Ordinary men don't give up everything to retreat to the hills to meditate and preach!"

He shakes his head. *Please*, he wants to beg, *please* ... But he doesn't have to, he doesn't have to beg or explain because he sees now that she too is shaking her head. Now she is rushing towards him and now she is standing next to him at the window without looking at him but he can hear her voice lift and flutter like a sail in the wind.

"Don't be so scared," she says softly. "Sometimes you just have to trust isn't it? Can't you see yourself like how we see you? You don't have to be anything else. What you are is what we need."

And maybe that very night she went to him in his room. Did not knock did not hesitate just opened the door and walked in and there he was sitting up in his bed and she knelt before him on the blanket—a gesture at once forceful and demure—and took his hands and why in my imagining of it why are they both crying? Does he think at first that it is his mother come to him after so many years in her daffodil dress and if so then should I be even more unnerved at having to imagine this scene for you? Who I ask you wants to picture their mother unpinning her hair their father unhooking hooks and fumbling with buttons —and on top of that if below the surface lurk the unexamined longings of the motherless father and the fatherless mother ...

It is more than I can bear.

But here is the very least I can do for them. You see I could not save them. In the end I could not save them from each other or from themselves. No child can do that for their parents. Perhaps no one can do that for another human being. After everything all you can do is to tell the story and in the telling of it to redeem.

So I will tell you that they felt saved that night. She from her past and her present and even from that other future she had imagined: the tooth-sucking and the pitying looks for the single mother and her anak haram. Why should she not have this man? The safety and certainty of him the gratitude in his trembling hands? Didn't she of all people deserve some happiness at last? After all these years of crumbling to ash in the fire of those glances, of thinking maybe they are right, maybe this is who I am and this is what I deserve—now she stepped out from that heat into a cool green morning. *No, this is who I am,* she thinks. They were all wrong after all. Cyril Dragon—who calls himself an ordinary man!—has created her and named her.

And he? From what did he feel saved? From too much knowing and too much thinking. From the loneliness of the reluctant idol. From the weight of his past and the monotony of his future.

Now seeing them glowing with that born-again bliss most of Cyril Dragon's followers cannot help but feel lifted up. To remain impervious to it one would have to be a heartless wretch. Inside their own lungs their very breath bursts into blossom. They—Rupert and Hilda Boey, Harbans Singh Gill and his wife Gurmeet Kaur, Thomas Mak and Bee Bee, Selwyn and Estelle Foo, George Cubinar—turn to each other in wonder. That joy could be so contagious; that joy could broaden the spirit and bring with it so much unconnected hope. After all these years of feeling bitter and besieged, righteous and grim, they remember now: *the greatest of these is love.* They watch Salmah watching Cyril watching her. The gaze and the gaze-back: it is as rich as brandied fruit cake.

And the girls, yes, do not forget the little girls with their murky predilections and fantasies! Their bodies—scalp to fingertips—quick to the mysteries of romance. Waking up like the trees and flowers and little animals beneath the wand of the Spring Fairy in the stories. Waking up as though from the hundred-year slumber in *Sleeping Beauty*. Kiranjit Kaur and the giggly Mak twins and most of all Annabelle Foo. Watch the way their pupils dilate and their eyelids flutter. How they love a good story! And what is unfolding before their eyes if not the grandest and most ancient story in the world? Even without knowing what it is they want it for themselves. Before the pocked and stained mirror in the girls' dormitory Annabelle Foo acts out scenes from her own future. Bats her lashes and dips her fine pointed chin at her reflection. One day it will all be hers. Those looks those whispers that heat. Only the face of the handsome prince remains to be filled in.

Persuasion

Mama asks Reza a hundred questions: question upon question first thing in the morning last thing at night and every time they are alone.

"You like this place isn't it Reza? You're happy here? It's nice to have other children to play with all the time isn't it? You like that boy Leo? He's the same age as you, don't you think he'll be a nice playmate for you? You like the big garden? So much place to play isn't it, not like KL? So nice ya the fresh air? All the flowers and the beautiful butterflies, you like to see them or not?"

She is not asking because she wants the real answers. Sitting next to her he has pulled his brow down low over his eyes but he sneaks a look and sees her gathering up the tears in herself the way she does. He knows what she needs. Better than anyone else he knows. What to feed her when she will not get out of bed for days (hot Milo and kaya toast). How to listen when she needs to tell him things he does not understand. How to help her choose her outfit for a party. How to answer her questions just enough to satisfy her needs but not enough to be telling lies.

He holds out an open palm to offer this up: "The other day I saw a butterfly as big as my whole hand."

She smiles brightly. She squeezes his shoulder and says, "If you are happy then Mama is happy."

But as she says it she must realize that in fact he has not said he is happy. She could tell herself there's no need to insist on the exact wording. She could let it go. But some vestigial maternal instinct niggles her.

"You really like it?" she presses. "Is there anything ... I mean, sometimes you're so quiet. Is there something you don't like?"

Reza frowns so hard his eyes almost disappear into his skull. He presses his lips together as though afraid the truth will trickle out. Then he says, "I don't like the food. I want to go to A&W. I want to go to Kentucky Fried Chicken."

He is pleased with this. He can already see in her face that he has hit upon just the right thing.

"The food!" She laughs her high airy laugh. "The food!" Delight sparkles in her eyes. "You mean that's all? And here I thought it was something really terrible! The food means no problem lah. I'll ask them to make something nice for you."

He looks up at her encouragingly. Maybe she will be happy here. In KL people made her cry. Neighbours and relatives and colleagues talked about her: "They're saying I'm a bad woman," she used to tell him, "They're simply making up things about me, they love to gossip." They talked about her but not to her. At parties the other ladies would put their purses on the empty chairs near them so that she had to sit alone.

When she started packing to come here she told him, "Nobody knows us there. We can start fresh."

It's true nobody knows them here. Nobody knows he's the boy with no father. Nobody has brought him meehoon at ten o'clock at night because they saw his Mama go out at five o'clock and not come back. Nobody has invited him into their house to watch TV because Mama locked him out to loiter by the monsoon drain when some brand-new Uncle was spending the afternoon with her.

"Feeling happier now?" Mama says. "Don't worry, vegetarian food also can be nice! Okay?"

"Okay," he says. "Okay, Mama."

The Whole Truth

is not that Reza is desperate to go to A&W or Kentucky Fried Chicken. The whole truth is that while his tastebuds yearn for hamburgers and breaded chicken skin his stomach burns from too much Cyril Dragon. The way he talks: one minute lord-and-mastering it and the next minute everybody's too-kind grandfather. Pretending to care so much about people he just met. Bending down and holding your hands and talking too close to your face. Just thinking of it Reza feels geli. And the way he looks: that milk-pudding skin that curly-girly hair. Like a man in ladies' clothes. Reza wants to take a coin and scratch out Cyril Dragon from the picture. He never had a problem with any of Mama's men not even the one with the turban and the chest as fluffy as a towel but this one is different. He doesn't tell dirty jokes he doesn't talk cock or try to make you laugh he doesn't smoke cigarettes or do any of the man things. No: Reza simply cannot see what Mama sees in this lady-man who has no stories of military adventure or daring escapades but only a lot of stupid lembik talk about God and love. The way they look at each other! And they are not even ashamed. Far from hiding it they keep trying to catch Reza's eye as though they want to share a joke with him. As though he is part of whatever disgusting thing they are cooking up.

He is sitting on the sofa in Cyril Dragon's office where he is pretending not to pay any attention to the two of them. He takes a ballpoint pen from Cyril Dragon's desk caddy and uses it to poke a row of holes in an index card. Who knows what they are saying it is all just mumble-jumble. One row of holes two rows of holes. Harder and harder he stabs the index card until he can feel the pen nib boring through the wood of the desk underneath.

Krishna Buddha Jesus Muhammad Guru Nanak Blah Blah Blah. Loving-kindness blah blah blah. Leading by example blah blah blah.

And Mama encouraging the man's bullshit by acting like a cheeky schoolgirl. Twinkling her eyes at him and asking, "One thing I tell you, this God fler is a real trouble-maker yes or not? I mean why did He say different things to different people if He wanted us all to live in peace?"

The only thing that could be worse than Mama's school-girl act is Cyril Dragon's response. Because instead of roaring with glee like Mama's other men used to do—instead of slapping his thigh and shouting out in delight instead of jumping to his feet to mime a fistfight with God—Cyril Dragon smiles an irritating patient smile and murmurs more nonsense.

Suddenly she whips her head around to look at him. Reza slipperyfishes his gaze out of her grasp. She says, "Reza do you need something else to do or what?"

"No."

"Then please stop that. You'll break the pen and spoil the desk."

He's not going to look at her. But just to shut her up he stops poking his index card holes. Instead he starts a drawing of Cyril Dragon. In the drawing Cyril Dragon is naked. His whole body is as hairless as Reza's own. His dicky bird dangles darkly like an overripe banana and he has dribbled piss down his legs; he is looking down at the puddle like a retarded baby his mouth and eyes and all making big piti-ful Os that you just want to pour sand inside. As soon as the drawing is finished Reza colours over the whole thing with a thick black marker pen. Nobody else will ever see it but he knows it is there. He knows exactly what is underneath the big black square.

Star Boy

When it came to boys Cyril Dragon couldn't rely on his own childhood memories. Never having been like other boys, he had avoided their company and even now remained slightly frightened of that alien species. Yet somehow this had never mattered with Leo. Of course Neela had always been there nudging and urging the boy: "Tell Cyril your joke," "Show Cyril your drawing," "Why don't you ask Cyril?" All he'd had to do was to show a modicum of interest. Laugh at the jokes and ask a question here and there. Once upon a time Leo was the opposite of Reza: responsive pliable eager to please. The way he'd beam and arch towards the slightest attention like a plant seeking sunlight.

He'd given Leo an old Ladybird book once. Some silver-fished thing he'd found in a second-hand bookshop and taken a fancy to for its illustrations. It was a book about constellations and each one was drawn in realistic detail in the night sky: the bear with its soft eyes and velvety fur; Pegasus soaring on his terrifying wings; gallant Perseus rushing to the rescue of beautiful Andromeda. Leo would've been four or five years old. His face had lit up like a whole galaxy when Cyril had put the book in his hands. "For me, for me!" He'd ran and shown his mother but he'd struggled to read it and Cyril had sat down and helped him with the words. *Myth-o-logy. Zo-di-ac. He-mi-sphere.* That was a hard one with the *ph*. Cyril felt Neela watching them from the kitchen doorway willing the boy to do better to prove himself, to surpass some imaginary average. The fierceness of her ambition puzzled and terrified him. *What is it you want?* he wanted to ask her. *What is it you worry about?* But these were not questions for him to ask her, so instead he tried to allay her anxieties with praise: "Well done, Leo! Clever boy! How quickly you learn!" At this Leo would flash his shyly proud smile. Lashes lowered. Tongue pushing at one corner of his mouth.

A few days later he'd seen Leo on the porch at night squinting at the sky. "Where got?" the boy had demanded. "Cannot find the horse with wings. Cannot find the hunter with the big shield." Cyril had dropped to his knees and laughed and laughed and laughed with delight and to his own surprise a kind of pride. For he too had as a child expected to look up and see the real beasts and warriors and princesses in the sky in all their finely detailed glory. "I thought the same, Leo," he'd kept saying, "I thought the same! At one time I was also looking for Cassiopeia's long locks and the swan's cruel eyes!"

But was it pride he felt or merely the satisfaction of seeing yourself reflected in another human being? Yes yes it could after all only be that. The oldest human need and nothing wrong with it. Cyril was laughing and Leo was laughing together they were laughing and their eyes were locked because Leo felt it too this *oh you also*. Simple as that. Of course Leo could not have put it into words but you could see that was all he was looking for. No grand theories necessary here. The point was that it had been so easy to connect. Just one battered Ladybird book. If only it could be as easy with Reza.

New Reading Matter

In theory there are two of them to keep each other company. Isn't that how it is supposed to work? Cyril has heard tell of the effortless camaraderie of children. Yet when he urges Leo to make friends with Reza he gets a puzzling puzzled look, then a rapid flutter of those thick lashes, indeed almost a flinching, followed by a stony stubbornness. What is wrong with suggesting a friend? *You are not the prince of the Muhibbah Centre,* he wants to say to Leo. But of course it would be useless to scold.

Instead he repeats gently, "At least try. You have grown up here, Leo, but you must try to imagine what it is like for a boy your age to come from Outside. It would make such a difference to him to have a friend. At least try to be kind."

Nothing. The more often he asks the more blank Leo is becoming. Staring at him with those eyes like huge windows in an empty house. And the way he looks at Reza! What strange biological tribalism is it that makes a dark child jealous of a fair one even when he has grown up in a paradise free of false notions of Race?

At one point Cyril almost says, *When you were lonely I read to you and played with you. Remember? Now you should do the same for Reza.* But he cannot quite bring himself to burden the child with such blithe pay-it-forwardness.

How easily Salmah could use the boy as an excuse: I cannot stay after all—it wouldn't be right—my son is unhappy—you must understand my son comes first. But no, the nagging obligation to win the boy over is all his. As though only by doing so would he truly deserve her. But even that does not explain his desperation. He wants the boy to look at him without suspicion and mistrust. Just once. Just one hard-won look. For the boy and his mother are a dyad. You only have to be in the same room and you can feel the heat of their bond. Salmah will never belong entirely to anyone else. Cyril's only hope is to shift a molecule here and there to insert himself. Turn the dyad into a triad.

But when he presses Salmah for suggestions she murmurs, "No need lah." Out of more than politeness whether or not she knows it: the boy is hers alone. Has been for all of his nearly six years. Competition baffles and threatens her but without putting words to her feelings she is aware of a fluttering in her veins a tingling a prickling. No no no you don't need to go out of your way for my son. Emphasis on the *my*.

"Please," he begs. "I simply cannot bear to see a child so unhappy. Surely there must be something we can do."

And so—to stop the begging and to make him happy—she shrugs and tells him "Anything also can. My boy"—again that *my!*—"is not fussy," she says. "He can keep himself busy for hours with one comic."

Cyril has seen the type of comics of which she speaks: *Dandy* and *The Beano* for example which disguise horrifying violence as slapstick comedy. How are impressionable young minds to draw any link between those cartoon punches and the reality of hard knuckles bruising soft flesh and breaking brittle bones? No. Not even for Reza will Cyril bring such rubbish into this house. Instead he takes out subscriptions to *Look & Learn* and *World of Wonder*.

"For you," he says to Reza. "Your Mama told me you like to read."

Reza looks from the magazines to Cyril's face and back to the magazines. Cyril has left them both open: one at an article about an entire family devoured by man-eating ants in Africa, another at a chapter of *The Moonstone* in comic-strip form. A good long while Reza stares at these pages. He takes a step forward but does not touch them. When he looks up he is smirking and once again Cyril is taken aback by the dark streak of I-know-something-you-don't in his smirk.

Purporting to be the headmaster of a small private school Cyril sends for forms from the Asia Foundation. After a few months giant boxes of American books begin to arrive: all twenty-one volumes of *The New Book of Knowledge*; sixteen volumes of *Basic Science*; the entire *Childcraft* series; a complete reading program constituted of such intriguing titles as *From Elephants to Eskimos* and *From Bicycles to Boomerangs*. With George Cubinar's help he unpacks the boxes straight onto the library shelves. He bides his time. When the perfect moment presents itself—Reza all by himself on the staircase drawing patterns in the dust with his big toe—he puts a hand on the boy's shoulder and says, "Come. I've got something to show you."

Reza stands in front of the heaving bookshelves and clicks his tongue this way and that. He taps that relentless tongue on the roof of his mouth. He presses and unpresses it against the insides of his cheeks. All of this distorts his face so that Cyril is unable to determine if he is smiling.

A small noise at the doorway makes both of them turn their heads.

"Oh," Cyril says lightly. "It's just you, Leo!"

But his laughter sounds jagged to his own ears and he sees from the expressions on the boys' faces that they have noted all his small involuntary movements: the stepping away from the bookshelf, the tensing of his shoulders, the folding and now the unfolding of his arms.

"Come, come," he says. He extends an arm as if to draw Leo into the room. "Come and see. I ordered some new books. You also like to read, I know."

Leo drags his feet in. His eyes run across the rows left to

right left to right left to right taking in all those ordered and numbered volumes: *From Codes to Captains, From Coins to Kings, From Pilots to Plastics. Folk and Fairy Tales. Life in Many Lands.* Then he steps back and looks at it from top to bottom over and over again moving not just his eyes but his whole head up and down up and down. Now his breath is so fast and shallow that Cyril can hear it.

"But," Leo says, nearly breathless now, "but where is my astronomy book? Where is my book with all the stars? With the bear and the lady and the other lady? With the big pot and the small pot?"

Cyril exhales. "Oh!" he cries out. "Is that all? The book has not been moved! *The Stars and Their Legends.* There it is, where it's always been!"

He reaches out to run an index finger down the spine of the book and at once an idea comes to him as though conducted through the cardboard.

"Look," he says. "Now got some more books about stars and planets. See this one. And this one also."

He pulls them off the shelves: *From Bicycles to Boomerangs, World and Space,* one volume of *Basic Science.*

"I think one of these books even tells you how to make your own telescope," he says. "Shall we find the page?"

But Leo will neither nod nor shake his head. He presses his lips together and blinks hard as a cat at Cyril.

"Well," Cyril says. "Anyway these books are here for both of you. Whenever you feel like it you can just come and take what you want."

He pats each of them on the shoulder before going back up to his office. That evening out of curiosity he stops to look in the library on his way to the dining room. As far as he can tell the new books have not been touched. But *The Stars and Their Legends* is gone. Where it stood on the shelf there is now the slimmest of gaps. A missing milk tooth.

He doesn't shift the books on either side to close the gap. He thinks perhaps it has just been borrowed. *Tomorrow it'll be back,* he tells himself.

But he knows it won't be. Leo has taken it to mark the end of something. To say: *Once upon a time I was the one for whom you bought books. Once upon a time I was your pet. Well you can take all that but you can't take my book. This book is just mine.* He feels the cold missingness of it: again like the surprise of that soft empty gum in a six-year-old mouth.

Spine

Annabelle Foo has been tracking the movements of *The Stars and Their Legends*. To be more precise: she has been tracking its stationary state. For three days the book has been lying on Leo's bedside table in the children's dormitory.

"We're not supposed to bring library books up here," she announces. "They're supposed to stay in the library."

"Who says?" Leo replies.

"Tsk," Annabelle says and rolls her eyes theatrically. "Don't simply pretend you don't know. Library books belong in the library."

Leo looks at her without a word. One. Two. Three. Four. Five seconds. Then he says:

"This book is mine."

"Yours! Since when? All this time it was in the library and now it's yours?"

"I'm the only one who looks at it."

"So? It still doesn't belong to you."

"If you're suddenly so interested in books why don't you go and take a different one? Got five hundred books now in that library."

"Five hundred books!" she repeats. Then gleefully, "Wah! So many books Cyril Dragon bought for that boy."

Leo's face crumples as though squashed in a fist. He closes his eyes and shouts.

"He didn't buy them for that boy! He just wanted to buy them, so what?"

A malicious smile steals across Annabelle's face. The greenish light of it flickering in the shadows.

"Okayfine," she says. "He simply went and bought five hundred books. Not for that boy. But I'm not simply going to take books without asking. I'm not like you."

"Then sit there and read lah. Sit there and read and mind your own business."

"I'm minding my business what. If somebody steals from the library it's my business. It's everybody's business."

"I already told you, I'm not stealing." Then suddenly he springs to his feet and rushes from the room. In the doorway he cries out without turning around. "Why can't you leave me alone?"

She hears his bare feet on the stairs bam bam bam bam like war drums all the way down. When she can no longer hear them she sidles up to his bedside table. She picks up the book. It must have come from a second-hand bookshop to begin with. Look at its spotty yellow pages. Its soft corners. Somewhere along the way someone tried to protect its spine with Sellotape but now the Sellotape itself has turned brittle and is breaking off in pieces like the wings of a dead beetle. She pinches the curling top of the spine between a thumb and forefinger. Slowly she peels it back. Satisfaction floods her small chest. She thinks of Leo's face when he will see his precious book mutilated. She lays the spine neatly beside the book in one long piece.

Fritters

The fish is not fish and the sambal belacan has no belacan
in it. The egg in the beehoon is tauhu dyed yellow with
kunyit and the thing that looks like chicken will crumble
like cake between his teeth. Behind closed doors Mama has
tried to explain it all to him: they don't believe in killing
animals now. Animals are God's creatures too and when
people don't value their lives then slowly-slowly they stop
valuing each other's lives also. If you kill the goat because
you need to eat it then why not kill your neighbour because
you need his land? It will be hard at first Mama says, for a
while it will be hard for us because we were used to eating
flesh foods but then we will get used to it like everybody
else. It's better this way. You are only six years old Reza and
you don't understand everything but one day you will understand.

You are only six years old you are only six years old
youareonlysixyearsold. Suddenly in the last few weeks
Mama has been repeating like a mantra what all these years
she did not seem to notice. All these years she accepted
then expected his beyond-his-years wisdom. Reza the tiny
gentleman. Reza the man of the house. Reza the defender of
his mother's heart. Always she has said to him: you got to
be strong for Mama because Mama got nobody else to
depend on. And always he has stepped up. Stiff upper lip
and steady hands. He has hot-Miloed her and brought her
Panadol and massaged her feet. He has opened the right
letters and thrown out the bad ones. He has counted out

coins for the bills and when there has been money left over to buy a late supper from the curry mee man he has put only two fishballs in his own bowl so that she might have three.

But here in this musty mossy house he has shrunk and she has grown. Now he is only six years old. His mouth waters like a six-year-old's at the thought of those forfeited fishballs. He did not even have a birthday this year. Oh sure Cyril Dragon made a big fuss about the chocolate cake he'd asked Leo's mother to make. Like as though it was the only chocolate cake the world had ever seen and to look at the other children's faces it well might have been. "Cake cake!" they'd all said, nudging each other and pointing. But there had been no candles for the cake and he'd not had any presents because the latest news was that Happiness was not about Things. Even the birthday meal he'd not been able to choose and what would he have chosen anyway? Those horrible bondas? Fat mealy slices of fried yam? They'd come out with vegetable pakoras and everyone had oohed and aahed. There was no ketchup. You had to eat them with a funny green chutney or nothing at all. Happiness is not allowed to be about Things now but he still has a magazine cutting of an advertisement for the Airfix set his father promised him before everything broke.

After the so-called birthday party his mother had taken him aside and pleaded with him. "Don't be rude Reza just please don't be rude. Cyril Dragon is doing so much for you! At least show some appreciation. Don't make people feel bad when they are trying so hard!"

Why should he? She is welcome to show all the *appreciation* she wants however she wants to show it but why should he? She's the one who's going to reap the rich and disgusting rewards of any appreciation not him so let her be the one to stump it out. Now again she takes his hands and says, "I know you say you don't like the food here but at least just try it out and see okay? Can or not?"

He blinks at her. "It's not just *trying out*. We're going to stay here forever and ever isn't it? Isn't it?"

Yes. From now on he is going to be only six years old. He is going to abandon all pussyfooting.

She turns away from him and lifts one corner of her mouth in a coy little smile. He doesn't want to see it but it is too late and now the sight of it makes him want to pick the scabs off his knees. But then she turns back to him with a deep loud sigh and says, "I told you isn't it, I'll show them how to cook something nicer. Okay? Okay, Reza boy?"

He shrugs and averts his eyes.

One week later Reza is holding Mama's hand in the lunch buffet queue and looking at a tray of what he forgets cannot possibly be real prawn fritters. He should not forget; by now he should know that the possibility of prawn fritters is exactly zero. But remember: he is only six years old now! He can be six years old. He can give Mama what she wants. Giving her what she wants is in fact all he knows how to do.

Is some small part of him still aware at this point that he is performing? That he is an old man playing the part of a six-year-old? Or has he given himself up completely to the role and has it opened its maw and eaten him alive?

"Hot hot hot," Mama says about the chafing dishes. "Don't touch don't touch." As any mother might say to any small boy. And perhaps Reza thinks, *Suddenly now you have to warn me about hot pans? Have you forgotten how I used to make Maggi Mee for us at the stove when you couldn't get out of bed and there was nothing else in the house? Have you forgotten how I used to take the tiffin carrier downstairs to the curry mee man or up the road to the mamak stall and bring back boiling soup and mee rebus?*

Or perhaps he doesn't think that at all.

All the way down the table he says "No no no" to everything. Every inch the petulant small boy. No noodles no cabbage no yellow rice even. "What?" says Mama. "You love yellow rice!" But brand-new smallboy Reza is saving all the space on his plate and in his stomach for the promised treat because brand-new smallboy Reza trusts in people and their promises. In front of the tray of golden-brown fritters he points and says, "I want that." The voice warbly. The whole pointing arm rigid from shoulder to fingertip.

Mama puts a fritter on his plate then seeing once again that he has hardly anything else puts another.

"More," he says. "Put more, I want more."

"Why don't you eat first and then see if you want some more? After you don't finish means wasted only."

"No," Reza insists. "More. I'm hungry."

In her hurry to keep moving so that others can serve themselves Mama piles them onto Reza's plate: three four five six fritters. The other children stare goggle-eyed: fried foods are supposed to be rationed. Two pieces per child.

In his seat at last Reza sinks his teeth into the not-so-crisp batter whose sogginess and rancid oil smell he has already forgiven in anticipation of what awaits inside: the solid bite of it the solid chewy sweet prawny bite. In that brief glorious moment he remembers the floury fritters of Ramadan bazaars and the fat buttery tiger prawns of Chinese wedding banquets. He remembers the tempura prawns of dinner parties at the club when they were flush.

And perhaps then he remembers the life he had with Mama before they came here: men coming men going but always always in the end and in between it had been the two of them—Reza and Mama, Mama and Reza in their own bubble. When there was nobody to take them anywhere and nobody to pay for a treat Mama would call a taxi and they would go to town and there would be these things: prawns crabs cuttlefish chicken drumsticks.

All these thoughts at once exhilarating and devastating must wash through him as his teeth attain the centre of that first fritter. Then the disappointment: inside the batter is something cold and mushy and boiled-tasting. It smells of dusty weevilled spices and cloudy lukewarm water. Of other people's bathrooms.

He forces himself to swallow and holds the other half of the fritter gingerly between thumb and index finger as if it were somebody else's used tissue. There he sits for a good ten minutes before Mama noticing his plate says, "What is this, Reza? You've not eaten anything. I told you not to—"

"But," he says. Trying to force the words out the same way he forced the fritter mouthful in: at the exact same point in his throat fritter and words lumpify themselves and stick fast. Like a big wodge of long hair caught in the bend of the bathroom sink pipe. Waiting to be fished out. The unbudgingness of it not quite painful but sickening. Then he draws in a big breath and gathering up all the air inside his head uses it to expel the words: "I don't like it."

The other children watch intently. Their own food untouched. As dinnertime entertainment it is a little more tense than the usual offerings. Annabelle Foo whispers to Kiranjit Kaur, "I think so he must be used to English-type food lah."

"Try it with the sauce and see," Salmah says.

"I don't like it. It's not prawns." Braver now that the first words are out of the way. Willing and able to elaborate.

Though he believes himself to be speaking quietly and discreetly the one they call Mrs Arasu whips her head around and bursts out laughing while clapping her hands. Reza never liked her to begin with but now he hates her. She is not soft like fat people usually are but hard and shiny like a bead. Tall and thin and bucktoothed with a mean little hairbun no bigger than a ten-cent fishball that she nevertheless confines in a hairnet in what even Reza age six recognizes as a fine example of wishful thinking. Her lips are always oily even when she has not eaten in hours. Her skin fits too tightly around the whole hard mass of her.

"Listen to the poor innocent boy!" she shrieks, turning to Reza. "You see," she says to him with too much patience— why should he need so much patience when he is not even crying? "You see we don't eat prawns here because eating dead animals is not good for the body and the soul. But these fritters are even tastier than prawns isn't it? These are cauliflower fritters but one bite and I guarantee you, you will never look at prawns again, wah so tasty they are, just like prawns but better than prawns, mmmm!"

She tears off a hunk of fritter with her teeth like a caveman devouring a boar leg and chews avidly, all the while maintaining eye contact with Reza. Perhaps it is this terrifying spectacle that dispels the last of his reticence. Or perhaps this is the moment when his whole body realizes what it means to be a small boy and not only steps up to the task but goes leaping clean over the abyss. He shoves his plate across the table. It goes crashing into Annabelle Foo's and she giggles nervously as though they are playing a game of plate carom and she is losing. But Reza takes no notice of her. He jumps to his feet with the oily hand held away from his body in disgust to shout, "No they're not! They don't taste like prawns at all! They taste like dogshit! All the food here tastes like dogshit and catshit and horseshit!"

The children hold their breath. The whole perfect oval of Annabelle Foo face aglow with something between horror and admiration. The Mak twins on the brink of vomiting from the excitement of it. But Reza is not nearly done.

"You're all pretending to like it! You're all just bluffing! I don't want to eat your horrible food! I don't—"

"Oh dear," says Cyril Dragon who has rushed from his place at the head of the table to their side. He puts a hand on Reza's shoulder and says again: "Oh dear, Reza."

Genuine sadness weighs down his words. His face sags. His eyes look tender and puffy. The children wonder would he say oh dear and put his hands on their shoulders if they too refused to eat? Out loud Annabelle Foo cries, "Wah!"

Even Neela has come to the kitchen doorway to watch the show. It's entirely possible that if Cyril's eyes had not fallen upon her when he looked up from Reza's side he would not have said what he said next. But there she is leaning on the door jamb looking upon the scene with those slightly despising eyes and that slightly pugnacious chin and it is more than he can bear.

"Neela," he says, "the fritters are soggy and tasteless. See, even the children are complaining, and children always love anything deep-fried. Your cooking is becoming terrible."

It's this last accusation that silences the entire room. All the hissing and muttering stops. People freeze mid-chew. Neela stands to attention, searches his face for something she doesn't find. Swallows hard. Then she says, "Children where complaining? Only one. Only one children complaining."

"Yes!" Mrs Arasu cries as if the horse she picked has won. "The fritters are exactly the same as they always are. Let us be fair to Neela!"

The ultimate slap in the face for a man of such high ideals: to be reminded to be fair by a woman like Mrs Arasu. A petty busybody who is never fair unless it suits her own purpose. Even she can see where the real fault lies here. Cyril is shaken. He stands up as if to deliver a speech at a funeral.

"I'm very sorry," he says to nobody in particular. "I'm really very sorry, I got carried away, this type of conflict deeply upsets me."

He says to the clock on the wall: "Neela, I'm sorry, I'm sorry. I had no business, really, you do so much for us, slogging away in that kitchen, you always do your best, we all know it."

Then he bends slightly to address Reza again. "It's all right, it's all right. You're not used to the food, of course. It will take time."

He might have got away with it had he not at this point laid an absentminded hand on Reza's curly head. Immediately Reza swats the hand away and bares his teeth at Cyril

Dragon like a wolf caught in a trap.

"Go away!" he shouts. "Go away and leave us alone! As if you can make me eat this dogshit food! You're not my father! I don't have to listen to you! I don't even like you!"

"What to do, what to do," Mrs Arasu is saying to Bee Bee in a razor-blade voice that carries expertly across the room. "The poor boy has never had a mother, I mean she must have been busy with *other things* all the time isn't it?"

"Reza," Mama murmurs, "sit down right now." She tugs at the hem of his shirt like a demure wife begging her husband not to bargain so much with the salesman. On her face not cool authority but a weary smile.

"I told you," Reza shouts, "I told you already isn't it? I don't want to eat this! I don't want to stay here! I hate this place and I hate this food!"

Then Mama's awareness of her impotence finally overcomes her. Before she can stop it her left hand is reaching under the table and pinching Reza hard on the thigh. She knows that Cyril Dragon who has gone quietly back to his seat is trying to catch her eye. She pulls Reza back down into his seat. She leans over and hisses between her gritted teeth:

"You are embarrassing me. You are making a fool of both of us. I am so ashamed! I don't know where to keep my face. I am ashamed to be your mother. Why couldn't I have died the night you were born? Now shut your mouth and stop crying and eat."

His eyes are big enough now to swallow her whole. Though nobody has touched his face his cheeks blaze red. *I wish I could have died*, she said, *I wish I could have died*, and now that the words have taken shape he must swallow them. All the times he brought her back from the dead and now she has said to him: *because of you only I want to be dead*. Now everything has changed. Now she does not belong to him anymore.

There is nothing to do now but eat this whole plate of

soggy batter and slimy cauliflower—someone has dragged it back to his place and here it sits in front of him. No magic wand in the world will disappear it so eat it he does, stuffing as many pieces as he can into his mouth at one time so that his mouth is so full it will not close. The salt of the fritters mixes with the watery salt of tears and phlegm in his mouth. He gags and eats and eats and gags and everyone pretends to ignore him because that is one thing adults are very good at doing: pretending. Half of the tears running down his face are tears of sorrow and the other half are the tears that are forced out of the corners of your eyes when you are close to vomiting.

The Unwilling Confidant

"The thing is," Mama says to him, "the thing is I have never been so happy, Reza boy."

He'd been wandering down the path by himself when she surprised him. Sneaking up behind him and spoiling his solitude. He pulls a dry leaf from the nearest shrub and crumbles it between his fingertips. But she won't stop.

"I know at your age boys don't like to hear about all these things. But you've never been like other children. I feel you're mature enough for me to confide in you. Am I wrong?"

There is no right answer: the only way to stop her from telling him what he doesn't want to hear is to be what he is not, i.e. a child like other children. If he stops up his ears he will be immature; if he admits he is mature he has to listen to whatever horrible confessions are already making him wince before he's heard them. He tries to hedge his bets by shaking his head only imperceptibly.

"I knew it!" she says. "I knew I could trust you. Can I tell you something?"

He meets her eyes with an expression she chooses not to interpret as accusatory.

"There have been so many men isn't it? You know how they sweet-talk me at first. But in the end? In the end they are all the same. They think just because I talk English, I drink wine, I smoke cigarettes means they can use me and throw me away. You saw how your own father left like a bloody coward, like a dog in the night. No balls to tell me he had found a younger fresher woman. But Cyril Dragon, Cyril Dragon is *different*. I knew it from the moment I first saw him. No, I knew it before that. When I first heard about him, when I first heard his name."

She lowers her eyes and chuckles at the recollection.

"I just had a feeling," she goes on. "I had a sense. Like as though—hai, we Muslims are not supposed to believe in all this but what to do? I've never been the kind of Muslim they wanted me to be. I can't just follow the rules and go by the book. I had that feeling like ... like I knew Cyril Dragon in a previous life. Like I was supposed to come here because we had some kind of unfinished business. Oh, Reza, don't be shy, one day you also will grow up and find true love!"

He covers up an involuntary wince by rubbing and rubbing at his nose as though it is itchy. Either she does not notice at all or is completely convinced by the pretence, for already she is proceeding.

"Then when I came here and actually saw him—oh my God, I cannot even describe it! To see him, to talk to him for the first time ... and even when we are just sitting quietly together, even when neither one of us is saying one word. It is a feeling I have never had, Reza, a feeling a person cannot get even from the finest champagne in the world, it is like being *bathed in bliss*, for him to just put his hand on my hand, just like this"—and here she demonstrates while Reza struggles not to snatch his hand away—"just that! So you can imagine all the rest."

Imagine all the rest! *All the rest.* Dim glimmers of filthy talk rise from the back rows of the school bus to the surface of his memory. Disgusting rumours circulated by the Standard Six boys on the school padang. He knows how to distil the cloudy brew down to its essence: women have a hole and into that hole men can put their fingers or—believe it or not—their *thing*. That is what men and women do when they are alone together—of all the many activities they could choose, e.g. reading comics eating assam watching TV chewing gum playing cards, they choose to take off their underpants and fit their private parts together. And now his mother tells him to imagine it as though it is something good and beautiful.

"The first time Cyril Dragon kissed me, oh, Reza! You cannot imagine it, of course you cannot, you are only a small boy."

She goes quiet for a few moments as though lost in thought. He drives the toe of his shoe into the earth. All the rain has made the soil rich and yielding. A chocolatey smell wafts from it so thickly he can almost see the swirls of it like in a cartoon. When she speaks again her voice is bright and brassy.

"Do you know about men and women, Reza?"

"What?" he says. It is not a *What? I didn't hear you* or even a *What? I'm not sure what you mean*; it is an incredulous *What? I cannot believe you are taking us down this horrible path.*

"Maybe—maybe you are too small." She sighs. "You are so small but I have no one else to talk to, no one to pour out my secrets to. What to do?"

There was a time when he would have said, *Tell me Mama tell me*, and he would have covered her tight fists with his hands and laid his head in her lap. But now he has had enough. It is Cyril Dragon who has brought upon him this Had Enough feeling. Cyril Dragon with his too-muchness and that hoity-toity way he glides around like everybody's saviour and his smug earnest face when he looks at Reza. Like they belong together for life. Like he has replaced Reza and is Mama's everything now. Nobody ever looked at Reza like that before. It makes him want to throw sand in both their eyes and run like the wind while they are blinded. It makes him want to gnaw through the trap. These fantasies must be apparent in his face because Mama says, "You want me to stop talking, I see."

He is assailed by guilt. There is no winning. Under his dark eyebrows he raises reluctantly beseeching eyes to her.

"Well," she says. "Well, you know that in your fairy stories when the princess falls in love with the prince they get married and they live happily after. But it is not the wedding dress and the ring that joins them forever. A piece of paper cannot make them man and wife. Cyril Dragon and Mama cannot get married because of the man-made laws in Malaysia. But we belong to each other. We have shared everything. We have shared ourselves, our bodies, in the way that men and women share their bodies when they love each other. I know, I know, Reza, you don't like to hear about all this, it's normal, when I was your age I also didn't want to hear. But I am telling you so that you understand: Cyril Dragon and Mama have given themselves to each other. We have sealed our love in God's eyes. We have become a family. I am telling you because I feel sometimes you feel shameful or what. You feel embarrassed that your Mama goes with men but they are not your Papa and they are not my proper husband. Well, I cannot change the past. I made mistakes, I trusted people I should not have trusted. But this time it is different."

Reza keeps his churning thoughts to himself. How could any six-year-old—let alone one who has been his mother's sole caretaker—spell out such thoughts to that selfsame mother? But one day when I am six he will ask me: "You know what I was thinking about the whole time she was talking about their True Love?" And I will shake my head to say *No no please don't tell me* but Reza will very conveniently interpret this to mean *No I don't know please tell me.* The words always on the tip of my tongue: *Don't talk about Papa like that!* But myself too much of a shit-eater to say them out loud. How he dotes on you! Made you his special pet the day he met you. Loves you better than his own flesh-and-blood son. If Reza knows all this he will not give a damn. "You know what I was thinking about?" he will ask me and then with a filthy little chuckle he will tell me this story:

"I was thinking about one of Mama's other men, this hairy Indian bugger who used to hang around the house few years before we came here. Lawyer or something. Loaded. Used to fill up the kitchen cabinets with imported biscuits and chocolates. Anyway, Sundays they used to stay in bed until afternoon. Wouldn't even come out to eat. Well one Sunday she must have got hungry. Maybe by then she was starting to get bored with the fler's bedroom tricks. Sends him out to hunt-and-gather for her. Fler doesn't realize my room door is open one tiny crack. Comes out totally naked. I still remember the shape of him: squat torso and thick thighs but not one ounce of fat. Built like a wrestler. That tiny crack was enough for me to get a big eyeful of his dicky bird. As fat as a German sausage but no more than three inches long. Dangling here there everywhere. I swear to God the thing was wet. In fact his whole body looked shiny and oily. Fler walks into the kitchen and bends down to get the kuali and stands there stark naked making nasi goreng. Not a care in the world even though his sausage is hanging right in front of the spitting kuali. Now that's balls for you. Hahaha! So the whole time she's going on about The Act of Love and how she and Cyril Dragon have been joined by their genitals, I'm thinking of this other fler who was ready to sustain second-degree burns on his cock all for the sake of his hungry woman. Hahahaha, no, actually I'm thinking, *It's not the first time you've sealed the deal that way, Mama.* But what to do? Our mother is a whore. Just got to live with it I guess."

And that, dear reader, will be too much even for me (feeble doubts notwithstanding). "She's not," I will protest, "she's not what you say!" (Oh the poor dear boy too prudish even to say the word *whore*—I feel for him now.) "She loves Papa. She doesn't do all that anymore. She changed after she came here. What men has she gone with since coming here? What men?"

"Hah!" Reza will respond. "You don't know her like I

know her. That's why Mama's got two sons, don't you know? One to love her and one to know her. Oh, the things I know about her! Even when I was sleeping she used to creep up to the dorm and pick me up and carry me out to the porch so that she could tell me all her so-called secrets. The whole time I'll pretend to be sleeping. That's what she did when I told them how disgusting their food was one time. Came up in the night to tell me grandmother stories and then beg sorry, sorry, I shouldn't have shamed you in front of other people. I used to feel shy for her because she didn't know how to feel shy herself. That's how she's been her whole life. Simply does whatever she likes, and then she'll come and sweet-talk you, butter you up, bribe you. 'Oh, I'm so sorry, oh please forgive me.' Why would I forgive her when I already knew she would never change? You'll know it too soon. Wait and see. Just wait. It won't be long."

But where is my share of the sweet-talking where is my buttering-up where are my bribes? I will wonder when I am six and he tells me all this. And alone I will wrestle with my multifarious feelings the same way Reza once wrestled with his.

The Prize Students

2023

Though there may have been precious little sweetness and buttering Mama did know how to take the helm of my life as necessary. The manner and methods of seizing control were different but the ends, the ends were always whatever she wanted for whichever reason she wanted it. Her pleasure. Her comfort. Her safety. It was she who decided many years ago that my job at the neighbourhood tuition centre was giving me gastric. "You know how you are," she said to me. "You need more peace and quiet. You should give tuition from the house itself. Enough. No need to go up and down every day and on top of that every Tom Dick and Harry is teaching there and you have to smile politely and do all that small talk with them. Tension lah."

See how neatly she does things. Everything wrapped up in its smooth packaging: "every Tom Dick and Harry," "all that small talk." She herself had taken the necessary steps to maintain our public image: "everything I do, I do for you only," she said when she took to wearing the tudung.

"You don't mean to tell me that if you don't wear it, people will drive their children through the traffic to some other tuition centre," I'd said at the time.

"Everybody already knows that if the Ministry sacks a teacher it must have been something very serious," she'd said. "If there is any trouble the owner won't think twice about letting you go next term. You don't know these people. If we were Indian or Chinese, that's different. It's because of who we are, Yusuf. It's because of what they all know about us. They'll be frightened you're going to lure their children into some kind of funny cult while pretending to teach them English. You can be sure they're carefully studying what homework you give the children."

"I'll be sure to assign only the best translations of the Quran and the Hadith," I'd said, but she didn't find that funny. I could have pointed out the hypocrisy of covering her aurat solely for career reasons and not even her own career at that—but who was I to talk? Who was already ducking into the downstairs toilet during the fasting month to eat rolled-up Kraft Singles? Who was popping Cadbury's Nutties from his trouser pocket into his mouth in the afternoon and then pretending to break his fast at dusk?

Over the course of the next fifteen years Mama graduated from the mini-tudung to the tudung bawal to the tudung labuh which then grew ever longer and darker (shoulder-length chest-length waist-length even as she grew thinner and thinner and had less and less of a body to hide) and was finally joined by the jubah; as she became first an occasional and then a regular attendee of ceramahs at the neighbourhood mosque; as she joined PERKIM and sallied forth on all-expenses-paid trips to convert kafirs and buy cheap leather handbags all over Southeast Asia.

And why not? Why not please people and buy top-quality designer knockoffs into the bargain? There are clear benefits to abjuring thought in favour of peace of mind. My mother has aged gracefully and blissfully. Look at the unclouded whites of her eyes—fresh and clear as a baby's—look at that smooth brow. Now look at my ruined face. All the grey at my temples. All the broken capillaries in my eyes. The tremors and stammers and dropped stitches of my mind.

But even Mama's tudung couldn't protect me from spies and snoops in this era of googling anybody you have just met. Nor from the types of questions that might innocently or not-so-innocently fall under the umbrella of small talk among our people and the assumptions deductions and conclusions that would ensue from my answers or lack thereof. And then there were the dangerous little facts I might accidentally reveal: one minute you think you are telling a harmless tale about a coveted childhood treat or a punishment or scolding you endured in your boyhood and the next minute a slip of the tongue or the brain has given you away. Of course I have had a lifetime to practise the art of concealment but why should Mama trust in my skills? Why should she ever have faith in my ability to sift and sort and shut up as needed when my rat mouth once played such a key role in our downfall?

Having thus determined my isolation to be an utmost priority she still knew how to take matters into her own hands. No asking for help or sitting around waiting. Oh no. Like a general she drew up a plan of attack. Stationed herself in the tuition centre lobby and cornered the parents of the children in my classes. It wasn't hard for her to convince them: why pay so much for tuition when the class sizes at the centre were hardly smaller than government school class sizes? My son will have no more than twelve students per class! He'll be able to give each student so much more attention! He'll tailor his teaching methods to fit individual students' needs! All This For Seventy-Five Per Cent And Not A Sen More Of What You Are Paying Here!

A quarter century may have lapsed since her journalism days but she hadn't lost her persuasive skills. When she had successfully poached a good fraction of the tuition centre's clients she then turned her attention to her lady friends, i.e. the loudly upstanding and proudly prosperous wives of UMNO and PERKIM. Why you may well ask would one even have wanted to bother with tuition classes when one's children would be very shortly sailing into one's own alma maters which is to say the Etons of the East whose doors are never darkened by the children of the lesser races? And thenceforth to the UK US Canada Australia courtesy of our selectively generous gomen and *thence*forth into plum jobs at Petronas TNB TM and whatever miscellaneous gomen and half-gomen agencies would guarantee them, Datukships and seats on the boards of directors? But there you have it. Mama sayang. Ice to an eskimo sawdust to a lumber mill: she could sell anything. She knew how to appeal to the keeping-up-with-the-Datins instincts of Datins. "Datin X is sending her son for my son's classes," she would tell Datin Y, and to Datin X, "Datin Y is sending her daughter for my son's classes. My son's classes are not like other classes around here. He offers all the classics and the English poetry and whatnot. You won't get that at the tuition centres." And their kind had always needed pukka English for their swanning around London and New York isn't it? Not for those children of fatcats the anticolonial grandstanding against the language of the penjajah. The so-called National Language was for the plebes and the jetsetting classes knew it.

Yet it was Amar Mama seemed to think of as her greatest catch. *Which bigshot's son was he?* you might ask. Which Datuk which minister which tycoon? None of these: when we first knew Amar's father Dawood he was only an assistant at our neighbourhood mamak restaurant. Dawood was the nephew of the childless owner and so after the requisite number of years of disparaging him in three languages (Tamil, Malay, English, all three beautifully suited to the task) in front of all his customers—useless bloody boy, failed his Form Three and had to repeat, failed his Form Five, a real dunce, his poor father was at his wits' end so I took pity what to do what to do—the uncle handed the business down to Dawood. By then (one had to conclude) the useless edges had been sufficiently rubbed off for Dawood to manage the operation.

I remember the way Mama's face glowed the day she came home and announced: I got Dawood's boy for you.

You could have mistaken her for any of the barren fairy-tale women who finds a baby in a flower bulb or a haystack. Was it just the unwarranted level of joy that unsettled me? Cold fingers lightly brushed my heart and then were gone: my head told me *Why not, the boy is in secondary school now, good idea.* Couple of years later the sister followed suit: it was only fair that if the boy was getting English tuition she should too.

All the stages Amar has gone through since he came to his first tuition class: the downy moustache the five o'clock shadow the Bollywood action-hero stubble. His sister Amira battling acne enduring braces and specs and now look at her: contact lenses and lip gloss and nicely hour-glassing out her T-shirts and jeans.

When he started attending my classes his face was still smooth.

"Boy," Mama would say to him on his way in or out of the house. "Study hard."

He'd smile shyly then, eyes lowered as he rushed past.

For ten years at their father's restaurant she'd been patting the chair next to her and calling out to Amar and his sister Amira: "Boy! Adik! Come come. Sit with Nenek for a few minutes. Tell Nenek: what you want to be when you grow up?"

Polis. Princess. Fireman. Flimstar. Doctor. Scientist. Heart surgeon. Marine biologist. We saw their ambitions grow and crystallize as they grew older.

They've neither one of them been bad students although it must be admitted that Amar is not one of my best. Solidly average. Now What Do You Want To Be When You Grow Up is no longer the stuff of distant fancy but a harsh round-the-corner reality.

Of course they have one significant advantage: they have shed their Tamil skin and emerged into the full glory of being Malay in Malaysia. Dawood's uncle was as Tamil as Tamil could possibly be and spoke that powerful high-flown form of the language one encounters almost uniquely among the mamaks; Dawood himself is black as a prune with the frog face of a Tamil film village buffoon; yet by the rules of the national Race race he and his family have been able to reinvent themselves as Sons of the Soil. They have no idea I am the exact opposite sort of animal: however hard they scrambled into that coveted Bumiputera box I have tried just as hard to sneak out of it. The difference was that theirs was an undertaking people applauded and cheered or at least countenanced with a shrug of resignation; mine is a dangerous secret for which I can be reported. I am Malay in name (as far as anyone knows) and Malay in face yet shedding my Malay skin to emerge as—what exactly? Nothing at all. A skinless wonder. Pink and raw. Liable to be destroyed by the slightest exposure to sunlight. Not that Dawood and his family are privy to any of this. To them I am the upstanding Encik Yusuf. A model Malay son. Pity not married no children. (Never too late though. Inshallah.)

In Dawood and his wife the conversion to Malayness is only partial. Which is to say that as long as you see the wife only from the back—baju kurung *check* tudung labuh *check*—you might mistake her for a Daughter of the Soil; but the minute they open their mouths you can hear the heavy beads of their Tamil accent hanging from their Malay. But their new identity has reached its apotheosis in their son and daughter. It helps of course that they have not inherited their parents' looks. They say some of these mamaks have Pashtun or Kashmiri blood in their veins, the physical traits of which may skip a generation or two: in Dawood and his uncle that blood must have run deep as a subterranean river but in those children and in particular the boy! Ah, the boy. Lush curls that glinted gold-brown in the sun. Hazel eyes cherry lips the complexion of a Pre-Raphaelite muse. They are the sort of specimens any race in Asia would rush to claim in the unspeakable mission to improve its stock.

Amira is the one they have ambitions for. Her father's gunning for Law or Medicine and thanks to the grand family Malayfication the girl can safely expect a generous government
scholarship. Actually whom are we kidding—thanks to the grand family Malayfication even the boy can expect a scholarship though he may have to content himself with a BA in fisheries or food science from the University of the Wideopenprairies whereas with a little luck she will make it to Cambridge or LSE.

Once a week for all these years they've sat in my tuition room. A schoolteacher has them in his class for a year, before with a great sigh of relief he fobs them off onto the next poor sod wipes his brow with the back of his hand and dusts himself down. It's people like me—the tuition teachers the piano teachers the senseis—who watch your children grow up. Never has this been truer for me than in the case of Amar and his sister. I was there when Dawood was swaggering from table to table of the restaurant beaming and handing out sweetmeats when they were born. I saw them when they were babies sweating in their mittens and booties. I saw them when they were toddlers scattering pieces of roti canai far and wide from their high chairs. I witnessed their first lisping squabbles I saw them show off their brand-new school uniforms. I saw them stand at solemn attention to answer my mother's questions about their ambitions.

We all saw how she looked at them and most especially the boy. We'd be having our roti telur and the children would be doing their homework at the corner table in front of the swivelling stand fan blowing about like nobody's business. Those poor children had to sprawl over their books to hold the pages down. There would be nonstop football on the TV and the fluorescent lighting made all the curries and deepfrieds look sickly in their chafing dishes but Mama never wanted to bungkus our meal to eat at home. She'd be watching that boy like he was a TV show and I'd be watching her watch him while pretending to watch TV.

Feeling sorry for the poor Nenek saddled with her stubborn bachelor son Dawood would push the children towards her: *Go and salam Nenek. Nah, take this drink to Nenek. Nenek has finished eating, ask her whether she wants coffee or tea.* Mama would turn on her best grandmotherly charm for them: the beaming countenance the *so handsome so pretty so clever* the sweets from her purse. "Aisehman," Dawood would stage-whisper to me when I went to settle the bill. "Kesian lah Nenek. Can see she is longing for grandchildren."

Then I would grunt a few indecipherable syllables and Mama would pretend to be so hard of hearing she was oblivious to the whole exchange. A casual observer would have had no doubt that Dawood was right. But Mama knew and I knew that her fascination with Dawood's goldenboy cherub had nothing to do with a desire for grandchildren. By unspoken agreement we had agreed to uphold this misconception because it was easier than anything else. Like this we went on for years: Mama eyeing the children pulling out treats pinching the girl's cheek ruffling the boy's hair.

"They will do very well in life," Mama says smugly. "Mark my words, one day Amar will be Somebody."

I mark her words all right. After all she's been careful not to outline how and why he will be Somebody. Loose screws notwithstanding our Mama sayang has retained that guileless instinct for what to leave out. One cannot even accuse her of lies of omission: all by itself her tongue knows how to tell stories that are Technically True. And why wouldn't those children succeed by all our favourite measures? Dawood is no pauper to begin with: from one 24-hour joint he has built up an empire. Three different branches. Workers from Bangladesh and Nepal and Myanmar. So his children are twice-sorted. Daddy's money plus the gomen gravy train of special rights. All they have to do is finish school without killing anyone or getting pregnant and they will be A-okay.

The Worried Father

Dawood comes to see me one afternoon. Just as I expected he feels he needs my advice and how can I refuse him? *Listen brother I just want a peaceful life can or not?* No. I brace myself and cock a sympathetic ear and he launches straight into his woes.

"Even I have to send him myself also, I don't mind you know," he says. "We parents can sacrifice for our children, no problem isn't it? Even UK or US cannot also, can try India, otherwise local U also okay, I always tell him, you just do your best, not everybody can be Number One, not everybody can be the leader, followers also we must have, yes or not?"

So far so easy to nod and smile. But then he goes on.

"You also can see what is happening I'm sure. Isn't it, Encik Yusuf?"

I draw in a big breath—fill my head with air—blow it all out. There.

Have I noticed the changes? What sort of buffalo head would not have noticed them? First the stubble allowed to flourish into a full beard. Though whether the stubble came before the robe and the kopiah I would be hard-pressed to tell you.

"What a breath of fresh air!" Mama said when the beard and robe first made their appearance. "Just the opposite of boys nowadays. Where can you find a boy his age behaving like this?"

Where you can find a boy his age behaving like this? I could tell her: I think you know where Mama. For they are not so few nowadays are they? You can hardly take ten steps without bumping into a school trip in which all the little boys are in robes and kopiahs and all the little girls are demurely betudunged and if you keep your eyes peeled you will find somewhere on their person the inspired names of their schools: Little Caliphs Al-Hidayah Seven Skies The Sunnah School (where your child can spend three years memorizing the Quran without the distractions of Maths Science History etc.). But I let Mama enjoy her little pretence.

"Young people, you know," I say. "Often they like to try this and that."

Dawood shakes his head like an indignant cat. "If it is cigarettes or drinking or even girls, then okay, I'll say aaah, never mind lah," he says. He lowers his voice to an urgent whisper. "But this?"

But what, Dawood? Does he know what I know? Does he know about the dirty looks his son gives me when I read Shakespeare or Joyce out loud? Does he know about the assignments from which his son demands special exemptions now? No excuse no apology. Just: "I cannot read this." Then it falls to me to suggest an alternative. Always this odd panic as I bow and scrape and always I am asking myself, *What am I frightened of?* The boy is barely seventeen years old. Is he going to report his tuition teacher to JAKIM for a poem that describes a woman's breasts? And yet I can't seem to quell my terrified need to keep him happy. As though—*no no* I tell myself *no no you are reading too deeply into all this* and yet ...

As though having first-hand knowledge of the price youthful zeal can exact I must be the one to save us all. I must do whatever it takes. If I believed in a God then I would be the one He had Chosen for this delicate mission. But there is no Chosen One. There is just a lowly tuition teacher sweating bullets under the burden he has taken onto his shoulders. And so when Amar comes in late and the only remaining seat is next to a girl I no longer wait for him to stand conspicuously goat-coughing in the doorway. Without anyone needing to say a word I clear my throat clap my hands and instruct someone to move so that Amar can sit with a boy. In the beginning there would be a little low-grade grumbling. A few raised eyebrows and perhaps an eye roll from whichever girl Amar hadn't wanted to sit next to. I would have to present my best shit-eating smile to them and murmur some soothing words about Respect and Compromise and how in Malaysia we understand Give and Take. But now they are all used to Amar's requirements. The other students know it is easier this way. Exams are approaching and nobody wants to waste time.

And Mama (who has an uncanny sense of what goes on in my classroom for someone who does not—as far as I know—spend those hours with an eyeball pressed to the door crack) has registered her approval.

"All the others are watching donowat on their phones and computers. All thinking about filthy things all day long. But this boy? So respectful. So pious. I look at how he is fighting to keep his mind pure and I just want to cry I tell you."

A joke danced on the tip of my tongue then: *I just want to cry too Mama but not for the same reason.* But from some mysterious place those cold fingers emerged again to flutter against my heart. When it comes to Mama and this boy my heart struggles to maintain its temperature I tell you. Best to bite my tongue is all I know.

"Ah, brother," I say to Dawood now. "Could be worse lah. He is not a drug addict or a Mat Rempit. He is not gallivanting or painting the town red like the ministers' sons and the sultans' sons. Don't worry so much."

Dawood shakes his head. "I don't want to simply argue, Encik Yusuf," he says. "But you don't know what all happens at home. In the beginning it was not too bad. If his sister wore makeup or whatever, he would quietly tegur.

Okay lah. But now! Even if she wants to go out with friends, you know lah, a girl that age, we also must understand. Let her live her life a bit. Natural lah. She likes to dress up a bit, makeup, jewellery …"

This is putting it mildly and Dawood knows it: Amira is in with a crowd of high-class girls who all look like they have stepped out of the pages of a glossy fashion magazine from a country uninhibited by the notion of modesty.

"Last time somebody came and said they saw his sister in Bangsar the boy goddamn wild. Called her—" He stops. Shakes his head again. "I think if you hear the type of language Encik Yusuf, you also will be shocked. The words he uses. And on the sister is one thing. Now, even his mother goes to the gate without covering the head also—just to check the letterbox or whatever!—she gets one big bloody lecture. If her sleeves slide down while she is hanging up the clothes outside, you won't believe the things that come out of his mouth. We ourselves don't know what to do anymore."

Be careful, be careful! I want to say. *Cut off his internet access take away his phone lock him up at home make an appointment with a counsellor!* But I don't want Dawood to sense my apprehension. I don't want him to start to wonder or speculate about the ghosts of my own past.

"No need to do anything lah," I say. "The less you say the better. Just leave it and he will move on when he gets bored."

He frowns. "Sure ah?" he says. "Anything else means I also will tell myself, just a phase lah. But this type of thing … They don't move on. They are all in it together you see. Like a club. The friends also … all like him. They go to the mosque for ceramah and meetings and whatnot. Now with the new government lagi teruk. Those ulamas think they will lose power so even louder they are shouting about the kufr lah, shirk lah, what-what Arabic terms he is using now, I myself cannot keep track. Our time all where people talked like that? Those days Malaysians had the true Muhibbah spirit."

He doesn't see me flinch at the very word.

"Race and religion were not such a big thing like now. People knew how to get along. Neighbours used to eat in each other's houses. People knew how to be friends. I really miss that Malaysia, I tell you Encik Yusuf."

That's right Dawood. People knew how to be friends. By which we mean that most of us knew how to express our real opinions only behind each other's backs and some of us knew how to swallow our bile and keep smiling when we encountered real opinions in unexpected places. In this way we convinced ourselves that Everybody Could Take a Joke and Nobody Was So Sensitive in those days. Everybody would laugh it all off and nobody would make a big deal of anything except for those very rare occasions on which we would pull out our parangs and butcher each other and set things on fire. But that is the best one can expect in this imperfect world is it not Dawood? Someone should have told my father it was the best we could expect.

"I don't know," Dawood is saying now. "Those days are gone. Maybe we just have to accept it. He is growing up in this new Malaysia, not that old Malaysia. So what to do? At the end of the day, he is still our son."

The words slip out before I can stop myself:

"Anyway, brother, what are you worried about? Your son and his friends will be fine. In this country nothing bad will happen to them."

He looks at me as though he's seeing me for the first time. In his eyes the bloodshot clarity of a man who finally understands what he's up against. He shakes his head again—more slowly this time—and smiles. Then he says, "After everything I've done for the boy. All my blood sweat and tears, just to give him and his sister a proper education. For us that was always the most important thing. Our children must study hard, come up in life."

"Who is to say he won't come up in life, Dawood? Such people are very successful nowadays. Running foundations, hosting TV shows and all. Some of them are given top posts. Let him find his own path. Doesn't mean if he wears a kopiah he cannot get a scholarship to study in UK or US."

But at this, Dawood puts his hands to his ears and shakes his head vigorously. "Ah no no no, please! That is no more my plan. I am not sending him overseas. I need to keep an eye on him here. He will go to UK, he will join donowat jihadi nonsense, next thing I know he will be going off to Syria or whatever new place they all want to go and cause trouble. No thank you. He wants to spit in our faces like we are dogs, never mind. Better he stay here and spit in my face than go somewhere and bomb innocent people!"

For a moment we stand there looking at each other. We breathe. Then in a calmer voice Dawood says, "Only thing I wanted to ask ... You ... you cannot help us Encik Yusuf?"

"Help you! Help you how?"

"Maybe ... I thought maybe ... you can talk to him. Long time you have been his teacher, you see. All of us have a lot of respect for you, you see. Even Amar. At one time lah. Because you are well educated, you read so much, your English so powerful ... His mother and I thought, maybe he will listen to you. If *you* tell him to concentrate on his studies. If you tell him all these flers, in their own way they're just as bad as the drug addicts and the drunkards. After all, these flers are also trying to pull him away from his studies, trying to spoil his life."

"No. They're not trying to pull him away from his studies Dawood. Say what you may, these boys are not playacting for our benefit lah. They really believe their way is the correct way. Nothing you and I can do to change it."

He sighs. "Maybe you are right. Maybe you are right. But ... I am frightened. I myself don't know why I am so frightened."

Out loud I say, "Different generation, different mindset lah, Dawood. You yourself said isn't it? We had to play by different rules to come up. Their generation they don't have the same ideas. No kowtowing to the West, no trying to ape Western ways. He can have his education and *also* be a good Muslim. We should be happy for him isn't it?"

But to myself I'm thinking about Dawood's nameless fear. I'm thinking about his unerring instinct. About his stomach that knows how to lurch at the thought of a zealous son although he has not yet seen it happen: he has not yet seen how the piety and certitude of the young can blaze through your whole life leaving nothing but smoke and embers in its trail. He knows nothing of the concrete possibilities. And yet he has homed in on the truth with no hesitation: there is nothing more dangerous than a young person who has appointed himself policeman of the world's morals.

Trail

Amar and Reza, Reza and Amar. They swim in and out of my dreams. The one's face blurs into the other's. Sometimes Boy Reza grows up into Young-Man Amar and sometimes Boy Amar grows up into Young-Man Reza with an Adidas duffel bag. Sometimes I find myself face to face with the Ghost of Amar Future who upon closer inspection seems to be an artist's projection of Present-Day Reza. But as this face comes into focus I realize it's not Reza not Amar no neither one it's just a man no longer young but not yet old. A gently ageing specimen like me.

"Try with your internet," Mama says. "You know how to do the Google and all that."

So obvious that even a seventy-three-year-old woman can call up the words and yet I swear to you it had never occurred to me. But there it is as soon as she has spoken the words: the seed of an idea. The germ if you will because I always like a word that can multitask and what we have here is the possibility of both growth and disease.

It turns out there are people who will take your money and an old photograph of your missing person and age him or her for you. Not the police (who in their right mind wants to go poking the hornet's nest we call the police when it is not absolutely necessary? No bloodshed no kidnapping no fire therefore no police thank you very much) but private companies. In the red photo album in the TV cabinet there are photos of Baby Reza and Small-Boy Reza and then a significant lacuna but then oh yes *then* in the back of the album on the very last page where you are unlikely to look because after all those empty pages you will have thought there is nothing more: there is a photo of Reza in those last strange months. Our aunt took it apropos of nothing at all one afternoon in her sitting room. It was printed on the matte photo paper that was in vogue in those years and the colours have gone all funny as they do: a thin wash of pink over everything. But the fading and the discoloration cannot obscure Reza's refusal to humour our pestering aunt.

"Ala, smile la sikit," she'd begged. "Working at Pizza Hut, surely you know how to say 'cheese,' can?"

Then she'd laughed alone at her own lame joke. In the photo Reza is sucking in his cheeks and frowning. His arms are sullenly folded. At first you might think he is doing the exact opposite of what she wants; indeed that was what I thought for many years each time I turned to that secret page to confirm that the photo was not a figment of my imagination. But when I was the same age as he is in the photo I had a sudden realization: he could have ignored her entirely couldn't he? He could even—truth be told—have got up and walked away. It would have been much more in keeping with his character at the time: *Sorry, don't feel like it.* Our aunt would have been powerless against his whims as she always was. But he chose to sit and stay and look at the camera. People are always more complicated than our memories make them out to be. And so it is that I have this photo now. But I don't have USD200 to blow on a professionally aged photo of my brother.

As though Mama's hectoring is not enough Ani has begun to attempt a nudge here and a hint there.

"They always say it is good to make old people happy. God showers with blessings those who are kind to old people."

I laugh pointedly. "My mother is not that old," I say. "She likes to merepek but don't be fooled, she's doing it for attention."

But Ani shrugs. "If it is attention she wants, then attention is what will make her happy isn't it? I'm saying let her have whatever makes her happy." Her single-mindedness —in a less charitable mood one might even call it mulishness—astonishes me into a moment of silence just long enough for her to seize her advantage.

"Hasn't she earned it?" she presses on. "She gave birth to you and fed you and clothed you and brought you up properly. I'm sure when you were small you also wanted lots of attention."

I could stop her right there. I could tell her the whole story. *Oh I wanted their attention all right. How I longed for it.* But it's much more efficient to agree.

"You're right. I wouldn't lose anything. I'll never find him anyway, but I can give her the small happiness of my effort, it's true."

Knowing what Ani does not know about the calculus of attention and love and gratitude I know that in the end I will do it not for Mama but for myself. To satisfy my curiosity. The question is what if I actually *could* trace Reza? My internet as Mama calls it did not exist in 1988. In those days one would have hunted down old friends and acquaintances. Written letters. But to whom could Mama have written? She had made no allies in life. That left only prayer which I am sure she bravely tried but prayer—let us just say that the internet is a surer thing.

Of course the first question is what name he goes by.

Let us recall the name he inherited from the good-for-nothing real-not-real probably Australian father. And would you look at that! This side I have prepared myself for a long and arduous search but that side he is quietly sitting on the staff of a vegan cooperative cafe in Melbourne in 1998. Can you believe it? He must really have gone looking for his father. I think of him as he was when he left. His barely-needing-to-shave face, his Adidas duffel bag. I think of his heart holding his secret hope—small and flinty as an arrowhead it is—of his father saying all the things one might want a father to say after twelve years. And as I think of it the finest of cracks appears in my own heart. All those years I thought he had everything I wanted when actually he was as full of longing as I was.

Here he is more troublingly in what appears to be a Dickensian eviction process in 2000 (picture it: the dreadlocked vegans in their bean-smelling pot-smelling squat). And here he is in 2005 on the board of an anti-GMO activist collective and there next to his name is an email address. So simple in the end. Of course who knows if it still is his address but it is a beginning. I write it down on a little pad of paper. I stuff the pad into a drawer.

One of these days. One of these days. Nothing really so urgent about it. Mama is not dying. Reza is not dead.

Teacher Training

"The most important job of all!" Cyril Dragon tells George Cubinar when he first puts him in charge of the children's education. And it's not the practical matter of keeping body and soul together; not the vegetable garden that brings in their meagre income nor the sporadic pamphlets they sell to spread their message as and when the spirit moves them. "The children's education must come before all that. The children are our hope and our light! In a way it is already too late for us. We are set in our ways. Our thoughts move along old familiar paths. But the next generation will have known nothing else." On the future curriculum: English Maths Science, the rudiments of the National Language, and—the keystone—a class called One God.

Having already been a disappointment to his actual father George Cubinar is terrified of disappointing the surrogate father he has found in Cyril. But though he wants nothing more than to please, he balks at taking on such a crucial role.

"But sir—"

"Please call me Cyril," says Cyril Dragon for the nth time. "We are all equals here."

"But Cyril sir," says George Cubinar, "I have no teaching experience whatsoever."

"Plenty of time to learn!"

Truth be told nothing delights Cyril Dragon as much as training up a younger version of himself. Piling into George Cubinar's lap all the books that inform his own ideas about how to build a just and reasonable society from the bottom up. Rousseau. John Dewey. Ivan Ilyich. Poor George Cubinar so badly wants to please and impress that he is unable to admit he cannot make head nor tail of any of these texts. That he slumps over them in the dim light of his monk's cell picking at his chin pimples to keep his eye-lids from drooping. At the appointed hour every morning he goes dutifully to Cyril Dragon's office to sit face to face with his mentor-hero. He prays Cyril Dragon will not notice what a woodblock head he has. And when Cyril looks at George's punch-drunk eyes—like a cartoon character like that with the big-big stars circling around him—and exclaims, "Ah! How grand to be young and discovering all this for the first time! How wonderful!" George knows his prayers have been answered.

Picture it: Cyril Dragon putting his arm around George Cubinar's shoulders at that long dining table. "Our future rests on these shoulders!" he announces. All George Cubinar registers is the feeling of Cyril's thumb on his shoulder muscle. His own father nevernotonce put an arm around him like that. Perhaps George Cubinar chooses not to understand or perhaps he really is incapable of understanding that he has been saddled with the job nobody else wants because he's on the bottom rung: the youngest one with no real expertise to speak of. Perhaps even Cyril Dragon chooses not to see this; or perhaps Cyril Dragon truly believes the job of educating the young is best entrusted to the recently young if only because their memories of youth are still fresh.

But to George Cubinar the fact that he has been selected is everything. The turning point of his life. Never in his life has he been good enough and now: *Our future rests on these shoulders.*

In these disjunct perceptions of weight and consequence and in this unequal esteem—lies a recipe for disappointment that neither Cyril Dragon nor George Cubinar cares to notice for the moment.

George Cubinar looks at the small faces of the children. Blank and blunt as pebbles they are. All his life he has been at best baffled and at worst terrified by those pebble-smooth faces that give nothing away. Four of them altogether: Annabelle Foo then Kiranjit Kaur and finally those discomfiting twins. "One day you'll have a whole classroomful of them," Cyril Dragon says. But George Cubinar is not terrified anymore. Perhaps mildly nervous and perhaps not even that. He is home now.

Stargazers

A four-foot parcel arrives from America. Inside the cardboard box is a wooden box with a hook clasp. Inside the wooden box is a telescope: a beautiful shiny black-and-white contraption nestled in a green baize bed. Cyril Dragon sets it up himself on the front porch. He swivels it this way and that on its stand. In great excitement he turns to George Cubinar and cries, "Just think of it! The ancient Greeks, the Hindus, the Arabs, the Chinese, even the Freemasons and the Rosicrucians! Has any civilization or religion in the history of the world been immune to the night sky?"

For weeks Cyril Dragon has been outlining and fleshing out his plans. They should be investing more time more money more effort in the future he says. They should be broadening the horizons of the next generation. Exposing them to the best that the human spirit of inquiry has to offer.

Three years have passed since Cyril Dragon entrusted George Cubinar with the futures of the Centre's children. In the privacy of his own head George wonders, *Why now? Why is this the moment to pour what little money the Centre has into flashy new tools for horizon-broadening.* But his questioning does not extend to: *So, now you have set your sights on making that boy your real and proper son I will be reduced to an egg for your omelette.* This he will not allow himself to think. For George Cubinar does not hate Reza. All his grief spins around Cyril Dragon as he tells himself *It is only to be expected. All the great leaders must have disappointed their followers left right and centre because doesn't everyone want to be the chosen one? But even a mother hen has limited space under her wing. At some point surely she must push one chick out to fit another in.* It must also be that he is older and stronger now and Cyril Dragon knows he needs less coddling. Perhaps—George Cubinar told himself as he was leafing through the optical instruments catalogue Cyril Dragon had told him to send for—perhaps it was not such a bad thing to be taken for granted. Perhaps it was even an honour. A promotion to an even higher level of trust. He ordered the Criterion Dynascope.

When it arrives Mrs Arasu takes one look at it and wants to say to Cyril Dragon: *Take it from me, nothing you do is going to impress that boy. How much did we pay for the bloody thing?* Cyril Dragon tut-tutting over the accounts and suggesting Cuticura instead of Yardley if ladies really must have their talcum powder and then in his desperation to impress Salmah getting a telescope from America! As though the child has any interest in astronomy. Mrs Arasu knows a spoiled brat when she sees one. Greedily the child laps up all the special treatment without showing one ounce of appreciation.

But she never does say it. And now here they are all lined up to take turns with the telescope on its inaugural night. "Good good good," Cyril murmurs and steps back and folds his arms. But look at the expressions on their faces! Reza yawning and rolling his eyes. Annabelle Foo scratching at all the bites on her shin. The twins whispering secrets as usual. Kiranjit glassy-eyed with the strain of staying up past her usual bedtime. Only Leo is making any effort to be inscrutable and this in itself Mrs Arasu knows is remarkable in a six-year-old is it not?

No need to bother also, Mrs Arasu wants to say. *Now itself can close it up and send them upstairs.*

But Cyril Dragon is not a man who changes his plans.

"Okay, George," he says like a film director.

In attitudes varying from resignation to obedience the children step up to put an eye to the lens.

"It's just the moon," George Cubinar says apologetically. "Next time we will look at one of the planets. Or maybe even—"

"Just the moon!" Cyril Dragon wails. "*Just* the moon! But look at it, children, look at it! To think they were walking around up there just a few years ago, same time as some of you were learning to walk down here!"

Embarrassment wells up in George Cubinar's throat. Of course he didn't mean *just the moon* in that way. He wants to make a joke of it he's trying oh he's trying so hard to find the joke and now he's almost got it but no, Mrs Arasu has jumped in.

"To think," she says sourly, "that some nations were sending people to outer space while our countrymen were busy butchering each other."

Estelle Foo snaps. "What a thing to—"

"Okay okay," George Cubinar says hurriedly and then pretends he was addressing the children. "Keep moving, don't take too long, everybody must have their turn."

He's calmed his voice nicely somehow. Now he is establishing his authority again.

"Come on then, Reza," he says.

He has to nudge Reza forward and even then the boy will not walk but stumbles and flops towards the telescope like a poorly controlled marionette. George Cubinar suspects that he places his head in the designated position and shuts his eyes and counts to five before turning away. *So what?* George thinks. He's not going to make a big deal of it. A scene is probably what the boy wants.

Annabelle Foo squints through the lens and smiles to herself. The other children know what is coming. And there it is as if on cue. The hands clasped to the chest. The gasp. The turning to Reza who has the misfortune of having gone just before her. The Beijing-opera blink-blink-blink of those flashing eyes.

"Wah! Did you see, Reza? Did you see the moon's face? A sad sad face!"

Reza snorts. "There's no face. Those are just craters."

"No, Reza, come and see properly."

She reaches out to take his hand but George Cubinar steps in. "Come come Annabelle, it is Leo's turn now."

Annabelle stops. Her mouth hangs open. She blinks first at George Cubinar and then—as though she has just realized something—at Leo.

"Oh," she says. "Oh, okay."

Stepping away to join the other children she holds her arms close to her body like somebody's fastidious grandmother forced to use a public toilet on an outing. She keeps her eyes on the ground and gives Leo a wide wide berth.

George Cubinar says half-heartedly, "Your turn, Leo."

But Leo does not move up to take Annabelle Foo's place.

"Come on, Leo," says George Cubinar. "Getting late already. Come and look quickly, before you all have to go to bed."

Still Leo does not move. He shakes his head. "Don't want," he says.

George Cubinar looks helplessly at Cyril Dragon expecting another subtle dressing-down. But Cyril Dragon refuses to look back at him. He smiles only at Leo: first a small sheepish smile and then broader and broader until at its limit it has turned into the disarming grin of the organ grinder the performer of tricks the market square purveyor of miraculous cures.

"Come, come, boy!" he says. "You are the one who has always been so fascinated by the stars and the planets! Now finally you have a chance to see them properly so don't be silly. Don't sulk, don't be stubborn, come and look."

Leo stands at attention. His face is perfectly still. He does not even blink.

"No," he says.

"No what?"

Leo beetles his brow at Cyril Dragon. "I'm not interested in it anymore," he says.

Cyril Dragon's smile freezes. A faint note of cruelty slowly colours its eerie glow. George Cubinar feels he should do something say something anything but again he doesn't know what. He feels the chill in his nostrils: the night is turning. No good to be outside past this time they say. Damp settles on everything. Cyril Dragon's eyes beam unforgiving through the mist.

"Not interested?" Cyril Dragon says. "You don't want to learn? You prefer to be stupid and ignorant? You want to be the village idiot? Everybody else will write *Scientist, Astronomer, Physicist* under Occupation, and you will write *Village Idiot.*"

Nobody laughs. Not even one nervous giggle breaks the silence. Leo looks right at Cyril. His eyes are unafraid but his tightly closed lips tremble.

"Yes," he says.

The silent universe expands. The air thins so much so fast that they are left dizzy and lightheaded. Above them the stars whirl in widening circles. Any minute now gravity will lose its hold on them and they will drift and float like astronauts: all of them except Leo who stands solid and heavy and earthbound as a boulder.

Suddenly Cyril Dragon's face seizes up. He runs a quick hand from forehead down to chin as though to smooth it back into place.

"Okay," he says quietly. "Okay then. Nobody is going to force you."

It is perhaps the most unnecessary sentence he has ever spoken because if there is one thing everyone can see it is that Leo will not be forced. Just look at him standing there. Unmoved and unmoving. He is a law of physics. He is the blind wisdom of the universe. He will never look through that telescope. Even George Cubinar can see that. He doesn't know why but the realization makes him want to fall down on the damp grass right there and sleep and sleep.

A Tentative Alliance

Leo's mother tells him, "He's just another bastard child like you but he looks at you like as though he's ten feet taller than you."

But she is mistaken. Reza hardly looks at him at all. Leo's mother might for some mysterious reason want them to be enemies but you cannot be enemies with someone who does not see you. At most you can be not-enemies-not-friends.

He ought to satisfy his mother but try as he might he has been unable to secrete the desired amount of jealousy. Maybe he should pick fights with Reza. If nothing else she would let herself get swept up in the excitement of it. She would egg him on.

"Oh," she says, "Oh his mother thinks just like that she can find a father for a child or what? Everybody can see what she is trying to do. Yesterday they arrived and today they are the queen and the prince already is it? Don't forget Cyril Dragon has known you since you were *born*. Who is that boy to him?"

But here is what Leo at six years old knows better than his mother does: you cannot make somebody love you. A person can change their mind about anything at any time. They can turn their heart inside out like a T-shirt and there will not be a thing you can do about it. If he made an enemy of Reza, Cyril Dragon would only sigh and say, *Such a pity. I always thought Leo was such a nice boy but I was wrong.*

If he cannot please his mother and he cannot win Cyril

Dragon back then what choice is left? He may as well try to friend Reza isn't it? Because if Reza friends him they could be a gang. There are two of them now after all. Leo is no longer the only boy against Annabelle Foo and Kiranjit Kaur and the Mak twins. They could teach those girls some lessons. They could catch some of those furry-furry cater-pillars and put them in the girls' socks-and-panties drawer. They could make ghosty noises in the dormitory at night. They could lie in wait in the corridor and pull down their trousers to show the girls their backsides. Lots of ideas Leo has. All he needs is an accomplice.

But how to friend this boy who shields his narrow eyes behind his long eyelashes? Real girly eyes he has. Once a long time ago Annabelle Foo said to Leo: "You got sissy-boy eyes." But that was before any of them saw Reza. Put a dress on Reza and everybody'll think he's a girl. Probably that's why he acts so tough. Has to make up for his sissy-boy face by spurning every one of Leo's small repertoire of friendly overtures:

– If Reza is digging a hole and Leo goes and joins in then Reza will stop at once.

– If Leo is passing time with a football and kicks it to Reza then Reza kicks it in the opposite direction. As far away from Leo as possible.

– If Reza is sitting shaking his legs on the front porch railing and Leo climbs up beside him then Reza hops down and goes inside.

Then one day Annabelle Foo climbs up on the railing beside Reza. It is the back porch this time and Leo is not outside with them but drawing rockets at the big wooden table in the kitchen while his mother picks the stones out of tomorrow's lentils. Through the glass window in the back door he can see and hear Reza and Annabelle.

"How come you always like to sit and shake legs all by yourself?" she says. "How come you never talk to anybody?"

"I don't feel like it," Reza says. "Why you care?"

"I'm just asking. You think you better than everybody else is it?"

"No I don't. I just don't feel like talking to you."

"You think you better than everybody else because you're mixed."

"I thought you're not supposed to use those kinds of words here? I thought you're not supposed to say who is what."

"But we still know you're mixed. My father said—"

"Leave me alone!" Reza cries. His voice suddenly so high and sharp that inside the kitchen even Neela looks up from her lentils. "Why can't you leave me alone?"

Annabelle eyes him narrowly. A curious smile plays at the edges of her face. She swings her legs and savours his distress. Then she says, "You think this porch belongs to your grandfather is it? You came here just a few weeks ago and you already think you can tell people what to do. I also can sit here what!"

Reza turns away from her to hide the tears filling his eyes. Through gritted teeth he says, "I hate this place! I wish we never came here. I want to go back to KL."

Annabelle folds her arms like an adult riding out a two-year-old's tantrum. She has just opened her mouth when the back door opens and Leo sidles out onto the porch. Her eyes flicker in his direction. But then she homes in once more on Reza.

"Why don't you just go back?" she says.

Reza's lashes come down like curtains. Then he shrugs and all the air goes out of him.

"I can't," he says. "My mother wants to stay here."

A funny feeling comes over Leo: as though he has entered a familiar room to find it completely alien. The furniture all new. The walls a different colour. Because all this time Reza has looked like one thing (What? A smallboy. A whiteboy. A cocky little smart aleck.) and now without warning he has turned into another. Leo clears his throat and says,

"Actually your mother shouldn't come here in the first place isn't it?"

He barely registers Annabelle's irritated shoulder twitch and *tsk*; so intently is he savouring the surprise slowly passing like an afternoon cloud shadow across Reza's face.

"What you mean?" Reza says even though Leo knows he knows.

"Because she's a Muslim," Leo says.

"She's not," Reza says. "We're not really Muslim. We believe in all the different Gods. I mean we—we believe it's all one God with many names. Just like what you believe."

"But," cries Annabelle before she can stop herself, "But your mother's a Malay! She's not allowed to believe that!"

"I thought you're not allowed to say Malay Chinese Indian," Reza says. "I tell Cyril Dragon then you know."

But his voice trembles as he threatens, and the trembling, while nearly imperceptible, is detected by his keen interlocutors.

"Tell lah!" Annabelle shouts. "Even Cyril Dragon can't save you if people find out about your mother."

"It's none of *people*'s business what my mother wants to do. It's none of *your* business either."

Annabelle says nothing. In the silence Reza and Leo can both sense the precision of her calculations: the corkscrew trajectory of something evil and brilliant from her belly all the way up to her brain. Ping! The spring is released and she shouts in triumph.

"You're scared! You just pretend you don't care but actually you're scared!"

"I'm not scared of people finding out about my mother! She's allowed to do what she likes!"

Immediately he knows he has said too much, for such is Annabelle's brilliance that she will hear both the spoken and the unspoken words. Sure enough she smiles and says, "Then you must be scared of something else. I don't know what you're scared of but you're scared of something."

Reza's whole body clenches. Jaw fists feet stomach bum-hole. Oh how he wants to punch this girl. He feels one fist rise.

"Why can't you just leave him alone?"

Like a boxing bell Leo's voice rings out. Reza and Annabelle turn their startled faces towards him.

"I was just teasing lah," Annabelle says. Her words fuzzy. Shame-muffled. "No need to be so serious!"

She looks from Leo to Reza and back to Leo wondering what tack to take now. She could give them her most charming smile. She could insult them both in one damning swoop. She could sow discord between them: *Reza hates you,* she could tell Leo, *so what for you want to defend him?*

But no. In the end she slides her small bum off the railing. She walks away without a backward glance. *Who wants to friend you anyway?* she forces herself to think.

"She's so irritating isn't it?" Leo says. "All the time wanting people to pay attention to her only."

"Stupid girl," agrees Reza.

This assessment completed and a shared position on the main issue established they find they have nothing else to say. They study each other. Not like foes not like friends but—Leo realizes it now—like shipmates on a voyage neither one chose. Tossed on the rough seas of their mothers' mysterious quests.

Naturally the metaphors are mine. It is the smallest of payments I exact from them in exchange for the privilege of having their stories live on. Narrator's rights. I was not there on that porch. I was not even born. But who is to say that a remembered past holds more truth than an imagined one? We say: *I remember.* But half the time we've stolen the memory. Scientists say the more often we remember something the further it veers from the original event. By that logic all the parts of my story that I did not witness may contain the most truth of all. If I was not there I cannot remember them and if I cannot or indeed have never been capable of remembering them then perhaps they are nothing but the truth. Not fact but true: the storyteller's oath.

And so in this perfectly true thread of my story Leo and Reza stand there considering each other in their curious forthright six-year-old way. With a hot-cold-hot flash of surprise Leo thinks: *He's just like me!*

What they note as they scrutinize each other's bodies and turn over the facts of the case:

– Leo has rough ashy patches on his knees and a long pale scar on his right shin.

– Reza's toenails need clipping.

– The pockets of Leo's shorts are so deep that the white cotton insides of them peep out under the hems.

– Neither one of them has proper parents i.e. the sort of parents other children have i.e. people or at the very least a person who is inarguably and irrevocably in charge of you.

I can't. My mother wants to stay here. It echoes in Leo's ears now. The I-give-upness of it. The whiff of here-we-go-again when he talks about his mother and oh how familiar it all is! Reza knows his mother's habits. He knows how to keep her happy and he does it—oh yes oh yes—he does it as though his life depends upon it.

They meet each other's eyes. They exhale. And now they see that they are on the same side and have been all along. Annabelle's only purpose was to open their eyes to this. Now she blurs and fades like an old water stain at the edges of this moment.

Without a word to each other they begin to walk down to the waterfall. Sauntering as only small boys can saunter. Kicking at rocks and roots. Snapping twigs from trees. Separately they choose smooth stones to hold in their fists. All around them unseen insects click and whirr. Birds bright as flags lift at their approach. Hefty jungle flowers droop from vines. The air is wet and mossy. A mist of smells swirls around them and sticks to their skin: green fern and sweet spicy bark, wild bean and ferrous earth.

Reza's Questions

"For example," he says. "For example when we used to be Muslim they taught me that Jesus escaped at the end. But in the Christian Bible it says he died on the cross. So how can all religions be true?"

"Ah, it's not like that," George Cubinar says. "God gave us different stories for different people at different times. God knew."

"God knew, God knew, if God knew so much then why couldn't He just make everybody believe the same thing? Why didn't God invent the best and most perfect religion the first time itself? Pooooor Cyril Dragon wouldn't have had to come and hide in this house just to say that all the gods are the same God."

"But you see God wanted us to have free will," George Cubinar bleats helplessly. "God did not want robots, he wanted—"

"I know what free will means, free will means whenever you're bored you can switch to something else. That's what Mama did, don't you know?"

Relentless Reza. Forever at George Cubinar's ankles.

"Didn't God create the devil and didn't He know when He created him that he was going to be the devil and he was going to tempt us and spoil everything? If God already knows what you're going to do then that's not really freedom what. He already knows if you're going to choose the right thing or the wrong thing. Yes or not?"

Poor George Cubinar. Ill-equipped even to handle the

standard-issue button-pushing and insurrection of the rest of his pupils let alone this terrifying boy. He stands there with his hands hanging by his sides his elbows bony under the dry skin, his front pocket stained with ink from his forever leaking pen.

"I mean to say," Reza continues, "even the part where you're going to pray to God and He's going to change His mind, He already knows that part also, isn't it? So since He already knows what's going to happen why do we actually have to pray? Is it just because God has a *big fat ego*? Just like Mama's old boss who liked people to tell him how wonderful he is, except even bigger and fatter?"

Annabelle Foo lays her face down on her desk and laughs into the intoxicating wood smell of it. The air hums and buzzes and George feels the whole class teetering on the edge of chaos.

"Oh Reza your brain is the most unique brain in the whole world!" Annabelle trills.

"I'm not trying to make anybody laugh," Reza says. "I'm just asking questions what."

He's allowed her admiration to spill to the ground uncaught. Around her feet it slops in an embarrassing mess. Okayfine there is nothing she can do to charm Reza; that much she is learning quickly. But is also nothing she can do to get any attention from anybody else: neither hanging on to Reza's coattails nor striking out on her own. Eyes wide open she lays her face back down on her desk.

Leo perches his elbows on the back of his chair and grins. Neela has told him: *If that boy can ask questions you also can ask questions. You also put up your hand and ask whatever you like.* But Leo feels no need to ask his own questions. He takes a proprietary pride in Reza's.

George Cubinar's hair is already thinning. The head hair is thinning before the face hair has had a chance to thicken. Five years ago—he thinks of those days as his *younger days* even though he is all of twenty-four years old—he was easy-going and malleable. Anywhere you wanted to put him he slotted in with a mild and beatific smile. But now he looks at Leo leaning back like a cowboy in the sun and he thinks, *Oh to give Leo one tight slap like he deserves. At least Reza thinks up his own trouble to cause but Leo? Leo is just an unimaginative shit-eater. A ball-and-arse-licker. If you have no balls of your own you can only lick someone else's isn't it?* And don't even talk about the girls. Stupid giggling creatures and that Annabelle Foo at six years old already wanting the world to fall at her feet and worship her.

These children are giving him prickly heat. After particularly difficult mornings he has to rush back to his tiny bedroom and lock the door and pull down his trousers and underpants. Itchy boils will be popping up all over his groin. Scratching only worsens the problem. He airs his balls and shakes his head. That boy and his questions!

One day when Reza's provocations nudge the class right over the edge of the cliff into wholesale pandemonium—George standing there like an idiot yapping "Stop it! Stop it! You cannot waste everybody's time simply asking stupid questions! Other children have to learn also you know!" as the other children express nothing but delight at this descent into madness—Cyril Dragon himself comes sailing into the room like a boarding school headmaster. *How?* George Cubinar wonders. *How did he know what was happening when he could not have possibly heard from all the way up in his office?*

Somebody has told him. For the first time since he left his parents' house George Cubinar feels his warm bath of trust cool a little. A shadow falls over the bathtub. A chill wind stirs the curtains. Footsteps in the corridor. The truth is one is always besieged. Even when one believes oneself to be surrounded by friends one is besieged.

"Oh dear," Cyril Dragon murmurs. "These children are completely out of control."

"But it's not—" George Cubinar begins before Cyril cuts him off.

"Never mind, George, never mind. When class is over just come and see me in my office, would you?"

George Cubinar knows the "never mind, George" is supposed to be a consolation—a ruffling of the hair a pat on the head—and yes once upon a time he would have been nosing at Cyril Dragon's hand like a bloody dog for these blandishments but now he cannot help but hear in it the same dismissal his father intended when in the recitation of his six times tables George had stammered "Six times nine is fifty—fifty- ... six?" and his father had closed his eyes and calmly said "Go away, George."

After class is over he goes as requested to Cyril Dragon's office. By this point nothing surprises him. Not *It's very important that the children actually be encouraged to question received wisdom because after all that is what we are in the business of doing isn't it? Questioning received wisdom? All the so-called truths and assumptions that are handed down to us ready-made?* Not *All this time you have been quite able to handle the class. And no not even I have to say I am a little disappointed.*

He cannot defend himself. What is left to say? He tries to tell Cyril Dragon about Reza's callous childish questions —"The oldest questions in the book surely," George Cubinar says, "I mean to say haven't these questions been adequately dealt with by now?" He tries to raise an eyebrow in such a way as to suggest that he has like Cyril Dragon read all the dealings with all these questions but Cyril Dragon only says with a superior smile:

"Well. Perhaps if they had come from an adult we could say they were banal, but surely from a child of his age they are extraordinary? After all hasn't he arrived at these questions all by himself? When a child simply parrots scripture or dogma we know it is nothing but brainwashing. But when a child is asking questions he has not heard others ask—well, aren't they wonderful questions, actually?"

Wonderful questions it seems. *Never mind, George. Consider it a blessing in disguise: now you know where you stand.*

And so when Cyril Dragon takes to speaking in public about Reza's "well-oiled brain"—"despite all our attempts to indoctrinate him, haha!"—George Cubinar tries to ignore the felt-wrapped dig at his own teaching and the fact that "despite all our attempts" is just another way of saying *You are no match for this child, George!* He tries to remind himself that to know where one stands is a great blessing indeed.

"A razor-sharp well-oiled brain," Cyril says but these days he no longer tries to put his arm around Reza's shoulder because even he knows how that attempt would go.

For years Leo will think of it as a Reza-sharp brain. But now he and Reza are friends Leo is no longer jealous of how Cyril Dragon will do anything to please Reza. Everyone can see Leo's selfless admiration: that rare ability to be truly happy for someone else glowing right through his skin like he's turned into some rudimentary phosphorescent organism. Like he's cancelled himself out—his very selfhood. Ceased to exist. Exists only in and through Reza. Like the most saintly of Catholic saints fading to nothing but their Christ-love. *Imagine that!* George Cubinar says to himself. *If that boy of all people can manage not to be jealous—*

Leo's love for his friend blinds him. He cannot see how Reza most of all hates the way Cyril Dragon smiles down from on high while praising others. He cannot see that Reza deserves none of this praise. How he takes it from Cyril Dragon and flicks it to the floor like a palmful of snot. George Cubinar sees it. He sees it and saves it up in his bulging purse of blessings-in-disguise.

Family Walk

Why oh why after the big boxes of books and the telescope and the microscope for the classroom and the binoculars for nature walks—why after all these things following so close on the heels of Reza's arrival—why (suspecting everything he suspects) does Leo do it? He should know better. He does know better. But he does it anyway.

This is how it happens: sitting at the long table in the kitchen while his mother grinds rice for idlis he sees them setting out. Cyril Dragon and Salmah not quite hand in hand but close enough. Behind them the boy looking like as though they have forced him. Dragging his feet. Hands pushed deep into his pockets.

Just before they disappear down the stone steps Cyril Dragon turns and looks at the back door. What to call that look? A faint hint of a smile in it but not a joyful smile. One kind of look. Seeing it, Leo has a funny feeling in his stomach.

What he should do is one or both of these: 1) sit quietly and mind his own business; 2) pull that strange look of Cyril Dragon's close against his beating heart and keep it there and never ever show it to anyone else as long as he lives. Because (and part of him holds this thought briefly) it's okay that Cyril Dragon loves Reza more isn't it? As long as Cyril Dragon throws Leo some scraps every now and then?

But the other part of Leo rejects this consolation today. And weighing these two parts of himself against each other Leo chooses unwisely. What to do? He is only a six-year-old boy wondering what message he has been given. What he feels is a mixture of panic—what if he would be welcome to tag along on this walk what if he misses the moment what if it's already too late?!—and curiosity.

"Like an idiot you got up and followed," his mother will accuse him later. "Like a bloody nitwit! How easily people can make a fool of you!"

"People," she says but they both know she means Cyril Dragon. All his life Leo's mother has made him understand that no one but Cyril Dragon has the power to lift him up. Now he sees what she has never spelt out: no one but Cyril Dragon has the power to crush him also.

From the front porch Annabelle—who is supposedly playing a solitary game of batu seremban—sees him go. With her eyes she follows him and when he slips from her view she stands and steps to the edge of the porch to find him again.

Instinctively Leo adopts an aimless gait. His own body surprises him. His unsupervised feet taking their own selves towards Cyril Dragon and dragging Leo with them. *What, what, tell me the right answer and I'll be good* his whole body begs.

Who is to say that Cyril Dragon's look had not been a searching and optimistic one? He might well have been thinking *Where oh where is that boy because he would make such good company for Reza.* He might have been wishing that Reza had someone to show him all the smallboy things—the eggs the nests the weightless bodies of dead butterflies and dragonflies—because when Cyril Dragon tries to show him it is false and awkward for everyone involved. Who better for the task than Leo? Leo knows all the trails blindfolded and backwards. He can scramble up and down the bramble-choked slopes and run the rocky paths all in his Japanese slippers and never so much as twist an ankle. These hills have been to him the mother who dresses and undresses in front of her babe, who scrubs her back and oils her skin and empties her bowels as he watches, who lets him study her at her mirror arranging and painting her newly woken face into a mask for the rest of the world.

He is right behind Reza now. Close enough to see the down that grows in a V shape along the top of Reza's spine. Close enough to hear Reza humming tunelessly to himself to keep Cyril Dragon's voice out of his ears. But Leo knows that all Reza's efforts are in vain and that in fact Reza can hear just as much if not more of Cyril Dragon's words than he can. "You cannot imagine," Cyril Dragon is saying to Salmah, "You cannot imagine how lonely I have been. You are the only one who sees me as I really am."

Then Salmah's indecipherable soft murmur. Leo sees her turn towards him. The shine of her eyeball in the dusk. The flutter of her lashes.

"Please," Cyril Dragon begs—and who could have imagined that Cyril Dragon could ever beg anyone for anything!—"Please stay. Stay with me. I cannot go on without you. For so long I have been waiting, without knowing what I was waiting for!"

Leo allows himself to be thoroughly distracted by this melodrama. No longer paying attention to his own feet he steps closer and closer and closer to Reza until his toe catches Reza's heel. Reza freezes. In the three long seconds between this uninvited contact and Reza turning around— slowly oh so slowly like a slow-motion gangster in a Hindi film—it becomes clear to Leo that Reza has been aware all along of his presence. When he turns around he is looking right at Leo.

"What?" he says. "What do you want?"

But, Leo wants to say, *But I thought we were friends now!*

"Why you following me?" Reza says. "What's your problem?"

Leo blinks at him and he blinks back. "I thought ... That

day we went for a walk what," he says. "Remember?"

"*Remember?*" Reza mocks. His face contorted in scorn. "*Remember? Remember?*"

"We went for a walk!" Leo insists. Refusing to be made fun of. "Of course you remember! I thought ... I saw you going again so I thought ... I just thought I'll also come lah!"

Reza is holding back a smile. "You're such a busybody!" he says. But then he does smile and it is not an unkind smile.

By now Cyril Dragon and Salmah have turned to look. Now Cyril Dragon is taking a deep breath. Now retracing his steps back along the trail towards Leo now smiling apologetically at his feet. Behind him Salmah folds her arms and draws shapes in the earth with the tip of her shoe. Leo cannot see the shapes but he knows what they are: a stick figure of Cyril Dragon. A stick figure of Salmah herself. A heart.

Cyril Dragon stands next to Leo now. Crouches on the balls of his feet and rests his elbows on his knees. Behind Leo, Reza rolls his eyes at his earnestness. Cyril's face is everything and nothing: confused and guilty and ashamed. Frightened and doubtful and sorry. When finally he opens his mouth he says, "Leo, I know—we know why you want to come along but you see this is ... We wanted to go for a little private walk."

No we didn't, Reza thinks.

"Maybe next time—" Cyril begins. Immediately he realizes what his mouth is about to promise. Leo and Reza see him stop himself.

A heavy juddering fit-to-burst cloud in Cyril Dragon's chest. Too many unspoken promises already broken. He has never actually lied to Leo, and yet—how has it come to pass that the boy is standing here looking at him with an air of, yes call it by its name: betrayal. He never meant to mislead anyone. Hasn't he cautioned people against unreasonable expectations and unsustainable dreams? *I am only an imperfect human being,* he has always told them. Just like all of you. And this boy ...

He never wanted so much power over this child. Never asked for it never wanted it does not want it now. But the thing has fallen to him and what can he do but comfort himself with this: *It is for the best. Better for the boy not to harbour any false hopes.* He puts his hand on Leo's shoulder and says in what he thinks is a reasonably gentle tone: "You go home. You go back to the house."

Still Leo hesitates. Stands there looking from Cyril Dragon to Salmah to Reza who shrugs. Then back again at Cyril Dragon.

"Go," Cyril says now. "Be a good boy."

Leo grins an impish last-ditch grin. "I'm not a good boy!" he says.

And suddenly Cyril wants to slap him. His anger takes him completely by surprise: a hot high hum behind his eyes. How dare he, how dare this child intrude like this! That was the whole problem with children. You gave them an inch and they took everything. Everything. Without even realizing they were taking it. As though you had owed it to them all along. He cannot trust himself to speak at first. Once he opens his mouth there will be no going back. In front of him the boy waits like a jackass with that grin untouched. That irresistible innocent gap between his two front teeth: once the sight of it gave Cyril a tiny tender twinge but now he feels the fondness twist itself into fury. And this change shocks him, nearly breaks him.

"What?" Leo stupidly says. Perplexed by the expression on Cyril's face.

"There is a time for making jokes and a time for being serious. Now is not the time for joking around. Go back to the house, okay?"

"But I just—"

"I said *go*! Don't talk back to me, Leo. You are old enough to feel shame, aren't you?"

Reza backs away slowly as though from a fight between two playground rowdies.

"Well?" Cyril says. "Aren't you?"

"Cyril ..." Salmah says. He feels her breath on his back. But now he cannot leave it.

"I'm waiting, Leo. Are you or aren't you old enough to feel shame?"

Unblinking and fierce the boy finally whispers: "Yes."

"In that case you should know that it is shameful to stay where you are not wanted."

What has he just said? "Where you are not wanted." To this boy of all people. His mother the unmarried cook. Himself so acutely aware of his Unwanted status. Cyril Dragon's heart shrivels. But Leo does not flinch. He clenches his small jaw.

What is Leo supposed to do with all his swelling-welling feelings? His but-I-was-here-firstness and his you-wait-and-seeness? His flicker of but-I-thought! under its protective veneer of who-cares-anyway? He can see what Cyril Dragon apparently cannot: Reza has no use for Cyril Dragon. It is Cyril who lingers where he is not wanted. What is the point of playing this game Cyril Dragon has initiated? It is an illusion. Cyril the sole player who does not realize he has already lost.

"Okay," he says. "Okay I'm going."

He shrugs. Then he turns around and lopes back down the trail without a backward glance. They watch him go: the thin ankles the thorn-scratched calves. They watch him and feel all their different feelings. Cyril his guilt. Salmah her curiosity. Reza his panic: now he is trapped alone with these two. *Wait!* he could call out to Leo. *Wait, I'so coming!* But duty holds him back. For Mama's sake he must try to play his part. He must go where he is supposed to go and eat what he is supposed to eat. He cannot take any more tears any more scenes. He has to play his part but dear god he doesn't have to enjoy it.

On the front porch Annabelle sees Leo drag his feet back up the path. She springs up and slips her seven stones into the back pocket of her jeans. *Ha!* she says to herself. *Thought you were so great is it? Thought you were Cyril Dragon's special pet? Thought you were Reza's best friend? Ha!* With nowhere else to take her small but tasty triumph she scampers jauntily up to the girls' dormitory to savour it in solitude.

Orange Squash

"They have become," Mrs Arasu says and she delivers it like an accusation, "like a *family!*"

For it is true that Cyril Dragon now sits with Salmah and her son at every meal. And what Mrs Arasu means is: *like the rest of us don't exist.* Because Cyril talks to Salmah and Salmah talks to Cyril and the boy leans his head on one hand and gapes and stirs his food clockwise anticlockwise up-and-down side-to-side and together they are a tableau vivant of the Modern Family.

If you try to talk to Cyril Dragon as you did before—about History or Religion or the Great Philosophers—he must always invite Salmah into the conversation.

"That is how couples are, what," Mrs Arasu says. "That is why Catholic priests cannot marry. Yes or not?"

"Aiyah don't worry lah," says Gurmeet Gill. "It's young love! New love! Just give them a couple of years, they'll be tired of each other just like all the other married couples."

"I only feel bad for the boy," Mrs Arasu says. "So awkward for him! So embarrassing! To see his mother flirting and carrying on like that. Poor boy doesn't know where to hide his handsome face."

The adults turn to look at Reza just in time to see little Annabelle Foo slip him a folded note with a smirk. Reza takes it and without opening it—the sheer pleasure of this cruel triumph flaring his nostrils, his lip curling complacently—crumples it into a tiny ball which he flicks across the table right over the shoulder of his oblivious mother.

Annabelle's face flushes and puffs up with unwept tears. Pouting furiously she bows her head so low it almost touches the tabletop.

Mid-sentence, Salmah pauses and turns to her son.

"Reza," she says, "what's the matter? What for you kicking me?"

"I'm thirsty!" he says brightly.

"Thirsty? Drink your water then!"

"The water here tastes funny," he says. "I don't like it. I want orange squash."

"Orange squash!" Salmah cries. "Do you see anybody else drinking orange squash?"

"Wait," Cyril Dragon says. "It's okay. It's true Reza, actually we keep it for special occasions only, but ... it is hard to suddenly come to a new place like this isn't it? So many new rules and regulations. Too many. Most of the other children do not remember anything else. But you—I think it is okay if you want a bit of orange squash. We must do what we can to help you adjust. Am I right?"

Reza looks squarely at Cyril Dragon. He does not say yes or no. He does not smile or shrug or blink. He's not going to do anything to make this easier.

Cyril Dragon looks all around him as though waking from a dream. Then his gaze steadies as though it has alighted upon a familiar face in a foreign land.

"Ah, Leo," he says. "Do me a small favour, Leo. Would you please run to the kitchen and ask your mother for one small glass of orange squash?"

Leo does not move. He's remembering *where you are not wanted*. Words spoken not by Reza but by Cyril Dragon. It's not Reza who is betraying him and pushing him further and further out of the tent. Leo would get the orange squash if anyone else had asked but he won't do it for Cyril. No more doing somersaults and handstands trying to be Cyril Dragon's pet.

"Leo," Cyril says. "Did you hear me?"

Leo scowls at his plate.

"Have you no respect for your elders, Leo? What is happening to you?"

What is happening to you? Leo wants to ask.

"I'm not asking for much, Leo. Just one small thing. I have ... we have all of us done a lot for you and your mother. You can't even go and get a glass of orange juice?"

Oh Cyril! How easy to judge him from this safe vantage point. How impossible for even a stranger predisposed to sympathy—let alone a reader—not to believe the worst of him in this moment. Go ahead and say it: in those words— *done a lot for you and your mother*—there is bullying, there is menace, there is even perhaps blackmail. There is the insistence of the privileged and powerful that the powerless be grateful to them for ... for what? Their mercy? Their forbearance when they could destroy their inferiors at a whim? But if you had known Cyril you would understand that this was a moment of weakness. The unreasonable anger all adults feel when a child defies their authority had loosened his tongue. Cyril did not actually believe that Leo and Neela owed him eternal gratitude. He did not believe it—but in a way what does that matter? What Cyril believes and what Leo hears are two different things. And Leo has heard the threat. Leo is picturing himself and his mother living in a cardboard box under a bridge. And the picturing is pushing him to his feet.

Already he's perched on the tips of his toes, he looks as though he might blow away in a breeze. He suffers regularly from dry skin but today his lips are so parched their silvery colour heightens his audience's impression that they are looking at an apparition.

They are all so transfixed by Leo that nobody notices Neela enter the room until she is standing right behind Reza. With both hands she holds the glass carefully out as though what is in it is not orange squash but something disgusting and possibly dangerous. She keeps her eyes on the glass but her face is oh so dark and so still. As still and dark as the sea on a moonless night. Watch that black water because any minute now something will rise from it.

"You ordered orange squash?" Neela says above Reza's head, and all who are familiar with Neela's ways—which is to say everyone except Salmah and Reza—note the unprecedented word choice: *ordered* instead of *asked for* or *wanted*.

Reza turns around and smiles uncertainly up at Neela.

"Take," she says without smiling back.

"Reza," Salmah says. "Say thank you—"

But Neela has already turned on her heels and left. There Leo still stands as though waiting for further orders. There Reza sits with his orange squash clasped in both hands and not a sip tasted. Here Cyril Dragon smiles left right and around the room in a futile attempt to reassure and restore the lost ambience. But it is Neela who still fills the room. Her presence so sharp they find themselves putting their hands to their cheeks as though startled to sense the nearby sea: the way the ground begins to shift beneath the feet. The swell in the air. The cold salt smell of it.

All's Fair

"Do try to make friends with him," Cyril Dragon had begged Leo when Reza first arrived. Leo had mistaken this for some selfless yearning to see them both less lonely, but soon enough he had seen that it was all for Reza and only Reza. It was Reza whom Cyril Dragon wanted to see happy and Leo had been reduced to a device that might help him achieve his aim. But what a fine lesson Leo is teaching his teacher now. Oho oho! You thought you could with surgical precision excise one boy and replace him with the other. Exit Boy A, enter Boy B? Watch me snatch your prize away from you.

From the window in his office Cyril Dragon sees them every afternoon playing with the goats. Scratching the animals' velvety flanks. Gathering handfuls of grass to feed them. One day Leo kneels to peer under the billy goat and soon both boys are kneeling and giggling. They look away and giggle then peer again and giggle some more at what they have found. Cyril Dragon smiles to see them but it is not a smile of sweet recognition. It is a smile of wonderment: *So that is what it looks like to have a friend!* A smile of awed discovery. It trembles like the wings of a butterfly fresh from the chrysalis.

So believe me when I tell you that it is in the spirit of a naturalist that he begins to shadow them. Not a spy. Not the jealousing villain of the piece. He simply wants to observe, to catalogue and classify. The habits and predilections of juvenile male pairs. Their favoured trajectories and territories. Here is where they turn off to throw stones into the waterfall. Here is how they wade fearlessly into the water even on the mistiest chilliest of days. Here is how they horse around and giggle and splash each other almost like girls—in fact if there were girls in the vicinity behaving in this manner these very boys would hardly be able to stop themselves from mocking and jeering.

Here is how they pluck dry grass from the ground and roll it up in small rectangles of paper. Here is how they light them with matches they got from don'tknowwhere.

The sight of the two small boys coughing and sputtering on their handcrafted cigarettes gives Cyril a tiny jolt. He turns and strides unseen back down the trail. Silent as an owl. Light in his bones but heavy in his heart.

He has been at his desk for what seems like hours when out of the corner of his eyes he catches—far down below at the top of the trail where it meets the stone steps—the movement of the boys' return. Singing and swinging twigs and branches through the high grass. He follows their approach. On the top step they stop. They bend to study their ankles and knees and shins. They twist to look at their calves. What are they searching for? Leeches? Scratches? Cuts? Whatever the case they appear delighted with their finding or not-finding.

He tells himself again: *It is not as though there was a competition. Leo has not actually taken anything from you. Just because they are friends does not mean you cannot still win Reza's heart.* Why then is he unable to shake this sense of defeat?

Tracksuit

For a former Scoutmaster Harbans Singh is deplorably unpunctual. Three times a week he takes the children on their Nature Walks and three times a week they shuffle about on the front porch waiting ten-fifteen minutes for him to turn up.

"Needs extra time to take his bath," Reza says. "Fler is getting so fat he's having trouble reaching his toes. He's got to lie down on the bathroom floor, put his legs up, wash his feet with the long-handled brush."

"No lah," Leo says. "You don't know ah? Gurmeet washes for him. She soaps him she scrubs him she bathes him nicely and then she dries him with a soft towel and puts powder."

The children guffaw. Annabelle Foo the loudest of all but even—I regret to admit—Kiranjit herself. Laughing at her own parents to get into the good books of those two charming clowns. Except it will never work. Already it is amply clear that they cannot give two hoots about anyone else. Their two-person club is all they need. There is nothing more pathetic to them than a person who has failed to understand that basic fact.

"You guys can be professional comedians I tell you!" Annabelle Foo says. "Last time my parents used to watch TV to see people like you."

She loves them she hates them she cannot leave them alone. They do not even look at her.

"Some more the fler got terrible gas lah," Reza says. "You

walk past the john only you can hear his thunder. Most people only got morning thunder but his is all-day thunder. All-you-can-breathe buffet. Of course lah he's got to sit on the throne for an hour before taking us for our walks, otherwise he'll be simply letting fly. Nature walk but all the nature will be dying."

Annabelle Foo collapses against the railing in helpless laughter. When she recovers, a strange expression comes over her face. A sort of slow rolling brainwave. Very deliberately she reaches out one leg and hooks her foot around Reza's ankle. They all see him freeze but he does not turn around.

"Eh!" she says. "Your tracksuit top so nice lah. From where you bought?"

Now he turns his head unhurriedly and blinks a lazy lizardy blink.

"Why? You going shopping is it?"

Effervescent giggles from the front row seats.

"No lah, just asking what."

"I brought it from KL. I brought all my things from KL. Satisfied?"

Annabelle Foo knows she should let it go now but ...

"Oh, your mother bought for you ah?" she says.

He turns his whole body to face her. "No. My father bought for me. It's imported from England."

But his voice shakes a bit and he looks at his feet as he speaks. Annabelle offers an encouraging "Wah!"

But her smile is sly. Not a smile at all; a smirk.

"Eh what's your father's job anh?" she says. "You never told us also."

"He's a businessman."

"Ohhhh, international mat salleh businessman. Wah, that means he can buy for you anything you want, hor? So lucky!"

Reza shrugs.

"What toys he bought for you before?"

His eyelashes flutter as he mumbles, "Lego, Airfix, Matchbox cars, everything."

"Waaaah. Sure lah you want to go back to him rather than stay here. When is he going to come?"

Suddenly Reza meets her eyes and with unexpected ferocity says, "He's on a business trip in Europe. When he comes back he's going to fetch me."

Again Leo feels that shifting and twisting in his chest. A month ago he would have snorted *Bullshit lah you!* But slowly slowly starting with the day Reza said "I can't go back, my mother wants to stay here" an invisible hand has been reshaping Leo's heart. Now he sees what is happening with a new clarity. This mixed-up boy with the greenish eyes has become not the enemy or the rival his mother sees but someone he must protect. But he must do it so cleverly that Reza himself must not realize he is being protected. Reza is proud and his pride is not just the pride of one boy in front of another: it is the special pride of the half-white child in a country that still—shamefacedly or subconsciously—worships whiteness. Leo understands this and understands also that he—a dark-skinned ragamuffin an Indian bastard child a gangster boy to look at—should want to squash that half-white pride. It would be in the natural order of things for him to do so. But he does not want to. He does not want to and whatever his mother says there is nothing to do about that. With a dim sense that he is betraying her he says, "No, he won't fetch you. I won't let him fetch you. If you go I'll be left with all these idiots." He juts his chin at the awed bright-eyed girls.

"Aiyo, true also, huh?" Reza says. "Then how?"

They laugh. Even Reza himself. And with a flourish Leo finishes: "So you better tell your father you're not going anywhere. At least for my sake, friend."

As the heavy-breathing shape of Harbans Singh ambles towards them along the path from the back door like some winter-fat English woodland creature in a book—a badger perhaps or a brown bear—they arrange themselves into two desultory rows and prepare to hear all about stamens and pistils. When no one else is watching Reza gives Leo a shove. A shove at once forgiving and grateful: a shove to seal a deal.

But recent developments have assuaged Cyril's sense of loss when he sees the two boys together. Namely: a bubbling. A pulsing. A greedy new life that will not be denied. Cyril Dragon one, Reza nil. At least that is how it must feel to Salmah because she does not tell Reza about me. The nagging guilt draws up fiery baritone burps from her belly. Her ankles swell and her skin secretes silky oils. On Nature Walks she struggles to breathe the thin hilltop air. Slowly slowly my growing bulk ousts my brother from her lap. I knead her bladder with my see-through hands. I drive my knees into her ribs. I do everything in my power to make my presence felt. She cannot stand or sit or lie down without pangs and twinges and if she lies on one side I convince her she must roll over onto the other. She suffers from heartburn and headaches and rashes. She scratches her stomach skin. She disgusts Mrs Arasu in whom these things have always retained the faint distaste they induce in girls of twelve or thirteen. *Can't the woman at least wear looser maternity dresses? Can't she complain a little less and can't she stop rubbing her stomach like an emperor who has just eaten a whole suckling pig in front of his starving subjects?*

But Salmah remains blissfully unaware of these uncharitable thoughts. She smiles and rubs her stomach some more. At night she props herself up on two pillows and stares at the changing light on the ceiling: first the grey-black of 10 p.m., then the true black of midnight, then the deep blue of 1-2-3 a.m., and finally the purply grey of creeping dawn. *Speak!* I command from her depths. *Speak of me! Acknowledge my existence!* And though her waters swallow my voice my mother understands that I am plotting and scheming. Here I come. Here I come, Reza and Leo.

Vegetable Lorry

MARCH 1977

Leo has promised Reza: *wait and see*. When the van comes to take our vegetables to the market the flers will bring something special for us. Only thing is we've got to hide-hide when we eat.

Twice a week the vegetable lorry comes to collect our Pure Wholesome No-Pesticides No-Chemicals Goat-Manured vegetables (plus a few plantings of Mrs Arasu's prize roses and hydrangeas) for the market in Tanah Rata and the lowlands. We are prolific and reliable suppliers because if you take care of God's earth it will blossom and bear fruit for you. We are only the Stewards. Everything comes from Him.

On the back-porch railing Leo and Reza kick their heels. Leo twitchy and nervous as a young Romeo arriving to pick up his lady love in his car for the first time: Will it pass muster? Has she already ridden in bigger shinier faster cars? He tells too many jokes in a too-high voice while next to him Reza wears his cool heavy-lidded proof-is-in-the-pudding face. *Produce the goods first and then we'll talk my friend.*

In the kitchen Neela is mashing up greens with her heavy wooden masher. Thump thump thump thump. The sweat tracing the line of her gritted jaw. Not difficult to picture her hefting the thing over her shoulder to bring it down like a club on a man's brow. The vegetable men know to avoid her eye. They know to deal directly with Leo. With him they have developed a good business relationship. A bit of bargaining then the money handed over at the end. Loading up the sacks into the lorry while Leo watches them arms folded like an overseer. Finally the commission.

"Hey big boss!" they call out to him. "Apa macam?"

But today Leo does not want to be a small boy for hey-big-bossing and handshaking. Today he nods at the men and says, "This one my friend. Like orang puteh only isn't it? See the eyes. See the hair."

"Wah, very handsome," the vegetable men agree. "Boleh cakap Melayu sikit-sikit?"

Leo steps in front of my brother and answers for him: "No. He can talk English only."

"Oi!" Reza says in English. He steps forward and shoves two hard fingers into Leo's temple. "My foot! I can talk Malay better than you lah!"

"Came from where?" one of the men asks Leo like a tropical-fish enthusiast admiring a rival's latest find. Reza may as well not have spoken.

"Came from KL," Reza says.

The men look at him as though he were a statue come alive in front of them.

"From KL!" one of them says. "Orang puteh kah?"

"He's mixed," Leo says. His proprietary air undiminished by Reza's stubborn resistance.

"Mixed what?"

"Oh, you know," Leo says airily. "Different-different things."

Then—like an invisible hand has run down his face or the magician's fingers have snapped before it—something tougher comes over his features. "Eh," he says, "you all brought anything for me or not?"

The men chuckle and thwap each other's shoulders like as though his regular request is suddenly the funniest joke in the world. One of them hops up into the cab and emerges with a plastic bag. In the bag is a nest of newspaper bundles. One-two-three-four, Leo counts them.

"Okay, big boss?" the man says. "Special for you today. Because when you got new people you must spend your new friend a bit. Isn't it?"

Leo sticks out his jaw and blinks. "How you knew I got a new friend?" he says. "You didn't know until you came today what."

"Ha!" the men say. "Ha! We know everything! You don't worry, we know everything. Okay boss, now we got work."

They set to loading the vegetables into their van.

That sly sidelong glance Leo gives Reza as the two of them stroll off.

"Eh," he says. "Even the vegetable-lorry flers simply fascinated with you, you know or not? I tell you! White skin means you're like a God, man!"

Reza dismisses this with a casual "Aaaaah!" but a dark satisfaction flashes in his eyes just long enough for Leo to savour it.

In the shade of the back porch the two boys crouch to unwrap their loot. A bundle of jumbo fishballs. A bundle of chicken wings. A bundle of char kuay teow with prawns and cockles. And a bundle of lap cheong.

"*Pork* some more!" Reza crows. And Leo knows he has done it. He has scored. Because it is not just non-veg he has produced but pork: the unholy of unholies. The flesh most guaranteed to offend. Reza looks at him with the wonder and respect with which an apprentice might have met the eyes of Da Vinci. The *told you* he has been saving on the tip of his tongue he holds back. He sucks on its secret sweetness.

Neela Experiments with Truth

"Bosom buddies," Mrs Arasu says. "Boys will be boys, after all. Look at them! Just look at them. Salmah and Cyril Dragon busy with the new baby so just nice for them. They're having a field day."

Easy enough to mistake her tone for pleasure or admiration or even affection. But Annabelle Foo recognizes it for what it is. Not a call to action nor even a warning but a slow boiling-over.

"Rules are rules," the adults repeat to each other. "It is for them to keep their children under control isn't it?"

This question lodges itself inside Annabelle's brain. *Children under control.* Again and again and sometimes all through the night it flashes like a lighthouse before her eyes. She stares and blinks and rubs her eyes and rubs her eyes again. When she looks at it closely she sees: it isn't about the pork and the chicken and the mutton.

Once Hilda Boey cleared her throat and shuffled her pigeon feet under the table and said, "Aiya. After all we also used to eat everything what." She didn't dare look at the others but fixed her bulbous eyes steadfastly on a spot on the ceiling. Her mouth turned down at the corners as though she knew she was speaking of distasteful matters. Annabelle looked at this pigeonfoot fisheye toadmouth lady and saw—not what she expected to see, not shame for her meat-gobbling past—but anxiety. Impatience. Hilda Boey was in effect lifting up the edge of the carpet for the others and exhorting them: sweep-sweep faster-faster sweep the secret under, no need to go and tell Cyril Dragon everything. And now hearing the adults talk about *rules* and *control* Annabelle understands that Hilda Boey is not the only one and that this is what the rules are for. For maintaining the God's-in-his-heaven all's-well-with-the-world peace that is the reward of those who do not question why.

Hilda Boey did not want to risk all this and neither does Mrs Arasu who now surveying Reza and Leo's long sunlit field day feels her palms itch with the urge to slap a soft boyish cheek. Why could these stupid children not just respect the rules? Mrs Arasu feels her universe wobble and teeter. She sees how fragile it is—a robin's egg balanced on the end of a juggler's stick—and how even two reckless boys could crack it irreparably. First the private jokes. The snorting and giggling during Morning Meditation and Evening Devotional. Then gradually, rules are flouted more and more openly. Here the gong is ringing for Evening Devotional and there they are grandly sauntering down the trail with plans of their own. Contraband treats are savoured on the front porch: chewing gum, Chickadees (chicken-flavoured!), Coca Cola. There is talk of the smell of garlicky meat on the boys' breath and fingers and once even an unconfirmed report of half a burger hastily swallowed on the porch in between the Chickadees and the Coca Cola. "Haiya," the women sigh. "They're children only what."

It is a different story when the newspaper bundle of chicken bones is discovered. It is Annabelle Foo who finds it in its shallow grave under the back porch. Pulling apart the layers of newspaper. Touching the knobby end of each bone with a curious fingertip. The smooth cartilage and the loamy marrow. She ponders her options. She brushes the soil off the newspaper and places the whole bundle delicately among the rhododendrons. Up high where the flash of newsprint will catch someone's eye.

Within a few hours they find it. George Cubinar takes it

upon himself to pull the boys aside.

"I'm afraid this is going too far," he ventures in a regretful tone.

But the boys push their hands into their pockets and refuse to meet his gaze.

"Small-small things we can close our eyes," says George Cubinar. "After all with a newborn baby in the house we don't want to bother Cyril Dragon with every other thing. But *this*—"

He looks at them long and hard. If the boys were looking at him they would take great delight in counting the number of times the bulging vein in his forehead pulses before a despairing sigh finally bursts out of him.

"If this goes on I will just have to burden Cyril Dragon with it," he says. "You know meat is violence. We cannot take life just to fill our stomachs."

The boys look at George Cubinar and see a limp noodle. His forelock hangs foolishly over one nervous eye.

"Cyril Dragon's parrot," one of them says under his breath, and as keenly as George Cubinar studies them he cannot tell which one it was. The eyes in their heads! Like glass marbles in the sunlight.

There is no actual question of going to Cyril Dragon. Protecting Cyril Dragon from the truth: that is the unspoken goal in pursuit of which everyone must be united. So Mrs Arasu is appointed emissary to Neela. Tamil woman to Tamil woman: easiest (or so everyone thinks) to settle it this way.

"Who knows which one is influencing the other one," Mrs Arasu says to Neela. "Either way you must put a stop to it. Your own son! Surely you don't want his soul stained with meat."

But Neela too at once recognizes my father's tongue wagging in another's mouth. Not *unclean* or *filthy* but *stained*. Mrs Arasu says the word and she hears Cyril Dragon's pet phrases: *The stain of violence. The dragging down of our dream.*

Bloodlust tainting our collective spirit. Such things cannot be allowed in this house.

"Such things," Mrs Arasu is saying, "in this house ..."

Neela puts one hand on her hip. "They are eating it outside the house isn't it?"

One small part of Mrs Arasu wants to laugh at Neela's deadpan retort. She has seized the letter of the law in her fist and like a Stone Age bare-hands fisherman she is shoving the whole wriggling length of it in Cyril's face: *Here it is, look at it, this is what I think of your rules.* But the larger part of Mrs Arasu wants to plant two tight slaps one after the other on Neela's smooth cheeks.

"Come on," she says. "This is a serious matter."

"Oho," Neela says. "You didn't eat mutton chicken fish before? From small itself you have been pure vegetarian clean-clean holy-holy is it?"

How dare you talk to me like that! Mrs Arasu thinks and already the forbidden words bubble up into her head—*cook, servant, bloody uneducated*—and she relishes yes relishes them.

"That time was that time," she says. "But now we know better it is our duty to teach the country, yes or not? If the wisdom is there we must pass it on. Every generation must give the next generation what they themselves did not have."

"Ha! Okay fine," Neela says. "But why are you coming only to me? Oh, she is so special because she gave birth to Cyril Dragon's baby, is it? Is that what you think?"

Mrs Arasu cackles. "As though I decide who is special and who is not special according to whom they spread their legs for!" she says.

The words have come out of her in Tamil and suddenly there's a menacing intimacy in the air. Whether it's the switch to Tamil or the crude image that stiffens Neela's shoulders Mrs Arasu doesn't know. She doesn't know about the nurse who laughed while Neela screamed in labour, and said, "That time when you spread your legs for the man, never cry, now only cry is it? Now is too late lah!" She doesn't know about the kuchu-kuchu-kuchu whispering and the nudges and sidelong glances and the asking Neela not once but twice when the father was coming to sign the papers.

All Mrs Arasu can see is that she does not need to add *You should be grateful we let you in and allowed you and your bastard son to stay this long.* The sour half-smile has already wilted and dropped off Neela's face. She holds Mrs Arasu's gaze for a few seconds and then with an air of facing her on the battlefield she has chosen she too speaks in Tamil.

"How old are you? Sixty, sixty-five years old. Sixty years you lived like everybody else, five-six years you have been here but already talking so big. Like as though you don't even know the woman you were five years ago. As though even your shit now will be too good for that woman to smell."

Now Mrs Arasu is truly shocked. As far back as she can remember no one has ever spoken to her like this.

"Is this the way for a woman to talk?" she says.

"A woman?" she says. "You mean the language *you* were using was so courteous? When it suits you, you will say women must be like this, like that. But who washes your backside, who scrubs everybody's shit"—Mrs Arasu's nostrils flare at the way Neela is flaunting the very word she objected to—"whom do you use like a bloody buffalo? Don't you just mean, is this is the way for a low-class woman like me to talk to a high-class woman like you? Because *you* can use whatever language you like, but it should only go in one direction isn't it? All the beautiful fairy tales you people spin, everybody is equal it seems, nobody is anybody's boss it seems, you think you can fool me? My answer to you is yes, this is the way for a woman to talk. This is the way for a woman *like me* to talk."

"Tsk tsk tsk, such anger," Mrs Arasu says. "Why is it you

are so angry? Aren't you living a good life here? A roof over your head, three meals a day, everything safe and stable, why can't you be happy with it?"

Neela laughs bitterly. "Oh, you're asking me about life and happiness now? No, you just came to put all the blame on my head and my son's head, that's all, so no need to ask grand questions now. Fine. You want me to tell the boys, I will tell them. But first I will tell you one thing: the temple priest's no-onion no-garlic pure vegetarian food and the poor man's koddal curry feast, it all turns to shit in the end. And whether it is the priest's shit or the poor man's shit, it smells like shit. Shit is shit. I am the one who cooks and I am the one who scrubs the toilet so who knows this better than I do?"

Mrs Arasu sees the glee with which she spits out the word each time now—*shit, shit, shit, shit*—and thinks, *What more can you expect from this type of people?* For one brief moment she imagines frogmarching Neela straight up to Cyril Dragon's office. Telling Cyril Dragon how she talks about Salmah. Feeling the thrill of her power over Neela. But why should she waste her time fanning those flames? Two loose women. Let them enjoy the silly competition between themselves. She felt no solidarity with either one of them.

After Mrs Arasu's footsteps have faded, Neela lowers herself onto the wooden stool she uses when she has to grate coconut. How tired she is. How heavy her body feels. Look at it, look at this body, even the way it is sitting: feet planted wide apart, knees spread, elbows on knees. Like a peasant woman or a primitive clay sculpture. Who was to say that whatever she could wrest from the outside world would be better for Leo than the little they had now? That world might well be even crueller to people like them. All the streams all the tributaries that once came together to carry her along and deposit her here: now she is here she cannot imagine trusting herself to that unstoppable river again.

She thinks about what it would cost Reza and Leo if Cyril Dragon learned of their transgressions. He would not kick her and Leo out for a few chicken drumsticks. That much she knows. It is not about these menial childhood sins at all. It is about how foolish the children of people like her can be. Hasn't it always been like this? With an apologetic wave at their erstwhile human playthings the lord's children take their rightful place in the world. That is how it was for her. That is how it will be for Leo one day too.

Her son can take care of himself what, she thinks. *He has everything on his side. White skin. A pretty mother not afraid to shake her backside to get what she wants. Probably a rich family somewhere they can run to if anything happens. What does my son have? Nothing. Even what we thought we had was just an illusion.*

A Mother's Warnings

Even after her first warning their grandstanding and their gasping hiccupy laughter seep through the back door into Neela's ears every evening. They've even made up a clever but tuneless song:

> *Murtabak and char siew pau*
> *Eat the pig and eat the cow*
> *The Dragon says all gods are one*
> *But what if all the gods are none?*

She doesn't know exactly what she feels listening to the two of them. When the Tamil word *kadupu* pops into her head she looks at it like the out-of-place ornament it is: cheap and ready-made and ill-suited to the setting. It isn't jealousy she feels. It's not that she begrudges Leo this small lovely prize he has plucked for himself, this friendship that in his eyes is a perfect berry. He and he alone found it hidden on a high branch of the tree where everyone else forgot to look.

"Whatever I tell you just doesn't sink into your head is it?" she asks him one evening. "Lolu-lolu-lolu I can bark but it is like I am barking at a stone wall." She's summoned him into the kitchen and closed the door behind him.

Outside in the corridor Reza drags the toe of his shoe through the fine floor dust. Hears the long low snarling and knows nothing good is transpiring in the kitchen. Tells himself it's not his fault, has nothing to do with him.

"But I did what you said!" Leo protests. "Where got empty packets and bones anymore?"

"*That* you are doing very well. Both of you have become very clever nowadays. But I am not talking about that."

"About what then?"

"After everything I told you, still you are hee-hee-ha-ha following behind him like a real Tenali Raman. Everything he says you'll nicely laugh. Everything he does you'll try to copy. But no matter how hard you try they all treat you like dirt. They treat you like a servant. After all your mother is a bloody servant isn't it? So of course lah you also became a servant. What to do, servant means servant. Cannot be avoided. They don't know any other way."

Leo hears the change in her voice: all the sting and spit gone out of it.

"You think for Cyril Dragon you and that boy are equal?" she now asks.

"What do I care?" he says.

"Oh, what do you care? The world treats you like dirt but *you* still want to go and lick that boy's boots. So nice ah the taste?"

What happens next happens so fast that neither one of them will later be able to remember the order of events: Leo's face crumpling as though he is about to cry; the question *Why can't you just shut up?* bursting out of him; Neela's hand flying up and clipping him on the side of the head. Or maybe the hand flew up before the question tumbled out. Or the question tumbled out first before the face crumpled in shock at it.

Neela's eyes spring wide open when her hand makes contact with Leo's head. Leo's head drops a full forty-five degrees like he's one of those spring-necked toys. But instead of bouncing back he is clutching his ear and snivelling while she holds her slapping hand with her other hand as though nursing a wound. She can't deny it: the feeling of whacking the credulousness out of him is physically satisfying. Look at his face now! The stupid innocent posturing but right beneath that the too-bright eye and the wobbly chin. She sees a future in which she will crave this feeling. Whenever the option presents itself she will take it: she will whack him for being stupid she will whack him for trying to be clever she will whack him for trusting too much she will whack him for distrusting her views she will whack him for his sullen silences she will whack him for talking back. Something has changed forever.

"Bloody idiot!" she snarls.

"You were being rude *first*," he whimpers.

She looks at him without a word. All of him: the curly hair—so much thicker now!—the broad forehead the dog eyes the stubborn little chin. Now she is crying too, her eyes full of tears.

"I'm trying to *help* you," she says. "I scold you like this because you are my son. You know or not, everybody is laughing at you behind your back?"

At this Leo does bounce back. "No!" he cries. "Enough of it! It's not true! You're the only one who thinks like that! Always looking round to see who-who is laughing at you. Simply blaming other people for everything. You're the one who made *yourself* into a servant!"

From deep in their sockets her eyes blaze. "Nandri keta naayi! What do you know about my life? Everything I've done for you and you dare to blame me."

"What 'everything'? What is the 'everything'? Okay fine I'm just an ungrateful dog. So what? What you want me to do? Stop talking to Reza? When he talks to me I just say 'Sorry I don't friend you anymore'? I only have one friend here and you want me to not-friend him?"

She turns and busies herself at the sink. "Go," she says to the dirty pots. "Go with your great hero of a friend. Go and do what you want."

She knows he won't hang around trying to make guilty amends like she would've done with her own mother. It will suit him just fine to take her words at face value: he will go and do what he wants. She hears her mother's voice saying, *You poor thing, if you were only going to have one, and in such wretched circumstances, you should at least have had a girl.*

Her mother could never say enough about those wretched circumstances. And about the shame and dishonour she had supposedly brought to her family, as though they had been so grand and highly reputed before. It was true of course that what was a time of joyful anticipation for married women had been marked by fear and misery in her case. One day her desperate efforts to brush aside her worst fears had given way to the unmistakable truth: she was pregnant. The blood rushing to her face then settling into a slow sickening dread. But the dread turned to resignation and then even to defiance and so she carried him for the nine months in which he went from her biggest-smallest secret quietly fluttering in its private sea inside her to an announcement scrawled across her body. Wherever she went the announcement was the first thing people saw and she in turn would see the calculations in their eyes, the equations the implications the hesitations.

The night he was born he'd hung from the doctor's hands so pale and still she'd thought he might be dead until that first wail was coaxed out of him. When she realized he was alive after all her heart tumbled over and over itself like a stone some unseeing person had dislodged in their hurry. His skin so thin she could almost see right through it when she held him for the first time: here were the blood vessels blue and red, here was the cage of thin bones that held his langsat-sized heart. Watching him suspended in some mysterious glowing in-between place—not yet this world but no longer the other—she felt her own body, her *self*, shrink into insignificance. She became distilled superhuman courage. She could sink a knife into anyone to protect him. Carry anyone's balls scrub any shithouse sell her body just to give him a chance at a different life.

What-what she couldn't afford to buy for him after they left the hospital! He had no singlets or mittens or socks. No soft brush for his hair. No proper safety pins for his nappies. No blankets no basket. He was a those-days baby. Swinging in a sarong hung from the rafters. When they took him down they would spread out the same sarong on the floor and he'd lie in that and follow them with his clever eyes.

Nobody told her boys could suffer just as much as girls. Rich boys and poor boys did not live the same lives. Master boys and servant boys. Boys with a father and bastard boys. Boys could also suffer and she would not be able to say I too went through this let me show you what to do to survive. What did she know about surviving in the world of men? The posturing and the fighting like dogs to see which one would end up on top? What chance does her son stand against that boy and his bum-wiggling mother? Why not let him be the sidekick he wants to be? If you'd told her on the night she was born that one day she'd be the kind of mother who itches to give her son one tight slap just for being happy she'd have laughed in your face.

And while she is in the kitchen thinking these thoughts Leo and Reza are outside on the back porch. What remains of Leo's fight with his mother is difficult to measure: a few tear stains on his cheeks, some well-concealed fears swirling in his chest. Reza's company may not have erased but it has successfully distracted.

"When I grow up and leave this bloody place you know what I'm going to do?" Leo is saying. "I'm going to open a nasi kandar restaurant. I'll have fifty-sixty of those big metal pans. Rows and rows. Mutton-chicken-prawns-fish every single day."

"That's nothing," Reza scoffs. "I'm going to open a restaurant selling *only* meat. *Just* meat and no vegetables. No rice no roti no noodles. Even the drinks will be meat."

They laugh until they are so weak and dizzy they have to

put their heads between their knees like passengers on a crashing aeroplane. Far below them in the valley the first yellow lights are appearing in twos and threes. Standing at the sink Neela sees the bent-double boys and the twinkling lights and closes her eyes.

That night she will lie awake for hours in the room variously called "Where Neela Stays"; "The Small Bedroom"; "The Room Next to The Kitchen"; and sometimes in a slip of the polite tongue, "The Storeroom." Finally she will rise and climb all the way up up up the stairs to the boys' dormitory where she will kneel at Leo's bedside and brush his hair away from his eyes. She will lean forward and breathe in his smell: a combination of dark dodol and wet moss. How small he will look: the bubbling pout of his newborn mouth not yet completely faded. *Please* she will beg no one in particular—for that is among Neela's great secrets: that alone in this house she has no belief whatsoever in a just and benevolent God—*please if a heart has to be broken let it be mine and not his.* He trusts so easily and so much and in the end they will think nothing of flinging his trust to the ground and grinding their heel into it. *Sorry*, she says right into his sweet waxy ear. *I'm sorry Leo. In the end I could not protect you.*

Foretellings

I am ten years old when Father Vincent Dubois crosses our threshold for the first time. A driver has brought him all the way from the Catholic Priests' House. In one hand he clutches a sheaf of cyclostyled sheets. He is a solemn liver-spotted man with that perpetual nod-bob-nod of the head that comes to some people in old age. Combined with his straggly Confucius beard it makes him look like a disillusioned billy goat. Seen it all with those cataract-clouded eyes and just wants to be left alone to graze in his pasture. And yet here he is climbing up to my father's office and then coming down with him to lunch. Gout and a delicate stomach will not let him eat tauhu or ghee or spice which rules out just about everything on our table so Neela brings him a glass of buttermilk and a fed-up look.

But Father Dubois is not here to luxuriate in our hospitality. "You must be following the news," he says. "Even without TV you must know what is happening."

"Oh!" Cyril Dragon says. "I take the *Straits Times* and the *Star.* I keep track, certainly, but when it comes down to it, politics does not concern us. Politicians are the same all over the world. You will never change the world by supporting one politician over another. It's a filthy game of money and power."

"It is not about supporting or not supporting politicians anymore," says Father Dubois. "Things are going from bad to worse. They are not just cracking down on people who speak out against them; they feel threatened by everybody now. DAP men, Catholic priests, Protestant missionaries, even some Muslims. Nicely calling for sanctions against South Africa, but doing the same thing here in their own backyard. One law for Malays, another law for everybody else."

"That, at least, is nothing new. That's been going on since 1970."

"It's getting worse, though, Cyril, it's getting worse. They're getting scared and when they're scared they'll do anything. You must have heard about what they did in Memali back in '85. Sending in tanks and all that, slaughtering those people just because their Islam was not the official Islam or whatever. Why would they hesitate to do it again if they felt like it?"

"I can guarantee they won't send tanks up here. I am not getting mixed up in their politics. We are not inventing a new brand of Islam. They can't be bothered with people like us."

"People like you? But you are one of us, Cyril!"

"One of you! I am not one of you. *You* are one of *us*. We are all members of the church of mankind. We are all children of the same God."

Father Dubois's goat head nods and bobs this way that way. Who can say whether he agrees or disagrees? But then he clears his phlegmy throat (pipe smoking and a damp climate have not helped his tendency towards catarrh) and says, "You know those famous lines, Cyril? First they came for the communists, then they came for the trade unionists, and so on?"

"I know those lines. But they won't come for us."

"How many hundreds of years have there been Catholic priests and nuns here with no trouble, Cyril? All the schools we built, all the orphanages and charity homes we started, and now suddenly overseas priests cannot get visas to come, and even the ones who are already here cannot renew their visas. This is how it starts. They make things a little bit difficult first and then—"

"With all due respect, I fail to see the problem. You can do your charity work in France, in Ireland, in Italy, you have no reason to be here. You are not of this place. You have no ties to this piece of land. Why not go and do God's work elsewhere? It is different for us. We are all Malaysian. So, they won't bother us and we won't bother them."

"But if they think you have broken any of their laws," says Father Dubois, "they will not hesitate. You know they torture people in those cells? Their tactics are brutal. Remember all the times we have begged them to show mercy. Our vigils and our prayers and our protests years ago. All no use."

We bow our heads in memory of the two Australians and three Frenchies they hanged despite the best efforts of the nuns and priests. We too prayed at the time for their souls by which I mean not the souls of the two Australians and the three Frenchies but the souls of the takers of life. For the taking of a life—Papa said—was the world's only mortal sin.

"You must be aware," Father Dubois presses on, "I mean surely you know that there is much in your teachings and in … in your *lifestyle* to which they can raise objections. They go after Malaysians too, you know."

As he says "lifestyle" Father Dubois puts his two fleshy thumbs together with great precision and looks at my mother. It is only the quickest of looks, barely a second long so that if you had no inside knowledge of which laws applied to which people in our country you might have thought him merely distracted by a sudden movement. But everybody in the dining room has that inside knowledge. Father Dubois does not look at my mother again but we are now all acutely aware of this not-looking. A dozen subdued conversations fall away. The quiet noise of cutlery fades. My mother picks up her water glass and slowly drains it: godok-godok-godok the only sound in the whole world is the water moving down her throat. An avid undeniable thirst. A primeval thirst. Selwyn Foo turns his head away as though he cannot bear the sound of it.

Finally my father says, "My dear Father Dubois, they are not going to march in here with tanks and guns just because we have one Muslim in this house. In Memali they had four hundred people, you realize. The government has bigger fish to fry. I fail to see how anyone would even know that Salmah used to be Muslim. And she is still Muslim after all. She herself will tell you that she has not left the religion into which she was born. We are all Muslim and we are all Christian and we are all Buddhist and we are also all Hindu. So, far from abandoning one faith for another my wife has merely broadened her faith to include all the manifestations and all the teachings of the one God who loves us all."

"That may be the way you see it. That may very well be the way you see it. But I guarantee that *they* will not see it that way."

"Then what do you propose we do, Father Dubois? What is your plan of action?"

"I do not have a plan of action, Cyril. I am only here to tell you to be careful." He has brought his stack of sheets to the table with him and now he thrusts it at Cyril Dragon. "Read and see," he says jabbing at the top sheet. "All of you should read. It is all in here. What they do to people. Everything they have done. We should all be very afraid." He looks around desperately but fails to catch anyone's eye. In groups of two or three the other adults sit engrossed in their own conversations in that dim dining room. Father Dubois watches the condensation trickle down the sides of his glass to form a ring on the wooden table.

"It is *you all*, not me, who could pack up and leave tomorrow," he says. "It is not as if you have to wait for orders from anyone higher up."

"But I've done nothing wrong," my father says. "My conscience is clear. Why should I run away?"

Father Dubois draws a deep breath. "In that case," he says, "if and when the need arises we must stand up for each other."

"And how will you stand up for me, Father Dubois, when you believe I am a heretic?"

"Well, I may not agree with all your teachings. But if they come for you—"

"If they come for me then what?"

"I will pray for you, and I will tell the world about it."

"Ah, well, *that*! I will pray for you even if they do *not* come for you. Surely we do not have to wait for them to come for us before we can pray for each other."

My father crinkles up the corners of his eyes and smiles with his whole face at Father Dubois. You might—if you knew him only as well as the Reverend Father Dubois does —be impressed by his confidence or even offended by his arrogance. But the truth is that a long-buried memory is rising like Neptune from the waters of his belly. Dripping and shaking itself off so that its shape reveals itself against the white moon: a bleeding boy a bonfire of tyres and twisted metal a circle of black-booted soldiers. The feeling of his bony knees on the wooden floor of his father's house. The smell of burning rubber and the sight of an old man's striped cotton underpants stained with blood. His skin gives off a faint chill. His crinkled-up eyelids flicker and tremble as though something is hovering right above his eyeballs threatening to touch them. After Father Dubois leaves he sets his own glass on the face-down stack and returns to his office. That night he will remind Harbans Singh to lock the back door as well as the front door, and his dreams—of tanks and spears and flaming torches—will infect my sleep.

Water seeps through the top sheet of the stack rendering a small ring of letters visible. When everyone has gone upstairs for Evening Devotional, I move the glass and pick up the stack. I read quickly, my brain skipping over some words and latching on to others for their novelty. Around me the room seems to fall into a deeper and deeper darkness. On the fifth page I am stopped short by this description:

> *The cells lack the most basic of comforts, being of cement with no linen or furniture.*
> *They are badly lit and ventilated and are infested with insects, especially mosquitoes.*
> *The detainees, who are kept in solitary confinement, are deprived of any basic hygiene needs and are not allowed out of their cells except for interrogation.*

I read it over and over again. As my brain unpicks the unfamiliar phrases—*solitary confinement, basic hygiene needs*—the meaning of it dawns upon me. I flip through the rest of the sheets with shaking hands. The kicking of stomachs the bashing of heads the breaking of fingers the forcing of needles under fingernails nails into genitals bottles into anuses: all this I force down so fast I start to feel sick. I read about a man made to duck walk frog jump crawl like a baby piss like a dog. I read about a man forced to wear a tin over his head while the guards hit the tin with a stick. I read about interrogators who pick up a man in a throttle-and-lift manoeuvre that leaves him drooling for hours. I read about elastic bands flicked at ears and nipples. Faces prodded with toilet brushes and heads shoved down filthy squat toilets for flushings and reflushings. I read about apopletic interrogators who themselves sweat and shake and—like Selwyn Foo after the May 13th mob burned his older daughter alive in their car—cannot stop screaming until someone hits upon the magic words, except the magic words in the case of the interrogators are not a prayer but a surrender. *Yes yes yes* says the prisoner finally *yes I did it* and only then does the screaming stop.

When I have reached the last page I rearrange the stack as I found it: face-down, empty glass on top. I swallow my bile I run up the stairs I slip into the prayer room halfway through Evening Devotional. No one notices that I am shaking and sweating like a fever patient about to vomit. When I open my eyes I see my father seated cool calm impassive facing his followers as he always does and for the first time I hold him responsible. Here I am struggling not to bring out my lunch and there he sits high on his mountain preparing to take his last stand but here is the awful truth: we will all have to take it with him.

For now no one else seems to be aware of this. And yet Father Dubois's visit slips into the workings of the Muhibbah Centre and lodges itself there. A tiny speck of grit. For a few days our ears pick up the funny noise the gears are making. One more crumb of foreign matter, one curious poke or prod and the whole thing might detonate. Springs and metal will fly in every direction. But then we get used to the faint grinding. Our ears begin to tune it out. Click click. Whirr whirr. Surely that's what it has always sounded like.

Descent

Seeing the black van snaking up the hill at 2 a.m. on October 28th—its headlights lighting the way like the eyes of some predatory beast—Father Dubois tried to dispel his I-told-you-so thoughts by reading the Gospel aloud but the Word of God froze on his parched lips. Father Dubois was eighty-two years old with a feeble heart and a failing prostate so do not judge him too harshly for this small detail: there at his desk he wet his trousers thoroughly. He felt the warmth of it trickle down his pyjama legs into the sheepskin slippers his sister had sent him from Normandy the previous Christmas. He contemplated the distance between his desk and the corridor telephone. *Anyway what's the use?* he asked himself. *Will ten minutes' warning make any difference to Cyril? No use no use.* And then, since Father Dubois had from his fifty years in our country acquired an ease with our local lingo, he summed up the situation with a shrug and a *What to do.*

I too was sitting up sleepless that October morning, though I made no attempts to self-soothe with the Holy Gospel. Oh no. By then there was no Word of any God that could comfort me in my sickening hour of regret. By then so much had happened that had I known of the van beaming its way up the hill I would have thought of it as the necessary final destruction of our filthy world. Like Shiva the Destroyer in the Hindu Mythology we'd studied, the black van was coming to obliterate. It would be neither sufficient punishment for my sins nor salvation but only our inescapable collective fate. I was sitting up in bed in the Boys' Dormitory and I was the only one there. I was thinking of the boys whose beds were empty and I was thinking of my mother who that evening had produced from somewhere a suitcase I did not remember. I was considering drastic measures. What if I leapt from my bed at this hour what if I ran to her and begged: *Take me with you Mama please just take me wherever you are going.* But it would have taken more courage than I had left to speak to her at all in these last few days let alone to go barging into her bedroom in the dead of night. She was sick and tired of most of us. She was a powder keg, a she-wolf licking her wounds. When she opened her mouth it was like looking over the rim of a volcano. Sparks and a livid glow. You could feel the heat of it hit your face.

My father was not in that bedroom but perched in his attic office. An eagle in his eyrie. Alone and exposed in what had been his refuge. Like me he had not sought out the Word of any God tonight. He sat at his desk not because he had anything left to do at it but because there was nowhere else to go. Police or no police, his work was done. Things were falling apart and the Centre would not hold. All Papa could do was sit and think his thoughts. Reza had already packed his bag. "I'd rather die than come with you," he'd said to Mama. He'd never forgiven Mama for dragging him here in the first place and now layered on top of that old grudge were new betrayals.

What a tricky bastard I can be. Why this beating around the bush this pussyfooting this hiding behind my coy Chinese fan? Let me at last say it out loud: I was the one who betrayed him.

I was, I was. It is almost a relief to admit it. Nevertheless I shall show you the aftermath first so that you will not look at my mistakes and think all the usual rot: *oh you were just a boy, oh these are just small-small childish sins,* no, none of that please. There is no moral to my story but there was an ever after. An unhappily ever after. A bitterly ever after. And that is what I am giving you a glimpse of before I reveal my small-small childish crimes.

"You know I'm going back where you've always wanted to go," Mama had said to Reza. "Back Outside. Back to civilization."

A note of panic in her voice. Of tell-me-what-to-do-and-I'll-do-it. Her goldeneldest was the only one she wasn't sick of, and he didn't want to come with her.

"But what can you do on your own out there?" she pleaded. "You all didn't sit for your government exams, no Form Three, no Form Five, nothing. It's better for you to try to catch up, take some courses, get some qualifications, and *then*"—you could see she still had trouble conceding it, still could not accept the fact that she had run out of time to Start Over and Make Amends—"and then," she said quietly, "you can go."

But by the time the black van was lumbering up our hill Mama's panic about Reza had subsided a little. He was eighteen years old and had neither money nor friends. It would be easy to call his bluff. When the time came he would follow her just as meekly back into the world as he'd followed her out of it twelve years previously. For now there was nothing for him to do but incinerate his frustrations cigarette by cigarette on the back porch. At least all the toilet-puffery could come out into the open now. Compared to the shithouse, the porch was a downright glamorous smoking spot. Like two factory-strength chimneys they were—Reza on the porch and Mama upstairs downstairs in and out, in short wherever the hell she pleased—and not a word anybody could bring themselves to say about it.

There on the back porch Reza was sprawled as the black van beetled closer and closer to the house. But Reza's eyes were closed and so, unlike Father Dubois, he did not see its lights slicing through the night. He did not hear it either for his head was full of its own voices there on that porch where he had sat with Leo when they were small boys and when they were not-so-small boys and when they were nearly men. There where they had sat listening to Leo's mother taking out her steady plodding rage on the mortar and pestle and the batu giling and the coconut grater, all the old-time cook's tools of sublimation. The back porch in the golden light of all those bygone years was a very different place from the back porch in the dead of night. To the soundtrack of a thousand small creatures—the shrill warnings the low mourning calls the dark rustlings—Reza lit yet another cigarette like it was the funeral pyre of the old innocent back-porch years.

Three simultaneous last puffs on the back porch and in Mama's locked bedroom. The smoke from Mama's Virginia Slim snaked across the room and spread its despairing fingers across the inside of the door. Reza lifted himself up onto his elbows. He took a deep breath and opened his eyes. And at the exact moment that he opened them—so that forever afterwards he would retain a lingering suspicion that it was the snapping open of his eyelids that had set the final events in motion—we heard the hammering at the door.

All of us heard it but none of us wanted to be the one to answer. In the end it was Harbans Singh who dragged himself out of bed: there was that trademark stomp-and-shuffle of a heavy man on a wooden floor. When I heard the rumble and growl of his "coming coming coming" sinking down the stairwell I crept out to crouch on the first-floor landing. The moment he opened the front door the night air rushed in to fill the vacuum, the cold violence of it making him catch his breath before anyone had said a word. The back door slammed: even Reza had come in to listen.

A strange man's voice. Then another. We heard them say my father's name and my mother's. We heard Harbans Singh's gruff "Yes yes." The men pushed past him into the front hall. Their shoes on the wooden floor ruptured the quiet like a sudden downpour. If I had not stood up they would have walked right over me. They were not what you might imagine if you are given to such imaginings, if fuelled by one too many Gestapo-KGB thrillers you imagine uniformed fellows with lean lantern-jawed faces barking furious commands. No these men moved fast but their faces were calm, or even—dare I say it—tired. One of them was paunchy and balding. The other three were not far from school-leaving age. They looked around in bewilderment as they climbed the stairs as though they'd set off on a different excursion altogether and were surprised to find themselves in a dusty colonial bungalow in Cameron Highlands.

They must have expected a bit more excitement because when my father met them on the attic landing—his hands up, and on his face the wistful smile that he had worn all his life—they stopped short and looked at each other. The young ones waited for the older one to speak. A good five seconds that senior policeman stood and looked at my father. When he opened his mouth the words fell out with a slap on the wooden floor between his and my father's feet.

"Cyril Tertullian Dragon?"

"Yes," my father said. "I am Cyril Dragon. I am the one who called you about the … about the incident. But I'm sure we were already on your list, yes or not?"

"We have orders for your arrest under the In—"

"Yes, I know," said my father, and held out his wrists for the handcuffs.

Here was his last stand: exactly as I had imagined it and nothing like I had imagined it. For my anger at him had by now been muddied. The horror of Father Dubois's cyclostyled sheets still lurked in the back of my mind and I knew my father bore the blame for dragging us all into his reckless heroism. But other calamities had befallen us in our last days at the Centre for which I could only blame—what? God? No. As I was unable to believe in a God who knew exactly how we would behave in any circumstance. He'd conjured up and then punished us for behaving as he knew we would—I was left with no choice but to regard our tribulations as the random cruelties of a blind universe. My father was both responsible and not responsible, both despot and victim.

The policemen trudged through the house opening doors. Their boots were heavy and dusty and their manner weary, as though they could have really used a break from the drudgery of arresting people. You could tell they were resentful that we had all politely rounded ourselves up because now there was no way for them to go through the motions without looking ridiculous. Annabelle Foo stood between Selwyn and Estelle, who for the first time in her daughter's eighteen years had combed and neatly plaited the girl's hair as though she were a much younger child. Paralysed by terror, gratefully, desperately (*oh comb-comb my hair, for eighteen years I never had a mother and tomorrow I will once again not have one!*) Annabelle had let her do it. Someone should have taken a photo to immortalize their brief resemblance to a normal family: two proper parents and their cherished offspring. Rupert and Hilda Boey were pressed close to each other mouthbreathing loudly like two stranded walruses. Harbans Gill was grunting his unnecessary commentary at Gurmeet: "Well, this is it. Our time is up. Flers have come for us." Mrs Arasu had put on a saree for the first time since 1970. Thomas Mak, thin, white, trembling from an emotion none could identify and all feared, was trying to steady himself by shutting his eyes and chanting Buddhist mantras in his head. Bee Bee was frantically trying to shush her twins and Kiranjit whose shared response to terror was apparently to giggle hysterically. This row of docile dissidents was bookended by Mama, who in her lipstick and kebaya and mother-of-pearl combs looked like she was heading off to a kenduri, and Neela, whose hair was so neatly oiled and bunned that she must have stayed up all night awaiting this moment.

When the youngest of the men took out a pair of hand-cuffs and stepped towards Neela my father said, "Please, no, no, she is our cook." His voice was shaking. He could not bring himself to say *just our cook* even then. Even if it might have saved her.

"Cook or driver or gardener is not my problem," the old-est man said. "If she is one of you then we are under orders to arrest her."

The handcuffs clicked shut.

"But she is not here for our … our *teachings*," my father said. He looked at Neela then and she looked at him. Un-flinching. Unblinking. Without shifting his gaze he went on. "She came here to … just to make a living. She had no … The boy had no … You know, she had a child to bring up all by herself."

The man in charge grunted and shrugged. But my father would not give up so easily. He cleared his throat and this time spoke in a steady voice.

"Please. You know who she is …"

But his hands shook, even if his voice was now steady. And seeing this—my father shaking after all I had done to protect him!—I felt my blood turn to ice. The blue-green chill of it spread from my chest down to my belly and up behind my eyes.

The policeman held up one imperious hand at my father. Stop. Enough. A schoolteacher silencing a small boy. He did not even bother to meet my father's eyes.

It was not supposed to be like this. Papa had told Father Dubois: *They have bigger fish to fry. They're not going to come all the way up the hill for a handful of people planting vegetables and praying for world peace.*

But then you see it only takes one dirty rat to start sniff-ing and twitching its whiskers and the whole swarm will come gnawing at your heels.

We all knew why they were really there. Why they had

sent the black van instead of just the normal police to follow up on the incident. And had we had any doubt we would have known from the way they not only avoided my mother's eyes but gave her a wide and judicious berth.

When they had handcuffed all the adults they stood and looked at each other. Uncertainty clouded even the senior one's eyes. He opened his mouth to speak and we all saw it: that moment of hesitation. What the bloody hell were they going to do with us? But the moment was brief. Before anyone else could speak he clapped his hands and said: "Take them also to the van."

A fiery ball of fear tore through me singeing my flesh from the inside on this chill night. Maybe it would kill me before they got to me. It was real and it was happening: they were sending us all to the lockup. Thanks to Father Dubois's cyclostyled sheets nothing needed to be left to my imagination. I knew the details. I had the facts.

The van doors opened as though by magic. Obediently we clambered in for our coach excursion. Two by two straight lines no talking please. Nobody even looked at anybody else. You see by the time the police came for us we were all afraid of each other. Or if not afraid then at the very least we hated each other. We sat in that van as the three younger men huffed and puffed in and out of the house with boxes of Papa's papers and we did not speak. Not one word. The shared air in the van turned stale from our breaths and still we did not speak. The passing minutes throbbed in our veins until with one bark from the bossman they all climbed in with us and the engine coughed to life.

They'd left the lights on in the Centre. All those sad yellow windows bearing witness. *What now?* they seemed to ask. Whose desires whose dreams whose schemes will rescue us next? Through the van's small back window I watched the house shrink. We'd left it all as it was. The sheets and blankets on the beds. The books on the library shelves. All the inspirational signs on the walls. *God Is Love. We Are All The Chosen People. Be The Change You Want To See In The World.* Whoever landed up here next would walk through the rooms like a tourist through the ruins of Pompeii.

Down down down the hill the black van spiralled like a weighty marble. Round and round and round the curves. The drunken-sailor moon rolling from one side to the other. We were dizzy but numb. Terrified but resigned. We rumbled past Father Dubois quaking in his wool socks behind the window of the Priests' House. Past the tea plantation and the horse paddock and the reservoir. Past the deserted wet market and the closed roadside stalls. Like cows in the back of a lorry we looked out around us. Wall-eyed and panting. The froth thick in our sour mouths. We were bodies in motion governed by the universe's most elementary laws. The sons among us would be punished for the sins of their fathers and the fathers for the sins of their sons. Oh say it, say it: the sins of mothers and daughters too. Our collective lapses. What we had done and what we had failed to do.

We reached the main road and picked up speed. The hill receded further and further into the distance. At the exact second it disappeared from view my life at the Muhibbah Centre was irrevocably over.

About ten minutes afterwards we reached the police station. I would like to tell you that I turned to look at my father one last time as they unloaded us children. That Papa wore a weary but loving expression. Tender forgiving eyes and a worried mouth. That he drew his breath in and his shoulders up as if to say *Remember all I have taught you and may God be with you.*

Oh god how I would like to tell you all this! I would like to have forgotten—by which I mean that I would like to have remembered it all differently.

But the truth is that although I knew Papa was looking at

me I did not turn to meet his gaze. *It's all right* I thought to myself. *Papa understands. It's the others I won't see again but that doesn't matter.* My whole body understood I had left those people behind forever. Like a boy in a trance I stepped out of that van onto a new planet. Record the exact hour of my arrival: three thirty-five by the police-station clock. "Sit, sit," said the young policeman assigned to babysitting duty. Then he began to clear space for us to lie down. Patting the armchairs and the sofa. Pushing chairs together. "Tired?" he said. "You can sleep here until morning."

But none of us lay down. Stiff as ice sculptures we sat under the framed portraits of Dr M and Mrs M. I recognized Dr M from the newspapers that had appeared daily in the downstairs hall of the Centre before Selwyn Foo whisked them out of my father's sight and into the archives. The strategy may or may not have worked to shield my father but I, despite my dread, had forced myself to study the face of this man issuing his cool veiled threats in his cool veiled language. Unity. Harmony. Sensitive Issues. National Security. Every day he had smiled up at me over his meaningless meaningful words and now he smiled down at me from his portrait. No, you could not even call it a smile. A contortion is what it was. A grin a grimace a menace. Fattening battening, forever waxing never waning. Look at it: it was ageless and unchanging. (In fact not merely ageless but like all true dealmakers-with-the-Devil aging in reverse. One day it would appear to fade but then—like the grin of the Cheshire Cat's sinister cousin—it would rematerialize when we least expected. In 1987 we could not have foreseen in concrete terms the grand comeback Dr M would make thirty years later but by Jove did I feel it in my bones when I contemplated that rictus.) After we had all returned to dust its unwholesome gleam would still be there proclaiming dominion over the world. *The woods are lovely dark and deep but I have promises to keep and blood to suck before I sleep. I have only just begun* it said. *Watch me grow.*

I remembered the way this face had chipped away at the veneer my father's faithfuls had tried so carefully to maintain for sixteen years. The pictures exposed their true colours and reeled in the ugly words from their darkest hidden places: Mamakutty. Mamakthir. Typical bloody Kerala conman. Trying to be more Malay than the Malays. Each time a word like this came out of a mouth they would look at each other wide-eyed realizing what a shoddy flimsy thing they had taken sixteen years to build. Not even a house of straw. Even a medium-sized not-so-bad wolf could blow this shelter down. Or a gust of wind from the wrong direction, no wolf required. Fearful whisperings and mutterings had sprouted like fairy rings around the contraband newspapers and now all the predictions—both about Dr M and about ourselves—were coming true in every way.

PART 3

Latifah

As night turns into morning turns into afternoon various aunties and uncles arrive to rescue the other children one by one. Our original keepers go home to their beds handing off the baton to a new shift of freshly showered policemen. Reza dozes off on the tattered sofa and wakes up and dozes off again while I sit in the same hard wooden chair watching him. We bear witness to many tea breaks and coffee breaks and kueh breaks. *Don't you want to lie down adik don't you want to sleep a bit* they ask me to their credit but my hands stay clean: I reject all their kindnesses. A slightly more comfortable chair. Karipap–kacang puteh–goreng pisang–Milo. And well yes the invitation to pray in the surau. The stomach food and the spiritual food Reza and I both refuse. The implications of our refusal to pray are (once again to the credit of our keepers) kept beyond our earshot.

At the eleventh hour she arrives to snatch me and Reza from the wide maw of the law. When she arrives—heels clicking tongue clicking bosom heaving—we do not for one moment fall for her pretence of altruism and deep family feeling. We sense each other's makenomistaking: she comes to conquer us for the objective Truth of Islam; to claim us for Malay identity; to take no risks with the Family Reputation; to win once and for all her lifelong battle with my mother her first cousin the prodigal the profligate the slut the whore.

With a flouncing and a fluttering she comes. *How could*

your mother do this to you astaghfirullah? An opening wide of eyes and arms.

"Of course you remember me," she says in a voice that brooks no dissent.

But Reza refuses to play the game. "No," he says. "No, we don't remember you at all."

She turns sharply to speak only to Reza in Malay: "I used to come see your mother even when you were living in that rented room in 1974, 1975. You at least should remember."

"Which rented room?" he says in English. "There were a lot of rented rooms."

She shakes her head and sighs. We know what she is thinking: *3) Malay but cannot speak Malay.* Add it to the fast-growing list of grievances: *1) Muslim but cannot speak Muslim; 2) bad attitude.*

"Well," she says carefully. "There were a lot of rented rooms because your mother could never stay in one place, yes or not? You can say that she, ah, likes excitement. Ha!" She flares her nostrils and presses her lips together to indicate her feelings about the particular kind of excitement she means.

Latifah is Mama's *first cousin.* You would think from the way she says it that it means the first Cousin who ever walked this earth. The proto-Cousin. The original one-and-only Registered Trademark accept-no-imitations Cousin. "You can call me Mak Long," she says and we know she means: you should be grateful for the privilege.

We have scarcely had time to put our bags down on the Persian carpet in her sitting room when she puts a hand on my shoulder and says, "You no need to worry about anything now. Islam will bring you such peace, you'll see."

We blink at her. I can sense our blinks alternating: first me then Reza then me again. Closed-open open-closed closed-open. If we do it for long enough we could hypnotize her perhaps. But she blazes on undimmed.

"Your mother will be okay. The authorities know she is a

Muslim. Just tersilap jalan a bit. They won't keep her long. She will come back and she will be a good Muslim this time, you wait and see. She will learn back her religion. Allah won't just let her go like that. We are all praying for her."

Who knew there existed this other language that shared all its words every single one with English? Each word in this language denotes something unrelated to its English meaning—*bread* might mean "moon," *sleep* might mean "coconut," *banana* might mean "house"—and it is my job to learn the new meanings. Already I am beginning to understand the basics. *Your mother will be okay* means "Your father will be punished." *The authorities know she is a Muslim* means "They know he was engaged in the illegal conversion of Muslims." *She will come back and she will be a good Muslim this time* means "No need to speak of what she was before." But how does one *learn back* one's religion? There is only one possible answer: *religion* means something else in this language than what I have always thought it to mean.

Latifah must sense my confusion because now she says, "Every human being is born Muslim, only thing is some are led astray. But they can always come back. Isn't that wonderful? Even you. You just need to revert back to Islam."

She beams at us. Then she claps her hands like a dance teacher.

"But for today," she says, "you come and eat first. Uncle is not at home but we don't have to wait for him. You must be so hungry. So long didn't eat!"

A silent servant carries heaped trays and brimming jugs into the dining room as though there were nothing more normal in this household than a full meal at five o'clock in the afternoon. "See how much Fauziah has cooked?" Latifah says. "Take, take." Reza fills his plate and I gingerly fork slices of fruit onto mine. I arrange them into an elaborate and sprawling configuration to make my plate appear full but there is no fooling Latifah. Frowning she hoists one tray right under my nose.

"Take!" she barks.

"We ... I mean, I ... don't eat meat," I say.

She purses her lips. "Oh?" she says at first. Then, "This one not meat. Just prawns."

"We don't eat animals. If it's an animal then we say meat."

"We? We? Who is this *we?*" she says smiling brightly again. "How come your brother can eat but you cannot eat?"

Without looking at Reza I say, "My father taught us not to eat animals."

"Your father! Your father! So loyal to your father, hmm?" Her smile grows wider and more honeyed by the second. "Your father should be very proud of you. But let me tell you something: some animals you can eat and some you cannot eat. We Malays can eat prawns. Understand?"

"Please, I don't want to eat it."

Again she purses her lips as though considering her options. She rests her elbows on the table and laces her fingers.

"Okay," she says at last. "Fine. If you're not used to it then I won't force you. I don't believe in forcing people. But you must slowly change your habits. You must follow Allah's law. Not any other law."

With that she lifts one of the jugs and fills our glasses with a milky rose-coloured drink.

"Air Bandung," she says. "Try it. You'll enjoy it. No meat." She blinks innocently at me.

At the sound of a stifled snort from Reza she fixes him with the narrow appraising stare of one who is refining and revising her list: *4) Not just bad attitude but downright biadap.*

Just Say It

Latifah urges us: "All you have to do is say it you don't even have to say it in front of me you can say it quietly in the privacy of your own room with Allah as your only witness but once you say it oh once you say it! You will feel such peace."

She stands at the kitchen counter heaping sugar into her Horlicks. Her face already fully painted at seven in the morning. Her calves bulging pale as jumbo onions beneath the hem of her pink nightie.

Reza watches her from under his heavy eyelids. She smiles and smiles at him.

"Take, take," she intones. Something of the Buddhist monk in her voice and manner.

She pushes loaded plates at us. By eight o'clock in the morning she has already slavedriven Fauziah the cook to produce kuih and nasi lemak with options to rival a roadside stall: prawn sambal cuttlefish sambal chicken curry fried chicken ikan bilis hardboiled eggs cucumber. Day after day I help myself to only the kuih and day after day she tells me: "You know, isn't it, Yusuf, Allah created the fish and the birds and the animals for us to eat? Allah Himself told us which one is clean, which one is unclean. Those that are clean we should thank Allah and eat. Isn't it? Uncle is spending a lot of money to buy all this good food for you boys. If you don't eat he will think, 'What lah this boy, so ungrateful!'"

"I'm not hungry," I say.

"Not hungry! How can, a growing boy like you not hungry! First time I'm hearing such a thing! Eating only kuih! After get diabetes then you know."

It is a war of attrition. Latifah is going to wait out our stubbornness. Her plan is to fatten us and stroke our neck feathers and lull us into compliance. We will be the happiest prisoners in history. So happy that one morning we will wake up and recite the Shahada.

All day long the whole world pours out of the TV screen in a great unceasing gush. The Alleycats and Search and Ramli Sarip and Francissca Peter whose latest album might be banned because she didn't think to take off her crucifix necklace for the photo. Sheila Majid in her miniskirts. Michael Jackson in his tight leather trousers. *Dynasty* and *Drama Minggu Ini* and *The Cosby Show*. Oprah and Anil Kapoor and Margaret Thatcher and Ronald Reagan so charmingly embroiled in the Iran–Contra affair. *It's marvellous what Milo can do for you while Chartered Bank keeps your (parents') money rolling rolling rolling.* The TV is to this world what Papa was to the Centre. An expert guide. An explainer a sorter a soother. All you have to do is listen and trust and you will know what you need. Fab washing powder. Yomeishu for energy. Scott's Emulsion for your children. Darkie toothpaste for teeth like the grinning black man but Hazeline Snow for whitening your skin. Hamama for cleaning your Muslim bottom without getting shit on your fingers.

In our bedroom Reza folds his arms under his head and stares at the ceiling fan. Sometimes he blows out narrow streams of air as if he were smoking imaginary cigarettes. *Look at me!* I think. *At least look for one second! Stop pretending there's nobody else in this room with you!* I direct the full force of these thoughts at Reza's head. First a whisper then a hiss then a groan then a bellow: the loudest thinking in the history of the universe. I kick my heels against the bedframe. But my small experiments yield no results. Reza's only movement is to stretch and refold his arms.

One night I say to him, "Actually we may as well say what she wants us to say isn't it? After all we believe in Allah what. We believe in God no matter by what name. Isn't it?"

With big unblinking eyes Reza looks at me. As though only now he is realizing that I am also here in Latifah's house. He shrugs and says, "Do whatever you want."

"But ... but I'm just saying there's nothing *wrong* with it. Right? Papa always said all religions are good. He always said people are wrong to think that if—"

"I said do whatever you want. You already know I'm not interested in what your stupid father said."

Before I can weigh the value and risk of them, the words stumble out of me: "It's not my fault! It's not my fault we're here. You can't be so angry with me! We would have ended up here anyway. They would've sent the black van because of—"

"Why don't you shut up and recite the Shahada? Save everybody your agonizing. You've always wanted to sit at the right hand of God. Well here's your chance! You can become a good Muslim boy, stamped and sealed by Allah himself, and you'll never need to think for yourself again. It'll be just perfect because you've never been very good at thinking."

I shake my head violently. "No! I won't. I'm not going to do it. I'm not a hypocrite! I'm not going to lie to her."

Reza grins broadly. The cruelty of it—all those white teeth that harsh gleam those flinty monkey eyes—makes me lift a hand to shield my eyes.

"Hah!" he says. "There are sins far worse than lying. As you know."

"I'm sorry," I say. "I hug my knees to stop the shaking. I'm sorry, Reza. I know, because of me, all the bad things happened to ... to everyone."

"Oh you don't want to say anybody's name is it? Scared to hear which names will come out of your mouth? But who are you thinking about? Who is this 'everyone' suffering such terrible fates? Most of them will be okay lah, slowly-slowly they'll all get out of prison, they've got relatives, they can find jobs, they can live in some middle-class taman somewhere and have nice quiet lives and everybody can pretend the last twenty years never happened. But do you ever think about Neela? When you're lying awake thinking about what you did, do you ever think about the woman who cooked your bloody rice and dhal?"

"But Reza—"

"Hah! Don't *but-Reza* me. You've never been able to put yourself in other people's shoes and you won't start now."

"Don't say that Reza, please, it's not true …"

But was I capable of imagining the afterlife of Neela daughter-of-a-man-whose-name-I-never-even-knew?

What did I know of where she had come from and where she might have gone afterwards? I, a ten-year-old boy who had known nothing but life in a dead Scottish tea planter's house on a hill. Somewhere in this new country to which we had all been spirited Neela was living a life. Picking stones out of rice chopping vegetables grinding spices and trying not to think.

Reza laughs and shakes his head as though he doesn't need to hear my thoughts to reject them wholesale.

I lie down and bury my face in the pillow. Within minutes we are both asleep.

In the morning almost as though she has been listening through our door Latifah announces, "Uncle and I have decided maybe you better go for kelas mengaji Quran while waiting. After all how can you choose properly if you don't know what you are choosing? You can start the classes this week itself. The ustaz is teaching every day at the mosque, just nearby, don't have to go far. Then by the time you go to school in January, Yusuf, you'll know a little bit already. And Reza, what for wait until your birthday? Already you have so many things to decide. At least you can have one less burden. Just open your heart and your mind and leave the rest to Allah. Of course you won't go to Yusuf's same class, don't worry. We'll send you for special private classes, just you and the ustaz. He'll tailor it to your pace, no need to wait for the small flers. You'll pick up very quickly, everything you studied when you were small will come back just like that, wait and see."

As she delivers this speech she puts a hand to her chest. Her voice quivers. Her eyes grow misty. "Isn't it, Reza?" she says softly. "Yes or not?"

Reza's only answer is to lift his eyes to the kitchen clock. Tick tock tick tock. His fingers drum a complementary beat on the sticky plastic tablecloth. A lizardy pulse throbs in his throat.

(Re)Education

The ustaz is a small neat brown man with piercing eyes and hairless hands. In his nasal monotone he imparts his soul-saving secrets: how to wash your bumhole after taking a shit; why pigs are unclean; why the Chinese are unclean (they do not wash their bumholes and they eat pigs—who can argue with the algebraic logic of it?); why boys and girls should not mix; why Muslims and non-Muslims should not mix beyond the exigencies of living in a multiracial country. (*What to do? We have to live with them. We got no choice.*)

My whole body burns to hear it. My tongue writhes itself blue-black inside my mouth. I am sitting here like a piece of slime. Betraying my father with every breath. With every lazy muscle. With every word not spoken.

On and on the ustaz goes. About Muslims and kafirs. About the hell that awaits those who reject Islam. Its unique and diverse punishments, its infinite torments: renewable skin for repeated burnings-off; pus-and-blood beverages; trees that sprout bowel-boiling devil-head fruit. "Ohoho!" Reza would say if he were here. "So the most Gracious the most Merciful is not after all all that Gracious or Merciful—though he is impressively inventive!

But Reza is not here nor will he have the opportunity to air his scepticism and scorn before the ustaz because the special one-on-one sessions Latifah promised/threatened to arrange for him never materialized. One week Latifah was weakly pressing Reza to come downstairs for the ustaz;

the following week Reza had a job at Shakey's Pizza and nobody ever again spoke of the ustaz to him.

Perhaps that is why the ustaz fixes that narrow knowing look on me.

Or perhaps he looks at me like that because he knows who I am. Torn between the shame of being a blood relative of Salmah Majid and the titillation of sharing the gossip, Latifah might well have chosen the latter. I can picture it with no trouble: the lowering of voice and eyelids then the dropping of heavy hints.

Or my suspicions are unwarranted and the ustaz is a genius of observation and deduction.

Those who refuse to accept the Truth when it is given to them. Those who turn away from the Straight Path. Druggies drunkards gamblers adulterers but above all—here the ustaz looks right at me—Apostates. "To be born into Islam, to know of its glory, and then wilfully to turn away—there is nothing worse," the ustaz says. And then again for effect so that even the note-passers and delinquents sit up and touch the backs of their tingling necks. "There is nothing worse. The hottest fires of Jahannam are reserved for such people."

Asylum Application

One Monday morning, bright and fresh and early, Ani approaches me with a problem of her own. She's prepared herself like a student sitting for an exam. Washed and combed her hair nicely. Scrubbed her face. Put on her best Snoopy T-shirt. Here is what she presents me with: a young niece hoping to seek her own fortune in Kuala Lumpur. Hoping to avoid the clutches of the agencies since she has her auntie already settled in a good position. After all there is always freelance work and then you are not just stuck with one job: a bit of cleaning people's houses a bit of dishwashing at the kopitiam a bit of waiting tables at the thosai stall and you get to keep your passport. Escaping indentured servitude, having a little limited freedom of movement: she'd be living the migrant worker dream. *Be careful she doesn't get spoiled*, I'm almost tempted to warn Ani.

"Very good plan," I say. I arrange my features into an approving smile. But Ani doesn't nod and rush off like she usually does when I have agreed to a new brand of washing powder or a costly type of fish Mama's been craving. She sits. She stays. She nods awkwardly and her smile takes on that horsey look it acquires when she's holding something back: lip pulled up high over her overbite, nostrils slightly flared, skin stretched tight across her cheekbones.

"Everything okay?" I ask her.

"Yes tuan. Thank you tuan. But I was wondering ..."

"Hanh, what?"

"It's just ... you know ... a young girl on her own ... She

has just turned eighteen, until now she's always been under her parents' roof ... My own sister's daughter, you know ..."

"Ah."

"I mean, how to ask her to stay by herself, tuan?"

I'm already working out solutions—who among my acquaintances might be strong-armed into letting out a room in exchange for the services of a part-time maid, very nearly full-time if for instance the dishwashing and table-waiting could be saved for her day off, if they were so generous as to give her one—but Ani is spoiling my plans before I have even had a chance to lay them.

"Even renting a room in a Muslim house also, tuan ... You hear so many terrible stories nowadays, you see all those incidents in the news ..."

"Tsk tsk, very difficult to trust anybody nowadays, that is indeed the problem."

"That's why, tuan"—and from the way she's brightened I can see that my sympathy has given her the courage to take the bull by the horns—"that's why I thought maybe ... Once she has a steady income she can even pay you a bit of rent of course ..."

"You mean ... stay here?"

My eyes are blinking fast my wheels are whirring calculating the pros and cons my rights as a bossman. Isn't this place small enough already with only the three of us and me giving tuition classes in the dining room? Isn't this my house don't I alone have the authority to decide what happens under my roof ...

And then I look at Ani sitting there in her dough-coloured pasar malam Snoopy T-shirt knowing she has asked so much probably too much. I recall the little I know of her village. Her parents her brothers and sisters and their various children packed into a hut on the edge of the rice fields from which they try to wring a living. The provision shop to which they are summoned when Ani phones from Malaysia wanting to talk to them. The money she scrimps and saves so that they can have a decent meal and new clothes for Hari Raya.

I am no hero or saint: since our long-ago years in the hills raising money for our annual causes I have minded my own selfish business. I rage privately against the worthless buggers running the country yet take no action to fight for justice anywhere. I know about the storm-tossed boats heaving with desperate starving people, those who drown and those who make it to shores where they have the great good fortune of being allowed to work from dawn to dusk seven days a week. I know about the ones who sleep on hard floors the ones whose bowel movements are timed the ones who endure beatings and starvation and even sometimes die from their injuries. I know about the police who accost them and empty their pockets and their wallets for having neither the passports their agents are holding nor the papers the government is sitting on comfortably while waiting for bribes. I know about the bosses who dismiss them with no pay when they have the poor judgement to contract diseases or sustain injuries. Faced with these iniquities one sighs and shrugs and gets on with one's life.

But those are faceless and abstract figures in the gloom whereas this is Ani who having quietly said yes no longer dares to meet my eyes. How would I face her daily knowing she was pondering the fate of her sister's daughter? Maybe the girl wouldn't come at all if I said no. Or maybe she would insist on coming and end up living packed into whatever hovel she could afford with ten other girls all at the mercy of some creepy hint-dropping landlord, and every day Ani would go about her work wearing a long-suffering face while never bringing up the subject again.

It's not often Ani and I sit looking at each other for whole uninterrupted minutes. I see all the small changes that have appeared over the years she has been with us. The grey in the loose curls at her temples. The fine lines at the corner of her eyes. The deeper lines around her mouth.

I nod slowly. "Why not?" I say. "There's space for another mattress in your room, isn't there? And even if she has other jobs elsewhere she'll be an extra pair of hands. Mama's getting older, you and I are not getting younger, and it might be helpful for us to have a strong young person when we need her." What I mean to say is that in exchange for the free lodging the girl can expect to do a few chores here and there.

"Of course, tuan, of course!" Ani cries. "She will be so grateful to have a roof over her head, and in the same house as her own aunt, she won't fuss about anything, she's a good girl, you'll see. The whole family will be so grateful to you, tuan. They will be so relieved. They know what decent people you and your mother are, and how lucky I am to be working in this house. They will pray for God to bless you richly."

I wonder if your young niece will be more observant than you, Ani, or perhaps simply more ready to call a murtad a murtad. Never having seen me pray you could have concluded by now that I do not crave the prayers of others either (let alone the blessings of their fickle gods), but no: the combination of my secrecy and your—what? blindness? discretion?—means that we must play these roles.

Despite Ani's endorsement Mama frets when she learns of the arrangement. And who can blame her? Some of these girls nowadays are sharp feisty young things. One hears stories about the maids who take advantage of kindness: yammering on their phones all day long if you don't confiscate the bloody things or answering back when you tell them what should be done and how to do it.

But Mama need not have worried because Hana is just as Ani described her. Meek and grateful. Intent on earning her keep. From the first day itself scrubbing here scrubbing there without anybody asking her. Hardly speaks and will not so much as lift her head to meet your gaze. Hurries off as fast as she can if by some accident she finds herself in the same room as me. After she has been at our place for a week I realize I would have trouble picking her out of a crowd. No distinguishing features whatsoever as far as I can tell.

When I ask Ani if she's settling in all right Ani vehemently assures me she could not possibly be better. Everything is perfect. The mattress is the most comfortable mattress she has ever slept on. The food is copious and delicious. The house is peaceful and beautiful. My mother is the saint of saints the very best old lady she could have ever hoped to meet. And the jobs are already popping up. A vegetable seller at the morning market needs a helper. Two of his customers wouldn't mind having a once-a-week cleaning. The Chinese restaurant three doors down from Dawood's could use another pair of hands to pack takeaway orders.

Stepping out of my tuition room one Saturday I find the girl bent over a handout left behind by a student. When she hears me behind her she jumps as though I've caught her stealing from the pantry.

"Sorry, sorry, tuan," she says. "Actually I came to ... I was just—"

"You were looking at that paper? It's just a short section from a famous book. Pity it's in English. If it were in Malay you'd be able to make sense of it, wouldn't you?"

"I ... Actually, I can't read very well. I'm not clever. I wasn't good at school."

Now that she's standing before me I have a chance to look at her face. It's a pleasant face. It has not yet set into the angles and lines of an adult's face; the features are not so much flat as soft. Still finding themselves. The beads of sweat on her nose and above and under her mouth remind me of the faces of schoolchildren on hot days. The ones I see waiting at bus stops in their school uniforms or walking down five-foot ways to their parents' shops and kopitiams.

"Not clever!" I say. "There's no such thing. If you had a bit of time you could learn to read properly just like everybody else."

"Oh ... No, tuan ... I'm really not clever, my whole family told me so. And anyway, I have no time now. I have the job at the market, then cleaning people's houses, then evenings I'm at the restaurant."

"Just a few minutes here and there will be better than nothing. You can do it on the days you don't clean houses, or on Tuesday evenings when the restaurant is closed."

"But ... the books in this house, even the newspaper ... I don't know English."

I see the house through her eyes: this solid comfortable house with its shiny floors its clean water gushing from taps its flushing toilets kitchen cabinets full of colourful mugs settees scatter cushions dining table and matching chairs and most absurdly of all its books, oh, its books, lined up magnificently on shelves made and acquired especially for the purpose. There were people in this world who owned shelves made especially to hold the books they also owned, none of which were school textbooks: to understand this she had slid three of those books off those shelves one after another. Opened them. Found them to be in English. Put them back.

"I'll buy you some easy books in Malay," I say. "Maybe a newspaper once in a while. I can even try to help you with your reading when you have time."

Her eyes blaze like the windows of a house on fire. They light up the whole room and yet she doesn't forget her manners.

"It's okay. No need lah tuan. But ... but if you would be buying anyway, I mean for ... for your students or whatever, then ... thank you, thank you tuan, I will try my best. I'm not clever but I'd like to try, just try and see if maybe I can do it now."

"Yes. Yes, you don't lose anything by trying."

The next day I buy three books: a primary-school reader,

a book of fairy tales, and a simple book of fables. I put them all on her flat little pillow in the room she shares with Ani. The blood tingles in my fingertips and beats hard in my face like as though I am about to perform in front of a crowd and it's then I realize: this is the first unsolicited kindness I have ever shown another human being. Who can say how it will go? The possibilities are wide open. The only way to discover them is to walk out into that dazzling circle of light that awaits me onstage.

Self-Discoveries

In the moments she steals from her day Hana sits with her three books. Brow knitted and finger tracing the lines as she reads. But like a fish in a pond she slips away when she senses my shadow fall over her. I have not had so much as a chance to clear my throat and re-offer my pedagogical services. You would think I was not the one who bought her the books in the first place so convinced does she seem that it is a great secret she is keeping even from me. I cannot deny that the irritation and the disappointment are there even as I try to swat them away: you cannot force, in the end it is her choice, etc. etc.

So how is it that little by little I find my heart softening towards her? She is not the ingratiating type. No attempts to insinuate herself into Mama's good graces by complimenting her clothes or massaging her feet. One gets the impression that if she could have one superpower she would choose invisibility but not for the purposes of righting wrongs or catching villains. Light-footed silent quick and so slightly built that you could almost miss her inside her clothes. The T-shirts and trousers appear to be walking around uninhabited by a person. Yet when she enters the room my joints do a funny jellifying thing: *weak in the knees* people say and always I thought it was just a way of talking but no it is a real softening of the bones.

It is as if by offering her one small shred of education I have claimed her for my own. Go ahead and laugh; I myself am laughing at the ridiculousness of it. But perhaps when you have never done anything for anyone this is what a first act of charity does. Tethers the object of your charity to you forever even if they cannot see it yet. If I had been feeding a stray cat downstairs in the car park or a bird on the balcony from my hand I would feel the same way would I not? Here is my cat here is my bird we alone have a special bond no one else can see.

And just like such a cat or such a bird Hana herself does not waste her time philosophizing about our connection. The cat eats the fish head you have set down the bird pecks its grains out of your hand without naming you as the source. Yet at the customary hour they wait eagerly and when they catch a glimpse of you their little hearts soar. So it must be that Hana does not need to think *It is tuan who bought this book for me* each time she opens one but the feeling oh yes the feeling is there vivid and keen if she lets down her guard. This is why she avoids me: this shock at the intimacy of it.

When I think of it the skin on the back of my neck awakens and I find myself teetering in a strange and unsettling way between monstrous cruelty and mad love. Do you know what I mean? It is as though as that trusting pecking bird perches on the palm of my hand I realize that I could stroke its feathers with one gentle finger or I could crush it to death: here I am suspended in that moment when both seem not just possible but desirable. And then to rise and rise to pull myself up to the peak of the wave before it comes crashing down always on the side of love. The blood rushing right to the head and the breath knocked out of me. But my hammering heart full of loving kindness.

You have jumped to inevitable conclusions. You think I am spouting pure bullshit to hide something ugly. You think of course that I have outlined for you the reactions of all my body parts except the one that really counts here. The one between my legs that is really leading this dance. I say loving-kindness and you hear filthy lust. But that is not it. As much as Mama hoped when Ani first came to us many years ago that such a thing might be possible for me. I still remember her shameless whispers: "Think about it. What's wrong? She's a good woman. Strong and kind. You could have a good life with her."

Of course it is only desperation that could drive a middle-class mother to matchmake her son with an Indonesian maid. She had given up on me by then. Not daring to ask questions and not wanting to know anyway. But she need not have worried because my preferences in that regard have always been rather orthodox. I was not as she might have feared secretly lusting after lorry drivers or messenger boys. With Ani she finally dared to make a last-ditch effort and I laughed in her face.

I felt nothing at all for Ani. Nothing between the legs nothing in the joints nothing in the belly. But I knew only the first option. What I feel for this waif I did not know was possible. When I teeter between love and the impulse to destroy you must realize that I do so because I am afraid of this kind of love. It will destroy me. Perhaps this is what mothers feel for their babies. I am no mother nor even a father but I imagine it must be like this: this fearsome sensation of a tiny living thing entirely under your power. I even feel—now you will really think I am raving—that I played a part in her creation. Not in the biological sense but in some more mystical way. There was a space that needed to be filled and like a god I conjured her up to fill it. I conjured her up with my unnamed longing and now here she is pulling on rubber boots five sizes too big for her—her legs rattling around like sticks in them—to go off and scrub someone's porch. Here she is skulking back from the pasar malam with a fistful of hideously ugly hair clips she's spent her extra pennies on. (Why does she feel she needs to hide them behind her back? Out of habit perhaps. Or perhaps out of fear that her auntie will scold her for wasting money on colourful plastic rubbish. Or perhaps out of some misguided notion that a grown man's eyes should not be insulted with the sight of red Hello Kitty clips.) Here she is slipping past me on the stairs so close that the smell of her cheap astringent shampoo fills my nostrils and splits my heart clean in two. Tomorrow I will give her a few ringgit to buy herself something more forgiving to the hair.

The Knotty Problem of the Non-Mahram Freehairs

Some weeks after Hana's arrival Mama asks me why Amar has not been attending my classes.

It's been a while since I went into his father's restaurant. Easy enough to avoid him since these days Mama prefers to sit at home and have the food brought to her. I send Ani to ta pau our roti or if it's my turn I just walk a little further to the other mamak place. Mama grumbles a bit—"It's those new Myanmar flers, they never put enough egg in the roti telur, so stingy for what, next time tell Dawood to make sure the Indian boy does ours"—but she runs her tongue battery down within a few minutes.

"Dono lah," I say to Mama now. "Maybe sick or what."

"But it's been so long!" she cries. "So many weeks!"

I lift my eyebrows. "Yes ah? Tsk tsk."

"We are living in terror of the boy, Encik Yusuf," Dawood said the last time I saw him. When he clutched my arms all I could see were the bags under his eyes and the white hairs suddenly proliferating in his eyebrows.

Mama tries another angle: "Can't you ask the girl where her brother is?"

Told me I don't know how to protect our women, Encik Yusuf. Said people are looking at our family and laughing.

And then your fine upstanding not-like-the-other-boys Amar slapped his father, Mama. "Just like that," Dawood said. His shoulders sagging at the memory. The breath ragged in his throat. "His own father! There's no point anymore. Everything is lost. My son is gone."

"Ask her lah," Mama begs. "Ask her where her brother is."

"Why don't *you* ask her, Mama? She doesn't bite."

In the moment before she turns away it dawns upon me: Mama is afraid. Afraid of what Amira might have to say about the situation but more than this she is afraid of Amira herself. In some way Amira in her immodest clothes is dangerous to Mama in her modest clothes. Even though —ah, no, especially *because* Mama was once a very long time ago herself a sexy young thing in smoky eye makeup and a see-through kebaya. Amira is no longer an unthreatening little girl in a Hello Kitty T-shirt: when Mama looks at her she sees that past version of herself that she has spent thirty-plus years trying to deny. Our whole lives spent pretending none of that ever happened—oh we excel at the National Curriculum's key subject of Not-Talking—and now here comes this girl blundering into our field of vision in her corset tops. *Too close too present too obvious no no no take Amira away and bring Amar back.* Except Mama you have forgotten to see it from any perspective but your own: what Amira is to you Amar is to me. You see your dissolute youth in her; I see my priggish childhood in him. And so why should I be surprised by the news Dawood comes bearing one fine day? I know what it is to believe that the world should bow down before your rules.

"The thing is," Dawood says, breathing hard, "it's because … aiyo how to tell you also I don't know, brother!"

I meet his gaze unflinchingly and the whole confession comes tumbling out of him.

"You see Encik Yusof, my son has decided that he cannot come to this house because you … you are living here with women not in your family and they don't even cover themselves properly. I'm only telling you what he says, brother! I told him, 'Mind your own business, why do you care what other people do in their own house?' He said he won't set foot in your house as long as this is happening. It's much worse since … since the young girl came. That was when … that was the last straw for him."

Neither one of us speaks for a few long moments. In the back room Mama horks up a gobbet of phlegm. In the kitchen Ani washes a pot with a great clattering and banging. Finally I take it upon myself to speak.

"I sympathize, Dawood. Must be weighing on your shoulders, you wanting to give your son the best education you can give him and him refusing to take it. Of course I won't charge you anything for these months he hasn't attended his classes. I wish there were something else I could do."

Almost physically he leaps at the rope I didn't mean to dangle.

"But, brother, sir, Encik Yusuf, that's what! That's why I came to see you only. I thought, well, maybe if you were willing to ask the—you know—the ladies who are not related to you ... to cover their hair ... just when other people are around?"

"What?"

"I mean ... of course I meant just to satisfy the busybodies! It's not ... I am not the one judging you, brother. But as you know, people will talk. People got nothing better to do what. Our Muslim brothers are the worst. Forever must jaga tepi kain orang. Everybody's business is their business. But I'm suggesting ... It's not just for my own selfish reasons you know, not just for my son so that he can come back to your classes. Of course that too lah, but ... you know how it is once the talk starts. Maybe it's safer if you don't give them anything more to talk about, yes or not, after all it's a simple matter of taking a few small precautions ..."

It's the *anything more* that gets his message across loud and clear. Without meeting my eye he slides the arrow in. Selamba only. Nicely done brother nicely done. The most impressive element of this is that Dawood and I have never discussed my past. Until today I never knew what he knew or indeed if he knew anything at all. And perhaps he doesn't. But all he had to do was introduce one ounce of doubt. The neighbours and the parents and all those who greet me with a beaming-booming *Encik Yusuf!* Do they know or do they not? Are they just waiting for me to slip up? For the chance to expose me? Because it is one thing to agree on a logical level that the sins of the father shall not be visited upon the son and quite another to sense in your gut that the son carries the seeds of his father's hubris in his blood. In summary: I must be more Muslim than the Muslims or face the (possible) consequences.

I rub my hands together vigorously to conceal their trembling. "Thank you, Dawood," I say. "Thank you for your advice. You're right, it won't cost me anything to satisfy the busybodies."

An overwhelming relief washes across his frog-like features.

"Ah! That's what I myself was thinking. My son is a real bigmouth, you know. By now—"

"No need to say any more. I will tell the maids. I suppose ... In other families too the maids take off their tudung at home ..."

"Of course, of course, but you see the problem here is, you're an unmarried man, living just with the old lady, then tengok-tengok got two unmarried women in the house also. It makes it all look ... And then you know on top of that ..."

He stops and shrugs. It's all I needed. It's the only reason I brought up the question of what happens in other houses. To see if he would say without saying it: other tuans in other houses didn't grow up in some kind of hippy-trippy free-love cow-worshipping 1970s cult. *On top of that ...*

Reversion

At seven o'clock each morning Reza comes downstairs in his Shakey's Pizza uniform. He drinks his Milo and puts on his shoes and leaves Latifah's house. He starts work at eleven so one can only conclude that he wanders the wilds of Damansara until his aching feet take him through those heavy doors into that air-conditioned kingdom of dough and cheese. Well after the azan Maghrib blares through the house he returns to wash his face and eat whatever is put in front of him.

In those long intervening hours Latifah has me all to herself. Uncle's authority is frequently invoked but the man himself is rarely sighted within these walls. "Uncle kahwin dua," Fauziah the maid whispers to Reza one morning in the five seconds he takes to down his Milo and beat his daily retreat. I am to discover the layers of meaning of this whispered confidence: first, the definition I dig up in the dictionary—*Uncle has married two*—and then, over the years to come, the particular variety of two-marrying that is a hallmark of the UMNO Melayu Baru species. For the males of this species are not proudly polygamous like their counterparts in the rural hinterlands whose wives embrace the sisterhood of the harem. Oh no. The Mercedes-BMW-Volvo-driving Malay husbands of Bangsar and Damansara and TTDI take their second wives in secret having bribed the right officials or bought the right loopholes to escape the first-wife's-permission requirement. They marry their secretaries on business trips they marry their daughters' classmates they marry in Thailand or Indonesia; in sum they marry as and when they wish leaving their first wives the consolation of money and luxury. And what are all these middle-aged women knocking about in their mansions with their maids and drivers and unlimited bank accounts supposed to do with themselves? Shopping and lunching and high teas at the Shangri-La can only fill so many hours.

My appearance in Latifah's life is therefore most fortuitous: I am now her entire purpose. Her sole undertaking. And what a worthy undertaking I am: a salvation project. A low-hanging soul waiting to be picked for Allah. Reversion not conversion she repeats each time she raises the subject. Just going back to the natural relationship of every human being with Allah. Here she gives me the warmest of Nice Auntie smiles indeed a smile so loving-giving so saintly so radiantly generous that her eyes narrow to slits and her mouth widens to reveal the purple gums and the premolars.

In order to achieve this blissful state intended by Nature it appears that I will have to make an offering to God. This is not how Latifah puts it—she does not speak of offerings burnt or unburnt or sacrifices or altars—but my mind nevertheless conjures it all up. The bearded man of God with his golden scissors. Here he comes to whisper in my ear. Here he comes to snip the most private and precious part of me because that is what God wants. One might conclude that He is a fickle and capricious God who concocts different nonsense rules for different people for the sheer fun of it.

In the dark, Reza's scornful response comes back to me: *If God really is omnipotent and infinitely merciful then why doesn't He come and tell them who is right and who is wrong?*

If God really is omnipotent and infinitely merciful then why are my parents still in prison? If God is omnipotent and infinitely merciful then why must I submit to those golden scissors? Why will this omnipotent and infinitely merciful God not save any of us? Latifah may be wrong about God but does that not mean that my father might have been wrong also? *Send me a sign* I beg my father's God. Any sign. Any small sign.

All you have to do says Latifah is pronounce the statement of faith. It is between you and Allah. Just say you believe. The rest slowly-slowly you can learn.

I may as well tell you: I never said yes. My silence was taken for acquiescence because after all they knew what was best for me isn't it? I was a child and you cannot let a child make their own decisions where life and death and eternal damnation are concerned.

Late one night I stop pretending to be asleep. I sit up in my bed.

"You're awake also," I say into the darkness.

It's not a question. I know he hears me.

"What am I supposed to do?" I say. "I believe or I don't believe they're going to make me convert. I've got no choice."

His breathing quiets down to an almost-silence. As though if I can't hear him breathing anymore I will forget he is there and shut up. But tonight I am not in a shutting-up mood. I ask him, "Where do you go all day long?"

A long breath slides out of him.

"I said I was sorry," I say. "You don't know ... You don't understand. There was a reason why. But you don't care. You don't want to hear it. You just want to be angry. How long are you going to be angry?"

He turns to face me in his bed. I feel it more than I see it: his breath coming infinitesimally closer louder warmer across the space between our beds.

"I'm not angry," he says.

"Then why do you ignore me? Tell me what I should do. Tell me."

"You have to do what you want," he says. "I'm not your

father or your mother. I've got my own life to live."

And just like that the space between us closes as surely as if he has zipped it up.

Right up to the last minute I am looking for that sign. I give Papa's God a chance and a second chance and a third chance. But He is a cocksure God all right: He squanders all His chances and lo and behold here I am with thirty other boys in the special room at the hospital and there is no sign but the green shower caps we are given.

My blood is spilled for Latifah's God: one two three drops. A thimbleful. A peg. A cup. Who is measuring? Certainly not me. A terrible pain burns between my legs and an even worse pain burns between my ears.

Now the God of the Jews and the Muslims will only need to check inside my underpants to recognize me as one of His own. But how will my own father recognize me? When he comes back from prison he will see in my face that I have become a stranger. Worse than a stranger: a traitor. For the sake of keeping the peace I have failed to stand up and speak. I have sided with that other God: the God who divides instead of unites. The God who like a ten-year-old boy chooses you for His team but not you or you or you. The Red-Queen God who dizzies you with unanswerable riddles and then cuts off your head. The God who will eat up our country and sit back to belch flames. May that God be satisfied with my sacrifice. May my missing foreskin distract Him from the doubt in my head. Verily, if God sees all, distraction is my only hope.

The Minister Lets Fly at a Press Conference

JANUARY 1988

The minister has a too-small head and a tight wrinkled-up face like a monkey's ball sack. His skin is blotchy his over-oiled hair sticks up in three places and he has brownish stains between his teeth. He is not what you would call a commanding or imposing figure and yet even on the English news he can talk big and beat his chest making some people shake with rage and others quiver in their shoes. His loose-lipped unconjugated English gives him no pause or cause for hesitation let alone shame. Datuk Monkey Ball Sack just has to open his mouth and everybody drops what they are doing and listens. Datuk Monkey Ball Sack frequently features on the front page of the newspaper (no need to give it a name since now there is only one newspaper) while my father is sitting in a jail cell and my mother is being rehabilitated.

"Fauziah! Fauziah!" Latifah calls. At once we hear Fauziah's fast light feet on the stairs. Breathing hard and dripping water from her fingers she appears in the doorway. Latifah jerks her chin at the TV and says, "Please make it a bit louder."

According to Datuk M B S the problem is that Women Nowadays have too much what do you call it independence. They think life is a what do you call it Hollywood filem that they can just go and fall in love with anybody and there will be a beautiful sunset and everybody will live happily ever after but we all know isn't it that that is not how real life works? In real life what do you call it research and what do you call them scientists have shown that mixed marriages do not work and in most cases fail because of cultural and religious differences. "What do they expect?" Datuk M B S asks. His face stretches out in a funny way: widened or spread and almost threatening to split open along the seam. We all know that we are happiest when we stick with our own kind. Less friction. Fewer problems for everybody.

But then here comes this what's his name Dragon talking nonsense and like a snake quietly spreading his seditious ideas and his heresies: questioning the special position of the Malays and—the worst of the worst I tell you the proof that he is doing the devil's work—putting Hindu and Christian and Buddhist gods on the same level as Allah! This man this what do you call him Dragon knows that even if the vast majority of Muslims reject his lies still the young the poorly informed and the confused may fall for him. Look at this Salmah Majid look at her life story her missing father her mother ahem let us just say that her mother was not how mothers should be and not the type of role model a young girl needs. In short Salmah Majid was the perfect victim for Cyril Dragon and we all know that he preyed on her of course but she being a Malay woman should have known better.

"Hai, hai," Latifah says. "Can understand or not, Yusuf? Aisehman, listening to him I feel even more sad now."

"Salmah Majid has disrespected Malay Culture," says Datuk M B S. "She has done what Chinese women are usually known for i.e. sold herself to the highest mat salleh bidder. Is this to be the only way in which Malays will catch up to the Chinese? Ask them to learn business acumen or work habits cannot but when it comes to throwing away their morals Dr Mahathir need not worry the Malays will not be left far behind. Imagine a Malay woman leaving her religion like that! Tak sedar diri is all there is to say. Zina, murtad, what sins are left for this woman? In the end who are the real victims?"

And then of course Datuk M B S answers his own question: "The real victims are the children. Just as Salmah Majid's own parents failed her she has failed her children and what more can you expect when people grow up with no proper role models? These are the social problems our community needs to solve. According to Tafsir al-Qurtubi the apostate is allowed anywhere between an hour and a month to repent. But Salmah Majid's repentance will not change the fact that her children are caught between this and that with no roots no culture to call their own nothing to hold on to. That mistake can never be undone. Those children do not know what they are. They are half chicken, half duck. Half cow, half goat. Look at them! They cannot fit in here nor there cannot fit in anywhere."

But how *can* anyone look at them? Those two boys are not there at the press conference. They are cloistered in the home of a good Muslim relative where Datuk M B S can say all he wants to say about them while they say nothing back.

And the older boy knows how to close his eyes and stop up his ears but look at the younger boy. Look at him hearing about himself on television. Discovering once and for all what he is. He may look in the mirror and see a boy but other people looking at him see a grotesque miscarriage of nature. A mistake that can never be undone. Half chicken half duck half cow half goat: four halves and still not whole.

Chicken

"You don't know," the Malay ringleader says at recess. "You just don't know these people."

His name is Azmi. A stocky spiky-haired fighter of a fellow. He stands in his usual spot under the angsana tree surrounded by the usual mix of sycophants and impartial bystanders. In my two weeks at a Sekolah Kebangsaan I've learned the lay of the land and its tribes: Malay–Chinese–Indian–Other. We can be friends but our friendships are governed by rules that—judging by the amount of general uncertainty surrounding them—are emerging before my eyes for the first time in history. Brand new rules. Fresh-skinned. From the way they are spoken about I gather that for a long time they were mere embryos; then they were foetuses; and now here they are to greet us in the clear light of day.

"But what for?" argues a boy called Rizal. "What would Mr Ho get out of ordering non-halal chicken?"

"What he gains," Azmi says, "is the pleasure of watching all of us Muslim boys eat haram food. The sheer fun of it. You don't know. These kafirs live for that kind of thing."

Somebody cackles with appreciative laughter.

Suffian says, "Look, the food fair is next week already. There's no time to cancel and order the fried chicken from somewhere else."

"So what if we can't cancel the order?" Azmi says. "We just have to boycott the fried chicken."

Like a sports coach gauging the morale of his team

members he looks from one to the other of us. "Yes?" Azmi insists. "Yes or not, Yusuf?"

I jump to attention but find nothing to say. I am still getting used to answering to Yusuf. Yusuf bin Abdullah: a new name for a new life. Yusuf bin Abdullah is Malay because his mother is Malay. And therefore Yusuf bin Abdullah is also Muslim. This much I know about him because Latifah has laid it out in no uncertain terms.

But Azmi has already pointed out: "If your mother is Malay then your father should have a Muslim name what. Then you won't be bin Abdullah like a convert." Azmi has my number all right and today he is watching me closely on the matter of the suspect chicken.

"Ha!" he says now. "Surprised only this fler. Well? Are you going to eat the Chinaman's chicken?"

"No," I say and I know as I say it that this is God's truth: I will not be touching that chicken, although not for Azmi's reasons.

"See!" Azmi says. He claps his hands together once. "Even Yusuf agrees. Who else is with us?"

"It's not that we're against you," Rizal says. "But if we boycott our own stall and tell all the other Malay boys to boycott it too, we ourselves will be the losers. All the other classes will raise more money, and we'll have no chance of winning the trophy."

A murmur rises from the small crowd.

"Wah!" Azmi cries. "You yourself are thinking like a Chinaman! Money money money! Why bother with Allah's laws when you can win a trophy if you don't follow them? That's why Chinese people have no religion, didn't you know? All they care about is a fat bank balance and a full stomach."

"Why don't we just ask Mr Ho about it?" says Suffian. "If there is a doubt, why don't we ask him?"

"Hah! *Ask him* indeed! Of course he'll lie! In the first place he's doing this on purpose! We're not going to ask him. But maybe I have a solution."

"Oh?" Rizal says and folds his arms.

"After all, look how many of us there are," Azmi says waving his arm over the crowd. "So we pool our money. We buy our own halal chicken. We tell all the Muslims what's going on and we open our own stall."

Another murmur. Suffian and Rizal exchange a look. Suffian shrugs. But Rizal's mouth and eyebrows show no desire to compromise.

"Well?" Azmi says. "The bell is going to ring anytime now."

"Fine," Suffian says. "Fine."

Rizal shrugs a defeated shrug.

"Oh," Azmi says, "but there's one thing. We can't breathe a word of this to the non-Muslims. Not one word. Does everyone here understand that?"

A sea of nods. A chorus of Sure and Okay. But Azmi does not let it go so easily.

"If they find out," he says, "finish for us. The whole thing will be a flop. It's us against them. If your tongue is loose, well, your loose tongue is choosing a side."

The bell rings and we scatter.

Food Fair

APRIL 1988

Like a fighter cock Azmi struts around, setting up his stall. A big sign in Rumi and in Jawi: *DITANGGUNG HALAL.*ﺣﻼﻝ. A small notice in Malay advising All Our Muslim Brothers to exercise caution in their selection and consumption of food at this fair: *Remember that if you buy and eat from a stall despite not being 100% sure then you have committed a sin!*

With his hands on his hips Mr Ho watches and shakes his head. He wipes sweat off his forehead with the back of his hand and says to no one in particular, "I wish you all had just asked me!" But when Azmi meets his eyes they look at each other like two boxers who have faced each other across a ring many times before this final defining match of their careers. Sweat drip-drip-dripping down their faces and not one word coming out of their mouths.

By nine o'clock the heat is unbearable. Meat-smoke clogs the air. Loud American songs blare from the speakers. The same bloody boys who refuse to eat the Chinaman's chicken jigging their buttocks up and down to Madonna and Michael Jackson. Azmi mouthing the words to "Bad" as he carefully extracts his own uncontaminated Muslim utensils from his backpack.

Azmi stations a sentry next to our class's main stall. "Stand here and warn people," he says. "If they look Malay at all you tell them the chicken is not guaranteed halal. You tell them"—he jerks a thumb towards his own stall—"to buy from over there. You stand here for an hour and then it'll be somebody else's turn."

At first I manage to avoid declaring an allegiance. I move vaguely between the two stalls standing ten minutes here ten minutes there. I pretend to busy myself but if you looked closely you would see that I was unhooking and rehooking the plastic bags from their nail, rearranging the bottles of Maggi tomato sauce and chili sauce, neatening the stacks of pink tissue just so, checking the flames under the woks every forty-five seconds. Sure enough after twenty minutes of this Azmi grabs me by the elbow.

"What are you doing? How can you just play around while others are working?"

"I'm not playing around, I was ..."

He hands me a pair of tongs. "You stand here and help to serve. Remember, don't give drumsticks unless people ask for them."

"Why are we serving the other pieces then? We should have just bought drumsticks isn't it?"

He gives me a long pitying look. "Bodoh ke? Drumsticks more expensive lah."

"But we're charging just as much for the other pieces!"

He laughs and slaps his forehead. "You want to make money or you want to do charity?"

Case closed.

I had no breakfast this morning and now the sight of the chicken bones in the dustbin—black tendons still hanging from them and the knob ends still wearing their skin—turns my stomach. Some of the bones have been discarded with strips of pinkish flesh clinging to them. And the smell of it! *No!* a small part of me thinks. *Your bloody tongs are not enough!* And then suddenly like a punching-bag toy the face of Umar bobs up into my head. Umar-the-Mamak who last week said to Chee Seng Eh *Lend me your ruler I can't find mine!* and then lined his hand with his handkerchief to take the ruler from Chee Seng's pork-fed hands.

I think of him and take a pink tissue from the stack. I too will line my hands. Do not be mistaken, Papa would not have approved of the pink tissue. That way (he would have said) lie the Fear and the Hatred of Brahmins of all faiths. The Hindu Brahmin the Muslim Brahmin the Jew Brahmin: all driven by disgust for others instead of love and non-violence. But faced with Azmi's hubris might not Papa too have sought some small private consolation in the knowledge that he was out-holying the haram criers? How satisfying it is to look at Azmi's smug face and say to myself, *You think you are better than the pig-eaters but alas you are wrong. In God's eyes you are no better at all whereas I! I have the truth. Straight from God's mouth into my father's ear.*

Look at them all queueing up. Look at their blithe chicken-hungry faces quickly clouded by the sentry's intervention. Look at the creeping gnawing doubt before the Muslim boys sidle over to our side. Look at the confused indignant faces of the Indians and Chinese and the weary faces of the Others and the Chindians who are already used to being interrogated for not-fasting and for ham-munching. Stupid fools.

A voice in my ear makes me jump.

"What are you doing? The tongs are not hot."

It is not God but Azmi. Eyeing me narrowly. The wheels and gears turning turning turning behind those eyes or am I imagining it? What could he possibly conclude from a piece of pink tissue?

"I know the tongs are not hot," I say. "I just don't like to have oily fingers."

"Is that so?"

An hour later he is at my back again. He speaks in Malay now. "Makan dulu. Nanti pengsan." He hands me a plastic bag with a chicken drumstick in it.

I press my hands to my sides. Before I can formulate a response in Malay the English words tumble forth. "Not hungry. I had a very big breakfast."

He reaches out and lifts my forearm. He hooks the handles of the plastic bag onto my stiff fingers. "Don't simply bluff," he says.

The plastic bag makes it impossible to hide the shaking of my hand. There is nothing for it but to say, "I don't like chicken."

He smiles. "Don't like chicken? Everybody likes chicken!"

As though from a great distance—my vision blurred my hearing dimmed—I am aware that the whole crowd is watching us now. The queue at the official class stall, the queue at Azmi's stall, the queue at the rojak stall on our left. Through a long dark tunnel Azmi's voice comes to me: "Malays eat chicken. Chinese eat chicken. Indians eat chicken. Mat Salleh of course eat chicken. But you don't eat chicken. That means what are you?"

My head is shaking *No no no* from side to side all on its own. I could give in now. I could pretend I am someone else. Not Clarence Kannan Cheng-Ho Muhammad Yusuf Dragon but someone who eats chicken. I could eat now and vomit later. Or I could get up and fight like Arjuna in the Gita. God's voice in his ear too. I open my mouth and speak clear as a bell. "I'm a human being. That's what I am. Why do you care what I eat?"

All the arrows from my quiver but Azmi is undaunted. He folds his arms and leans back. He sniggers.

"Oh, I see. You're a human being. I see! I see I see I see."

He looks around to catch all the eyes he can catch.

"Did everybody hear?" he says. "Yusuf here is a human being."

Faint laughter bubbles up here and there.

"What for you all laugh?" Azmi says. "It's true what! He is a human being. But I think I know something else about him."

And why wouldn't he? There have been articles and letters to editors and protests outside the Masjid Jamek after Friday prayers. Why wouldn't Azmi be starting to put two and two together?

Like a true master of oratory he waits for perfect silence. Then he says, "Ya, I know something about Yusuf. But now is not the time. All these people are waiting for their chicken."

He claps his hands to break his own spell. "Come on come on! No need to stand there staring. Look at the queue!"

I unhook the bag of chicken from my fingers and put it on the table. I wipe my fingers on the tissue and drop it in the dustbin. When I pick up my bag and go nobody stops me.

It Seems

By Monday morning the stories are flying.

It seems I am the illegitimate child of a famous Malay rock star and his high-class North Indian Brahmin mistress. Brought up a strict Hindu vegetarian until the government caught hold of my mother.

It seems I am the son of apostate hippies who went to America for studies and came back smoking ganja and drinking alcohol and avoiding meat.

It seems I am an orphan. Muslim by birth but accidentally adopted by a Buddhist couple from Thailand. One fine day an official going through old paperwork noticed the mistake.

It seems my Filipina mother secretly converted to Islam without telling my Eurasian father. It seems my father has taken up a court case.

I did not want to come back to school after the food fair. I tried to make a deal with Latifah: "Let me just study with the ustaz and I will never cause you any trouble. I will pray your prayers five times a day minimum. I will fast for Ramadan. I will even slowly-slowly get used to your food." But at this Latifah balked. "You think the ustaz can teach you mathematics and physics and chemistry?" she cried. "What are you going to do with your life? Join PAS or Al-Arqam? Become a missionary? You don't want to go to school, fine, I'll take you back to the authorities and see if they got place for you in a charity home somewhere."

That was that. I went to my room to sit and wait for Monday morning.

I would have to warn Reza. Of course he would tell me I was a fool; "You should have just shut up and eaten the chicken," he would say. But he would at least see that we were in the same sinking boat. Once the school found out my true identity he would have no peace either. Already—just beyond our field of vision—the forces were gathering. Ready with their prayers and the enforced piety and their vigilance.

The whole week all I saw of Reza was evidence that he had used his bed: on Saturday morning a rolled-up newspaper tucked between mattress and wall, on Sunday morning a blanket kicked to the floor. In the dirty clothes pail his uniform waited for Fauziah to collect it.

On Sunday night I did not let myself lie down. At twelve thirty Reza crept into the room wrapped in his cape of pizza smell.

"Reza!" I whispered.

He stood in the middle of the floor and stepped out of his public skin. I could hear the clink of his belt as it hit the floor. The zip. The rustle of his trousers. Now he peeled off his T-shirt and freed the trapped scent of his own sweaty skin. Dense as a cloud of birds it rose into the thick night air. But not one word did he speak. Even his breath was silent.

"Reza"—my voice low and pleading now—"Reza, I think they know who I am. The boys in my school I mean. I think they know who we are."

He unhooked his towel from behind the door. He opened the door and with his hand on the knob turned around and said, "Is that right? Tell them if they've figured it out they should tell us. Because if they know who we are then they already know more than we do."

He stepped out into the corridor and was gone to his cool bath.

I lay awake arranging and rearranging my options on the weighing scale hoping each time for a different reading.

Monday morning during PE Azmi struck.

"Tell the truth," he said. "You're not Muslim."

"What?"

"Don't play for time. Are you Muslim or not?"

"My name is Yusuf bin Abdullah. What more do you want?"

"Were you brought up Muslim? How come you don't know anything? I've been watching you."

Closer and closer he stepped.

"You don't know how to read the Quran properly. Even verses people learned in Standard One you don't know. You don't know how to wash before praying. Actually what are you? Are you a new convert?"

Suddenly I saw how much shorter than me he was. How much smaller. A strutting bantam. With one punch I could take him by surprise. I pushed my hands into my pockets. I pressed my lips together into a grim and supercilious smile.

"Who do you think you are?" I said. "What gives you the right to be judge and policeman of the whole world?"

He was taken aback. Turns out I was not after all the meekling I appeared to be. But he could not back off so easily. Got to save face what.

"I don't know about you," he said, "but I was always taught that Muslims got to help each other do the right thing. Strengthen each other's iman. Guide each other. Siapa machine cili, dia yang rasa pedas, right? If you are feeling the burn you must be guilty."

He grinned around at his audience. With one or two of his most reliable acolytes he made eye contact. Then he turned back to me and in a louder steadier voice said, "We're all waiting. Now please tell us once and for all: Where did you grow up? Who are your parents?"

My fist shot out to his face before I realized what was happening. Immediately, regret lodged like a hot coal in my throat. Azmi on his knees with his face in his hands.

Boys crowding around him and others holding me back as though I had any intention of punching him again. Mr Joseph the PE teacher blowing his whistle furiously. Someone pinning my arms behind my back. Next thing I knew I was sitting in the headmaster's office receiving a warning.

But it was not the headmaster's warning that haunted me that night; it was my own cowardice. My failure to speak the truth even after so many chances. "Who are your parents?" Azmi had asked me point blank. I knew very well what I should have said: *My father's name is Cyril Dragon. We are all one people under one God. I am neither Muslim nor Christian nor Hindu nor Buddhist. I believe in one God whose only commandment is loving-kindness to all creatures. I believe in one God who wants no blood shed in His name no anger no labels no walls.*

Violence is the worst sin Cyril Dragon used to say. The only sin.

What would he have said if he had seen me hit Azmi?

The Anointed One

What does Dawood say to his son to make him come back? Perhaps he is frightened enough of his own son to tread carefully. *I spoke to Encik Yusuf and he understands his mistake. He can't just sack the women and send them home just like that but they'll be covering their hair from now at least so you won't have to see that.* But one can just as easily imagine Dawood choosing to focus on his main objective. *Okay fine. You said you can't enter that house because Encik Yusuf is not related to those women yet they don't cover their hair. Well now they're covering their hair so you've no excuse.* And living under his father's roof on the profits of his father's empire the boy would've realized the game was up. Ideals are one thing but having enough shame to get out of the house and get a job is entirely another.

One thing is clear: he is not happy to be back.

"Boy, so nice to see you again!" Mama calls out to him on his first day back. But he barely darts her an obligatory glance. Grunts a greeting no one can make out through his bushy beard and strides past her. Gone are the days of bowing his head so low to salam Nenek that you could only see the curtain of his lashes.

He knows we are following only the letter of the law. He knows the minute his back is turned nothing can make us follow the rules of his exacting God. He knows we are still (at best) a house of sin waiting to happen. But he doesn't have a leg to stand on. Not a strand of hair is visible from under Ani's tudung when he comes to the house. She does not just refrain from speaking to me or making eye contact; she stays in the back room. Hana leaves the house and comes back nicely betudunged from her various jobs. Between the housecleaning and the Chinese restaurant she keeps her tudung on to sit bent over her books and her newspaper in the kitchen. As far as I can tell I had only to say the word for both of them to embrace this new requirement wholeheartedly. "People are talking," I said. The moment I'd said it both women hung their heads in shame as though their responsibility for my reputation had been weighing on them all along.

In his habitual seat in the back row Amar glares at me with his now-familiar mix of detachment and disgust. His blank eyes his lip curled. Leaning as far back as he can with his arms folded. Silently refusing to look at my photocopies of John Donne and Elizabeth Barrett Browning. How he can barely bring himself to touch a piece of paper with a Shakespeare sonnet on it. Oh the shameless literary canon of infidels. Everything hanging out. All those boners masquerading as poems.

Like this he quietly comes and goes for a few weeks. Here but not here. I wonder what Dawood will do when he fails the paper. I make no promises or guarantees after all. The man can't come here asking for his money back. Best thing is to keep quiet and let the boy warm his seat and fail the paper. It might even be a good awakening. With no other options he might settle down and start listening to his father about practical necessities like earning a living.

One day out of the blue Mama summons him as he's leaving. Either she's forgotten the snub (today she is wearing the bonnet and with it comes the unreliable memory of the bonnet wearer) or forgiven it. She's positioned herself strategically in the front hall. She sits in a pool of sunshine with a pile of Malay women's magazines in her lap.

"Come here," she says. "Come and sit with Nenek like you

used to when you were small."

Seventy-year-old Nenek in a bonnet: he cannot rely on the excuse of not talking to marriageable women outside the family or whatever it is these flers say. He stares at her with startled eyes.

"Nenek wants to talk to you," she says.

He shoots me a panicked look. But why should I save him from her? Thinks I'm filth and then wants me to help him. Ha!

"Ish, takut apa?" she giggles. "You've known Nenek from small isn't it? You know Nenek doesn't bite. Nothing important, Nenek is just feeling lonely."

I see it happen right before my eyes: all the firebrand stubbornness goes out of him. Even living in his father's house and eating his father's food doesn't do this to him but Mama with her yellow-toothed smile turns him into a little boy trained to respect the elderly. He sits.

"Your whole life Nenek has been watching you, you know," she says.

Words that have never in history reassured any human being. He stiffens and folds his arms.

"Tsk, nothing bad lah. But today Nenek wants to tell you something. The reason Nenek has always noticed you is because you look like Nenek's son."

At the sight of his wide eyes she throws her head back and laughs.

"Not this son, lah. Not your teacher. Nenek had another son. My older son. Looked just like you! Ask his brother and see."

But he doesn't ask and I don't answer.

"My older son—his name is Reza—passed away. He drowned in a pond when he was eighteen years old. But a mother can never forget. A mother can never get over it."

"Mama—" I begin but she holds up a finger and I think: *Why do we owe this boy the truth anyway? Let her tell him what she wants. Whatever suits her fancy today.*

"It was the biggest tragedy of my life," she says. *My*, not *Nenek's*: I can tell from the barely perceptible double take that Amar too has marked the change. "I think of him every day. But at least ... at least now I don't just think of his body when they dredged him up. Sometimes of course I do. But other times I manage to remember him as he was. Young. Handsome."

An infinitesimal nod from Amar. For a while she bathes him in the high beam of her yellow-toothed grandmother-hen smile. Then she says, "You're hoping to go overseas?"

He shrugs. "Depends on my father," he squeaks. Suddenly he sounds like a pubescent boy again.

"Ah."

They nod in concert. She leans forward.

"You must study hard lah in that case. Because you're a good boy. You won't be like these other youngsters who go overseas and get tempted by the orang puteh way of life. It's boys like you who should go overseas. Because you will keep your iman and your culture and not just that you will show them a good example. And like that you can lead them to the beauty of Islam. I'm not saying everybody lah. But a few will see the truth. Isn't it?"

He's still nodding. Perhaps he never stopped.

"Boys like you are so rare, when we see one we really want you to be successful."

He scratches his head like a loveable cartoon idiot.

"Sitting here so lonely all day long, every day, I can't help it, I start thinking of old stories. I know it's silly but I feel like you're my grandson because you look so much like my son."

She chuckles to herself. They sit in silence until she sighs and says, "I better let you go lah. I'll see you next week. Think about what I said, okay?"

He puts both his hands in his lap like a child posing for a studio photograph in the 1960s.

"Ya, Nenek," he says. "Thank you. Bye."

Then he gets up and walks to the door. I could swear his walk looks different now. The tentative swagger of a boy just learning how to perform the rituals of manliness.

Born-Agains

After so many stagnant years our household is changing.

Slowly, Hana is losing her watchfulness. Her skittish distant manner. One morning before leaving for the market she even tells me shyly, "My reading is faster now, tuan. I read all the books several times already. Can finish one whole newspaper article. Sometimes cannot understand everything, but can read."

So surprised am I by her addressing me voluntarily that I find I've frozen with my butter knife in midair. "Well done!" I say. "I'll buy you a few more books this weekend!"

We stand there smiling at each other for a few seconds. Feeling ourselves turning turning turning towards the warmth and the light. We breathe deeper and slower. We look at each other with an unfamiliar mix of surprise and relief in our eyes.

Nowadays she leaves in the morning and comes back at night but she is nevertheless emptying me out and refilling me. She is the tiny beating heart at the centre of the house. At the centre of my days. At the centre of me. I had given myself up for dead but look: my eyelids are stirring my fingers are twitching. The great frozen expanse of me is waking up after what was only a deep sleep. When I hear her packing her lunch in the kitchen I go and prepare my breakfast to keep her company. Those few minutes of companionable morning silence are a balm to both our spirits. All the small intimacies of our routine! I leave the butter and the butter knife out for her after spreading butter on my bread. I switch on the hot-water dispenser. I put out two mugs. There is nothing unseemly about this: Mama and Ani have their breakfast later that's all. I take out the pine-apple jam Hana likes. I stir my coffee I tap the spoon against the rim of my mug three times I lay the spoon next to her mug ready for her. These small-small things make her life that tiny bit easier and I know watching the blur of her spread the butter and spoon out the Nescafé that she notices and appreciates the thought. In the hall mirror she pins and adjusts her tudung. Tucking in all the wispy hair that frames her face. Standing so close to the mirror that her breath steams it. Must speak to Ani about taking her to the optician.

Life is after all about trusting and believing. If you simply wait even the most arid soil will one day yield a sprout whose seeds you had no idea were sleeping under the surface. Now it has leaves now it has a tight bud now—you rub your eyes and shake your heads—it is blooming into something not of this earth. All the hothouse hybrids of history's greatest botanists pale beside it. It is as lush as a peony and as bright as a flame.

Look at Mama: we all thought she was incapable of love but all she needed was time and patience. Look at her next to Amar which also has become a regular event. Bonnet days or no-bonnet days any days she asks he obediently takes his seat. One day as he is sitting with her for those five minutes after his class she says to me, "Yusuf! Go and bring the photo album, can or not?"

I myself cannot believe it. "What? Mama, I don't think—"

"Just bring it quickly. It's in my room on the top shelf of the cupboard."

Why do you bother hiding it there, Mama, I should have said, *when everybody knows you look at those photos every chance you get?*

No point embarrassing her in front of the boy. I go and get the album. It's an ancient one. The kind with ring binding and inside those thick black pages with sheets of parchment between.

"Come, come nearer," she says and without a word the boy slides closer to her. She opens the album.

"See?" she says. "That's my Reza. In those days we used to take our babies to the studio to make these pictures. Six months old he would have been. See his curly hair and his light-coloured eyes? I told you isn't it, he looked just like you. You could have been brothers!"

Reza sucking his thumb in bloomers and a smock on his first birthday. Three-year-old Reza wolfing down an ice-cream sundae in a fluffy post-swim robe at the Selangor Club. Five-year-old Reza enjoying a root-beer float at A&W. Gap-toothed Reza grinning with a trophy on Sports Day at the fancy private school he attended while the Australian father was still paying for it.

"Ho!" Mama trumpets. She pats the photo fondly. "Here you can *really* see how you look alike. In the baby pictures it's not so easy. Especially since I don't know what you looked like when you were a baby."

She turns to Amar with the raised eyebrows of one who has just had a splendid idea.

"Next time you come," she says, "bring a baby photo for Nenek! Ask your mother. Sure won't mind lah she. Tell her it's for Nenek."

Amar doesn't say yes or no. Anyone else would let it go but not Mama in her blissful state of newfound love.

"Janji tak janji?" she says. "If not Nenek will have to come limping all the way to your father's shop to ask him! And you know how hard it is for me to get around nowadays. So better you save me the trip and nicely bring me a photo. Okay?"

He laughs then. First time any of us has seen him laugh in at least two years.

"Okay," he says.

He looks back down at the photo album. But of course

there is a dearth of photos after that Sports Day one. Shortly afterwards things turned rocky with the Australian father. Then the Muhibbah Centre years.

"Long time we didn't take pictures after that," Mama says. Amar stiffens his shoulders but lowers his eyes in appropriately solemn understanding.

She flips through the dark pages. A single colour photo floats to the floor and Amar bends to pick it up. A photo that was never properly fixed to its own place like the others.

"Ah, that one you will recognize!" Mama cries in high delight. "That one I no need to tell you who it is."

With both hands Amar holds the photo at a distance. But he won't look at it. He looks at me instead. A curious expression in his eyes. The tension of it is so great that even though Mama herself said she had no need to explain the photo she says, "That's your teacher lah. Encik Yusuf. On his Convocation Day at Universiti Malaya."

Amar turns to her. "Only one photo of Encik Yusuf?" he mumbles.

Mama chuckles. "Ah!" she says. "The second child always like that lah. When you got two children you got no more time to take photos and all that. I'm sure it's the same for you and your sister."

Oh dear oh dear "your sister" … but Amar does not appear even to have heard. He's turning the blank pages of the album with a frown on his face. He's thinking, *But no photos? Not one photo after 1975?* He's thinking, *Maybe there are a few in a different album.* When suddenly Mama says in a bright and trembly voice, "That's why I'm so happy I found you. I feel I'm getting a second chance now. It's true, I never did enough for my boys. I was young and stupid and busy with … with myself. But now I'm not young and I'm not stupid. Not everybody is lucky enough to get a second chance. Allah is the most merciful, the most generous, the most bountiful!"

He's rubbing his sweaty palms on his knees and getting ready to excuse himself but that curious expression has not left his face. A weight in his eyes. His feelers have detected danger—something unspoken some twisted scrapheap some submerged shipwreck between me and Mama—and he's trying to retract them but she won't let him. With the force of her narrative she pins him in place.

"You know," she says, "my Reza is very successful in his life, but he doesn't come to see Nenek anymore." Like he lives down the road she says it. Casually. Smiling benignly at Amar as though perhaps to say, *Haha! My very own reports of his death have been greatly exaggerated.*

Who can blame Amar for casting me the look of someone who has just seen a ghost? How he explains the inconsistency to himself I cannot say; for that matter I can hardly be sure how *I* explain it to myself. The tricks of an ageing brain or a little game she plays with all of us?

"That's not right, is it?" she goes on. "Learn this now itself: your parents are your parents no matter what. They gave you life, they feed you, clothe you, send you to school. It doesn't please Allah for boys to cast aside their parents."

She's turning the pages now where he left off. One by one by one until she gets to that last page. There's Reza glowering at Latifah in her overstuffed front hall in Bangsar.

"That's my son," she says. "Few months before ..."

Amar blinks his giraffe lashes at her in trepidation.

"Before he went off," she concludes.

The ambiguity appears to suit all of us. Before the threat of clarification looms Amar stands up. His white robe sweat-stained from all his palm-rubbing. She looks up at him.

"I better go, Nenek," he says. "It's already Maghrib."

Her oracular expression gives way to a granny grin. "You'll bring the photo next week?" she says.

He puts a hand on the back of the armchair to steady

himself. "Okay, Nenek," he says. "I'll bring it."

"If you promise something to an old lady," she says, "you must do it. Sure sure."

With no warning the crooked smile of his distant boyhood flashes out at us. It seems to take even Amar himself by surprise. Then slowly he stirs into that smile the immense relief of being released.

"Sure sure," he says.

That whole week Mama does not once ask me to track down Reza on my internet my Google my Facebook. She glows with new life exactly as though she were pregnant. As though just in the last week she has felt the baby's first kicks in her belly. And exactly like a pregnant woman she sees the rest of the world in a blur. Where before she used to drive me and Ani mad with her twice-daily *What day is it today?* now she knows exactly how many days it is until Amar comes again. And this time with his photo too. With that photo in her file, her application to be a part of his past will be that much stronger: it will allow her to imagine his babyhood in such lush detail it'll be like she was there.

Night Terrors

In my nightmares Papa sits in a dim cell. Just enough light to see the toilet bowl in the corner and the brown stains on the walls. Footsteps up and down the corridor. Guards in black boots. Never-ending rain on the roof. A stale damp smell. One hand spread on his paining chest. Does he pray all alone? Does he mouth the words in the dark? Somehow I cannot imagine him saying a prayer not intended for public consumption.

Latifah's voice in my ear: "Your mother will be okay lah. They treat women better. And the authorities know she is actually a Muslim. She didn't try to renounce her religion or anything. Just got off track."

But is that true in the first place and if it may in some mysterious way be counted as true then do the authorities know it? It is not what the minister on TV seemed to think. "Tak sedar diri" he said. *Doesn't know what she is.* If she doesn't know then will they be the ones to teach her?

And if even my mother needs to be taught a lesson what more my father? What will they do to him? What are they doing right now? "The father is in Kamunting," Latifah whispered to the most recent busybody makcik to pop in just to look at my face. The unceasing river of them with their hungry beady eyes their pretending to care the great oily force of their auntiesmiles.

Kamunting. The name sends a chill down my spine and I remember where I've read it: Father Dubois's ghastly sheaf of papers. *Solitary confinement. Interrogation.* A cell with only a bucket for a toilet.

I look for Kamunting in my Geography book but it's not on the map. In the library I search for days until I find it in a book on the history of Perak State. There it is. Kamunting. Just outside Taiping. (Chinese meaning: peaceful, serene, tranquil. Site of bitter and violent feuds between Chinese secret societies. Place names are always aspirational/wishful don't you know?) Highest annual rainfall in Malaysia. Once a major tin-mining area. Featuring the Lake Gardens where my father would not be picnicking under the celebrated rain trees.

"They treat women better," Latifah said. Therefore they treat men worse. However they are teaching Mama her lesson it probably doesn't involve needles under her fingernails or nails in her private parts. My god no it is not that I want Mama to be treated worse if Papa cannot be treated better. All I want is for her to be sorry. To say for once: *I made mistakes. I should have been kinder. Those who loved me I should have loved back. I should have thought more about others and less about myself.*

But only in my dreams would Salmah say such a thing. Instead it is my father who sits in the dark thinking *I could not even save myself in the end let alone the country.* Concentrate on the facts: they hang people for drug trafficking. Those they don't hang get the rotan. Concentrate on the facts: Papa was not trafficking drugs. For what he was doing there is no fixed list of punishments. But then they will make it up as they go along. Everything depends on their powers of invention. Therefore miracles are still possible! God sees all. God will not abandon me. Prepare for the worst. And hope for the best, i.e. for Papa to be in the hands of sympathetic and unimaginative policemen and guards.

Canteen Brawl

MAY 1988

"Son of a jailbird."

We have not spoken since the day I ended up in the head-master's office but I recognize the voice in my ear immedi-ately. He grabs both my wrists from behind. "I told my father about you, that you look Malay but you won't even eat chicken, and he said for sure you're one of that crazy fler's sons lah." His fingers digging into my wrists he looks around to all our classmates lining up before assembly.

"You all heard me right? Makes like he is better than everybody else but that's what he is. Son of a jailbird."

Jailbird. He says it like he has just learned the word. Enjoying it. Wondering at its poetic cruelty. He twists my arms to turn me round.

"Well?" he says. "You admit it? Your father is a jailbird?"

"They arrested my father because he is brave and they are scared of him."

"Brave! Hahaha! That means every madman outside the market must be brave lah then. And what about your mother? She also brave is it? So brave that she can throw away her own religion and pretend she's not Malay?"

A strange heat creeps up my body. Like I'm stepping deliberately into boiling water.

"Race race race. Religion religion religion. That's all you know. You are like wild animals the way you divide your-selves into packs and tear each other to pieces."

His eyes gleam with pleasure at my growing agitation. He grins and sneers.

"Wah, this fler can talk big man! Don't play-play! Your father is in the lockup and still berani kau cakap macam tu? We're the wild animals it seems!"

It is as though he has been sent to test me. *Am* I in fact brave enough to say what needs to be said even though my father is in jail? How much can I bear each time before I betray my father's principles? Because over and over again I will betray them. Two things happen simultaneously: my leg shoots out to kick Azmi's shin, and my mouth spits in his face. Already the Discipline Master is bursting through the staff room's swinging saloon doors already he is waddling at top speed in our direction with a rotan in one hand already he is standing before us tap-tap-tapping the rotan against his right knee.

"What is all this?" he barks. "Before school already got boxing match is it? So early also got energy to fight like this."

He is looking only at me. "You again," he says. "Warning not enough for you, must be you want a suspension ah?"

He draws a breath. Weighs his options. But in the end he is a slave to time and place and biology: what man of his generation (let alone a Discipline Master) can resist the temptation to swell himself up by deflating someone else?

"I'm waiting for an answer," he says. "You want a suspension or not?"

What he wants is not the real answer but the lie proffered in apology and atonement.

"No."

"No what? No your grandfather?"

"No sir."

"You get one more chance. One more chance, you hear me or not? Three wrestling matches and you'll be suspended."

He whips around and turns up his volume three notches.

"The rest of you get lost! Now now now! Line up properly! This is not a stadium! Blaaardy busybodies all of you!"

Crick-crick-crick his rotan crackles each time he whacks his own thigh through the stiff fabric of his trousers. Then he goes off on his unmerry way and I hear Azmi's voice behind me.

"I told you! His father is that cuckoo bird. The Cameron Highlands Dragon."

The bell rings. We walk along the grey corridors to our grey classrooms in unbroken monotony. A familiar uneasy stillness falls over the surface but the monsters lurking under it are now unmistakable.

Glow in the Dark

Tell me it did not happen.

Not Reza you will say. Not the Reza to whom you may as well have been a clump of dirt on the bottom of his shoe. But it did happen.

I am alone in the room I share with Reza. On my bed. Under the ceiling fan. Unmasked but unsuspended. There is no escape: tomorrow morning I am going to have to go back to school. It is late but I am wide awake.

The next thing I know the door opens. In the dark I see Reza's bare white feet before anything else. At once I am absolutely certain I cannot tell him a thing. I cannot let him see my distress and this is why: he is not my friend.

But he perches on the edge of his bed and faces me. Without meeting his eyes I know he is studying me.

"Hey," he says. "What's happening?"

He sounds like he really honest to God wants to know. This takes me so much by surprise that the words tumble out of my mouth:

"They know, they all know, the boys at school know who I am, they found out."

Then I can no longer speak. I fold my arms across my knees and bury my face in them. Clarence Kannan Cheng-Ho Muhammad Yusuf Dragon, aged eleven years one month twelve days, bawling like a three-year-old. From this twenty-five-year distance I feel myself slowly slowly backing away. Look at him also I want to wash my hands of him. *Dono who lah this fler. Sissy boy. Crybaby.*

"Listen," Reza says. Then he pauses as if he himself knows it will take me a moment to realize he is actually speaking to me. When I am looking up and blinking away my tears he repeats himself. "Listen to me. Are you listening?"

I nod.

"You want to know something?" he says. "I am only going to say this once so take it and remember it for the rest of your life. Understand?"

My voice is a whisper. "Okay."

"You don't have to care what other people think about you. What matters is whether you are doing the right thing. Not what the rest of the world says, not whether they point and laugh or decide to clap and cheer. I don't know why it's so hard for you to see that. I swear you were born looking left and right and all around to see what people think."

I'm shaking my head no no no.

"You know that, isn't it? You should know, anyway. You were like a ... like a dog trying to please your masters. Trying to please your father, trying to please God, always trying to figure out what exactly you had to do to get a pat on the head and a 'good boy.' Now you know all the attention and approval didn't come free. Maybe you thought the price was worth what you got, but the rest of us had no say."

And I know by the way he says "the rest of us" that certain details will never be revisited.

"But Reza, I didn't mean ... I tried to tell you even then, I thought ... I didn't know—"

"I know what you knew and what you didn't know. I'm not talking about that. But you didn't mind being a rat if it could make your father sit up and take notice. You saw what happened with George Cubinar but still you wanted to be a rat. You know what a rat is?"

"Please," I beg. "Please, I'm sorry."

"Of course you're sorry. Every damn fool can see you're sorry. That's not the point. The point is, you can choose to change now or you can ruin the rest of your life worrying what every Tom Dick and Harry thinks of you. But it's not just your own life you'll ruin."

There's nothing to say. I blink at my knees and choke on my saliva.

Suddenly he reaches out and puts a hand on my elbow as though to steady himself. Then we are both simply lost. When I say nothing he goes on.

"Please, for god's sake, listen to me. Just stop caring about other people."

"But that doesn't fix anything. I can't go back and fix anything."

He shrugs. A heavy smell of deep-frying rises off his skin.

"Every day we're in the news, Reza. Papa and Mama are in the news."

"I know."

"What's going to happen to us?"

"Us?"

I pull my arm away from his hand. I correct myself.

"What's going to happen to me?"

"What's going to happen to you is that you're going to grow up and one day you're going to decide for yourself who you want to be and what you want to believe. The thing is, Kannu"—he has to swallow after saying my name—"the thing is, you can choose what to believe. If one person tells you one thing and the next person tells you the opposite, you know what that means? It means they're probably both bullshitting. It means you yourself have to decide what is true. You can't sit there waiting for someone to hand you the truth because anybody who claims they can do that is a World-Class Grade-A Bullshitter."

Don't tell me all this I don't want to know it I need safety I need rules I'm just a child: what child can see all that, let alone say it?

Before we know what is happening to us his arms are

around me in a clumsy embrace and I am enveloped in that fug of rancid oil and low-quality melted cheese and mystery meat. (You see? How could I have imagined it all when I remember even the smell?) A flash flood of confused feelings: suspicion (is this all a trick? where is my snide cynic of a brother?) then relief amazement gratitude—and shame. I do not deserve this comfort. This kindness. Yet I am so starved for kindness that my need is bigger than me. I lay my head on Reza's shoulder and close my eyes.

He pushes me away and still holding my shoulders considers the sight of me.

"You're stupid," he says. "You're a fool, you're a bloody idiot, but you're not evil. You're just a stupid kid. It's not your fault you got carried away by other people's nonsense. They're the ones who built the type of world that encouraged spying and ratting and they're the ones, well, your father was anyway, the one who rewarded you for it. You were just a … actually, no, you were not even a pawn. You didn't even have that much use. So don't think you were so great and powerful that now you have to apologize for your mistakes. Pull yourself together and get on with your life. Just go to school and mind your own business and learn all the things you never got to learn before."

It's the most I've heard him say in four months. I couldn't have made it up. Could I? I remember the look in his eye. Not love exactly. Not anything so soft and pure. But something gritty and dangerous. Had it remained in the depths of him rather than working its way to the surface he might have exploded because, look, his eyes glow red from the blazing heat of it. That is what I remember most of all. The red glow in the dark even after he has let go of my shoulders and lain down on his bed. Even after he has closed his eyes. That red glow through the skin of his eyelids. But for that, the whole conversation might never have happened. But for that, there would be not a trace.

Chipped Mug

2023

A morning like any other morning. Radio Klasik FM blaring while Ani does the bathrooms. Mama's moist snore bubbling out of her room. Hana bustling around packing her bag. I saved her a leftover sardine bun today. I roll it up in clingfilm and hold it out to her.

"For your lunch," I say.

She freezes and blinks. "Thank you tuan," she says. "Thank you."

How keenly I once wanted her to say things like *You are so generous tuan you do so much for me I am so lucky to have such a good place to stay.* In my waking dreams she would tell me, *All those years growing up so poor, one day we ate and the next day we didn't, so many of us in that house, I never thought I would come to a place like this and find such wonderful people.* But I know now that this is not Hana's way. I watch her hold the bun awkwardly for a few seconds before quickly stuffing it into her bag. All the unspoken declarations and avowals we do not need to say out loud: between us what is not spoken is understood. These little things I do for her are a delicate dance. I want to demonstrate my feelings yet I must be careful not to embarrass her.

"Aaah, it's a small thing," I say. I know she understands what it means; how I remembered and planned for her lunchtime in her absence.

She's about to drink her coffee when I notice the mug I put out for her is chipped on the rim.

"Eh wait," I say. I reach out and touch the handle of it to

stop her. It's halfway to her mouth already and I don't want to be too forward; I won't take it out of her hands. "The mug is chipped," I tell her. "It'll hurt your mouth. Let me get you a different one."

She half stands. "Tuan, I can do it, I can do it, tuan," she says. And I understand her embarrassment and this insistence on the tuan: of course the sahib should not be fetching and carrying mugs or anything else for the servant girl to begin with let alone when he has already bought her books and newspapers and sardine buns. She wants me to know she does not expect it she is not that kind of servant girl she knows her place. But I too want her to know something: she is not just a servant girl in this house. She is not our servant at all of course being employed as she is by other people but, more than that, servanthood is not her state under my roof. She is not even a guest. She is family.

"Please, Hana!" I say. "Sit down. I'll get you a mug."

But she won't sit. She hovers. When I bring another mug she pours her coffee from the chipped mug into it—so as not to waste I'm sure because some tuans and some mems calculate every grain of rice every onion every teabag consumed by their servants, sometimes going so far as to mark the level of the coffee and the sugar on the containers each day.

"Sit down, Hana. Sit down and have your breakfast. Don't worry so much. All these things are small things." All these things are small things and—I want to add but know I do not have to— what is between us is so much bigger than any of this.

She butters her bread and sits down. Always she eats quickly and efficiently but the last few weeks she has added a new step to her routine that requires even more haste at the table: she's taken to wearing a bit of makeup. To escape her auntie's disapproval she puts it on only behind the closed door of the spare toilet although it is nothing garish or inappropriate for a Nice Girl. Just a bit of lipstick and cheap eyeliner all applied with the hesitation of someone experimenting for the first time. She buys it at the pasar malam and hides it behind her back like she does with the hair accessories. Poor innocent little thing! It is hard to begrudge her these few pleasures. Once when she was coming back with the stuff my eye fell upon it in her plastic bag but when we looked at each other she understood: I would not go carrying tales to her auntie.

How can this not awaken the memory of Mama painting her face in secret for all those years at the Centre? No matter what else Mama was being and doing and feeling (and oh fair enough fair enough that was a lot in those days) there is nevertheless something so heartbreaking in the painting of a face behind closed doors. How tuned in to my frequencies Hana must be, for like a mind-reader she says, "Kesian Nenek."

I jump slightly. It's not often we speak to each other let alone during these quiet mornings.

"Why, what's the matter?" I say. "Why are you suddenly feeling sorry for her?"

"Your brother," she says. "She misses him. He should come and see her. Other people's children live overseas and they come. Even I, I came here to earn a bit of money but I don't forget my parents. I've always said, once I've earned a bit I'll go back and make their life easier. Build a brick house for them. Take care of them in their old age. Like you, tuan. You keep your mother in your own house, you come back home to her every evening. That's the way it should be."

Not only is it the lushest outpouring of words I have ever heard from her it is also the first time she has allowed herself the liberty of commenting upon my morals. It's not that I don't hear her admiration: "Like you, tuan." I know what she is trying to say: *You are a good man.* But she is offering it as a consolation prize. Because she saw what my face did when she talked about her going back.

"Hana," I say—and her fingers tighten around the sardine bun because it is the first time I have said her name needlessly like this when I already have her attention—"you know that you can stay as long as you want in my house. You can make more money here, send more back to your parents. You can go and see them and come back. I ... we ... Nenek has become so attached to you. You have many brothers and sisters, don't you? And they're all living somewhere around there only?"

"Yes but—"

"Then they will be there with your mother and father. You know you can trust them. Surely earning more here and sending the money back is what would be most helpful for all of them."

What I should say is *Don't go. Please don't go. You have brought light and life into this house. Even in those hours you're not here we feel your presence everywhere. Your house slippers on the shoe rack. Your soap and shampoo in the bathroom. Your rolled-up mattress under Ani's bed. We wait and wait for you.*

Or even, *Like a bird flying into a house you've flown into my heart and I know you do not know where you are which way is in which way is out. I know the usual thing—the expected thing— would be for me to open the window and let you go. But what if you stayed? What if we came to a point where I could hold very still and you would come and eat from my hand? What if you stayed forever? A splash of colour in all the grey. A flash-dazzle-flurry in the shadows.*

When I look at her I see that her brows are drawn close together and her face is crumpling as though she's about to cry.

"Thank you tuan." Then suddenly she spits out the words: "I do feel very lucky to be in this house."

And now that I hear them coming out of her mouth I am no longer so sure they are what I want. The saying of them opens a small rift between us. An airless gap through which I cannot stretch my arm or throw my voice. It is almost as if she has said them to make this distance: *you are there tuan and I am here.*

She lifts her head to the clock and jumps up. "I better go, tuan."

She holds the sardine bun tightly against her chest.

"Go, go," I say. "Don't be late."

She turns and scurries off and I imagine the tears pooling on that clingfilm. A profusion-confusion of feelings swamping her and yes Hana yes this terror this denial all of these are only to be expected in the face of big-big feelings but do not worry do not worry together we will navigate these uncharted seas.

As Good as New

One day she blows back in like the monsoon. Wild hanks of hair escaping from her bun. Her eyes too bright. Her skin too shiny. Her hands like two frantic birds.

"Come, come!" she says to me when I walk in the front door after school. She pats the seat. "Come and sit next to Mama!"

I obey. It has only been six months since I saw her last but my body responds as though a girl has taken a seat next to me on the school bus. Everything curls in on itself: my shoulders my fingers my toes. I press my knees together. I stare at the loose elastic thread dangling from the top of one of my socks.

All these months I wanted her back I begged for it I prayed for it and now—

I force myself to look at her. Something is different about her but what? Of course her hair is a bit longer. She is thinner and paler. But it is not these superficial things. Something is different *in* her. Someone has hollowed her out and filled her afresh. I think of Father Dubois's cyclostyled sheets. But *they treat women better* Latifah had promised. Why then can I not shake the feeling that the person sitting next to me is not the Mama I knew in the hills but the fairy-tale magician's decoy daughter? The shapeshifting witch. The cyborg. To think that among my prayers was an ardent but I-feared-unrealistic wish for a completely different Mama i.e. one with whom my fantasy future would be possible. But this different Mama is not the one I prayed for, inspiring in me no soaring hope but only a deep unease. A tingling a lightheadedness a raising of hairs and hackles. I must not be tricked by her exact resemblance to Mama. I must not be lulled into a foolish trust.

"Aren't you happy to see me, Kannu?" she says.

Latifah frowns. "Yusuf," she murmurs. "We call him Yusuf."

Her smile perfectly unbroken, cyborg Mama efficiently processes this input and repeats, "Yusuf. Yes. Aren't you happy to see me?"

"Of course he's happy to see you," Latifah says. "His own mother! Which boy won't be happy to see his own mother after six months?"

I can tell you which boy. I'll give you two guesses and a clue: he's at work at the moment but he'll be back late tonight.

I ought to say it: *I'm happy to see you Mama.* But a stone weighs down my tongue. A stone in my mouth a stone in my belly a stone in my heart. Mama is back but while the old Mama would have been hard enough—so much to explain or not-explain, so much to ask or not-ask, so much to forgive or not-forgive—this weird new Mama represents the end of whatever dreams I was mad enough to keep alive even cautiously. She is here and she is real and the realness of her in the clear light of day forces me to see that nothing will ever be the same again. My old life is gone forever. There is no coming back or going back for any of us.

At lunch Mama eats fish and chicken like a professional flesh-eater. Like a person who never dreamt it was possible to abstain let alone actually stopped eating them. Such gusto such flaunting: she so badly wants me to look at her that the air crackles from the force of her intentions. But her attempt at telekinesis fails. I do not turn my head.

Afterwards Mama follows me up the stairs to the bedroom. We're alone for the first time in many months. Perhaps years. Have we *ever* been alone together just the two of us?

She sits on Reza's bed. "I've come back, see?"

What am I supposed to say to that?

"I'm sorry, Kannu," she says. I snatch this small good sign up as it flits by and cling to it: at least my name hasn't actually been erased from her database and replaced with Yusuf. At least she was just pretending for Latifah. "I'm sorry for what you must have gone through. But everything will be okay now. We won't stay here. I'll get a job. We can rent something. I still have contacts at the newspaper you know? My old colleagues, most of them are still around."

I don't want to look at her. All this puzzling about what is different is starting to give me a headache. My eyes are tired. My forehead hot and tight.

"Say something, Kannu. What do you think? What are you thinking about?"

"Nothing. I'm not thinking about anything."

"Please?"

"I'm not thinking about anything."

For a few seconds she seems to hold her breath. Then she squeezes her left hand with her right and exhales and says, "You and your brother just the same."

She looks at me with her too-bright eyes. The threat of her tears forcing me to keep mine locked away when all I want to do is to lie down on the cold floor and weep.

"Just the same, both of you. You think I'm a bad mother. Your brother, from small itself, he could look at me as if ... as if I was I don't know what. A beggar, a prostitute, something even worse. Tell me, if I'm such a terrible mother, then what about the mothers who beat and burn and starve their own children? It's time for you to know such things happen, Kannu, and—"

"What about Papa? When is he coming back?"

She freezes. Mouth open. Hands in mid-wring. "Is *that* what you're worried about?"

"You said everything will be okay. So that means—"

"I said everything will be okay, yes. That doesn't mean

I'm promising you a happily-ever-after fairy-tale ending, Kannu. I can't control everything."

"But when is he coming back?"

She throws her hands up. "How should I know? I'm not sitting at the right hand of Dr Mahathir. How should I know when they will let him out?"

"Then ask them."

"Ask them! Wah, so easy, huh? How powerful do you think I am? If I go around asking too many questions, straightaway I'll be back in the lockup, you know that? They won't think twice."

A silence rolls in like a smell. Downstairs the kitchen clock chimes. Latifah calls out to Fauziah to stop the roti man. Fauziah runs to the front grille with the house keys.

"I'm sorry," Mama says. "I know you want everything to be like before. You want everything to be as good as new. But what can really be as good as new? Not me. Not you. Not even your Papa. The best thing we can do is move on and make a new life."

"And just forget about Papa? Pretend he never existed?"

She covers her face and through her hands says, "Hai, hai, Kannu! How you immediately jump from A to Z! Who said anything about 'pretend he never existed'? He will come back when he comes back."

When can I cover *my* face? When can I speak through the cover of *my* hands? On what future date in what parallel universe will I get to be the child and she the adult? *Some things never change after all* I realize bitterly as the wet sound of her sniffing through fresh tears fills the room.

"And then what?" I ask her. "How will he find us?"

She shakes her head and blows a great puff of air out through her mouth. "We'll leave a trail of crumbs. Like in Hansel and Gretel like that. Okay? Happy?"

And despite all my resolve all my vows to remain vigilant our future stretches before us again just like that.

Mama and Kannu and Reza. Reza and Kannu and Mama. (Almost) A Proper Family. How can I scratch out a story I so badly want to tell myself?

Which Boy Won't Be Glad

Mama is in her room with the door closed when Reza returns that night. A week ago I would have said nothing to him. I would have pictured his cool mocking you-must-have-mistaken-me-for-someone-who-cares face. I would have heard his snort of derision and the low snarl of his laugh. But that was before *You're a fool, you're a bloody idiot, but you're not evil.* Before the 2 a.m. encounter I could almost have dreamt. Except I did not dream it and so now I hoist myself up in bed to tell him, "Mama came back already. She came back this morning."

He stops under the ceiling fan right in the middle of the room. He stands there and breathes in and out. His shoulders rise and fall, rise and fall. Then without a word he peels off his sweat-soaked Shakey's T-shirt and his trousers and drops them into the washing pail. He picks up his towel and leaves the room. I lie awake listening to the sounds of his shower but when he returns he hangs up his towel and lies down and turns to face the wall.

In the morning there she is sitting opposite me at the breakfast table. She smiles amiably and asks me, "Where is your brother?"

"Gone out already."

"Surely his job doesn't start so early?"

"Don't know."

For three days this continues. On the fourth night she awaits his return downstairs.

It is as though he knows the moment he opens the gate

that she is there waiting. He whistles and saunters. His light step nothing like the familiar nightly dragging of his soul from some twilight zone back into the unforgiving light of Latifah's house. But he says nothing to the figure framed in the doorway. At the door he stands and waits for her to let him pass.

"Reza," she says. "I've been back for three days already and I've not seen you."

"And?"

He pauses to savour her discomfiture then adds, "Oh that's right, I forgot, before you left we used to spend all our time having deep heart-to-heart talks."

As though he has pushed her she sits down hard on the sofa. "Is that my fault?" she says. "You were never around, you were always off on your own adventures—"

"I had my adventures, you had your adventures. So what for pretend now?"

"Who is pretending? I'm your mother, Reza. I know you have been suffering. But just because you didn't want to be up there in the beginning, you still blame me for everything? Have you simply forgotten how happy you were for so many years? You were happy, Reza! It's not that I was too busy with anything, *you* were the one who didn't need *me*. What you went through at the end, was that anything to do with me? Why is everything always my fault?"

"What's the point of sitting around arguing about what was whose fault? No need to suddenly make like we are some perfect golden smiling advertisement family. You get on with your life, I'll get on with mine."

He does not wait for a response. He is already halfway up the stairs and the noise of her tears fills my ears before I slip back behind our bedroom door and into my bed. I close my eyes but still I hear her. A wet choked weeping. She will be shivering on the sofa now. That ugly shivering of shock not cold. The jaw seizing up. The hands clutching at each other. The billowy sleeves of her caftan wet with snot and tears.

For me there was none of this. Just a breezy *Come and sit next to Mama!* She had saved up all her anguish for him. But why should I be surprised? That is how it has always been.

Five Times

Latifah's hawk eye on Mama. The extra telekung in her hand. The prayer mats already rolled out. "Dah nak azan, Salmah. Jom solat." Haven't I been giving in myself for the sake of a peaceful life? Then why does the sight of Mama kneeling in her telekung next to Latifah drive me into a silent rage? How they whisper their prayers in not-quite-unison. How they bend and bob—forehead to mat and up again—like poorly choreographed dancers in some school production featuring bedsheet-draped ghosts. If I am faking it all for a bit of peace and quiet couldn't Mama be doing the same?

It's the look on her face. Her eyes and her brow bear no sign of a grand internal struggle. No resistance no stubborn disobedience of the spirit. Nor even indifference or resignation. Instead what I see is a kind of foolish bliss. Like as though she is oh so sweetly relieved to stop thinking and just go through the motions. To—after all the believers themselves would use the same word—*submit*. But then I begin to wonder: was her face different before? I cast my mind back and her face has always worn this look: that maddening quarter-smile that unflappable anything-also-can cast of her features that wide-eyed deer-blinking before an always-new world for which every day she needs a guide. Someone to take her hand and lead her through the confusing alleyways of existence.

One afternoon after the Asar prayer I go to her room. I find her on her knees by her open suitcase. I close the door behind me and stand there with my back against the door.

"What do you actually believe anyway?" I say.

She smirks. There is no other word for it.

"Yusuf, Yusuf. Always so serious."

By now the name by which I was known at the Centre has disappeared into oblivion to join all the discarded names of the devoutly rechristened. But who has time to properly mourn lost names? There are so many bigger fish I am trying to fry in this wobbly-bottomed kuali three sizes too big for my smallboy frame. If I add even one more the kuali will tip over spilling its boiling oil and half-fried fish on me and then what? Third-degree burns. Lifelong disfiguration. So if it must be Yusuf then Yusuf I shall be.

"No, really, what do you believe?" I insist. "I'm asking. You think you can get out of everything by just calling me by a new name like I'm a new person?"

She smooths the top layer of clothes in the suitcase and sits back. "What do *you* believe?" she says.

"Don't simply answer a question with another question. For you everything is so ... so *easy*. You can just change what you believe like ... no, you know what, it is easier than changing clothes for you. You just do whatever is convenient."

She opens her mouth to say something then closes it. Then she says quietly, "We are all doing whatever is convenient for us isn't it?"

"Speak for yourself! Some of us do what we believe is right even when it is difficult. You, you can just waltz back in and talk Malay and pray five times a day and eat fish and birds and buffalo and who even knows whether you are putting on an act? Who even knows who you are?"

She shakes her head and smiles. "Who can answer such questions in this lifetime? If you really know who you are at eleven years old, then wah, you are better off than most people, man!"

I can feel it as though it is a physical thing happening in

my hands on my neck on my skin: the slippery-eeling of her. The sliding away. The slow slither that conceals her secretly fast mental chess moves.

"Are you a Muslim now? Do you believe that Islam is the only true path? Do you believe that there is only one God and he is called Allah and all the other names for God are names of idols?"

But she is the unbeaten champion of the answer-a-question-with-a-question contest. "Yusuf, didn't you also say the Shahada? Latifah said you masuk Islam no problem, she's only worried about Reza."

"No! I didn't say it. I never said it."

Even as the denial shoots its scorching way out of my mouth I realize what my mother has done: she has turned the tables. She has slipped into the interrogator's chair. Now she frowns gently and says, "Latifah told me you said it."

"She's bluffing."

And yet like the very best interrogators she has fed a fine thread of doubt into my workings. I did not say the Shahada of course. I would remember saying it. My not-saying of it was the defeat that Latifah refused to admit. But what if? Can I really trust my memory given the state of me these past few months? The nerves the anguish the nightmares the sleepless nights—and then of course there is the question of whether I have always kept track of what all I am saying exactly. So many parrotings of Latifah and the school ustaz and the other ustaz at the kelas mengaji, I mean to say can I swear (and on which holy book) that the Shahada has never come out of my mouth? Would I have been sure to recognize it? Still, it didn't count if I didn't mean it. Latifah said so herself. "There is no compulsion in Islam." And trickery is a form of compulsion. If she conned me into a conversion (all cons and no pros) then she cannot in good faith consider me a proper actual Muslim.

Enough is enough now. I didn't say it. (Though if I did it doesn't count.)

"Why would I have said it? How could I have said it? I don't believe God has only one name. But do you? Do you believe that?"

A minute ago she was smirking at me but the mirth is gone from her now. She sighs. She turns her head away. When she speaks her voice is small and distant.

"By the time you get to my age you will know there are no answers. Just questions. And that is the most frightening thing about this life."

Say sorry I want to shout *Just say sorry* but instead I press on like a bulldog.

"Everything Papa taught, it was all just a bit of fun for you?"

"A bit of fun! A bit of fun! Where was the fun, Yusuf? Where was the fun, you tell me!"

"Now you're bored with it you're moving on, it's just like what Reza said ..."

Just like what Reza said. It is as though I have cracked a whip: our shocked eyes meet and the air crackles with suspicion and blame.

"Oh?" she says. "Just like what Reza said? And what did he say? What did he say exactly?"

"I just mean—"

"No, no need to tell me what you mean. You want to know what I believe? I believe in a nice quiet life. You don't know, Yusuf, you don't know how they treated us, how they looked at us in the lockup. I thought, don't want to tell you lah what for you are too small." (Never stopped you before did it Mama? At one time you had no age limit when it came to who should hear what details. But okay.) "They said, 'You want to be Christian is it? Then stand like your Jesus on the cross lah!' For hours they made us stand like that. Arms stretched out, balancing on one leg. I thought I will faint, I will die, finish for me. I told them, 'I am not Christian, we did not follow one religion like that, I never renounced Islam!' But they just laughed at me. 'You don't even know who you are,' they said. 'Malay but simply following every false religion.'

"At first I was angry. True religion, false religion, what is that, who decides, I thought. But you know what? One day I started to think what if there is something to what they are saying? What if I am just confused, don't know who I am, what I am? Simply wandering here and there. After all I was brought up Muslim. Maybe you forgot that? Praying five times a day, eating meat, fasting during the fasting month, all this is part of my childhood. You cannot escape your childhood forever. You can try to run from it but it's there in your blood. I'm going back to my childhood a little bit, I'm doing what is easier for me, is that so wrong? Is God going to send me to hell? I don't know which laws were made by God Himself. What I know is if I don't live as a Muslim they will make both our lives miserable. So what do you want? You rather I quietly do my solat, get a job, go and rent a house for us somewhere, or you rather they come and take me away again? Come on lah, boy. There is a time for fighting and a time for surrender."

All this time I have been standing against the door. But now as she reaches the end of her speech I sink onto my knees and tighten my arms around myself. The terrazzo floor feels cold and hard under my kneecaps. I just want to know, to be certain about one right thing. I am weak and have a great implacable need to be held or my god even just to be touched. A need like an undertow or a vacuum. Like standing too close to a speeding train. The speeding train is my mother. As it sweeps past me I feel its equally implacable need echoing in the chambers of my heart whup whup whup whup. There we sit struggling to breathe and echoing in each other's hearts but knowing—a true knowing that admits no doubt—that there is no possibility of us touching each other. Not now and perhaps not ever again. For a moment the memory of my mother's touch glints in the dark catching what minimal light there is—her hand on my head my head on her shoulder and further back much further back my round still-a-baby head on her soft chest—and then it begins to fade. I gasp and gulp and squint into the wind to watch the train disappear into the tunnel.

Morning News

Saturday morning. Reza already gone for the day. The dead bodies of prawns and fish and one unlucky hen are thawing in their plastic bags in the sink where Fauziah has dumped them. Washing my hands after breakfast I avert my eyes from the watery blood trickling out of the bags. I am considering the desperate frozen claws of the hen—like two hands reaching out from the crypt—when the phone rings. Fauziah answers it and passes it to Latifah. "Yes?" Latifah says. "Yes. Yes." Then silence and her eyebrows rising like bread dough.

I count the seconds of silence. Five six seven eight. I'm holding my breath.

"Salmah?" Latifah says. "It's for you."

"Oh?" Mama says. "Let me wash my hands first then."

She shakes her eating hand over her nasi lemak plate. Grains of rice fall from her fingers. She rises and comes to the sink.

Somewhere inside me a signal sparks like a failing firework in the night sky and I find myself thinking *Stop it stop it stop acting like everything is normal.*

"Yes," Mama is saying into the phone. "Yes. Yes, that's right."

And then suddenly her voice dries up. She says nothing and nothing and still nothing. She turns to look at me with huge empty eyes. Her mouth is a tiny black o.

What have you done? I want to say. *What have you gone and done now?*

Click goes the phone back into the receiver.

"Yusuf," she says, her voice crumbling like rotten wood. The radio dims to static. The clock's ticking slows.

These days I like to make her say Yusuf at least three times before I'll answer. Mama might have remembered who she is in the nick of time but the guards' diagnosis is still true for some of us. *You don't know who you are.*

"Yusuf." Some instinct or premonition makes me look up at her after only two Yusufs this time. Still I take care to give nothing away in my face.

"Yusuf, I don't know how to tell you also …"

"Your father has passed away," Latifah says.

I knew this was coming. I look the news in the eye and think only, *Oh, it is you. There you are at last.* And yet questions—so many questions!—swoop down like a hundred crows onto the bright courtyard floor inside my head.

"It happened very quickly," Latifah says. "At the end he did not suffer very much at all."

At the end? Very much? In my head a danse macabre featuring drooling people with strangulation marks on their necks tins over their heads nails in their private parts needles under their fingernails heads stuffed into toilets—

"It was an asthma attack you see," Mama says. "You know he was always asthmatic. His lungs could not cope."

I look her right in the eyes and I repeat her own words: "His lungs could not cope."

The briefest of frowns clouds her face. Bewilderment quickly re-covered by the mask. She steadies herself and says, "We should thank God he did not suffer."

"Not very much, anyway. Not 'at the end.'"

She shakes her head at me. "Just be thankful, Yusuf."

~~Clarence Kannan~~ Muhammad Yusuf ~~Dragon~~ bin Abdullah, I hereby order you (by your new name) to be thankful to Allah (~~by his many names~~ by his singular name).

I picture my father beaten bloodied bruised. Because this I know as surely as I know anything: Mahathir's men did not whisk him away in a black van to take him to a five-star hotel. I picture my father lying broken on a grimy floor. Everything leaking out of him. Drip drip drip trickle trickle. All his hopes and all his dreams. All his faith. All his many faiths: his faith in God his faith in himself his faith in his country his faith in my mother and me and Reza. His faith in Love. His faith in faith itself. As it leaks out of him so in equal measure does it leak invisibly out of me.

Be thankful? I think. And suddenly there it is. That worm in the apple. The tiny gnawing mouth of scepticism. And it is Reza's voice I hear in my head now, not Reza-now but the Reza of five-six-seven years ago. *Let us thank God for inflicting upon us only a fraction of the agony He could have inflicted! O all-powerful and ever-loving God, Thou art merciful indeed! Behold the man who only lost one leg when Thou couldst have taken two! Behold the child Thou hast cured (with the help of chemotherapy and radiation) after its three-year battle with leukaemia! Hahaha!* Reza would say and slap his thigh. *What a fine fine fellow this God is! First He shits on your head, then He says "Pray to Me, make Me the most lavish burnt offerings you can afford, and if they should please Me I'll wipe off the shit!"*

"I know you are angry," my mother says. "I can understand that. I know this is very difficult to accept—"

"So tell me, Mama, is Papa burning in hell for being a kafir? Is he burning or did he recite the Shahada before he died?"

"Please, Yusuf. This is not the time."

Look at you, I want to say. *Look at you with your five-times-a-day Allah-this Allah-that. How many more ways are you going to find to betray him?*

"What happens when people die?" I asked my father once. I remember he steepled his fingers and pressed his lips together into a gentle and mysterious smile.

"What remains when we die"—and here a fire came into his eyes and he sat up straighter— "what remains when we die is up to each of us. What remains for sure is the good and the evil we have done."

And then he came out with the obligatory Shakespeare lines.

Poor Papa! Even the afterlife he was one hundred per cent sure of has turned out to be an illusion. His body still warm, and what he built—or thought he built—already gone. Who will honour his dream? Who remembers it as anything more than a utopian fantasy? A few mocking paragraphs in the papers and then nothing. He may as well never have lived. Make no mistake: I have betrayed him as well.

"There is nothing we can do," Mama says now. "We cannot change the past. We can only shape the future. We have to move on."

I stare at her with my stone eyes but my thoughts are racing.

"And all the others? Are they dead too? Did they kill all the others?" my mouth says.

"Yusuf, Yusuf," she whispers.

"Did they?"

"No, Yusuf. No, they didn't. Some of them are still in the lockup and some of them are living their lives just like we have to live ours."

"But where are they? Are they even going to come to Papa's funeral?"

"Oh, Yusuf! Even if they want to, I don't think they can."

"Why?"

She doesn't say it then but the answer is: because there will be no funeral. No burial on land or at sea. No cremation with its ensuing urn of ashes to scatter. Nothing at all. *This is my body. It shall be given up for you. But I mean literally given up. For here it is and now watch—look! No body! The magician's hands are empty! No evidence! No proof I ever existed! You can't feel pain or carry scars where there is no body to feel or carry. That was my body but this is my not-body. My now-you-see-it-now-*

you-don't, handful-of-coins-in-a-conman's-fist body. Astonishing, no? *Do this in memory of me.* Do what? In memory of whom? What memory? Nothing ever happened. Just an asthma attack. An act of God really. A natural and surely almost expected death. There were no nails or needles whatsoever. No red fingermarks on the vanished neck or rubber hose wounds on the evaporated legs. At the end he hardly suffered. Not that we know of anyway.

Here is the secret no one likes to admit out loud: you forget even a face you have seen every day your whole life. You forget.

Towards a General Theory

Who does not commit small sins of forgetting, of uncertainty, of untimely weakness? Do we all deserve to die for these sins in a puddle of our own blood and vomit on the floor of a filthy jail cell? Perhaps Papa only had a stub end of bad karma left to burn off to be liberated forever from the cycle of rebirth. Though admittedly he must have had more than those who die shortly after birth and who have to be matched up by the celestial Department of Family Engineering with parents who have sinned enough in their previous lives to warrant the grief of losing an hour-/day-/ week-old baby. Or perhaps Papa was so good that God wanted him back in heaven early. Papa is either in a much better place now, as Christians would say, or one with the Godhead, as Hindus might hope for, or if we are to believe the Buddhists, then he is in no place at all (which going by the evidence is a much better place to be).

The ceaseless bell of long-ago Reza tolling in my head: *You know what it means to have a strong faith? If you have been fully brainwashed, if you have nicely byhearted what they have fed you, they call that a strong faith.*

Reza who said nothing when Mama told him Cyril Dragon was dead. Who fixed Mama with his steely stare and let the news wash over him.

Hocus-pocus. Opium of the masses. A crutch for those who cannot accept death.

At school the boys give me a wide berth but theirs is not the hushed silence of sorrow nor even of awe. Their eyes gloat-glint at me. Their lips curl. I hear their whispers. *You-know-who lah. Did you hear? My father said they whacked the fler nicely then called it an asthma attack ahahaha!* Not one person says a word to me. Not the teachers not the ustaz not the imams not the neighbours.

I keep up appearances. I do my homework I take the tests I answer questions. What is the official logo of Bank Negara? Pokok pitis. *(My father is dead.)* What is the capital of Saskatchewan province? Regina. *(It happened in Kamunting.)* What are the three major Himalayan rivers? The Indus, the Ganges, the Brahmaputra. *(Bludgeoned. Mangled. Pulped.)*

I am Yusuf bin Abdullah in public and it is Clarence Kannan Cheng-Ho Muhammad Yusuf Dragon who is mourning his father. But in private I submit my inquiry: What were my father's dying thoughts? Could he think at all in those last moments? Or did physical pain leave no space for even a blur even a flicker of anything else?

So where was God while people were massacring innocents throughout history? He arranged all of it just so at the beginning of time but He might change his mind a bit here and there if ... if what? If we're good enough? If we grovel enough? If we lick His boots? If we kiss His holey arse?

One day when nobody is looking I take a tiny sliver of beef from the serving dish. Quickly I cover it with rice and then pop the whole thing into my mouth. It does not taste of violence. It is only strangely chewy and unyielding. I try to think of my father watching me from above. Watching his own son trample all over his vision for a better world. His broken heart rebreaking. Tears rolling down his ghostly cheeks. But the man I have conjured up is a shadow puppet on a stick.

After a week or so I experiment with chicken and then after three days with some mysterious grey rectangles that turn out to be slices of fishcake.

I hide my explorations from all of them. It is not just my pride that holds me back. It is also the knowledge that I would not be able to prevent them from interpreting my flesh-eating as a victory for Islam when it is in fact a victory for other forces: disappointment doubt resignation or whatever combination thereof we sometimes call reason. But I would never be able to convince them of my lack of faith. "Good good," Latifah would say. "Good for you. At last you're coming to your senses."

So I seal my lips. I unseal them only to slip slivers of flesh past them. Strips of beef. Chunks of chicken. Tiny prawns, and even—once in the deserted kitchen in which Fauziah has left the pots uncovered on the stove—a tiger prawn I have to divest of its delicate shell in the downstairs toilet. Nothing happens. The world does not tilt more sharply towards its end. No lightning bolt strikes me. Consider the first eleven and a half years of my life the control experiment. Hypothesis: the universe is indifferent to your actions.

Changing Places

There is only one person to whom I can take my new self. To him I carry the whole brimming bowl. The contents sloshing and threatening to spill over the edge. *My heart in my mouth* we like to say but the truth is my heart is so big it is taking over my whole body. There is nothing left of me but the loud hungry beating of it. LUBDUB LUBDUB LUBDUB.

"Reza," I whisper in the dark.

I put my fingers out into the silence. Spread them like feelers. It is not an unkind silence. Its heart is warm and velvety.

"You know how you have always said," I pressed on—as though he might have forgotten—"how you've always said there is no God and I've always been angry with you for saying that?" If I open my ears wide I can hear his breathing. "But ... but now I ... I don't think I believe in God anymore, Reza. Not like that. Not that God anyway. Not that kind of God. I think ... maybe ... maybe you are right."

A puff of air in the dark: is it mirth is it scorn is it ire? I wait. I wait and wait. What else is there to say? Then finally he speaks.

"It's up to you to decide what to believe. Don't let other people decide for you. I didn't and you shouldn't either."

"I haven't let anybody else decide. It's just ... it's just common sense, like you always said."

Again that puff of air. "Did I? I don't think I was so polite about it."

"But that's what you meant. You meant that anybody

who looked at the evidence couldn't believe in that God. Isn't it?"

He shifts his weight on his creaky bed.

"Isn't it?" I say again.

"Kannan," he says, and the way he speaks my name like that, not even shortening it to Kannu, my whole skin awakens in the dark and cloaks my bones lightly like something ready to take flight. "Kannan, it's like this—sometimes, no matter how sure you have been about a thing, something can happen to change your mind."

I run my hands up and down my forearms. Stroke my skin down. There there. Breathe.

"What?" I say.

He sighs. "Everything I ever thought I spat out at your feet, huh? I thought anyone who believed was a stupid fool. But ... something happened to me. I was ... I had ... No, I can't tell you about it. But something made me realize people don't just disappear when they die. And if we don't disappear but we're not here on this earth, well, then there is a Somewhere Else."

"You mean—"

"Please don't try to guess. I don't want to turn it into a game. I told you, I don't want to talk about it. But I don't want to lie to you. You've changed your mind and that's fine. Well, I've changed my mind too. Every person has the right to find their own truth."

I try to swallow this. I try and try but it sticks in my throat.

"You mean you believe in God now? After what happened to Papa, after what happened to—"

"It's like they always said after all. In the end they were right. Believing or not believing doesn't have to depend on what happens to you or to ... If someone believes, they'll believe *despite* the evidence. That's what faith is."

"So, so just like that you believe in *God*?"

"It wasn't 'just like that.' I've been walking and walking

and thinking and thinking. At first, when it happened, I thought no no it's nonsense, I'm imagining things. But it wouldn't go away."

"An *all-powerful and ever-loving* God?"

He draws in his breath. "I don't know. I don't know what kind of God, or if it even ... if I can even call it God."

"'It'? What's the 'it'?"

"A feeling."

"What kind of feeling?"

"What kind of feeling," he repeats, and the way he says it I know that he is smiling. "What kind of feeling, what kind of feeling. If I had to put words to it I suppose I would call it a peaceful feeling. A feeling that nothing good ever really goes away. Nothing is ever destroyed. So we have nothing to fear. Certainly not death."

"But suddenly you're so *sure*? You always made fun of people who were sure of anything."

"I know." In the dark his smile grows and grows. "I know I did."

"And now?"

"I don't know what to say. I don't know how else to say it. I had never experienced it so I did not know. When you're sure of a thing, you're sure."

"Never experienced what?"

In the street a cat begins to wail. A steady low sound at first then higher and higher and louder and louder like a Beijing opera singer like an approaching siren like a widow at her husband's funeral pyre. We can hear nothing else. It fills our ears and we are hypnotized. When finally the cat is far enough away for us to reclaim our thoughts I am the first to speak.

"So how come I haven't experienced it? How come Papa doesn't send me a sign? Anything, even a small sign? Because isn't that what you mean? Isn't that what you *experienced*?"

"Please. Please don't. I told you, I don't want to talk about it."

"But if what you say is true then Papa—"

"Papa Papa Papa. Not everything in the world is about your Papa, Kannu. He is not the ultimate authority. He is not sitting at the right hand of God. He could not save the world but he also could not destroy everything. Because of him I was too angry to see the truth. I was too proud. But now ... Well, everybody has to make their own way, Kannu."

Is that all belief is in the end? A switch that can be flicked on or off by random external events? *Each man has to forge his own path. Every person has the right to find their own truth.* My father's beautiful lies coming out of Reza's mouth. There is only one lesson to be learned: anything is possible.

Adidas Duffel Bag

Four months after her return Mama finds a job. Not a job with a newspaper or magazine no matter how lowbrow (for after Dr M's evisceration of the press even bottom-of-the-barrel newspaper jobs are hard to come by), not a return to life Before Cyril. For that life would bring with it the people who remember too many things: late coffee-and-cigarette-fuelled nights before deadlines, smoky bars and theatre premieres, cocktails at the club and Christmas parties and overseas trips, men who made promises and then went home to Canada and Australia and England. The person she is now is apparently best suited to being a sales assistant in a cloth shop. And not one of the big Indian-Muslim cloth shops whose managers would shudder at the thought of hiring a woman who ran off to experiment with idolatry and live in sin. For all they know apostasy still lingers like an inflammation in her body.

After her first pay cheque Mama turns to the next order of business. Combing through the *To Let* advertisements in the newspaper she quickly eliminates both the *Chinese tenants only* and the *Muslim lady only* notices and finds a Eurasian landlord with no racial preference who is renting his single-storey terrace house in Ampang.

He might recognize her name and her face but he won't care. She has transformed herself into a nice Malay lady working as a shop assistant to support her family. He only has to play the game and ask no questions. Pretend her husband is maybe working outstation or maybe passed away.

Pretend she is not a one-time party girl who favoured her gin and tonics strong and her skirts snug. Pretend she is not the former mistress of a cult leader. Nor a woman who bore a half-kafir child out of wedlock. If and when he has to confront the living evidence of her past he will—she knows the type—pretend to have seen nothing as long as the rent is on time.

She looks from Reza to me and then back to Reza.

"A fresh start," she says.

She means what she says: we will never again speak of the Centre except in undertones and allusions. She will live as though the last thirteen years never happened.

Latifah lends us bags in which to pack our few possessions: an old brown case with leather corners for Mama, a red tartan case for me, a green Adidas duffel bag for Reza.

On the day we are to leave, Reza comes downstairs to breakfast with his duffel bag.

"Wah, look at him," Mama says. "Ready and waiting already man!"

We will never speak of the look he gives her now but we will never forget it: a look not of forbearance nor of embarrassment but of undiluted pity.

He smooths down his hair with both hands and it is only then that I see his hair is freshly cut. His face shaved and washed. With no hesitation he announces, "I'm not coming to the new house."

We stare at him. No one dares to breathe or blink.

"What do you mean?" Mama finally says. "I've arranged everything, I've—"

"I'm going away," Reza says. "At least for a while."

"Going away? Going where?"

"I've made my own arrangements."

"Your own arrangements? With all the millions you've saved from your Shakey's Pizza job?"

"I've saved a bit," he says. "But I don't need much anyway. I'm going to a … a kind of ashram. A spiritual retreat. A place to take some time and think."

"A spiritual retreat?" Mama echoes. "You haven't had enough of that? A place to think? You mean you cannot think here?"

There she stops because he is already laughing and shaking his head like a madman or a child or a genius and it is clear even to her that nothing can come out of reasoning with him. This is simply what he needs now. It fits. It soothes. A familiar unease is creeping up on me.

But his laughter slows and then stills. And in his face I see for the first time in my life something I cannot bear to destroy or even touch. Something that must be lifted with two delicate hands like a fresh sheet of fine paper. Something that must be held up to the light not in scrutiny but in celebration. I may be losing the God he is finding but I cannot wish it otherwise. If it is a lie it is a lie that makes my heart race like a small bird's. *Dear God-who-does-not-exist: Watch over my brother. Protect his illusions. Shield the tiny flame of his faith with Your palms.*

After breakfast Latifah and Mama and I stand in a row at the front door to watch him go. Duffel bag slung over his shoulder. Long strides and no looking back.

The Open Window

2024

The truths you try to ignore until someone holds your head down in their icy waters. Hana hardly having time for the new books you have bought her. You convince yourself she's just tired from all her jobs. These books are harder also. It's understandable that she needs time to do nothing at all. What do they call it nowadays? Downtime. Me time. Self-care. Whatever it is her time is hers to fritter away just as her money is. It's all very well for Ani to fuss about her spending her money on pasar malam makeup but Ani isn't a young girl surrounded by tempting fripperies. Didn't we all make our own silly mistakes? Everyone has their own youthful follies in their past but Ani has entirely forgotten what it is to be young.

Likewise you explain away her hiding in the toilet after her morning Nescafé to paint her face before putting on her tudung. It's because her auntie grumbles, you tell yourself. But what's wrong with a bit of makeup? The country is full of stylish young tudung-wearing girls with painted faces. Hana goes from two basic tudungs in cream and beige to what must be a whole drawerful in pink and purple and floral prints to be tied and pinned in all the different styles with sparkly two-ringgit brooches and again you tell yourself: a girl her age likes a bit of colour. It's a wonder she stuck with those two dull tudungs for so long. And even on Sundays instead of sitting at home with her books she dolls herself up and saunters to the bus stop in her shiny black sandals. You cannot explain this so you choose not to dwell on it. Maybe it's another job or maybe she has friends and why shouldn't she?

Then one morning, as soon as we hear the click of the gate latch signal Hana's departure, Ani edges crabwise towards me and like a Russian spy in a bad seventies movie—not looking at me not moving the lips—mumbles, "Dia dah ada boyfriend dah."

"Oh," I force myself to say. For the briefest of moments I am weakened by the shock but almost immediately new thoughts flood the wound like white blood cells. So what if she has a boyfriend? She is young. At that age there are meaningless dalliances before they find or come back to true love. It means nothing. And anyhow why would I take her auntie's word for it? For all I know Ani saw her talking to some young lout across a fence and drew her far-fetched conclusions.

Now Ani lowers her voice still further: "Orang Bangla."

"The man"—she tells me though I refuse to ask—"is a construction worker who takes his lunch in a kopitiam next to the morning market. A nobody! A common labourer! When she knows she has better options this can only be a passing folly."

She sighs and adds, "Boyfriend okay I suppose, but orang Bangla? I just hope everything will work out."

"But ..." I turn off the tap. I don't say, *Work out? So for him she will stay? With him she won't worry about going back to her poor old mum and dad?*

"Now she says she wants to apply for a cashier job. She can aim higher she says. Wah, such confidence, tuan, such grand plans. Going to work at the minimarket, going to save money to get married in a year's time. I don't know how all these things got into her head."

I reach for the hand towel and dry my hands. I try to hang up the towel but it falls off the hook. Again I hang it and again it falls. I stand there holding it and thinking I know how all those things got into her head. I put them there. I told her she should practise her reading. I bought her books and newspapers. She took my kindness and my dreams—the dreams I had for her which I swear to you were primarily those of a brotherly guardian or even a loving father—and presented them with a curtsey to someone else. No, worse, she tucked them into her bra for a filthy lecher to fish out. Everything I did for her someone else is going to ... what? I balk at *reap the benefits*. I push away the thought. What benefits? It was not like that. I was not plotting and planning the whole time. I was not kind to her merely because I wanted to woo her my god no I was not. I am not like that. I am not one of those men about whom people joke that the strings attached are G-strings. Please. The girl is over a quarter century younger than me. Young enough to be my daughter and that is what she was: a child under my care.

"Are you all right, tuan?" Ani asks me. "I know, one worries about such things, I worry because she is my niece and you worry because ... well, you wouldn't want ... If anything happens while she's under your roof ..."

"Oh. No I was only wondering, how do they even talk to each other, the Indonesian girl and the Bangladeshi boy?"

"Ah, tuan, you don't know ah?" Ani says. "Conversation all no need lah. I hold your hand, you hold my hand. Only thing, I hope it stops with the hands. If she's holding anything else then finish."

She chortles indulgently like I'm a small boy and she's my auntie deliberately burning my ears with her raunchy talk.

In my stiffest least encouraging voice I say, "Hana is not that type of girl. You should know. She's a good girl."

"Tuan does not know what young people are like. Good girl also ..."

Then shouldn't you have a talk with her? I should say. But when I try to speak it is as though my numb and swollen tongue is blocking the passage of air into my lungs. All I can do is to grunt at Ani and leave the room.

I have already told you: there is nothing unseemly in my feelings for the girl. I loved her as a father would. A protector if you will. It is only this betrayal that I cannot bear. If she had even *told* me. She led me on letting me put out two mugs on the table and pass my stirring spoon on to her as though we were ... as though we were a family. Like a bird all right she flew into my heart and I should have known. I should have known you cannot simply keep a bird that flies in by accident.

However, my heart is cracking—along whichever fault-lines and according to whatever ancient pattern—it will not stop whispering to me: *You, Clarence Kannan Cheng-Ho Muhammad Yusuf Dragon, are not worthy after all. It is not within the laws of the universe for you to be loved.*

The End of Hope

We no longer sit together in the mornings. It was not I who thought to snub Hana just because she was living her life as any young girl might. What is there? I am not the type to lock my daughters in a windowless room or to feel my stomach burn at the idea of them belonging to someone else. Mothers daughters wives and all: why shouldn't their beauty bring joy to others?

But Hana it seems can no longer face *me*. Knowing that her auntie has confided in me she is now—what? ashamed? afraid? Even jumpier than she was when she first arrived. It is as though the moment Hana began to draw away from me she began to grow up. Before my eyes she is becoming a woman. Her walk less a little girl's mincing steps now and more an earthy gait with weight to it. Her hips and chest filling out. Even her hair growing longer and thicker almost overnight so that the bun she covers up with her tudung is as big and heavy as a bag of sugar. In my house there is a woman I hardly know. She looks different and smells different from the girl I wanted to protect and nurture only a few months ago.

Every morning I put out the two mugs I lay my spoon neatly next to hers I put the butter dish and butter knife on the table but no longer does she sit down and eat her breakfast. Nowadays she wraps it up in a steadily-more-grimy bread bag and takes it with her. If I tell her to sit down and eat she mumbles it's late it's late through barely stirring lips and runs off like the White Rabbit.

I try to ask Ani about this change.

"Why is she suddenly so frightened? Just because she has a boyfriend doesn't mean I'm going to eat her up."

But Ani is no longer garrulous on the topic of young love. She shakes her head and shrugs.

"Entah lah dia. Am I my niece's keeper?"

She bustles around in silence. Squirts soap into the mop bucket. Hefts it into the sink and fills it with water. But on her way out of the kitchen she pauses in the doorway. Without turning around or setting the bucket down she says, "I ... I just want to say I'm sorry for bringing her into your house, tuan. I thought she would be the quiet homely type. I didn't think she would ronda-ronda like this. Going here, going there, cannot stay in the house. She wasn't like this back home."

"Well, she didn't have a boyfriend back home, did she?"

At this she puts the bucket down and lifts a hand to her face. "I don't want to talk about that anymore, tuan. Please. I just don't want to talk about it."

I could remind her that she was the one cracking off-colour jokes about them just a few weeks ago but what would be the point of such pettiness? The poor woman is upset. Maybe it was all a joke in the beginning but the gravity of Hana's behaviour is starting to sink in now. I must find a way to reassure her.

"It's not our problem, Ani. It's not like she's bringing him here."

Now finally she turns and looks at me but I cannot decipher her expression. I've surely never seen it on any other human being. With this ineffable face this dishevelled hair these exhausted shoulders she picks up the bucket and walks away. I know I've not convinced either one of us. I've soothed neither her anxiety nor my ... what to call it? Even despair seems too flighty a word. It is a death. A small and quiet death. How would you know to look at me that I've been hollowed out and left standing?

It's not the boyfriend. It's not that. It's everything I've lost. Those gentle morning dances to the music of our shared spoon. The luminous indigo dawn outside the kitchen windows. The wordless understanding. The way our feet would line up when we passed each other on the stairs: she with some contraband trinket behind her back and me with only love in my heart. And most of all, the possibility of long years ahead of us. I would have joined the ranks of the people who say proudly, *Our helper has been with us more than twenty years*. The arrangements I would have made the forms I would have filled joyously the bigger apartment I would perhaps have bought—

All this must be laid to rest now. Now she will not even speak to me, cannot even look at me. When I have healed I will go back to being what I was: a lump of stone in a man's body.

Pledge

Of course Amar didn't bring the photo the week after Mama had asked for it. Even a standard-issue teenage boy—let alone a serious alim type—would have to be an unusual specimen indeed to dig up a baby picture and bring it just because his tuition teacher's ageing mother has asked for it. I myself fully expected him to brush everything off his shoulders like dandruff. Her asking for the picture and her advice and even what was either the fully exposed unravelling of her mind or the tender offering of her most painful secret: *he doesn't come to see Nenek anymore.* Amar would have assumed she'd let it go. But not Mama. Thick-skinned and poker-faced she reminds him week after week. She makes him sit with her. She leans forward and peers into his bearded smallboy face like an archaeologist on the brink of a great discovery.

Then one week she reaches out and puts a hand on his arm. He starts to pull his arm away then as though some external force is stopping him he freezes halfway.

"You mustn't think I'm just trying to be a pest," she says.

I turn and slip back through the doorway of the tuition room. *Leave them to it* I say to myself. I busy myself with my pile of marking. Were it not so stuffy in this room I would shut the door.

When he says nothing she goes on, "It's true there are many who live to be much older than me. But—Nenek doesn't know why—Nenek feels her time is limited. Nenek feels she won't see her son again. Not until the hereafter."

He studies the symptoms: the odd vacillation between first person and third person, the wide blank unblinking eyes, the declining comprehension of personal space. All things considered he's still unsure whether her son is already waiting for her in the hereafter or whether she'll go first and wait for him. But at least he knows now that "my son" doesn't mean his tuition teacher. In that one way he has become a member of the family. Like a sword the urge to shut the door of the tuition room so that I won't be able to hear her pierces me but in a moment the impulse has gone.

"I ... I've got pictures of my own son, of course," she's saying out there. "You've seen them, I showed you. It's just, I thought ... I hope I wasn't being a busybody, I hope you didn't think *Hai, this Nenek, why can't she keep quiet and mind her own family's business?*"

I can hear him draw his breath in like he's about to contradict her because what else is he supposed to do? She has pushed him into a corner in which our absurd and truthless laws of politeness dictate that he cannot say *Why yes that was in fact what I was thinking.* But she rescues him herself from that corner.

"I don't even mean to keep the photo, you know. I'll give it back to you straight away. I just want to see it, that's all. I feel—I'm sure you can tell—that you are very special to me. When I pray, I always pray for you too. That God will guide you and you will always make the right choices. A young man like you—such an important time in your life. So many decisions to make. I should have prayed for my son, you see, but I didn't. Among all my big mistakes that was the biggest. I didn't know at that time, but now I know."

Moments of silence. When she speaks her voice is decades older.

"If you bring the photo, then I will know I really have a second chance. I didn't give birth to you, I wasn't there when you were a baby, I didn't raise you, but at least if I have the photo I will be able to picture you. I will have that one small piece of your childhood. In my mind it will be like ... like I was there for one brief moment at least. I don't think I'm asking for so much, am I? Am I? Just to see a photo. Won't you bring it next week?"

When I come to the doorway of the tuition room I see that she has put the other hand on top of the first hand still on his arm. With his other hand he's rubbing the back of his neck.

"Sorry," he says. "I ... I keep forgetting. I'll bring it next time. I hope ... I'll pray for you too, Nenek. I'll pray for ... for you to find peace."

"Really?" she says. "Really you will pray like that?"

"Of course!" he proclaims. "How can I joke around about something like that? If I say I will pray then I will pray."

"Pray that God will forgive me, then. Pray that He will forgive me for all my mistakes."

She takes both her hands off his arm and puts them in her lap. He meets her eyes.

"I'm sure God has already forgiven you," he says. "Whatever you did in the past, you were a different person. When you come back to God you're a new person. Think of it that way. Even I ... I was one person before and I'm another person now."

For a moment it is as if he has thrown a cloak around the two of them. They sit there adjusting it around their shoulders. Then at last she says, "You better go now. I'll see you next week with the photo."

He closes his eyes and brings both his hands to his face as though he might already be praying. But when he takes his hands away he looks just like any other exhausted teenage boy who should be getting more sleep than he's getting. He stands up.

"See you next week," he confirms. His whole body signalling acquiescence or perhaps even subservience: shoulders slumped, feet turned in, head lowered slightly.

Before he shuffles off he turns around and raises his hand at me in a man-to-man wave. *I see you*, the wave says. We have a deal. Only thing is I have to figure out what the deal involves. That he will accept my eavesdropping as long as I acknowledge his godliness and his wisdom? Or more than that: my eavesdropping is not just acceptable but *welcome* if it means I will finally see that he is no small boy playacting at piety. He is a legitimate holder of the truth. Listen at the door Encik Yusuf and you may yet be able to follow me down the path to eternal salvation.

Baby Photo

2024

He brings them—not just one but a good half-dozen—in an album. Not like Mama's prehistoric one but the cheap cardboard-covered kind with plastic pages. Mama grabs it like a monkey. Turns to the first page and howls—yes purses her lips and howls to the heavens—in victory and vindication. For there propped up on a teddy-bear pillow in his Anakku pyjamas is a replica of six-month-old Reza. And not even a mother in sight to function as a reminder that this one does not belong to Mama. Here he is again sitting up with a dummy in his mouth and here he is in a sailor suit on his first birthday. On a red plastic tricycle. In his blindingly spotless uniform on his first day of Standard One. Accepting a trophy from the Chief Education Officer on school prizegiving day.

An entire childhood suspended in a glass bubble and dangled by a string before Mama's nose. Her eyes light up like a small child's upon seeing its first Christmas tree. She holds her breath. She reaches out for it.

"Could be Reza in these pictures!" she says. "Even I would have trouble telling you apart if I didn't know which pictures were my son and which ones you. Just ask your teacher and see."

Not for Mama the polite pretence that I am not listening. She calls out to me now: "Come, come, come and see!"

Come Amar's teacher come and see how much Amar looks like my son. And when I don't come fast enough she holds up the open album so that I can see the first two pictures from across the room.

"Yes or not?" she says. "Wasn't I right?"

"I wouldn't know. I wasn't there when Reza was a baby."

She doesn't bat an eyelid at my betrayal. "Ish, you another one. From the pictures, I mean. From the pictures you've seen many times."

I shrug. "Many babies look alike."

"Come on! You mean to say Chinese babies, Indian babies, all look exactly the same as each other? Exactly the same as these two? And I'm not just talking about the baby pictures! Look, look at his school pictures and all, see for yourself!"

I should just say, *You win Mama. You can pocket this purloined boy for your own. You can insert yourself into every picture just out of the frame just out of sight. In fact his own parents won't even mind because they no longer know what to do with this childhood. They cannot reconcile it with the young man who has come beanstalking out of it in his beard and jubah.*

But of course—by now you know me—I do not say any of that. I shrug again.

"I can see," I say casually. "Sure, there is a resemblance." Why am I doing this? Why must I pretend not to see what is before my eyes? "They could certainly be related."
(To myself: they could be brothers. Whereas me and Reza, me with my mata sepet and him with his Michelangelo's David head ... I really should have known better than to aspire to such heights as being Reza's brother. What was I thinking? Where in this lopsided family was there space for an equal love?)

"Related!" Mama cries. "They could be the same boy!"

She flips indignantly through the pages like as though if she just finds the right one I will accept her claim wholesale. I glance at Amar. He appears unperturbed by our hairsplitting. The faint sardonic smile on his face unsettles me.

"What to do?" I say to him. "Nenek is lonely. When you sit with her it's like my brother is sitting with her. Simple as that."

"I understand," he says. "I don't mind."

I'm about to give him permission to extricate himself and leave when he opens his mouth to speak.

"I wish ... I wish Nenek could explain to my parents that I'm not that bad," he says. "It's for their own good that I tell people what I tell them. We can't just ape the West, ape the Chinese, ape the Indians even, and then call ourselves Muslims. We have to keep ourselves separate. We have to protect ourselves. My parents don't understand. They are angry for nothing all the time. There's no need to be angry. They could find such peace, such wonderful peace could be theirs, if they would just ... just submit to God."

What to do with this speech, how to respond—my god never more than a monosyllable out of him and now this! Will Nenek explain to his parents? But trust Mama to have a handle on it already.

"Ah! The problem is they won't listen to Nenek either. You see they are frightened. People are always frightened of what they do not know and what they do not understand. And when their hearts are full of fear like that, it is not the right time to show them the truth. They will not accept it. But—listen to me carefully—it does not matter what other people think of you when you choose to submit to God. People can make fun of you, they can decide to drop you because you are too strange, you are no longer the person they were used to. So what? It doesn't matter. When you know you are following the correct path none of that should matter. It is a lesson I learned long ago. Long before you were born. People will say it's a phase lah, it's an act lah, it's all fake and soon enough the real Amar will come back. All you can do is close your ears and live the life God wants you to live. Do not be afraid."

When I see Amar's eyes uncloud themselves and his brows lift I suddenly understand he must have unearthed our story somewhere. And now Mama has delivered the avowal he was waiting for. Now there is no need to approach her with the was-was recommended for unknown substances and dubious situations. She has spoken, she has repudiated her past. She is a true Muslim.

"Yes! Yes, you are right, Nenek," he says. "You are right. What you say is very true. Very very true."

He jumps up with his books and notes and hurries away like a man with a mission. The photo album sits in Mama's lap open to the picture of Amar receiving his trophy.

Sacrifice

You can hear them all the way from the bus stop on the main road. A lowing. A bellowing. A hollowing. A disembodied vibration. A cosmic sound. A bovine Om from which flows a sacred river of spilled blood.

Sacred. Allow me my poetic license. The truth is I don't believe in sacred anymore at this point. I believe in neither the God who cries out for blood nor the God who looks down his Brahmin nose at anyone who allows a morsel of flesh food to touch his lips. By the time Hari Raya Haji rolls around, the novelty of flesh in my mouth has worn off. What began as a show of defiance to that motherfucker of a God who does not exist is now little more than a tedious duty to my principles.

Behind the mosque, they are supposed to be thinking of Abraham with his sharp blade poised above his son's tender throat. But they are not thinking of the levels of insecurity and megalomania required to issue such an order only to then stay that poor father's shaking hand at the last moment. *Haha! Just testing. Got you, didn't I?* In His Mercy he saves you at the very last second from the terrible situations into which he has shunted you. Neither are they thinking of the boy himself. Of the view through his terrified and disbelieving eyes. Of how *he* would tell this story afterwards. *So there I was walking along with Dear Old Dad when . . .*

They wield their knives with nary a thought for how such an incident might have changed—to put it mildly—

the father-son relationship going forward. How did those two ever sit again at the same table to break bread? *Best father in the world I have. Except for that one time—*

You can see for yourselves that I do not need Reza anymore. I—all my life his unwitting pupil—have assumed the mantle of the Unbeliever. When I refuse to go to the mosque Mama says, "Just go and show face and come home."

"Do the people who 'rehabilitated' you know that your Islam is all about keeping up appearances?"

She sighs and covers her face with both hands. Just look at her in her pink tudung. Today she has put it on to go to the mosque but soon enough it will become an essential component of her daily attire.

"Yusuf," she says behind her hands. When she lowers her hands her whole face is bright and clear. "In the end, I can't force you to do anything." She says it quietly as though she is speaking to herself. "Eating meat is not going to cause World War Three. It is just food. We cannot keep clinging to all that … all those superstitions."

"Superstitions? You are the ones sacrificing cows to your God and you call me superstitious?"

"Faith is between you and God, Yusuf. The rest is propaganda. Actually it doesn't matter what you eat or don't eat, how you pray, what you wear. So why not keep people happy?"

"Why should I keep *those* people happy and not any others? How do you decide which people you're going to please at which times? You flip a coin? You roll your dice?"

She draws in her breath and opens her mouth and closes it again. Two-three times she does this and then finally she says, "Don't think they don't know who we are, Yusuf. They are just waiting for their chance. You … you are playing with fire."

It is the same argument she will make when she starts covering her hair: the moment I'm not doing exactly the same thing as them they will suspect us of praying to Ganesha and eating pork sausages behind their backs. Then I remember the mob at my old school. The terror that seized my heart when I thought I would be denounced. And I think: if there's no God judging me for my hypocrisy then what do I lose by showing face?

So I go and I stand before the slaughtering frames: three of them like three goalposts in a row. Each one fitted with three hooks. From each hook hangs a cow. And all these cows in varying stages of carcasshood while in the wings more cows hoof at the ground and await their fate.

I wish I could tell you that I vomited then and there in the dust. Or better still, that blinded by a bright light I fainted and had to be carried home by some brawny-armed fellow in a kain pelikat only to open my eyes hours later to a new and invincible faith in the Lord God of all creatures great and small. But in fact I managed to hold myself together perfectly well. Even fed myself from the twenty-five or so chafing dishes in the buffet.

"You've eaten?" she asks me afterwards.

And close behind, the echoes from her new Muslim brethren: *Dah makan? Dah makan? Dah makan?* Perhaps they're only being solicitous. Perhaps that is all they see in her question too: a mother making sure her child has not gone hungry. In front of all our witnesses I meet her gaze. I smile.

"I ate."

She smiles back. We stand there looking at each other as though at our own reflections in a funhouse mirror. Is this how the rest of our lives will be? This tricky confounding dance?

A spot of blood on the hem of her baju kurung draws my eye away at last. We finally exhale.

A Brief History of
My Teaching Career

OCTOBER 1998

I am twenty-one years old and in charge of forty impressionable young minds. I am—or so I think—wiser than my father. Not for me the utopian manifesto or the radical retreat from the world. Didn't I see first-hand that you can't change the world in a single lifetime? No, I will work indirectly. I will harness their natural thirst for knowledge. I will sow grains of doubt so tiny they will be invisible to the naked eye. Then I will lead them to the great questions and leave them there to drink or not drink.

At first nothing is on the nose. In my classroom there is time for poetry:

I went out to the hazel wood
Because a fire was in my head ...

There is time for Shakespeare's bawdy winks. For Caravaggio's Isaac and for Bruegel's crowds. For Molly Bloom's cornerboys' Aunt Mary's hairy etcetera.

Not that the few who are listening understand any of it. Look at gormless lot of them, doodling and passing notes. The boys looking at dirty magazines under their desks and the girls vying to lure them away from the magazines. If only they knew how a single paragraph of Joyce would leave all those tame nudes in the dust.

That's when the headmaster warns me: stick to the syllabus Encik Yusuf. This may be a honeymoon year for your students but next year is an exam year. And it must be the warning that unravels me. I had no plans to talk politics as such with my students but in those days you had only to tell me not to do something and if you were priest king prime minister headmaster I would do it. Making up for lost time is what it was: I had spent my life obeying the rules handed down to me. So here I am walking straight from the headmaster's office into my classroom where I announce:

"Today we will study the Admiral Zheng-He."

And then I tell them to imagine the country we might have built if one person could be many things: male and non-male, non-Muslim and Muslim, Chinese and Malay. "Do not forget, children," I say, "that our Nusantara people never had any use for notions of Race until the English arrived with their clipboards and callipers and boxes to tick. Imagine if all these essences—Malay Chinese Indian Other—could flow one into the other sometimes forming entirely new substances. Think of how gula melaka stirred into santan makes something more delicious than either of its elements alone."

On one of my shoulders the headmaster issuing his warning, on the other shoulder my father delivering his lecture on the unity of the human race at the Registry Office mere days after my birth. (I won't tell you who occupied which shoulder; that is for you to decide.)

That first day the only response I get is row upon row of staring faces. They are too shocked even to blink. And every day I push the boundary out a little further. *Sikit-sikit lama-lama jadi bukit.* Oh I'm building a hill all right handful by handful of earth and it will be the hill on which I will— don't say it! When the father has already taken rebellion to its absolute limit what is left for the son? It will be the hill on which I will stand to preach. Yes. That's it. I will continue to stand up and speak the truth right through the second warning and then the third warning and then ... what? Odd that I have a sense of racing against time when I have no fixed goal no learning targets no shadow syllabus in my head. There are no milestones my students have to meet to demonstrate that they have sufficiently unwashed their brains.

I tell them the story no one has ever told them about the Communists: that they were not wicked eyes glinting in the jungle nor bloodthirsty madmen but warriors who refused to compromise with our colonizers. I tell them about PUTERA-AMCJA and the People's Constitution and the 1947 Hartal.

"Is this going to be on the exam?" asks a voice in the back. It's a pugnacious-looking young man by the name of Jeffri. Bears an unfortunate resemblance to Azmi from all those years ago: the close-shaved sideburns the slicked-down hair the square jaw. On either side of him his smirking sidekicks.

"No," I tell him, "but it's more important than anything that will be on the exam."

Someone snorts and makes a great show of turning it into a cough.

"You've learned all about our founding fathers," I carry on, "but did you ever learn that the M in UMNO could have included all of us regardless of blood and faith?"

To this Jeffri objects. "M in UMNO stands for Malay."

"Ah! But what does Malay even mean?" I ask the class. "At one time anyone who put down roots in this land became Malay. And once upon a time all the ancient kingdoms of Southeast Asia were Hindu. Even our own sultans of Malacca. There is nothing to be gained by pretending the universe did not exist before Islam."

Now they're all shifting in their seats and looking at each other.

So why stop there? When I look back upon this day I will remember a feeling of intoxication: the way when you are drunk you walk without knowing you're putting one foot in front of the other.

"How do we know who is right and who is wrong when it comes to religion, anyway?" I ask them. "How can we be certain there's anyone in charge?"

"You can't say that," Jeffri says. "That's a sin."

In that moment it's no longer me in the classroom at all but Reza aged ten. I unroll the whole splendid carpet before them: "Maybe there is a God or maybe there isn't; I cannot prove the universe was not created by an omnipotent benevolent God but I also cannot prove it was not created by a giant creature with a cat head and a potato body. Don't believe it? Well there you go. The only difference between us is that the list of gods in which I don't believe in is one item longer than the list of gods in which you don't believe."

And in my father's voice the finishing touch: "It is not just possible but eminently desirable that you believe one thing and I believe the opposite and that both of us coexist in harmony. But for this harmony to come about we must all remember where we come from at all times. We come from the same peoples. We come from the same places. India China and everywhere in between. Africa if you go back far enough. We come from the same stories, both true and cooked up."

Why couldn't I have told myself that what I wanted was, finally, a quiet life?

Gradually the volume of smirking and muttering rises. Around himself Jeffri has gathered a little faction to discuss the problem. *Encik Yusuf is touching on sensitive issues. Encik Yusuf is spreading anti-government propaganda. Encik Yusuf is inciting racial unrest.* After someone carries the tale to the ustaz he warns the Muslim students: "Be very careful. When it comes to religion nobody should be asking all these questions. These liberal modern types will only lead you astray." Soon no student Muslim or non-Muslim will volunteer to carry my piles of marking or take a message from me to another teacher. At recess time when I ask for volunteers to queue up for my curry mee not one hand is raised. When I enter the staff room the other teachers stop talking. At the PTA meeting that term the parents stare and whisper. As the whole thing balloons into a hoo-ha worthy of the Education Department's attention I stand before my students and recite:

Exiled Thucydides knew
All that a speech can say
About Democracy,
And what dictators do,
The elderly rubbish they talk
To an apathetic grave ...

PART 4

Tell Me Tell Me Tell Me

Reza and Leo doing everything they can to escape from me: it is one of my earliest memories. The slap slap slap of their Japanese slippers on the soles of their feet as they run away from me. I am only five years old so how can I keep up along the rocky jungle trails through the long grasses down the steep slope? I stumble and trip. I pant and wipe the sweat and spit from my chin. I call out to them.

Then the teasing and bullying.

"No shame ah you? Tell you on your face don't come also you must come."

And me blinking like a numbskull because I don't know what shame is. Annabelle Foo coming to my rescue.

"Leave them lah," she says. "Don't care about them. Each one of them just as bad as the other one!"

Annabelle Foo is tall and pretty and perpetually bored. What thirteen-year-old girl wants to be friends with a five-year-old boy? That's how bored she is. But instead of being grateful I spurn her offer of solidarity. I turn away from her and nose to the ground I follow the scent of my brother and Leo.

When the bullying doesn't work they resort to bribery.

"Stay at home like a good boy and we'll bring you back something from the river."

"Like what?" I say. Even I know there is nothing worth bringing back from the river. Plastic bags and straws. Broken bottles and wet cigarette butts.

Leo looks at Reza. Reza slips Leo a faint smile.

"It's a surprise," Reza says. "You won't know unless you wait here and see."

They stand there grinning at me. Arms crossed legs planted wide apart. I breathe in a long slow breath to absorb my defeat. I breathe out.

"Okay," I say. "I'll wait here."

I lower myself down to sit cross-legged in the dark earth of the trail and they fall over each other laughing at the sight. It brings them to their knees.

"Look at that," Leo says. "Just look at the fler. He's actually going to sit right here and wait."

"Well," Reza says clutching his stomach, "we said to wait here what. So he's going to sit here lah."

They're still talking about me as they stride off down the trail. I know the type of things they are saying because they say them to me outright oh yes they tell me *on my face* just like what Leo said. "You stupid fler," they say. "You know what they call people like you in Tamil?" Leo says. "Paavam. That's you. You're the most paavam of all the paavams. Following us around like a ... like a ..."

"Like a puppy dog," Reza will say then. "Except not so cute."

And Leo will reply on cue, "Ya, you must've got your good looks from your father."

It's not always to the river they go. Sometimes they walk the other way down the path, towards the Catholic Priests' Retreat House but of course they don't go all the way there to sit and have tea with Father Dubois. They stop and sit on the grassy slope from where they can see the tea plantation terraces. From their pockets they pull out all the snacks and treats Neela has smuggled to them from the kitchen. Newspaper bundles of omapoddi and murukku. Curry puffs and bondas soggy from being pocketed while hot. Fat golden raisins. Groundnuts. They munch and crunch and throw the groundnut shells off the sharp drop into the bowlful of jungle below. They make plans for the immediate future—finding a way by hook or by crook to get to the bungalow left behind by the American millionaire who disappeared —and the distant future. "The minute I turn eighteen," Reza says, "I'm getting out of this shithole. I'm going to Singapore. I'm going to get a nice cushy job with a big fat pay cheque and I'm going to marry a nice sexy Chinese girl."

"A nice sexy Chinese girl like Annabelle Foo?" Leo says.

Reza ignores him and continues, "Then I'm going to migrate to Australia. My father's from there so it'll be easy for me to join him. I'm going to have one posh bloody mansion with shiny floors, aircon, everything. And a garden outside full of grass and big-big trees."

Sometimes they go all the way to the sundry shop at the last turn before the Retreat House. "It's too far for you to walk," they tell me. "You'll never make it there. You'll die standing."

But I know the real reason: they only go there when they've managed to *roll up some cash*. That's what they call the coins they scrounge up by secret methods they refuse to explain. "'Where you got that where you got that,'" they simply repeat back to me in a whiny baby voice when I ask them. *Tell me tell me tell me tell me!* But when they have finished clowning they still haven't told me. They spin the coins on the back porch and hold them tantalizingly between thumb and index finger. But try as I might I am unable to discover even where they store these coins in the dormitory let alone their provenance. Not in their bedside-table drawers. Not under their mattresses. Not in the pockets of the shorts and longs folded up neatly in the cupboard.

At the sundry shop they buy Chinese salted plums or Hacks sweets. The terrible black ones in the transparent red wrapper. One of those was the only thing they ever saved for me and I coughed and coughed—"Look at the fler," Leo said, "cough sweets make him cough more!"—and spat it out in disgust. They buy sticks of chewing gum and packets of powder you empty into your hand and eat with a licked finger. And once—I can hardly bear to remember it—they bought a packet of cigarettes. Benson & Hedges in the gold packet. I could manage only a hoarse whisper.

"You got enough money to buy cigarettes?"

"Look at the fler," Leo says but they look at each other instead of at me. "Thinks we can afford to buy Benson & Hedges."

They've stolen the packet then. But from whom? Not from the sundry shop because the hawkeyed shop man would never have let them get away with it. And not from Mama because her brand is Marlboro.

"You stole it from the boys at the river," I say finally.

"What makes you think we need to steal?" Reza says. "Just because you don't know how to make friends doesn't mean other people don't know how."

Though you would think it must pale in comparison to the Aladdin's Cave of the sundry shop the river is their favourite place of all. That river with its underwater rocks that will cut your feet and its plastic bags caught on twigs and reeds. Its little waterfall splashing onto flat rocks you can perch on for a nice cold shower. The Malay boys from the kampung stand under the waterfall in all their clothes and smoke and horse around. Once when I went with Reza and Leo they crowded around us to ask us rude questions: "Are you from that madhouse all the way up the hill?" "Is it true you all share everything? Husbands and wives also?" "Is it true in your new religion you all sit in a circle and smoke ganja together?"

"No," I said over and over again. "No, it isn't true, it isn't true. It's all lies and you're all stupid." This the Malay boys loved. They clapped their hands and laughed at me and Reza and Leo laughed with them.

"How can you?" I said to them on the way back home that day. "How can you keep quiet and let them say those things?" But none of it bothers Reza and Leo. The river is their Place and this is what drives me. I must know why. I must understand the magic of the river. That is why I sit and wait for them right there on the trail. Of course they will come empty-handed. Of course they will laugh like jackasses at the sight of me still waiting.

George Cubinar Tries

FEBRUARY 1983

I might seem to invariably position myself in the one spot the big boys are most likely to traverse upon their return i.e. the back porch, but you would be mistaken: it is a free world and anyone can sit anywhere they like. Furthermore the back porch offers many advantages over other spots e.g. the cooking smells that drift out from the kitchen, the relative shade and protection from glare compared to the front porch, the fact that from it one can see far and wide without being noticed, and the many conversations audible from here as compared to the front porch which is separated from the living heart of the house by that vast empty hall. Here on the back porch there is for one thing the coming and going from the kitchen. For another thing all the windows—many of them open on fine days—are just above one's head so that dormitories corridors lounges and meeting rooms each offer up the creaks and hisses and gurgles of their workings to the ears of any quiet patient person sitting here on the back porch.

In the ladies' bathroom Estelle Foo is asking her daughter if she wants to be a prostitute or what. Otherwise why is Annabelle cutting her shorts shorter and her necklines lower? "Four inches," barks Estelle as though she might even now be standing there measuring with a ruler. "Four inches shorter you've cut them and what is your grand idea of cutting the neck of your T-shirts like this what have you got to show off you think you got D-cup breasts is it?"

In the kitchen Neela is saying "Please I will do it myself

it is faster," and then, after a muttered exchange I cannot make out, "Yes. Yes. Okay I will put less chilis. Yes I understand what you are saying." Then the other person—and now I can hear it is Mrs Arasu (assiduous guardian of our moral rectitude especially if she can in one fell swoop guard our moral rectitude and make someone feel small)—says, "Say it back to me so that I can be sure you understand." A pause and then Neela complies in a voice like a Standard One child standing up to greet the class teacher good morning. "Chilis and hot spices give us bad thoughts." Mrs Arasu refusing to let her off so easily: "What type of bad thoughts?" This time Neela does not bother pausing. "Angry thoughts greedy thoughts and the mans will be having dirty-dirty thoughts about womans." Mrs Arasu: "Not only the men, Neela, not only the men. You think women don't have thoughts about men?" On the back porch I can almost hear Neela swallow before she says, "No. No I don't think like that." Mrs Arasu insists, "You must do your job properly, Neela, it is a very important job, what we are putting inside our bodies is very important. Yours is the most important job, you know." But Neela does not say thank you or arch her back like a cat for Mrs Arasu's stroking. "Sorry," she says. "It is not an important job, I am not so important but I will put less chilis."

Shortly thereafter Mrs Arasu leaves the kitchen and Neela begins to wash a sinkful of dishes with a lot of banging and clattering. If Leo were not blessed with an uncommon wisdom I would perhaps warn him to stay out of her way when he comes back but he has never needed my warnings; he knows what to do and when to do it to avoid a good clip on the ear.

At that moment George Cubinar saunters round the back of the house and as though we have been bosom buddies since day one plonks himself down next to me.

"Ah, Kannan," he says. "How are things?"

"Fine," I say.

"Bit lonely isn't it?" he says. "Your brother and Leo are always going off and leaving you here by yourself isn't it?"

"I don't mind."

"Ah, Kannan. I know you're a proud little lad."

Little lad? Who talks like that?

I turn my head to watch him fiddle with the pen in his shirt pocket. Then in a moment of grotesque misjudgement he says, without looking at me, "Where do they go, anyway? You can tell me, you know, I won't tell anybody."

"What? I don't know. I don't ask them."

"Tsk tsk tsk," he chirps and his weaselly shadow of a Confucius moustache twitches as he says it.

After that he doesn't know what else to say. He sits there thinking his useless thoughts while I consider his twin infractions. Number one: believing I would choose to form an alliance with him behind the backs of Reza and Leo. Number two: trying to make friends with a not-yet-six-year-old boy when he is a thirty-one-year-old man.

While talking to me he picks at a scab on the back of his hand. Look at him: he is probably the type of geli fler who digs his nose with the little finger of one hand and collects the nose dirt in the other hand. Or worse yet wipes it off under tabletops and chairs.

The back door opens and Annabelle Foo pours herself out onto the porch in that clumsy-graceful way of hers. As though she's always falling and catching herself just in time but it's not like other people's falling it's a dance to highlight her coltish and uncooperative limbs. Knees and elbows everywhere yet despite themselves ending up in just the right places at the right times. Something self-conscious—even perhaps shy—about it and yet her lingering flickering gaze and the set of her jaw demand attention. This afternoon her face is bright with the held-back tears of a freshly endured fight with her mother. Splotchy red in the cheeks. Bright glassy eyes.

"Annabelle Foo," George Cubinar says. He's stopped his

scabwork and is now rubbing at his overlong sideburns. "You are like a springbok. But not a full-grown one. A young springbok still learning how to coordinate its legs. All the same, looking at you we have no trouble imagining the fine young lady you will be one day."

She sniffs the threatening tears back in. Gives him a slow sidelong smile. Yes he will do for now.

"Me so poor," she says and plonks herself down on the other side of him. "I try to improve my clothes a little bit also my stupid mother nearly wants to kill me. I'm supposed to wear shorts all the way down to my knees is it?"

"Ah," says George Cubinar. "Ah. The eternal problem of mothers and daughters. Your mother is only trying to protect you, you know."

She gives him this look—knitted brow narrowed eyes curled lip.

"Protect me from what exactly?"

His embarrassment at this question is obvious to both me and Annabelle but here is the difference between us: I find it painful whereas she delights in it.

"Tell me!" she squeals.

I am staring at George Cubinar wondering what the matter could be. Why can't he explain what he is thinking? A vague sense of the truth creeps towards me. The opposite of a glimmer: a cloud a shadow a darkening. It grows and grows. Not until many years later will I be able to understand why the sight of George Cubinar's discomfiture was too much for me: something is rotten inside George Cubinar's head. People who are pure of mind and spirit have no need to be embarrassed. He looks at the trees he admires the birds he studies his own too-clean fingernails.

All the time the bugger could not get his mind off Annabelle Foo's budding breasts. A man with a cleaner mind could have matter-of-factly said: *You are a pretty girl and your mother worries men will get the wrong idea about you.*

"It's nothing," he says. "All I mean is that you're still a

small girl and your mother wants you to dress like a small girl."

Maybe if he doesn't look at her—oh that expanse of perfect skin at her throat and chest—he can even convince himself she's still a small girl. But Annabelle Foo is no fool. She may be a dud at algebra but she has the devil's own nose for other people's weaknesses. *Well well well* she says to herself. A sly fierce spark in her eyes she lifts her face to the sky and says to no one in particular, "I'm not a small girl you know."

She leans extravagantly back. She folds her arms behind her head for a pillow and closes her eyes. By this point George Cubinar has scrutinized every plant and animal in the vicinity. He's prayed to God by all His many names to have mercy. He's not even breathing anymore.

"Not to say I'm going to get married this year, haha!" she presses on. "But I'm not a small girl. My *feelings* are not small-girl feelings."

She has opened one eye and is watching him closely. She sees me watching her.

"Ah, yes, that yes, naturally," George Cubinar says. His voice squeaking and swooping and breaking on the *naturally*. Having regressed to adolescence himself he observes, "Adolescence is indeed a time of intense emotions."

"You always use such big words, Uncle George," Annabelle Foo says. "Teach me also to talk like that lah."

"Hmm, hmm," he says. A pointer finger rubbing at the right side of his nose.

Were I old enough at six to know about such matters I might have said *Oh go on George. The nose is a poor stand-in. Why not unzip your trousers and go all the way?*

"Best way to improve the vocabulary is to read," he offers. Scratching again at his scab. "Read read read." His face contorted in a grimace he rubs at the left side of his nose now. "Ah!" he squeaks. "Sinuses giving me hell nowadays. Either the dusty house or something growing out here."

But he doesn't get up and go. He hunches his shoulders and curves his spine until his whole back is as round and hard as a crab shell. There's a boil on the back of his neck and before my eyes it's growing angrier and redder. Up and down up and down go the gentle hills and valleys of Annabelle Foo's chest. In and out in and out rasps George Cubinar's breath. I am six years old and I do not yet know the word *pervert* but I can feel it oh I can feel it all right and it makes me sick and sorry. It fills me with revulsion and pity.

Come Back

The bequeathing of his baby photos to Mama triggers an immediate and unfathomable transformation in Amar. He arrives twenty minutes late for every class and is out of the door in a blur as soon the last photostat copy is handed out and the last sentence written on the whiteboard. All Mama gets is a furtive look backwards and a raised hand. "Nenek," he mumbles over his shoulder. Not even an I'm-going-now or a See-you-next-week.

"Always so busy now!" she calls after him. "No time for Nenek nowadays."

At first it is a joke. But when his awkward laughter turns to solemn guilt (and who would not feel guilty? He may be a headache to his parents but he has a conscience. And as far as he knows he has abandoned a poor old lady who maybe possibly probably lost her own son many years ago) she can no longer bring herself to say it. A joke is one thing but the hard truth is a different matter.

"Mesti ada girlfriend," Ani says. Henceforth it is to be her preferred theory for all inexplicable changes in a young person. "Don't think these ultra-religious types are not interested in such things. They're the worst ones. By age nineteen they've got a wife and four kids. They feel they should settle down early to avoid temptation, don't you know?"

"It's true!" Mama says. "I've heard the ulama say as much. Get married early, then you don't have to fool around."

"Exactly. That's why I'm sure he's got a girl somewhere. A nice devout type in a niqab."

"Maybe."

(Of course as soon as she says it I picture the exact opposite possibility: Amar doing everything he can to hide his miniskirted tube-topped mat salleh girlfriend. Imagine, after all, the reaction of his sister! *Told me I couldn't wear makeup and now look at the half-naked floozy he's hanging around!* But even I who like to give competing theories a fair chance am unable to convince myself in this case.)

The next time I am at Dawood's I quietly ask him.

"How come your son is forever rushing around now? Before he used to sit and talk to Mother, now suddenly no time?"

He shakes his head in a violent arc like a cow being led by the nose against its will.

"Don't know, don't know lah, Encik Yusuf. I myself don't know anymore."

"But he's not giving you trouble at home anymore?"

"He's hardly at home to give us trouble!"

"At least that's something. A silver lining, no?"

He rubs at the inside corners of his eyes with one thumb and forefinger. "I don't know, brother. I don't know which is the cloud and which is the silver lining anymore. I don't know where he goes and what he does. If at all he graces us with his presence it's to put his clothes for wash. I take them out of the pail in the kitchen to smell them, can you believe it? While sniffing I'm thinking, please let it just smell of cigarettes, I used to think, please let it smell of beer. Nowadays I just try to close my eyes and my ears. Better not to know anything."

I hear the note of warning in his voice. I see the way he keeps looking past me at the five-foot way.

"Everything will be okay," I tell him. "Take it one day at a time. Time will pass and things will change."

At least the last sentence is inarguably true.

At home Mama begins to grow restless again. Picks up the old refrain: "Reza Reza Reza. When I think of how they lifted him up from the water ..."

I tell her to take a nap. I tell her to take her medicine. I tell her to breathe deep and clear her mind of dark thoughts.

And then another day: "Reza Reza Reza. At least try and contact him. It's not that I want him to come back. If he's happy I'm happy. I just want to know that he's alive and well."

One day my patience wears thin and I ask her, "But what if he's not, Mama? What if he's not alive and well? What then? Half the time you say he drowned and the other half the time you pester me to contact him. Which one is it? What if he did drown?"

Immediately her lower lip swells and trembles and I'm left feeling like I've slapped a small child. I sigh and close my eyes for five seconds. Then I look her in the eye and say, "I'm sorry. Of course he is alive and well! Why wouldn't he be? But we have nothing in common anymore other than the fact that you gave birth to both of us. And that has no bearing on the different lives we lead now."

"No. No! I cannot accept that." I see the crazy idea form behind her eyes before she verbalizes it. "I always thought —I still think—that if he could just come and spend some time with me, be at home for a while, see how we are, he will come back."

"Come back? Come back where? To stay here you mean?"

"Not just that lah. Come back to Islam."

Nothing could have prepared me for this moment. She has stepped outside the laws of physics and dragged me with her.

"What?"

"By the time he left he had started to believe. Isn't it?"

"Yes, okay, in a way, but not like that. Not in *Islam*. He ... he went to some kind of hippy Hindu ashram. Or Buddhist or something, I forget. Can you imagine someone like that converting to Islam?"

"Not converting, Yusuf!" she cries. "Not converting! Remember that he was born Muslim. I brought him up Muslim—more or less Muslim—even though his father was a mat salleh." Then remembering the smoky bars and the dance floors and the loverboys she clarifies, "It was no business of other people to try to guess what was between me and God. No matter what anyone else thought, we were Muslim until we joined the Centre."

So blithely so airily she says it: *the Centre*. The first time I have heard her say the word since we left.

"Mama, Reza is not going to come back and put on a jubah and grow a beard."

"Did I say he'll do all that? That is not the only way to be a Muslim. He always found his own way to do everything. It'll be no different with this."

"I thought you said you didn't need him to come back. You said if he's happy you're happy."

She freezes. I can see her struggling to stop herself from asking me yet again: *What did I do wrong what terrible mistakes why can my own son not even look at my face?*

"Yes," she murmurs thoughtfully to herself at last. "You are right. But I don't know why ... I just feel ... if only I could see him and say to him ..."

Today is not the day I will find out what she would say to him. The afternoon is hot and still and she begins to nod off now. The eyelids drooping. That blissful smile back on her face.

Castoff

"I knew it, tuan," Ani says. "I said to her, 'What did you expect?' This is why women should be careful, behave properly in public, don't go around holding hands and rubbing shoulders. Now look! Everybody knows she's damaged goods. As though any other man will want to give her second look."

"Damaged goods?" I say. "You mean—"

"No no no, I don't mean anything like that, tuan. I just mean everybody saw her with that Bangla boy didn't they? Holding hands and going everywhere together."

"But what happened?"

"Don't ask me! Who can explain the ways of men? One minute they act like they're so crazy about you, the next minute they're already bored and looking at some other woman with their tongue hanging out. That's just how they are."

"So he's disappeared? He's completely out of the picture?"

"She tried to tell me maybe he's gone back to Bangladesh. I said, 'Oh, gone back to Bangladesh without even sending you an SMS?' She said, 'Maybe some family emergency, maybe this lah, maybe that lah.' Finally I said to her point-blank, 'He hasn't gone back to Bangladesh, you idiot girl. He's found another woman and he's very carefully avoiding you. You'll never see him in this part of PJ again.'"

"But what about his job? Couldn't she ask around? Someone will know where he works."

Suddenly she seems irritated with me. Even sucks her teeth when all these years as much as we have considered her part of the family I cannot accuse her of not knowing her place.

"It's easy to give advice," she says. "But I suppose she's tired. Got no energy to go hunting high and low for him. And if she found him, then what?"

Well, I say to myself, *she could make a nice big scene, shame him in front of the foreman and all his coworkers, show them all what kind of a bastard he is.* But instead I just say, "True. Poor Hana, though, pity her."

"Aah, save your pity, tuan. She should've known better. Stupid girl."

Since she is clearly not getting any sympathy from Auntie I gather up my courage and go to her that evening. The room door is open. She's sitting cross-legged on Ani's bed folding clothes in her nightie. Sweating even with the fan blowing right in her freshly bathed face. She looks up when I come in then turns quickly back to her folding.

"Hana," I say. "Your auntie told me about your troubles."

She gives me a stricken look. Those big jet eyes under that narrow brow and that thin fringe.

"My troubles?"

"I know you had a ... a friend, and he's left you just like that."

"Oh, that. Yes. There's nothing I can do. If somebody doesn't want you they don't want you. So that's that."

"Well, maybe it's true there's nothing we can do to bring him back. I just wanted to say, you know I—we—are here for you. Nenek and I."

"Yes. Thank you. I'm very grateful to you. I'm very thankful to God for leading me to such good people."

I can feel her almost physically draw away from me as she says it. As though I were a dirty old man on a crowded bus. *Hana*, I want to whisper, I want to plead. I want to say her name softly and watch her turn to me in wonder. To open her eyes and see the person she has never seen before. But I am too afraid to try.

"Well," I say out loud. "If you need anything, please just ask. Don't be frightened of your auntie. You just ask me or Nenek. We'll do anything we can to help you."

She curves her body around her pile of clothes like a coconut shell a comma a cooked lobster. *Go away!* the whole shape of her begs. *Go away and leave me alone.*

"Thank you, tuan," she says.

Nothing changes. If anything she seems to wake earlier and earlier in the mornings. I hear her creeping around in the kitchen on slow quiet feet. I stay in my bed until she's left. Why would I want to embarrass her? If she wants so badly to avoid me then it would be cruel of me not to allow it.

Three Boys on the Brink

"I also come can or not?" Annabelle Foo asks and Reza not even looking at her charming smirk says "No need." *You just mind your own business thank you welcome goodbye* advises his whole demeanour.

At the top of the attic stairs we pause. Above us Cyril Dragon's closed office door. Below us the dusty sunlit shaft of that long long staircase. At the bottom of the staircase Annabelle Foo squinting up into the swirling motes.

Now Leo whispers to Reza, "Coming ah she? You managed to get rid of her or not?"

"I don't know about get rid of her but she's not coming," Reza says. "I told her off. She's standing like a coconut tree like that there at the bottom."

Leo slaps his thigh and I snort with laughter. The delight of being included in their gang sits like silk on my skin.

Through the window on the attic landing we clamber. But I don't climb out all the way. I confine myself to the windowsill perching gingerly upon its amble breadth. I can still hear Annabelle Foo shifting and breathing. Below me Reza and Leo are already sprawled out on the roof tiles like it's a grassy slope in a park somewhere.

"Wait wait," Reza says. "Anytime now he's going to warn us—"

"Don't," I beg. "Don't go so far lah. It's dangerous."

"Told you isn't it," says Reza. Then he and Leo cover their eyes with their hands and snigger.

But I refuse to be mocked into submission. I try again: "If you fall—"

"This fler is a real old lady," says Leo.

Reza takes his hands off his face to agree: "An old lady trapped in a small boy's body."

Annabelle Foo pads up one-two-three-four-five steps.

"You and your brother are opposites," Leo says to Reza. "One scared of nothing, one scared of everything. One full of questions, one full of answers. One badboy, one goodboy."

With a smirk Reza says, "You know what that means."

"What?"

On the staircase Annabelle Foo holds her breath as though somebody is about to reveal a great secret.

"He must have got it from *his* father," Reza says. "Hahaha!"

Leo guffaws. "Remember," he says to Reza, "when you used to tell me that your real father will come and fetch you one day? Or you'll go there to join him?"

Reza keeps quiet.

"Remember or not?"

"I suppose so," Reza says.

"I suppose so," says Leo in an English accent that Reza does not actually have. "Action only lah this bugger."

Reza smiles a tiny reluctant smile that Leo and Annabelle do not see: the one's eyes are closed against the sun and the other is on the staircase imagining whatever she wants.

"Anyway so what?" says Reza.

"I'm telling only."

"Telling what?"

"No lah. You know what, even though Cyril Dragon is not your real father, you're still his favourite. So bloody unfair! You're everybody's favourite. Isn't it, Kannu?"

In the distance I can see a finger-thin plume of smoke rising from the chimney of the Catholic Priests' Retreat House. I can see the plantation workers beetling about on the tea terraces and I can see a flock of white birds circling in the sky above them. I can see a cloud shaped like a dragon and another like the profile of a witch. Only I can see these things because Reza and Leo are keeping their eyes closed.

Into the silence Reza shoots a single bullet of laughter.

"Who said life was fair?" he says. "You would think my holier-than-thou brother would be Cyril Dragon's favourite at least, but what can I do if he isn't?"

Their eyes are still closed and their faces scrunched up against the sunlight so that no one perhaps not even they themselves can tell whether they are joking around or having a serious conversation.

Leo snorts. "Pity only you," he says. "Poor, poor thing. Cyril Dragon's favourite and your mother's favourite also. And as if that's not bad enough on top of that everybody else also trying to angkat you all the time. So clever this boy so handsome so active! And the way that Annabelle Foo looks at you! Hahahaha! You didn't ask to be so popular what!"

In and out she breathes on the stairs. Calm and calculating. Her breath wafting up to my nose with its cool poisoned smell of vinegar and green mangoes. She folds her arms and presses her lips together and thinks of the lessons she will teach us all.

Then—still without opening his eyes—my brother says something so wise and cruel that I will never forget it.

"The thing is," he says, "people pretend how much also they cannot help worshipping the mat salleh. They may not be allowed to say Indian-Chinese-Malay but just because you cannot say doesn't mean you cannot see. And Cyril Dragon can preach until he got no more breath about everybody being equal but he cannot cancel out that dubba-dubba-dubba in people's hearts"—here Reza pounds his fist on his chest—"when they see a white face. They cannot help it. Even if they don't want to admit it, I am like a small god for them. Like a movie star or a book hero floated down on a cloud and landed among them, and they all want to gather around me and touch me. Hahaha!"

"Hahaha hohoho heeheehee," Leo says. "Great fler lah you."

There follows a long pause. Then Leo says, "You still waiting ah?"

"Waiting for what?" Reza says.

"Waiting … to … to go back," Leo says. "Waiting for anybody to come and rescue you from here."

"Aaaah," Reza says dismissively. "I don't need anybody to rescue me."

"But you still miss it isn't it?"

"I'll tell you what I miss: lamb chops and beef steak. Prawns and crabs and lobster."

A creak on the stairs: Annabelle Foo shifting her weight.

"Joker lah you. Bluff only. Where your mother had that kind of money?"

"She had money what."

"From where? You didn't even have a father. From where she got the money?"

"I *had* a father. But also money from other people."

"What people?"

"People used to give us money."

Then without warning but very calmly very casually Reza gets up and walks to the edge of the roof. Right up to the edge he goes until—my shoulders stiffen just to see it, my arms hug my knees tighter and tighter—his toes curl right over it.

"Eh!" Leo yelps. "Baddava rascal, don't play the fool! Don't fall and die, okay? You slip now, I'm not going to come and rescue you!"

Annabelle Foo climbs another one-two-three steps. Faster this time yet still not far enough to see.

"I won't fall lah," Reza says. "I'm not that brave."

Nevertheless Leo slithers across the roof on his stomach like a jungle commando. As soon as he can reach Reza he slips his fingers around Reza's ankles like he's shackling up a prisoner's legs.

"Got you!" he says. "Now you cannot go anywhere."

All at once all three of us are laughing. Not sniggering not chuckling but laughing. Fresh cold air fills our lungs and we laugh and laugh and laugh as the white birds circle over our heads.

Annabelle the Beautiful

Annabelle Foo stands before the wardrobe mirror in the girls' dormitory. The mirror—grimy spotty pocked-and-chipped—has never met her expectations but now in the moment of her blossoming it falls shorter than ever. She knows she deserves a better mirror. Just look at the long milky length of her. The high gloss of her hair and lips. The pencil line of a nose and the finely pointed chin. The tiny waist. The fresh new breasts so delicately cradled—like ripening peaches in their tissue paper—by the white eyelet cotton bra on which her mother finally after months of pestering agreed to spend some of the family's Personal Expenses money. This stupid mirror mars it all with its oil smears and its spatterings of black dots.

Annabelle Foo knows that she is not like the other girls. Just look at that pathetic Kiranjit with her hairy upper lip and her Punjabi treetrunk legs. Or the Mak twins forever giggling like a pair of chubby fools. Tweedledum and Tweedledee all right. The bowl haircuts they let their mother boast about—*more practical mah!*—and the way they will amble about completely unaware of the lunch remnants decorating their person. Egg yolk crusted in a corner of the mouth. A grain of rice stuck to a collar. A splash of soy sauce on a wobbly stomach.

In the past—despairing of her isolation—Annabelle has attempted to forge alliances with one or another of the units of girlhood at the Centre. Before Kiranjit's moustache and unibrow became so distressingly apparent, Annabelle admitted the possibility of a … *friendship* seemed too strong of a word, but something in that direction at least. She had gone to Kiranjit with concoctions meticulously devised to delight: "I saw Alice Mak cleaning out her navel with a hairpin. Did you know that Elaine Mak keeps two sanitary pads in her bedside table drawer? Hahaha! Like as though she got her period already! Her body like one stick like that! The chest like a table!"

But Kiranjit had shown little interest in these vignettes. She had oh-ed and hemmed and then she had gone and grown hair—not just any hair but a thick curling carpet of it—all the way up her legs, and that grotesque moustache too, thereby obviating any possibility of an alliance. To be seen whispering and giggling—this is how Annabelle imagines true friendship, a lot of whispering and giggling —with such a person was to disgustify oneself by association.

Half-heartedly but without wasting time she had switched sides. She scrunched up her face theatrically and said to Alice and Elaine Mak, "Ee-yer, that Kiranjit anh, forever scratching down there you know. Every time during Lessons I see her. She thinks got nobody watching but from where I sit I can see."

The Mak twins had blinked their alternating blinks: the one's eyes opening when the other's closed. A united and perfectly choreographed front. Even looking at them Annabelle Foo gets the message: *We are two-in-one. No place for anybody else sorry thank you goodbye.*

No point hanging around such people waiting for scraps of female solidarity. *Am I that desperate?* Annabelle says to herself. Without ever having attended a girls' school or a ballet class she knows the rules of the female pack: what can I call it but instinct?

Still. Knowing the rules was one thing and loneliness was another. Annabelle does not think of herself as lonely but she will (when she judges it to be expedient) admit to boredom. "I'm so bored!" she pleads with Reza and Leo when she catches them sneaking off on some secret adventure. "I'm so bored of *these people*, you know." She flutters her derisive lashes in the general direction of the house so that her so-bored expands to include not just Kiranjit and Alice and Elaine but the whole Centre with its Devotionals and prayer meetings and meditation sessions in short all its lofty goody-two-shoes mumbo jumbo increasingly unable to satisfy her restless aching adolescent soul.

But Reza and Leo laugh in her face and saunter off. That they don't even bother to walk fast is the ultimate insult. Like the members of every boys-only club since the beginning of the world they are blithe and smug because admission to the club is by-invitation-only and members can feel secure in the knowledge that the guards—even when invisible—will keep all intruders out.

Daily after Lessons she carries her lament to George Cubinar. She stays back to tidy up the classroom straighten the chairs rub the blackboard and moan. "So boring lah nothing to do here I don't even have friends the other girls are so irritating."

"Dear dear," sighs George Cubinar as he backs out of the room. *Dear dear* all the way up the stairs and into the farthest toilet stall in the men's bathroom to pleasure himself while thinking of the silky underside of Annabelle Foo's arm as she rubs the blackboard and where else she might have similarly silky skin.

Oh go on and say it: I have no proof. I am adding my own thought bubbles thirty years later. But what if I told you I heard him? I stood in the corridor and heard the small noises of his self-love. There. Satisfied? I cannot be sure Annabelle Foo did not hear him too. She could be as skulky and slinky as I was.

What can Annabelle Foo do with the knowledge of her own beauty and its power? She has been left to her own devices. To stand and stew before this substandard mirror.

When they see George Cubinar watching her with his tongue hanging out the other girls will have to be impressed if nothing else. There will have to be that kind of awe people feel when they witness a feat they cannot even understand let alone accomplish. And the boys? They will realize how wrong they've been all along. She's not some sad wallflower after all. She's wanted. Desired. Hankered after. Even her parents: what's she been to them but a dish of rejected leftovers? They thought they were stuck with the second-best sister (out of two). But now they'll have to sit up and take notice at least. They'll have to open their eyes and see her properly for the first time in her life.

The Van of Iniquity

It's Annabelle Foo who first tells me about the vegetable van.

"Is it true?" I demand when I've managed to get them to myself. "Is it true you get lifts to town in the van?"

"Yes," Leo says. "So?"

"It's not allowed to go gallivanting here and there with the vegetable men," I say. "They're not like us. They—"

"I thought Cyril Dragon didn't believe in *people like us* and people *not like us*," Reza says.

"I don't mean like that. I just mean they drink and smoke and they eat meat."

"So?" Reza says. "Maybe we'll be a good influence on them what. Maybe we can introduce them to our way of life. Guide them towards the right path."

Between them and me there rises an impenetrable wall of laughter. The two of them doubled over. Myself stiff as a rod.

"In fact," Leo says in between fits of laughter, "in fact, that is the whole reason we have been going with them only. We are hoping to teach them about nonviolence brotherly love inner peace etcetera etcetera."

"That's right," agrees Reza. "But slowly-slowly lah. Like taming birds like that. We have to earn their trust first, otherwise they'll just fly away isn't it?"

"You better be careful," I say. But my voice comes out desperate rather than threatening. "It's dangerous to keep the wrong company. Instead of you being a good influence on them, it'll end up the other way round. *They'll* corrupt *you*."

"Not a chance," says Reza. "We have morals of iron and steel. Invincible morals. Yes or not, Leo?"

"Oh yes," says Leo.

"But why do you want to go with them?" I persist. "What's so great about going to town? What do you do there that you cannot do here?"

At this they look at each other with big-big eyes. *Oh boy* that look says. *Oh boy oh boy oh boy.* Then Reza says, "Name all the things we cannot do here. Those are the things we do in town."

Slowly the answer dawns upon me.

"You mean you ... you go to town and eat lamb chops and prawns?"

"Hahaha!" Leo says. "Listen to the fler! Lamb chops and prawns it seems! You think what, we robbed a bank ah?"

"If only," Reza says. "No lamb chops and prawns for us. More like 20-sen fishballs from the lok lok stall. Dried sotong from the sundry shop. But one time, believe it or not, those flers belanjaed us a Ramly burger. Best day I've had in ten years, I tell you."

"You're bluffing," I say. "Why would they simply spend money on you?"

"Because," Reza says, and here he bends down and puts his face close to mine so that our noses are touching. "Because they take pity on us. They feel sorry for us, that we never chose to live under your father's half-past-six home-made commandments but we still have to because we got dragged here. We had no say in the matter. They feel bad that we have to be deprived of our childhood. We have to be deprived of A&W and Kentucky Fried Chicken and TV programmes and cassette tapes."

It's his fearlessness that offends me. The unnecessary details and the swaggering.

"You can't *do* that!" I shout. "You can't eat dead animals!"

"What a good little stooge you are," Reza says.

"If people find out—" I begin but Leo cuts me off.

"People found out long ago lah. Not everybody is so kay poh like you. People know and they just mind their own business."

"No. It's not true! You're lying. Papa would never keep quiet about something like this."

"I didn't say anything about your Papa. *People* doesn't mean the great Cyril Dragon. People means people."

"And they don't tell him? The others don't tell Papa?"

"Hahaha! How could they do that to him?" Reza says. "The poor man would never live through the horror. Imagine his disappointment when he realizes that his precious Next Generation, Hope of the World, is screwing around with the eternal fate of mankind. By all means tell him if you want, but you yourself will have to dig his grave and bury him after that."

I back away from them as one might from a pair of armed madmen. Who knows what they might do if I turned my back to them? I must never take my eyes off them. Not if I can help it. If my father cannot face the truth I will have to do so for him.

Bungalow

To my most glorious Father Cyril Dragon,
This is to inform you that Reza Notyourson and
Leo Raj s/o Unknown have embarked upon a Spiritual
Journey to the MOONLIGHT BUNGALOW i.e. the former
abode of American millionaire JIM THOMPSON at Jalan
Kamunting, Tanah Rata, Cameron Highlands, Pahang,
Malaysia. To facilitate your police report please note that
Reza was wearing a grey T-shirt and brown trousers
while Leo was wearing a white Garfield T-shirt and blue
jeans when last seen. They were given a lift to the
MOONLIGHT BUNGALOW by two employees of HOCK
LIAN VEGETABLE AND FRUIT WHOLESALE SDN. BHD.
Yours sincerely,
Your ever-faithful Own Son,

(Clarence Kannan Cheng-Ho Muhammad Yusuf Dragon)

The viciousness of it oh the savage contempt of this note
they've left on my bed makes my eyes smart. Yet even before
I crumple it up and stuff it into the pocket of my trousers I
know this: I will not tell anyone where they have gone. That
afternoon I feed the note to the goats.

For one whole day after they first told me about this latest plan I was one hundred per cent sure I would tell on
them. I would tell Cyril Dragon and he would summon the
vegetable men and give them a warning. I would show Reza
and Leo who I really was: by no means a pathetic issuer of

empty threats. Don't play-play.

But the next day I was already a little less sure. And the day after that still less sure. And the day after that one ...

What was it that weakened my resolve? I am almost—almost!—an old man now sitting here trying to remember. So forgive me: I cannot fill in all the blanks. What I can give you is these fistfuls:

The way Reza and Leo nudged each other and whispered and chuckled every time they saw me for a few days after I made my threat.

Their humming and whistling.

Their refusal to make eye contact.

You would think all of this would have driven me straight up to my father's office but instead I felt a strange kind of tenderness. I saw them for what they were—boys playing devil-may-care mavericks—and the seeing awakened in me an instinct to protect them even from themselves.

When they are missing at Afternoon Meeting on the day they've left me the note a few people sigh and shake their heads although really as Mrs Arasu points out what's the big difference between horsing around in the back row and not showing up? At Evening Devotional they have still not appeared but Mama shrugs and smiles. "You know lah," she says. "Boys that age very difficult to control."

At the dinner table Papa asks me quietly, "Where is your brother?"

"Don't know," I say. "Maybe went somewhere or what."

Neither one of us mentions Leo.

At bedtime they have not returned. I am alone in the Boys' Dormitory quietly reading *The Screwtape Letters:*

> You will say that these are very small sins; and doubtless,
> like all young tempters, you are anxious to be able to
> report
> spectacular wickedness. But do remember, the only thing

that matters is the extent to which you separate the man
from the Enemy. It does not matter how small the sins
are provided that their cumulative effect is to edge the
man
away from the Light and out into the Nothing. Murder is
no better than cards if cards can do the trick. Indeed the
safest road to Hell is the gradual one—the gentle slope,
soft underfoot, without sudden turnings, without mile-
stones, without signposts ...

when Annabelle Foo slips in like a lizard and sits down on my bed.

"Where did they go?" she says without preamble. "I'm sure you know."

Trapped like this I can only play for time. "Why? Why should I know? How come you're so sure?"

"I'm sure they told you. They'll never go somewhere without boasting to you first. They got to make you feel left out then only got syiok for them. Otherwise no point. Don't you know? They pinch you pinch you and watch your face. Everybody can see it except you."

Everybody can see it except you. With those words Annabelle Foo opens my eyes and now I see it too: I am everybody's paavam not just Reza and Leo's. The pathetic trailing little brother with no friends of his own. The unwanted tagger-along. The boy too slow and stupid and green to be part of the boys' club because unlike Leo and Reza I have no yearning for that lost Outside life. No knowledge of it. One look at me next to them and *everybody can see it*: their streetsmart slang and their bugger-off confidence next to my oily hair my sloping goodboy shoulders my sad turned-in toes. There is only one thing to do with an accusation as on the mark as Annabelle Foo's.

"Shut up," I say. "Don't simply talk rubbish. You don't know anything."

"Then tell me, how come you didn't go with them?"

There can be no delay or Annabelle will seize her advantage. I open my mouth and begin to talk.

"This time was their turn. Next time will be my turn and one of them will stay back."

But even as I am speaking the real answer comes to me.

"Anyway the one who stays back is the most important one of all don't you know? I'm the most important member of the team. Because it's my job to answer stupid busybody questions and it's my job to keep the story straight for them. Anybody suspects anything then I only must quickly cover up for them. That's why they asked me to be the first one to stay back. They know they can trust me. They know I won't simply blab to every Tom Dick and Harry."

And then I grab my inspiration and run with it.

"Of course," I say, "that means they got to be a bit scared of me also. Because if I really want I can let out their secret. They know I got that power."

It is a great risk I have taken: Annabelle's mouth hangs open and her eyes blink at me. Any moment now she might say *Shut up lah you, as though I believe your bullshit. Power it seems! Real clown this fler. Living in a dream world.*

But she doesn't say it. She blinks once twice thrice more and in that soundless eternity I wait for it to dawn upon her that Reza and Leo couldn't care less if I told everyone where they are. That I can choose what to conceal and what to reveal gives me power not over them but over everyone else: it's everyone else who would be upset to learn the extent of their secrets. But Annabelle fails to grasp this after all. The minute she turns around and leaves the room I let all the air out of my lungs and fall flat back upon my bed as though I have been pushed.

Return of the Gallivanters

High in the sky the sun burns the next day and still no sign of Leo and Reza. Lessons are over. In the classroom George Cubinar made an elaborate pretence of not noticing their absence. But afterwards my father pulls me aside again.

"Kannu," he says, "If you know where they are you must tell us. You see, if they are in any danger ..."

I smile a secret little smile. "No," I say. "They're not in any danger. They'll be back soon."

A significant pause before my father says, "Then you do know where they are?"

I incline my head as though pondering the question. "But they're not doing anything bad," I say at last. "They're just ... they're just having a small adventure."

My father considers this. "All right. In that case it's all right. But if they are not back by midday we shall have to ... to get help. And then you must be ready to tell us whatever you know. Do you understand?"

I push my hands deep into my pockets and lift my smug face up to him.

"Of course," I say. "No problem."

I wait for them on the front porch with my worn copy of *The Vedas and Upanishads for Children*. By the time I hear them and look up from the book they are five feet away.

"Yo," Reza says to me. "No other work ah you? Sitting here reading the Bhagavad Gita since yesterday?"

"It's not the Bhagavad Gita," I begin before I realize I must not let myself be diverted from my course. I draw in my breath and say, "You better be careful. Everybody was looking for you."

"Oh ho ho," Reza says. "Trying to threaten us, is it? I'm soooo scared."

"Did you tell them where we went?" asks Leo but he doesn't ask it like he is worried.

"Why should I?" I say. "That's your business."

"Tell them or not, who cares?" Reza says. "What are they going to do, ask us to leave?"

Leo claps his hands and laughs.

"They won't ask you to leave," I say. "They'll make sure you never leave again. They'll watch you like hawks. Like owls. Like—"

"One thing, the fler knows all his birds," Leo says.

"What's the big deal?" Reza says. "So we spent a night outside. It's no different from camping isn't it? Lots of boys go camping. Boy Scouts and all that."

"If there's nothing wrong with it then why didn't you just tell them and then go? Why?"

"What's your problem?" Leo says. "You want something from us?"

"I want to come with you next time," I say.

They look at each other. Then Reza says, "What makes you think there'll be a next time? Why would we go back to the Bungalow? There's nothing to see there. It's a broken-down joint full of creepers and bats."

"If it was so boring then why didn't you just tell everybody where you were going? You didn't do anything anyway what."

"How should we have known it was going to be boring?" Reza says. "We thought maybe the kampung boys would come and offer us nice-nice dadah. Ganja, hashish, all types."

They fall over laughing.

"Where did you sleep?" I say. "Just in the jungle? With no tent or anything?"

"Yes," Leo says. Still weak with laughter and making a great show of wiping the tears from his eyes. "With the lions and the tigers."

"And the bears," Reza says. "Lots of bears."

"I'm not stupid," I say. "Where did you sleep?"

"Fine," Reza says. "Next time we go to the Bungalow you can come along. You also can be eaten alive by mosquitoes. You also can lie awake all night listening to your own teeth chatter while you imagine ghosts."

"I don't mean just the Bungalow," I say. "I mean next time you go to the river, or in the vegetable lorry."

"Sure!" Reza says. He throws his arms wide like a sultan welcoming guests to his banquet. "Anytime! Come along and see. We'll make it a grand outing for everybody! Happy?"

"You don't need to worry," I say. "Whatever secrets you've got will be safe with me."

"What secrets?" Leo says. "What are you talking about?"

"He means like eating *flesh foods*," Reza says. "He's going to keep a log book of every fishball consumed. Then what, Kannu? How much are you planning to extort per fishball? Ten cents? Twenty cents?"

"I'm not going to tell anybody anything," I say.

"You don't have to," Leo says. "Everybody already knows, just like your brother said. Except Cyril Dragon and we're not scared of him. But if you want to come with us then be our guest."

We stand there in a circle eyeing each other. No one wants to be the first to turn his back to the others.

For days I wait for Reza and Leo to be summoned to Cyril Dragon's office. But as far as I can tell no questions are asked. Even Annabelle Foo does not go a-pestering. At first it is as though everybody is doing their best to avoid the subject and then—even stranger—they all contract acute amnesia. Except that whoever cast the forgetting spell left me out. I alone in that mouldy house bear the burdens of sight and memory.

The Waning Honeymoon

Almost like this it happened: she woke up one morning and thought, *This is it. This is all there is. This is the here-and-now but also the happily-ever-after.* It always comes in the end. The restlessness and all its symptoms. The ache in her heart the hollow in her belly the pasty feeling in the mouth. When she can see the change so clearly in the mirror how come no one else seems to notice? Her hair hangs dull and dry. Under her eyes the puffy skin is worn to a sheen. Her lovely youth is lost. Gone forever.

Not that there is anything *wrong.* "It's not that I'm unhappy," she tells herself but the very reassurance begs the question: "Am I happy? Was I ever actually happy here? Or was I merely not-miserable and is that no longer good enough?"

She sneaks in women's magazines and hides them between the pages of Thomas Aquinas and Jiddu Krishnamurti. She thinks, *God what I would do for a cigarette. For a drink. For a night of* passion. *Real passion not just* loving-kindness *with no clothes on!* Loving-kindness. The brotherhood of man. We are all the chosen people. Some days the lingo pricks at her like so many tiny needles.

What she would do even for a good fight! A night of sobs so powerful your breath came unsteady and shivery for hours afterwards. And then the lustful reconciliation. There are no fights with Cyril. Once in a wild attempt to provoke him she told him, "Do you know, after all these years I still miss meat? Sometimes I dream about it at night.

Beef rendang. Nasi ambang. Daging salai. Just cannot beat the taste of real meat!"

But he had only given her his usual melancholy smile. "In some ways," he'd said, "you are the stronger of the two of us. It takes more strength to turn away from constant temptation than to live a clean life when one feels no temptation to stray."

"Aren't you shocked?" she pressed. "Aren't you disappointed in me?"

"It's not my place to get angry about someone else's weaknesses. Who am I, God?"

His smile had turned still more melancholy.

You may as well be, she had found herself thinking. *You're not animal and you're not human so what else is left? How much holier-than-thou can one get without attaining Godhood?*

To a different man she might have said, "I wish just once I could see you really angry. I wish you would fly into a temper. I wish you would shout and slam doors and sweep everything off your desk. I wish you would be greedy I wish you would be jealous I wish you would be cruel. Just once. *Just once!*"

But you cannot say such things to a God. You lower your eyes and swallow your wishes.

The problem with swallowed wishes is that eventually they will begin to fiddle with one's digestion. Unforeseen sotto voce phrases escape Salmah's lips behind Cyril Dragon's back: "My husband the saviour of the world." "My husband the messiah." "The laster-than-last prophet." "The messenger of God." "My great husband who is seated at the right hand of the Almighty."

She sees the way the others look at her when she talks like this. She knows what they are thinking: *How dare she! How dare she after everything Cyril Dragon has done for her. Plucked her out of God-knows-what shameful mess that made her run up the hill. Saved her dignity saved her life saved her soul.* But in one or two faces she also sees something else. A newborn-baby blinking. A puzzled squinting into the light. Because they hadn't realized this was possible. To question the questioner. Sure Reza did it but that was only because he was a child. Still growing. On his meandering way to the Truth. Before their tired eyes Cyril Dragon had dismantled everything: history race religion and even God Himself. But could he himself be dismantled? She extends a single prodding finger but Cyril Dragon does not even feel it. She picks up a stick and then another and another each one sharper than the last. Still he does not topple. But does he at last feel her attempts? At Morning Meeting and Evening Devotional he looks out at them as Moses or King Canute might have looked over the sea. His eyes give nothing away. His smile carries the weight of the world as it always has.

Paralysis

Twice in his forty-two years Cyril Dragon has been afraid: once while peering through the upstairs shutters of his father's shophouse on the May 13th, 1969, and now. This second time is not like the first. Not a single moment or even a single day, but a diffuse and agonizing thing. It stretches out his guts and tangles them in knots.

It began (as so many terrors do) with a smell. He remembered it from his father's pipe: tobacco. First in the lavatory she smoked. Spraying some foul floral concoction and then flushing to throw them off the trail. It was the flushing that irked him most of all: the childish deceit of it! Flushing when there was ash all over the floor. More often than not the cigarette butt was left bobbing in the bowl like the dropping of some tiny creature. Then—perhaps thinking *why should I hide like a hunted animal*—she graduated to smoking in the room—their room!—with the door locked. If he knocked she would call out "One minute please!" her tongue dry from the smoke. And then—because what was the point of the whole locked-door farce when the smell smacked him left right centre as soon as she had to open the door—she began to smoke on the front porch. Later she would say, "Where else? The back porch is Neela's territory isn't it? And aren't the boys always hanging around there? Did you want me to be blowing smoke into their pure young faces?"

But before all that, there she is smoking on the front porch and the sight reminds him of nothing so much as a wild animal. Something about her hunched prowling posture: like she's waiting to pounce. And the way she stretches her arms between cigarettes.

Yet it is not her emerging beast nature that surprises him. After all hasn't he always said *Man is a beast among beasts. We can choose to give in to our animal side or we can choose to tame it but first we have to see it acknowledge it understand it yes or not?* And the taming of it is a lifelong struggle. The company we keep the words we think and speak the foods we eat: these are the ways to tame the beast or to whip it into a frenzy. But the beast itself is not something to be feared because listen brothers and sisters: we are smarter and stronger than it. So let Salmah's beast come out and soft-foot the perimeter. Let it growl and mark its supposed territory. In the end it can be coaxed back into submission.

Except that he finds himself unable to speak in its presence. This is what chills his blood: he can open his mouth and make inconsequential noises that imitate language but he cannot form words out of what he actually feels. He says to Salmah, "Surely I do not need to remind you that the body is a temple."

And she snorts and rolls her eyes and says, "If the body is a temple then why shouldn't I burn incense in it?"

He lowers his eyes and smiles a pinched-tight smile. His tongue a feeble pink slab in his mouth. A flopping fish quoting scripture and fairy tales when right there at the top of his throat the truth is flaming and spitting and burning itself out: *You need cigarettes now because I am not longer enough for you. The novelty of The Dream The Vision The Movement has worn off and so—because you cannot separate me from The Dream—you are growing tired of me. Or is it the other way around? That our passion cooled first and with it your infatuation with our grand and unattainable ideals? Either way this much is clear: it was a package deal and now you are finished with all of it. Will I wake up one morning and find you gone?*

Moved on to your next stop? With two boys this time. A growing band of wanderers. And what tales will you spin of this life? What is the story you will tell yourself about us?

He knows he ought to pray. To leave everything in God's hands. Would that he could believe in that kind of God! There it is: the great lie of his so-called vocation. If sitting back and trusting God was all there was to it then why had he put them through all of this? Why had he made them leave everything behind to come here and claw moss off the walls with their fingernails and dig in the dirt with their soft government-servant hands? Surely at least some of them must have stopped to ask themselves these questions.

Supposing that fairy godfather of a God did exist—then what? He can think of only one request: *Take me back.* But even God does not meddle with the laws of time and space. And back to when and what? To the day Salmah arrived? To be relived over and over again for eternity? For in moving forward something is always lost. Further back then: to the May 13th, 1969. Let him stand at that window again. Let him hear the voice in his ear. But then let him stand up to it. Let him answer back: *I cannot. One man cannot save a country. One man cannot change the past or shape the future. And how many others will I gather under my banner? Five-ten-fifteen. Fifteen against the tides of tribalism; we may as well each live a good life separately quietly with no lofty ambitions.*

But the truth is that by the time he stood at that window on the May 13th, 1969, it was already too late. He was already who he was. The boy who could not ignore the voice in his ear. The boy who bore all the sorrows of the world on his shoulders. There is only one moment to which he should go back and that is the moment of his birth. Let him slip out of his mother and let her take him in her warm arms. Let her live. There: in her daffodil dress she cradles him and sings to him. He is cared for instead of being the eternal caretaker. He no longer bears responsibility for the ills of the world.

Drive

We choose our cause every year: Vietnamese refugees Bangladeshi flood victims famine in Ethiopia earthquake in Mexico there has never been any shortage of options. On an appointed day the newspaper articles Selwyn Foo has been meticulously archiving are brought out. All the adults vote but it is Cyril Dragon himself who makes sure we spread out our charity among all the nations of the earth. The Christians distribute Bibles with their bread he says and the Muslims will only help Muslims and therein lies the problem. If we are going to preach that God Is One and We Are All The Chosen People then we must back up our words with our actions and give equally to each and all regardless of creed. This year we have chosen the unlucky people of Chernobyl and thereabouts. The teatime snacks and sweetmeats for our annual charity drive (murukkus laddoos jelebis assorted urundai jam tarts butter cake chiffon cake fruit cake) are made in our own kitchen. Naturally since we ourselves are vegetarian our confections are pork-free egg-free no-beef-gelatine.

Every year the posters have borne the same succinct text:

ENJOY THE SWEETNESS OF GOD'S LOVE

ONE GOD

ONE PEOPLE

THE MUHIBBAH CENTRE FOR WORLD PEACE

But this year Selwyn Foo hems and haws at the organizational meeting before offering his suggestion.

"At least put a bit of information lah."

A moment of silence follows while everyone digests the fact that someone has proposed a change to the order of things. A small change perhaps but everyone can sense that it counts as a challenge to Cyril Dragon's authority. Let it not go unnoticed.

"Everything important is there," Cyril Dragon says. His own voice equally mild. "Those who want to find us will find us."

"It's not that. But we should put a bit of our history, our mission, that sort of thing. After all it doesn't cost anything extra when you're making your own copies."

"So much ink," mutters Thomas Mak.

"Ink!" cries Selwyn Foo.

In the heat his sleek hairpuff has gone limp and one forelock hangs down his forehead—but rather than detracting from his matinee-idol good looks this only accentuates them. As though suddenly conscious of the whole room's eyes upon him he draws himself up higher to step into his role: the accidental rebel the reluctant firebrand the dark horse.

"Here we are supposed to be changing the world and you talk about *ink*? Why call ourselves the Centre for World Peace if we are going to be like mice in our tiny hole? Might as well be the Centre for House Peace. The Centre for Thirteen People's Peace. The Centre for Its Own Peace. We've been here for more than ten years now! In the beginning we said start slowly-slowly, then later share our message more widely. But after a few years of distributing pamphlets: finish! Supposed to lie low to avoid the government radar, okay, fine, but for how long? What is the point then? We are only saving ourselves and nobody else. Are we ready to share our message or not? Tell me."

Another fidgety silence follows this impressive monologue.

Has Selwyn been concealing his true character all these years? If so, why is he disclosing it now? Why this dramatic monologue for such a small thing?

"Okay," Cyril Dragon says at last. But the subtext is clear from his manner: *Fine. I'm not going to be drawn into your petty battle. I'll be the bigger person here.* "Why don't you do the write-up in that case? You can print a few leaflets along with the usual posters."

"Myself where can do write-up?" Selwyn Foo protests. "I can run the cyclostyle machine no problem, but for the write-up, maybe George or Rupert ..." He waves a wild desperate arm around the room."

George Cubinar (veteran puller of short straws) can already feel his heart sinking when Salmah unexpectedly pipes up.

"Fine. I'll do the write-up. Why not? I've got nothing better to do. I'll help Selwyn."

The part of the Story of Salmah Majid in which she was a reporter for a third-rate paper at least must be true—the write-up turns out to feature exactly the kind of pomp and bombast guaranteed to impress our local readership: *the immanence of the Godhead in all teachings and all scriptures the Divinity of the Immortal Soul it is ludicrous to postulate that Objective Truth might be the sole preserve of one faith* blah blah blah. No one can deny that it elevates the Cakes & Sweets Sale into rarefied territory.

Selwyn Foo needs only to take up his yearly post in the printing room. (A post that is—along with the faces of his wife and his daughter—one of few remaining links to his old life. He knows his way around a printing press. And unlike the faces of his wife and his second daughter the cyclostyle machine is not a painful reminder of the missing piece of his existence.) All these years he has done it alone but this year Salmah says, "I wrote it, I may as well help you to print it."

The part of her story in which she used to work for the

Malay Mail: Selwyn remembers it as together they purple up their hands with that particular bygone ink. Fill their ears with the constant clank-chug of the machine. *Like a pro all right*, he thinks. As though reading his thoughts she says, "Brings back memories. Only thing now is I can't smoke to take the edge off." And even as she is saying it something takes hold of her and pulls out a cigarette and lights up anyway—just to see? or because she is genuinely unable to withstand the temptation a moment longer her willpower having been eaten away by that relentless machine?—and Selywn Foo appears at first to be greatly startled but then simply says, "Haiyo, no windows also you can smoke ah?"

She takes a long drag. Without cracking a smile she says, "What to do? My husband's extremes drive me to my own extremes."

Just to see. Only when Selwyn Foo shakes his head and chuckles does she allow the corners of her eyes to crinkle though her lips are clamped humourlessly around her cigarette.

When Salmah tells Cyril Dragon of her plan to distribute the flyers with Selwyn he covers his eyes.

"Please," he says. "What is it you really want?"

"I want to be like everybody else," she says. "I want to stop hiding."

"You're always mocking our whole vision," he says. "I don't even know what you believe anymore. Everything is a laughing matter for you, one minute you act like you've had enough, but the next minute you want to put up posters?"

"Just because people can laugh at themselves a bit," she says, "doesn't mean they don't believe anything. You say you want to tear down man-made rules but you've just made your own rules. That's the part that makes me laugh. I'll tell you what I believe: what I believe is that what I eat, what I wear, what I do or don't do, it's all between me and God. That One God that you're always talking about. I believe that if we all let go of our rules a bit, maybe we'll have some chance of peace. But that doesn't just apply to other people and other people's rules. It applies to us also. To you and all your flunkies. Now tell me: does that mean I can't go and distribute posters?"

He looks at her for a long time. When he speaks his voice is smooth and quiet.

"All these years you never wanted to do anything. Even ten years ago things were much more lax for Muslims. But just when trouble might be brewing ... I mean, why now, Salmah? Why now, when the government is already making noises?"

"Because I'm bored. I'm going mad with boredom. Is that a good enough answer for you?"

"To entertain yourself you want to put all of us in danger?"

"Oh, come off it! How you exaggerate your own importance in your head! You all like to imagine that the government has one whole chest of drawers just for files about the Muhibbah Centre for World Peace. Makes your life more exciting I suppose. But you know what? The government hasn't even heard of us. Don't worry, they're not going to send out half a dozen secret agents to shadow me just for putting up posters in town."

And so despite the many whispered warnings of his faithful followers—*But won't she be seen? People won't suspect she's a Malay ah?*—Papa does nothing to stop Mama from hopping into the Centre van with Selwyn Foo. There is nothing left to do. There is nothing left to say. Not even when Reza and Leo cadge a lift to town in the back of the van.

Reza and Leo have broken no promise by leaving me behind. It is not the vegetable van and they are not going to the river in it. Where Selwyn Foo drops Reza and Leo what they do where he picks them up: all of this is a mystery but when they come back in the van well after the dinner hour all four of them are in a fine mood.

"Of all things," Mrs Arasu says to Hilda Boey. "Not only condoning their behaviour but aiding and abetting it!"

As to who is aiding and abetting whom Mrs Arasu does not specify. Hilda Boey does not ask but only nods soothingly. "Hmm hmm hmm," she coos deep in her throat. She folds her arms over her belly and shapes her mouth into some semblance of an encouraging smile.

"Her two sons," Mrs Arasu goes on and nobody needs to ask whose sons she's talking about. She draws her lips back in a broad smile like a horse reaching for a perfect apple. "I tell you, each one matches his own face. One doesn't know how to lie or hide what he is doing even when he should, just like an Englishman. The other one so secretive, just like an Oriental."

She does this proud essentializing when my father is safely out of earshot of course which is just as well because if he could hear it he would wonder more than ever if his whole dream has been a sham and a waste. But for me it is an awakening: your very destiny is woven into the colour of your skin and the cut of your face. I have no secrets such as Mrs Arasu must be cooking up inside her small head. In truth it is Reza with his fine Englishman's face who has secrets.

Go-Between

I am still standing in the exhaust-fume wake of the receding Muhibbah van when Annabelle Foo pops up like the Devil himself on my left.

"Ha!" she says. "I thought you said you know everything about everybody? I thought you said you can go with them anytime?"

I refuse to look at her. "I can if I want to. I just didn't feel like it."

"So tell me then, where are they going?"

This time I widen my eyes at her to highlight her stupidity. "They're going to distribute posters. As if you don't know."

"Not my father and your mother lah. No need to play dumb. I'm asking about Leo and Reza."

"You think I've got nothing better to do than to keep track of their comings and goings?"

She smiles sweetly. Then placid as a cat she says, "Last time you used to be part of their gang, but now no more, hor?"

"So? I've got my own things to do sometimes."

She throws her head back to laugh. "Oh I see, your own things is it? Like shaking legs and scratching your backside? Like sitting in the library pretending to read the same book one hundred times? Like—"

"I'm not pretending. I like to read."

"I'm just saying, what for you so meek and mild? Scared of what?"

"Where got meek and mild?"

She rolls her eyes and sighs. "Come on lah. You talk big only, but actually you're like a mouse. Your brother and Leo got no time for you anymore so they just threw you away" —she flicks her fingers in the air like a nose-digger like that—"but instead of fighting back you just let them do what they like."

I'm drawing in my breath for a rejoinder when she says, "I know because I'm also like you. That's why I can recognize another sad case."

"You're nothing like me!"

"Haiyo calm down a bit lah. No need to shout. At least listen first then shout. My parents don't care about me. I tell you if I was lying down dead in front of them they'll just step over my body and keep walking. Your parents same what. You and me, our own mother and father also don't care about us. And now your brother some more. Same story. "

Like a boy with a sharp stick she has come poking into my shell. I want to give her two tight slaps. I picture myself biting her arm. The movement so sudden she will have no time to react before my teeth sink deep deep deep into that pale skin.

"Listen," she says. Her voice is different now, soft and full of susurrating menace. "You know why they go to town isn't it?"

"Why?"

"Okay then, if you want to pretend you don't know then I'll tell you. They are breaking all the rules. They eat meat in town. They drink beer. They smoke cigarettes. When they go to the river maybe they smoke other things too with those kampung boys. And you know what's the best part? They bring all those things back here to the toolshed. They eat meat in there, they drink alcohol, they smoke. Right here on the sacred ground of the Muhibbah Centre."

"Shut up your stupid mouth! They don't do those things."

She takes a deep breath before speaking again. "Fine," she says. "Here I thought you and me can be friends. I thought we can be on the same side we can help each other out we can make people respect us for once. But no. So fine. If you don't want to tell your father about it, I can tell him on my own."

The cold certainty of her *I can tell him* has not died away before it comes back to me in a flash: the sight of my father alone in his office with his face in his hands. She will see my panic in my eyes she will smell it on my breath she will hear it like a dog can hear the onset of an epileptic fit ...

"Go ahead and tell him," I say. "What do I care?"

It is a dangerous move. Just like that she could call my bluff. But it is the only move that has any chance of working because I know Annabelle Foo. If I beg her not to tell, I'm a gone case. I watch her closely. Two imperatives do battle in my breast: the first is to protect my father who is yes brave and strong but who has staked everything on us and is therefore as vulnerable to regret as any man who has ever staked everything; but the second which now twirls itself around the first like smoke threatening to choke it is this: I want Reza to get caught. I want to see him taken down a peg. To hear my father say to him: *You have disappointed me.* I want to see the light that shines in Papa's eyes when he looks at Reza dim forever.

Well I've rolled the dice. It's up to Annabelle now to decide.

When I see that first tiny hint of an almost-pout I breathe a silent sigh. Of relief? Of disappointment? Difficult to say. When she speaks her voice has lost its fighting spirit. It's low and quiet. Heavy as though with tears.

"I won't tell lah."

I don't make it easy for her but after a while she adds, "The thing is, I like Reza and Leo. Especially Reza."

She looks at me hopefully. Meaningfully.

"It's not that I want them to get into trouble," she says. "I don't know why we all can't just be friends."

"You can't force people to be your friend."

"No. But you said you can go with them anytime you want isn't it?"

"Ya, so?"

"In that case, next time bring me also."

"Just because they allow me to go with them doesn't mean they want the whole world to tag along."

"I didn't ask you what they want and don't want. I asked you to bring me."

We stand there looking at each other. She and I. Alike. Alert. Then out of the pocket of her shorts she extricates a folded-and-stapled piece of notebook paper.

"Here," she says. "Give it to Reza."

And finally it comes to me—oh dimmest of bulbs oh dullest of knives oh poor little fool—in a wash of heat and a lurching of the guts so acute I want to run to the john. How could I not have seen it? It is what Annabelle has been wanting all along. *Don't you know Mama likes men?* Reza said to me once years ago. *She's itchy like that.*

Don't say things like that, I said then. At the time I did not want to think about what it meant to like men or where exactly an itchy woman itched. Inside my head I drew up a list of things I would not believe and then I crossed them out with a big *X.* There. Gone.

Except it's back to haunt me. That *thing.* I look at Annabelle and wince. I still do not know exactly what it means to like men but what I do know is that it is a shameful and dirty weakness. It has to do with the shortness of Annabelle's skirts and the way she crosses her legs. The languid twirling of her hair around her fingers. The fringe allowed to grow too long and fall across her face just so she can toss it back. Her wet pink tongue and her sidelong glances. The too-big T-shirts always slipping down one shoulder to show off the bra strap.

I take the note from her. "Okay," I say. "Fine." I slip it into the front pocket of my shirt. Then I take it back to the Boys' Dormitory and bend the staples back. *Hi Reza!* it says in Annabelle Foo's bubblegum-sweet handwriting (a heart for the exclamation mark; little circles over the *i*s). *I can't stop thinking about you, what to do? Help me lah! Hahaha love Annabelle.*

From the empty kitchen I steal a match and burn the note on a saucer just to be sure. I crumble the silky ashes between my fingers and blow them away. As I do so I have the distinct sense of cleansing the house and the air and even my own body.

Ultimatum

"So how?" Annabelle Foo says. She has me cornered in the corridor outside the upstairs lavatory. It has been two days since she gave me the note for Reza.

I shrug.

"Don't know."

"Did Reza open my letter or not?"

"I didn't see him open it."

"Did you tell them I also want to come along in the van next time?"

I'm drawing in my breath to say *No not yet* when out of my mouth pops a fully formed lie unrecognizable to me (where has it been hiding? who planted it and watered it?).

"Yes I told them but they said cannot."

I watch her face. The foot-stamping exasperation of the princess who cannot have the moon quickly building to the purified rage of the queen whose mirror is telling her the inconvenient truth.

"Oh, they think they're so grand is it? Actually you know what? I don't need to ask their permission. When the van comes I also can talk to the men and ask them to give me a lift to town."

"Of course. But don't expect Reza and Leo to let you follow them around."

For a long moment she is silent. Then she says, "How come Reza didn't reply to my letter?"

"Don't know. That's his business."

"You gave it to him or not?"

"Of course I gave it to him! What else would I do with it? I wouldn't want to hang on to your disgusting letter."

"Why is it disgusting? How you know it's disgusting?"

"I know you. I know what type of girl you are. Only filthy things can come out of your filthy mind."

She throws her head back and hoots with laughter. "Oh, I'm the one with the filthy mind is it? And you? Sneaking around reading other people's letters, and just listen to yourself! You can only think of one thing! You're the one with the one-track mind! What were you thinking about when you read my letter? Never mind lah, no need to answer also. People who look at girls and say 'Ee-yer, I know what type of girl she is,' everybody knows what they're thinking about."

She folds her arms and studies me as though seeing me for the first time.

"So? After you read it? You gave it to him or not?"

"You asked me that already. I told you, yes I gave it to him. Satisfied?"

"So how come he didn't reply? How come he didn't say one single thing to me about it? Didn't even look at me also."

"I told you, I'm not in control of Reza. I can't force him to look at you."

But the old triumphal glint has crept into her eyes. For two days she has been weighing her options and refining her plans and now she thrusts her honed threat at me.

"He thinks he's so grand and special is it? Everybody sees his white face and treats him like God so now he really thinks he is God? You know or not, all I have to do is tell your father what they bring back from town and that's it. Last time you told me, *You want to tell, tell lah*, but you know what? If I tell, that's the end of your father. I bet he can take anything but not his favourite boy contaminating this whole holy house with *flesh foods*. Bringing *violence and death* into our life. And if it's the end of your father, it's the end of the Muhibbah Centre. It's the end of your whole life."

"Don't be stupid," I lie. "My father already *knows*. Everyone knows! It's not some big secret."

It's the only defence that presents itself to me in the moment but Annabelle sees expertly through it.

"Nonsense lah. Nobody can bear to tell your father. All sorts of things people hide from him, and you know what? It's not because they're afraid of him. It's because they feel like they have to take care of him. They can't bear to see what will happen to him if he knows. I just have to produce one piece of proof and your father will feel so shameful and so disappointed with his golden boy."

Her shrewdness astounds me. So clearly she has seen it: that I am afraid not for Reza but for my father. That I therefore fear Reza's exposure more than Reza himself does. Why else is she threatening me and not Reza? Reza wouldn't give two hoots. "Tell lah," he would say. Whereas I am the eternal sucker-upper. The toymaker's wooden boy who yearns to be real. The ungolden son who would settle for gold plating. She thinks she can get me to beg.

No way. I will not do it. I will not say what she wants to hear. She is shrewd but I am no fool and I know that such people are like dogs: the only way to handle them is never to show your fear. So I look at her straight in the eyes and I say again, "Go right ahead. Tell my father whatever you want. Nobody is going to believe you. Everyone knows you lah. Full of drama. My father will tell you to get lost and go to hell."

"Oh really? You think so?"

Even before she has finished speaking I have come up with a plan so brilliant it turns my mouth dry and makes my fingertips tingle. I will teach her. I will show everyone what type of girl she is.

"You can smile," she says. "But wait and see. I'm going to wipe that smile off your face forever."

I don't have to worry about her threats anymore. In one ear and out the other to float aimlessly in the air like dust motes.

Loose

Annabelle Foo thinks she has me up against the wall but the truth is that long before her note for Reza I already knew what she was, i.e. *asking for it*. Where did I hear that and who said it? As though all these phrases have been lying dormant waiting for the right season now they are sprouting in my head. Foreign implants. I myself have only a dim understanding of their meaning. Asking for what? What is the *it* in *asking for it*? Whatever it is the one who wants to give it to her is not Reza not Leo but George Cubinar. George Cubinar with his weedy moustache and his checked trousers. Underneath his earnest yes-man manner is this dirty secret. Annabelle Foo has only to sigh *Aiyo, poor me!* and offer herself up across the smudged surface of her maths exercise book—what a mess of cancellings and ink splatters and smears and Liquid Paper scabs!—and George Cubinar rushes to her side on bended knee. "Stay behind for extra help," he says. "I can tutor you this afternoon," he says. "You can be excused from the Nature Walk. We'll meet back here in the classroom after lunch."

And she smiles that pleased smile. "Sorry lah," she says. "I'm not so clever like the others." But her smile says, *I'm much cleverer than the others. I'm very clever indeed.*

In the classroom after lunch she sits next to him. She leans so close that her shoulder touches his. Her bare shoulder with the T-shirt sliding down. So wide she has cut the neckline that at times it slips down past both shoulders at once.

"I still don't understand," she says rubbing herself against him like a cat. "How many times you explain to me also I won't understand."

He backs away even if I am not mistaken moves his chair an imperceptible distance away. He clears his throat and still his voice is hoarse. "We'll just ... we'll just try that again."

"Thinks about her and touches his thing," Reza and Leo like to say. "Guess what," they say and their eyes dance about as they say it. "Sometimes we walk past his room at ten-eleven o'clock at night and we hear him. 'Yes yes oh yes,' he says and then faster and faster, 'yes yes oh yes yes yes oh yes' and all the time thinking you can be sure of it of Annabelle. Poor fler! Poor sad bastard."

Who knows if this is fantasy or slander or truth? Either way I feel no pity for George Cubinar. None whatsoever. Not *poor sad bastard* but shameless bastard. No pride, no self-respect. Why does he have to make his lusting after Annabelle Foo so obvious? If she wants to make a fool of herself must he also make a fool of himself? He's like an ugly insect that makes you want to squash it under your thumb. To pull off its wings and its legs one by one.

Sacrificing George Cubinar

It is also for Annabelle Foo's own good that I have to carry out my plan. Sure I will take some pleasure in it but my satisfaction and her benefit need not be mutually exclusive. She must not be allowed to do these things. She cannot be like this. Okay for now George rubs his thing in the privacy of his own room but then what? What comes next? Who even wants to find out?

So before Annabelle Foo can go to my father I go to him myself. I knock on the door and wait for his firm quiet *Come in.* When I go in he is so surprised he stands up.

"Yes?" he says. "Is everything all right?"

"Y-yes. I just ... I need to talk to you about something."

Knits his eyebrows. "Okay," he says. "Okay. Sit down, sit down."

But I don't sit and neither does he.

"You see, I wanted ... I should have come earlier but ... it's very hard to tell you—"

"What is it, boy? Just tell me."

His eyes are still not fully focused on me. He is distracted. A little put out by the interruption. Far far behind my eyes I feel the first faint prickle of tears. *Listen to me* I want to say but I must not beg. *Listen to me.* He thinks I am a smallboy come to talk about smallboy things. No. I will not be cheated out of my right to be heard.

I let it tumble out of me in a glorious rush.

"It's Annabelle Foo. She, I don't know how to say also, she's always looking at Mr Cubinar one kind, she always wants him to pay attention to her but not like how a teacher pays attention to a student, it's different, it's … I don't like it."

"My goodness," my father says and now finally he sits down. "My goodness."

But he does not say it like he has grasped the seriousness of the matter. That *my goodness*: gentle and almost mocking. A playing-along phrase to humour a child's fantasies. I have the urge to shout something anything that will break the perfect poise of my proud cruel father who thinks everybody is so wonderful, everybody except me. I cast around for evidence hideous enough to jolt him out of his complacency but what can I say what is it what is the thing I am looking for … Right there on the tip of my tongue it is, I can feel it like a small pill and if I concentrate hard enough on the picture of Annabelle in the classroom it will come to me. Speak! Speak now!

"I don't like the way she behaves, she wears short-short skirts and makes him look at her legs and then, and then he asks her to go for extra help and …"

I wring my hands and cast panicked glances out the window. From your great distance it is easy is it not to judge that lying deceitful boy? But I will tell you this: I was not acting. My anguish was real. My story took on a life of its own and possessed me entirely.

My father puts his fingertips together. Joins and unjoins them. Tap tap tap tap tap.

"They sit next to each other and she lets him touch her … her legs. Her *thighs*. And … and she likes it. She *wants* him to do that."

He stops tapping his fingers. His hands rest lightly together as though he is ready to say a prayer.

"How do you know that?" he says quietly.

My voice is not mine anymore; the words come from somewhere outside me from far beyond perhaps even from God himself.

"Because the other day I went back to the classroom to get my Composition book because I forgot it and when I reached there the door was open a bit."

"And?"

"I saw Mr Cubinar touching Annabelle's thigh."

But this image, hideous as it is, is only a recapitulation and already to my ears it sounds stale, so before my father can speak I go on.

"He was touching her thigh and ... and the other hand was on ... on her shirt. On the front part of her shirt. And she was smiling at him."

"Sit boy," my father says again.

This time I obey. I hang my head and say, "I couldn't stop thinking about it so I decided I should tell you."

To look at my father in this moment is to watch all the air slowly leaking out of him. His cheeks slacken. The skin under his eyelids sags. But I know something he does not know: this small disappointment serves to protect him from a far greater one. I have to stop Annabelle Foo before she comes up here and in three-four cruel sentences shows him how fragile his dream is. The younger generation in which he has banked all his hopes pissing on those hopes behind his back and the so-called Old Faithfuls paying lip service to his principles while closing one eye when it suits them. Beside all this what is the small shock of George Cubinar fondling Annabelle Foo's thighs? (Tell me: was I not right to bend the truth a little to save my father? In the end of course I only delayed the breaking of his heart. In the end I could not protect him.)

"You saw it?" he says.

I fight the urge to kick his leg or stamp my foot and growl *I already told you isn't it*. Go ahead then. Let him cross-examine me if he must. Let him ask me again and again as though I am a small child or an imbecile: "Are you sure? Are you sure you saw it?" All the time giving in to flights of fancy and look, look boy, here is a way out, here is a face-saving opportunity for you to retract your revelation and deny everything. I must speak calmly now and almost as quietly as him.

"Yes. I saw it."

He is silent for so long after this that I begin to wonder if I should get up and leave. But just as I am about to stand up he says, "Thank you for telling me, Kannu. I am very glad you told me."

Like that. He said my name. He must have said it before but I cannot remember; I have always been *boy* or *son* or *young man*. Not only has he said my name but he is looking at me. Looking at me for the first time in my life like I exist. Looking at me and *seeing* me. It is a sad look not a proud-father look but that is only to be expected: I have displayed the kind of bravery that can only make a father sad. And after all isn't this kind of sadness more rare and precious—more hard-won really—than simple pride? Annabelle Foo's twin sister Angela had to die to earn her parents' unending implacable grief but in dying she ensured that they would never see anything but her. I have not died of course but in my father's new gaze there is something of that eternal sadness.

"It is important for me to know these things," he says. "I do always hope that anybody here would come to me if ... if there is a problem. I hope that anybody would trust me like my own son does and not be frightened to come to me."

My own son. And the way he smiles: a wise and gentle smile that reaches across the desk and puts its hands on my shoulders.

"After all I am not God. I cannot be everywhere at once."

Still he smiles and now I see that the smile is in addition to being wise and gentle a deeply exhausted one. It is in fact the sort of smile one might expect God Himself to have.

"You must always come to me if anything is wrong. You must not be frightened."

A funny thing happens: although I was not frightened

no sooner has he said the word than I am frightened and I do not know why. I am shaky and shivery all over as though I am about to stand up and sing in front of a big audience. Frightened yes but admit it admit it say it out loud: my fear is tinged with excitement. An icy thrill. My father is still talking.

"It is for their own good that I must know about it if people are hurting each other, or even if … even if they are only in danger of hurting each other. It is so easy for one person to lead us all astray. It could destroy everything we have built here. Do you understand what I am saying, Kannu?"

"Yes Papa."

Against the rattan seat of my chair my thighs are sweating profusely. After another long silence he says, "Yes. Yes."

He says it as though he was waiting for my approval. As though my own *yes* has now decided something for him or given him some unspoken permission.

"Yes," he says a third time. "Yes, you will be my eyes and my ears. Isn't that so?"

Our culture has a vast vocabulary devoted to both the sin and the sinner: bodek angkat tripod ball-carrier ball-licker arse-licker. That is what you think I am doing, that is who you think I am. And you may be right after all that this instinct to seek approval is what brought me to my father's office but now as my father lays my solemn duty out before me something shifts. I am transformed. I have a purpose in this house: to save us all from weakness and disgrace. My whole body feels different. Awake. Alive. Resonant as a violin. The slightest vibration in the air will set me humming. I am ready. I am a part of something much bigger than my own self and my own life.

"Yes Papa."

My throat is like paper my eyeballs like ice. I am terrified.

Expulsion

The information spreads without anyone seeming to know the source: George Cubinar is leaving. George Cubinar has been *asked to leave*. For the first time in the history of our Eden someone has been banished from it. But neither Cyril Dragon nor George Cubinar himself issues an official statement. George Cubinar dusts off his one bag and packs it. Here in the Centre he grew into a man. Watched his feathery facial wisps develop into proper whiskers. Here someone had been proud of him. Not a father no he was never a real father of course. One has to be realistic and not expect too much of people. But thanks to Cyril Dragon George Cubinar had learned to feel safe and useful without the need for a diploma or a deadening office job. Learned to settle into this easy trusting God-serving example-setting life. Now what? Now his uncle will come and fetch him. His uncle whose letters fifteen years ago he crumpled up and threw out one after another. George Cubinar tries to picture the man he recalls grey or bald. Wrinkled and stooped. No matter: a car will be driven up the hill by a Eurasian-looking man of a certain age and George Cubinar will get into it.

What happened actually? Everyone wants to know. Adults children everyone. Then three days before the appointed Saturday, Annabelle Foo is called up to Cyril Dragon's office. She goes upstairs dry-eyed and comes downstairs puffy-faced and sniffling.

Despite my best efforts to paint Annabelle with equal if

not superior guilt it emerges that my father has taken her to be the victim of the piece. The whispered story makes its rounds: "George Cubinar 'did something' to Annabelle Foo. Poor girl." "*Did something* means what?" the children ask each other. I alone know exactly what it means. I am the author of the story but instead of their assigned parts one of my puppets has taken on a life of its own. I pluck at the strings. But it's no use; it's as though they've been snipped. Now I have to step back and watch in astonishment. Annabelle will not be shamed or stopped. Her filthy mind will not be fixed. Around me the adults shake their heads and say, "Who would have thought George Cubinar of all people could have had such a thing up his sleeve." On cue Annabelle disintegrates before their eyes into private nightmares and public sobs. She throws herself into the role of the Innocent.

But if I ever entertain any suspicions that she has lost her hold on reality I need only to catch her eye. I am the only one who can see it: that bright hard centre. Like sunlight on glass. It could almost blind you but the trick is not to look away. We look at each other—she and I—and nothing needs to be said. It is a win-win game after all (though not for George Cubinar). She gets the attention she has craved all her life, and thus satiated she shuts her mouth on the subject of Reza and Leo. I know that all I have bought myself is time but time is better than nothing. Some might say time is everything.

George Cubinar would have said to my father: "I never did it! Such a thing could never even enter my head!" It would have been his word against mine and my father would have chosen to believe me. Me over George Cubinar. My word over an adult's. Against my own status as an Innocent my father would have considered his lukewarm fondness and medium-grade protective instincts for George Cubinar. (Why not be honest? George Cubinar was never to my father what my father was to George Cubinar.) *From where would Kannan get the idea?* my father would have thought to himself. A boy utterly unexposed to the filth of Outside. Never even seen a film.

And so I enjoy my first taste of the power of the Word. I do not mean the Word of God but the Word of a child. I can make the world bend to my bidding. I can make my father open his eyes and look at me and hear all I have to say.

My father would not have revealed his informer's identity. "It has come to my attention," he would have said. Or, "A concerned member of our community has reported—" And George Cubinar would have sat there stunned. Half hearing the rest of Cyril Dragon's words as the faces of possible spiteful liars marched through his head in a grim parade. One of the other men perhaps jealous of George's daily proximity to the nubile young things he himself secretly lusted for? Mrs Arasu because her prudish heart was unpleasantly stirred up by all these girls' conspicuously imminent pubescence? Selwyn Foo giving in to a father's paranoia yet unable to admit to himself that even if anything had happened, his daughter—only look at her ever-shorter shorts and her constant feline posing!—bore at least half the blame? Who had it been? Who who who? Not once would my gormless moon face have participated in that parade. Goodbye George Cubinar. Good luck. Good life.

The Busybody

In mid-October we put up our sweetmeats-and-baked-goods stall in front of the Catholic church. This timing allows us to take advantage of both the Deepavali stock-uppers and the earlybird Christmas shoppers for in our business model as in everything else we are resolutely syncretic. We take the same spot that we have occupied every year for sixteen years because the Catholic priests will never report us for trading without a license. They may be suspicious of us they may consider us heretics or hippy-pagans but they will never report us because the enemies of their enemies are their friends. We are in this together: they and we against the forces of Islam and UMNO and everything-for-the-Malays. And so just outside their courtyard Mrs Arasu and Hilda Boey and whoever else wishes to help them spread out their wares in tupperwares and balangs and pre-sealed plastic packets.

Business is good this year. Who can say why? Perhaps the fame of Neela's palaharams and cakes has been subtly accumulating over the years and has now reached a tipping point. Perhaps Chernobyl has touched a nerve that other disasters did not. Whatever it is the cakes are sold out by three o'clock every afternoon and Neela is run ragged. A few customers place advance orders for office gatherings and Friday morning breakfast meetings and children's birthday parties and one woman even tries to order enough murukku to fill two suitcases to be sent to England with her daughter and distributed to all their relatives there.

"Our hot cakes are selling like hot cakes," Mrs Arasu says every day and every day Hilda Boey—sitting there with her big knees so wide apart the customers can see her panties—says flatly, "You really funny lah you."

Mrs Arasu makes note of the soaring demand and resolves to discuss it with Cyril Dragon. Perhaps for next year they should get hold of more cooks. Outside volunteers perhaps or even temporary paid help and then who knows how much money they could earn and to what great heights they could aspire. They could be like the Hare Krishnas or the Sai Babas: they could open branches and meetings halls in KL-Penang-Ipoh and maybe even overseas. The Hare Krishna movement has a venerable international history of course and the Muhibbah Centre has always had more modest aspirations but why should they limit themselves? Mrs Arasu believes with all her kiasu heart that Cyril Dragon's teachings could change not just Malaysia but the whole world if given enough light and air. Now people are hearing about them at last. Maybe Selwyn Foo's new posters were a good idea after all. Why be shy about their goals? It's the rest of the country that should be ashamed to admit what they are settling for. The bigotry underpinning their daily lives. Let them read and think for themselves.

One afternoon a Malay lady stops to pack a whole balang of vadai. A full five minutes she stands there nicely picking the fattest ones from the tray and yet it is not until her eyes begin to drift from the vadai that Mrs Arasu thinks to check that 1) the leaflets are hidden away, and 2) my mother who happens to be today's volunteer helper is not within reach of this lady's wandering gaze.

By design or by coincidence my mother is facing away from the road at that moment. Somebody has been remiss about the leaflets though: Mrs Arasu's eyes and the customer's fall at the same time on the stack right in the middle of the table.

Now this lady is not the first Malay customer at the annual stall in sixteen years. Many others have come and concentrated studiously on the edibles as befits our national character; whether they were genuinely unaware of the Muhibbah mission or were only pretending in order to be able to come and buy the famous vadai-murukku-jelebi nobody knew and nobody cared.

But just from the way this lady blinks her lizardy eyes as they fall upon the leaflets Mrs Arasu already knows that this is a different sort of character. With one oily hand (no plastic gloves tongs and all that in those days) the lady picks up a leaflet. Holds it between thumb and pointer finger as if she found it in the lavatory. At first her expression is just vaguely curious and then as she turns the pages a light switch goes on and something clicks and pops and the lizardy eyes turn bright and beady.

"Apa ni?" she says in a voice so nasal Mrs Arasu wonders if her whole head might be one solid rock with not a bubble of air anywhere in it.

Enunciating as carefully as a schoolgirl in an elocution contest Mrs Arasu replies, "All proceeds from the sales of these kuih go to charity."

"Charity? What charity?" quacks the Malay lady.

"Chernobyl. Ray-dee-ay-shun victims."

She thrusts the leaflet into the lady's hand so hard its pages flap in her face. After all the woman has already seen the thing isn't it? Might as well try and make the best of a bad situation. She adds, "All inside there, you just have to read only."

"Read of course I can read, but you all from where?"

"Can read means read lah!" Mrs Arasu's voice climbs higher and higher and Hilda Boey starts to look around in a panic.

Suddenly my mother steps forward and placing her hands carefully and neatly side by side on the table (a gesture Mrs Arasu will replicate every time she tells the story) she says, "From the Muhibbah Centre for World Peace."

The lady takes a moment to digest my mother's entering the fray. Then she says, "Christian is it?"

"Christian also can, Hindu also can, Buddhist also can ..."

Here Mrs Arasu fights the urge to pinch my mother under the table to make her stop but undeterred by Mrs Arasu's dear-God-please-shut-up vibes my mother finishes with a defiant flourish: "... even Muslim also can. Anybody can join our movement. We pray for world peace, that is all. Everything is in the leaflet, like my friend here said. In fact I only wrote that pamphlet. I wrote the whole thing myself. So if you want to know, just read."

The woman flips through the leaflet one more time.

"Hmm," she says. "So in past years you have helped Africa, India, Bangladesh. Not many Muslim countries unh? Chernobyl also not Muslim country. I don't mind buying your kuih but if the money is going towards something I don't agree ..."

She stops and looks squarely into my mother's eyes. "And you?" she says. "You ni muka macam Melayu, tapi you Christian ke? Serani ke apa?"

Mrs Arasu sniffs. Hilda Boey noisily chases flies off the stacks of vadai.

"Ee-yer!" she shouts. "So many flies lah today!"

"Why do you ask?" my mother says.

"I ask because I want to know. You're a Malay or not?"

My mother smiles her politest smile and replies, "I am not Muslim."

Without taking her eyes off my mother the woman says in her slow airless way, "Mmm mmm mmm, so anyway, I didn't know you all were collecting money for something else. I thought you buat business only. As a Muslim I cannot donate to this lah. I don't think I want to buy your vadai. I put back, okay?"

"Put back?" Mrs Arasu says. "What do you mean put back?"

"Since I cannot give you money takkan I want to take

them! What do you take me for? You think I'm a thief or a beggar, that I want to take food without paying? Come, come, I put back for you."

"Put back!" Mrs Arasu repeats, more shrilly this time. "You touch everything with your hand and now you want to put back!"

"Huh? Touch everything with my hand? Why, what's wrong with my hand? My hand probably cleaner than your kuih!"

Hilda Boey is standing up now. She plunges her fingers through her thin hair and works at her scalp in a kind of half massage half headscratch. A handful of people has gathered. No surprise knowing our Malaysian love of spectacle what. Anything will do. Car accident, police raid, moneylender's thugs at neighbour's gate—the more sensational the better.

Mrs Arasu knows that she needs to make some grand and flamboyant gesture to win the audience over to her side. She flares her nostrils and folds her arms. Not for nothing did she spend thirty-five years striking fear in the hearts of primary school children.

"Okay," she says. "Fine. You too cheap to pay for what you took means no need to pay. But we don't want your vadai back after you wiped your hands all over it."

She screws the red plastic top back onto the lady's balang with quick firm turns of the wrist and her mouth keeps going.

"Just because people are not Muslim you cannot donate a few dollars to help them is it? Then that is your prerogative. If that is what your great religion teaches you then everyone here should ask themselves—"

"Not to say just because people are not Muslim," the woman begins.

Then she must realize she has nowhere to go from there. She pauses for the briefest of moments casting about for some sharp weapon to wield against Mrs Arasu's unstoppable tongue. Her eyes fall once again on my mother's face. She juts her chin at my mother and demands, "So, may I ask what is your name?"

My mother bats her lashes and provides no clues to the workings of her brain.

"My name?" she says sweetly. "My name is Salmah."

She can hear Mrs Arasu and Hilda Boey stop breathing behind her. That sudden stillness broken only by the buzzing flies.

"Salmah?" says the Malay lady. "But Salmah memang Malay name what!"

"Oh," my mother says. "It's just a name. Anybody can have any name."

The Malay lady purses her lips and sniffs. "But how can—" she begins.

At once Mrs Arasu comes to her senses and swings back into action. With both hands she holds the balang of vadai out across the table to the lady.

"Fine!" she barks. "Take and go! Your few ringgit makes no difference to us in the end. But you know what?"

"What for I want the vadai?" the Malay lady protests. "If I'm not paying then I don't want—"

"You know what?" Mrs Arasu repeats. "God sees everything you do. Call Him what you want, that is up to you. But everything you do He can see. Just remember that. If you think your Allah wants you to turn a blind eye to other people's suffering just because they are not Muslim, then fine! You do as you think is right."

So hard she shoves the vadai at the Malay lady that the latter falls two steps backwards and grasping at the air in desperation to balance herself finds herself grabbing the unwanted balang. The audience senses that Mrs Arasu has pulled ahead by a sliver.

The unexpected silver lining of this brawl is that business that day roars more than ever. After the nosy lady leaves, the milling spectators poke around among the sweets-and-frieds. To peruse the leaflets and study my mother. As though by the cut of her face and the cadences of her speech they might know her whole story. How does a woman with a name like Salmah end up in hippy-dippy Christian-or-what utopian cult?

So they ask her quietly, "That means you're Eurasian?"

"Malay Chinese Indian Other, what does it matter?" she tells them. "I am one hundred per cent Malaysian!"

When the crowd has dispersed she says to no one in particular, "You see? I know how to regurgitate the great Cyril Dragon's script when I have to. Not bad huh? I also know how to keep up an act."

Mrs Arasu recovers quickly enough from her initial horror to reply, "Who is asking you to keep up any act? When you should lie you don't lie. You tell the woman your real name like it's nothing. Then proudly telling us you're keeping up an act. If you don't believe in our teachings you don't have to pretend, you know? Why not say, 'Yes I am Muslim, yes I am Malay'?"

"That would be lying," my mother says. "I'm not Muslim by that woman's standards. She would not consider me Muslim; she would consider me an apostate."

"And so? For the sake of a man you make fun of behind his back, you want to risk being charged with apostasy? What for?"

"Oh! It is not for his sake. Believe me, it is not for his sake."

It is the closest my mother has come so far to admitting that her marriage with my father is dead.

"Oh, so suddenly you are full of high-minded principles is it?" Mrs Arasu says. "You're standing up for your beliefs for their own sake? Tell me another one."

"What makes you think I have no principles?" Mama says. "Just because I'm not forever spitting out nonsense propaganda like the rest of you, you think I want to tell lies to save my own skin?"

Mrs Arasu draws her breath in and when she speaks her voice cracks.

"Please. Please, we have to be very careful. We have to stick together. Now that people know there's a Malay in our community it won't take long for the news to spread. The way things are now they won't think twice about sending someone to investigate us."

"So? Let them send someone then. Cyril Dragon himself has said he's not scared what."

"The problem is it's the rest of us who will get into trouble. That's how it always happens. In every situation you Naatukaran are let off with a slap on the wrist while the rest of us are drawn and quartered."

One might attribute her ill-advised recourse to the Tamil word—its Man-of-the-Land denotation so innocent its connotation so loaded with decades of resentment—to Mrs Arasu's shock and dismay. But my mother is not in the mood to be charitable. She shakes her head and laughs.

"Just listen to yourself," she says. "If only your great Cyril Dragon could hear you. All his preaching about one people one blood one God and after sixteen years of it this is still how you talk whenever he is not there!"

"Why?" Mrs Arasu says, spoiling for a fight now. "Are you claiming it's not true? Malays don't get special treatment?"

"Just listen to yourself!" Mama says again. "Us and them, us and them all the time. Why else do you say 'Naatukaran' instead of 'Malay'? You think I don't know it? How will you feel if I use the word keling to talk about Indians?"

"Oh please," Mrs Arasu says and turns away with a grandiose rolling of her eyes. "Spare me. Stop acting like you're the victim. Your kind own the whole bloody country and you're trying to tell me one word is some kind of atrocity. What difference would it make even if I said a thousand worse words?"

But her breath is unsteady her eyes are bulging right out

of their sockets and everyone can see she is trembling. *How dare she how dare that bloody Salmah how dare she drag all of them into the fire with her just for some purported reluctance to bend the truth? As though she is so honest and upright the rest of the time. Of all the times to choose to be faithful to the truth …*

Who is it who repeats that forbidden word Naatukaran back at the Centre? Surely not Mrs Arasu herself, which leaves my mother and Hilda Boey. Whichever one it is the end result is that we all hear about it. All except my father of course. And hearing it we—I—store it away for future use. In the meantime we ponder the implications of the incident. If we were paying attention we might be able to say to ourselves: *the end is nigh.* Because all things must come to an end after all—even the solid things even the sturdy things let alone the impossible things like dreams of Utopia.

Recognition

"I know what you did," Annabelle Foo says.

I am engrossed in my *Torah Stories for Children* on the back porch. Annabelle Foo has come out pretending to look here look there but we both know she came for me. I bat my lashes in confusion.

"What?" I say.

"It was you. You made up that story about George Cubinar. You were the one who got him in trouble."

"Prove it."

"Tsk. I'm not interested in proving it lah stupid."

"Then what are you interested in?" I ask her.

She gives me a long pointed look. "You want me to tell you what I'm interested in?"

"You want to tell me means tell me lah."

"I'm interested in your mother."

This is not what I expected but I run with it. "Hah!" I crow. "You're not the only one lah. Everybody is interested in my mother. A Malay lady who prays to Ganesha and Jesus, it's not every day people see such a thing."

Her smile turns sharp and narrow. "You're not supposed to say 'Malay,'" she says. "You're not even supposed to know those words."

"Who said? Nobody can control what they know and don't know. We can only control our actions."

Slowly and grandly she begins to clap.

"Wah!" she says. "So well you have learned your father's lessons."

I look away. If I were Reza or Leo I would spit into the grass now but I, I am not a spitting boy, and I would not be able to summon the spit now even if I wanted to.

"What do you want?" I say.

She folds her arms and now she too looks into the distance. "No need to talk about what I want lah," she says. "Instead of that let me make you an offer."

Let me make you an offer! Where she acquired the phrase no one can say. But while I am still turning it over in my mind she says, "Four eyes is better than two eyes. Yes or not?"

"What are you talking about?"

"Even the East German spies don't do their spying work all by themselves. They've got comrades and secret friends everywhere."

Now barely three inches separate her nose from mine. I shove her shoulder with the heel of my hand and turn away from her in disgust.

"Go away lah you stupid girl you."

"You're the one who's stupid Kannu. You want to make yourself so important but you don't know how. Let me tell you in simple English. Got a lot of things you don't even know about that you can report to your father. *Real* things I mean. You don't need to go around making up bullshit stories."

Then she watches me. She watches my eyes flicker this way that way. She watches in great satisfaction before offering, "Go and tell your father that my mother slaps me. Tell him that she *raises her hand in violence.* Whenever she feels like it some more. Not just once or twice in my life."

"What do I care? I'm sure you deserved it."

"I've not come crying to you lah. I'm telling you, if you want something to tell your father, you can go and tell him that. And then after that I'll give you more. I help you."

She leaves the second half unsaid but I hear it loud and clear nevertheless: *I help you, you help me.* I look at her standing there. One leg bent to rest the tips of the toes delicately on the floor. Lord Krishna in his flute-playing pose.

"So what do you get out of it?" I say. "*Poor Annabelle Foo, poor Annabelle Foo* not enough ah?"

She shrugs. "Not enough lah I suppose. Okay? Happy now?"

"Look, Reza is not going to kneel like a prince and ask you to marry him because your mother slapped you. Reza is not going to give two hoots."

"Hai, hai, Kannu. You really quite stupid, huh? I know a lot of things that you don't know. I can always go to your father myself. If you can't fix a day for me to go in the van with Reza and Leo, I also know the way to your father's office. I've got a few things to tell him."

A few things. Then itself I should have taken note of the phrase but I dismissed it as nothing more than talking big.

"Why do you keep threatening to tell about Reza and Leo?" I say. "I told you already isn't it? I'm not scared."

"You think you're such a good liar, but you're not lah, Kannu. Everyone can see: you're a small frightened boy. A mouse. A sneaky mouse with sharp teeth but still a mouse. You don't even know how to get your own parents to look at you."

Many times in my life to come I will remember this conversation and the feeling that comes over me in that moment: a surge from the bottom of my belly to the roots of my hair. I am like one of those see-through clocks: she has studied my workings and determined exactly where and how to introduce her grains of sand in order to cause maximum damage. But what hope have I got of doing the same to her? She is eight years older a whole foot taller and twice as strong. And though I do know what she wants I am powerless. Even as I deliver my desultory blow I know it: just like Reza and Leo she doesn't care what I think or say.

"As though *your* parents pay attention to *you*."

"I knew you would say that," she says, "but I don't waste all my time angling for it like you." She's laughing now as she looks at me. "Don't worry," she goes on. "You still got time lah. You can ask the van flers directly. You just tell them, my friend Annabelle wants to go with you next time."

"And? What will that achieve? You can go in the van as much as you like and Reza will still ignore you lah. You're pathetic."

"Hmm, hmm. I tell you what, Kannu: you worry about your part and let me worry about that part, okay?"

"I'm not going to do your dirty work. You want you tell Cyril Dragon about your mother yourself."

She's opened her mouth to retort when some new thought appears to stop her. She frowns as though seriously considering the option. "I could," she says. "Actually I could. It's only if you want to keep your new secret post as your father's right-hand man."

How to take this and run without admitting defeat?

"Fine," I say. "Fine, I'll tell him. But the next thing you want me to report better not be your own sob story."

"Oh, don't worry, don't worry. I got plenty of material for you."

And so we stand there regarding each other. Accomplices. Opponents. Same-boaters. Schemers.

Eighty-Three

Dawood falls on his knees and sobs in my front hall.

"I knew it would be like this! I knew it from the beginning, I knew it, I feared the worst. To have the police banging on the door like that! Have we become that kind of family? All the neighbours would have seen."

"It doesn't mean he had anything to do with it. They have to take every precaution. They'll round up everyone who knew those flers, everyone who's ever had a cup of coffee with them or talked to them at the mosque. They'll question them, and then they'll let them go. You wait and see."

"He had nothing to do with it," Mama says. "He wouldn't get involved with all that. I know Amar. He's not that type."

"Not that type, not that type," Dawood groans. "Who knows what type anybody is anymore? When he was small we would have said he was not the type who'll be walking around in a full beard and robe."

He lifts his whole arm to his eyes like a small boy being punished. "Eighty-three people dead!" he says under his breath. "Eighty-three people! To think he could have been mixed up in that!"

We've all seen the eighty-three faces. We know their names and ages and occupations by heart (we are after all a byhearting people). We've convinced ourselves we knew them personally—even intimately—because doesn't this man look just like our uncle and couldn't that student be the twin sister of the barista at that coffeehouse and look this young mother's children are exactly the same age as ours. The victims are Malay Indian Chinese Other even one Nepali and two Myanmar nationals but for once we have found common ground with migrant workers. We can all agree that the universal Muslim Extremist bogeyman is worse than any pendatang asing. We are in short more united than we have ever been since 1957. Impossible not to think of my father. Impossible not to whisper to the un-hearing memory of him: "One people at last!" At least for now. Turns out this was the price we had to pay for unity.

It is Malaysia's First Time. Our first real entry in the record books of violent terrorism and no one can argue we've not come in with a bang. Five nearly simultaneous explosions.

"When it happened," I ask Dawood, "what did he tell you?"

"Nothing! He didn't say anything. We all saw it on the news together. We didn't know what to think. After the bomb in Chow Kit we all thought ya Allah what will become of this country? Then see-see another one and another one and another one. Pudu. Bukit Bintang. Petaling Street. Mid Valley Megamall. Like a nightmare. I thought I must be dreaming. I saw he was acting one kind. Didn't want to look at us. Walking here walking there like a cat that just had kittens like that. Couldn't keep quiet, couldn't sit down. So I gathered up my courage and I asked him point blank: 'Were you involved in this?'"

"And?"

"He broke down and cried, I tell you. He said no. He said please believe him."

"Poor boy, poor boy," moans Mama.

Dawood goes on. "He said he might have met one of those flers once or twice but he didn't really know them. He said the one he met liked to talk big but he thought that's all it was. Big talk, you know? He told me, 'I believe in the Caliphate but I don't believe in violence. I don't believe in killing people, I keep away from all those flers.' But when the police came—"

His voice cracks.

"When the police came?"

"They said—my god, Encik Yusuf, my god, I don't know what to tell you also!"

"Just tell me."

"They said they were rounding up people who had expressed support for ISIS. I looked at him and said, 'What is this?' And later his sister tells me, on the Facebook they all had ISIS flags, they were pretending to shoot guns, they were putting all the jihad surahs from the Quran. Facebook and Instagram and Twitter and all that, you know all these things, Encik Yusuf?"

"A bit."

"You knew this was happening, ISIS in our own country?"

"Knew or didn't know, I don't know how to answer that, Dawood, I mean, I didn't go looking for proof, but ... you could say I never ruled it out. You could say I always assume these things are happening somewhere, even if I don't see them."

"Ah, you are wiser than me, brother, you are wiser than me! I never thought ... I mean there were always rumours that it was getting worse after the government changed, it seems the extremists were instigating people, I know, I saw how every little thing also they would point a finger and say look, they're sidelining Muslims, they're taking away the status of Islam, they're selling the country to the Christians and the godless people, but I thought those flers trying to round up Muslims to fight were ... I just never thought ... I mean, my own *son*, Encik Yusuf! Only when my daughter told me about the Facebook and all that, then only I started thinking about how he has been rushing around like an international businessman these past two-three months. I said to her, 'Why didn't you tell me before?' and she just looked at me. Because I swear to you, Encik Yusuf, if I had known, I would not have hesitated to go to the police about my own son. I would not have hesitated for one single minute."

"No!" Mama insists. "No, no, no. Don't you understand? It is just playacting for their friends. Each one wants to be bigger than the other one. Boys have always been like this. In another place, another time, they might have been competing to see how many girlfriends each one had. Now it is this kind of jihad talk."

"But then ... but then why was he so busy? What was he planning and plotting?"

"That I don't know," Mama says. "Maybe we'll never know. Could be that somebody was trying to drag him into it, could be he went to a couple of meetings and then got scared. After all he told you he'd met a few of them isn't it?"

He's rocking back and forth. Under his breath he's saying *astaghfirullah astaghfirullah astaghfirullah*.

"Pull yourself together, Dawood," Mama says. "It is not the end of the world. Everything will be fine. In fact this experience will be good for him. Maybe now he will be a bit more careful about whom he mixes with and how he talks."

"But everybody will come to know!" Dawood protests. "Even now everybody knows already. Neighbours friends relatives. People will talk and everybody will think he's an extremist for the rest of his life. People don't forget these things."

"They will. They will, Dawood, don't worry! And the boy himself won't be taken in by every nutcase leader. Instead of trying to show others how strong his faith is he will learn to think for himself," Mama says.

Dawood looks at her. Remembers perhaps that she speaks from experience. Whether or not he knows our past her words calm him a little.

"But people won't trust us anymore," he says. "They'll keep their distance."

He seems now to be persisting almost out of habit or obligation. We give him a mug of strong hot milky tea. We sit with him in silence. When we hear the Maghrib call to prayer we send him home.

It's not hard to find Amar's Facebook page. Real name real photo. But all the bluster about jihad is gone. Oh sure there are surahs. Surahs for calming your fears. Surahs for strengthening your faith. Surahs for warding off temptation. But nothing about jihad. Nothing about infidels. No ISIS flags. Of course he would have taken it all down in those hours between the bombs and the police arriving. Who wouldn't do the same in a panic? It doesn't mean anything. Seventeen years old. Doesn't remember 9/11. Doesn't remember the Gulf War. Just a boy caught up in somebody else's web.

That evening while Mama is watching the latest news reports on TV I go into her room and take down Amar's photo album from the high shelf where it sits next to Reza's. He faces me squarely from this safe remove of nearly two decades: the tiny steely-eyed baby on his teddy-bear pillow, the little boy pretending his tricycle is a speedy-fast zoom-zoom motorbike, the prizewinning schoolboy with his spotless scrubbed face.

Of course Amar is not part of this jihadi cell. Somehow—call it instinct—I have no doubt about that. It is not in his makeup. His rigid piety is cut from a different cloth. They release him with no charge the very next day. He comes home chastened and peakish to be fed bubur lambuk and a neverending string of questions by his mother: "Where were you going every day these past few months? With whom? Did the police ask you what you knew? Did you tell them everything? Are you sure? You gave them names?"

The day after that they release the identities and photos of the suicide bombers. I cannot look at those five faces without stripping the years away. Propping them up on teddy-bear pillows. Sticking dummies in their soft bubbling baby mouths. Sitting them on the seats of red tricycles. They are nothing like Amar on the surface. No beards no robes. A bunch of rough-tough gangsters at loose ends. A security guard. An engineering dropout. Two brothers running a satay stall and a car mechanic. Once they were babies and now they will hang. Their mothers will put their photo albums on high shelves. In secret they will take them out to turn the pages. Their mouths dry and their hearts overflowing with questions even after twenty-thirty-forty years.

And then I think of my father. The words *if only* come stealing into my head like jewel beetles. But if only what? If only he'd lived? By the time we left the house in the hills he had no hope of changing the course of history. One man cannot change the course of history alone. My father's idols—Jesus Gandhi Martin Luther King—lived in other times and other places. A tidal wave of followers rose up under those men. People were more desperate and braver perhaps. My father only had his motley dozen. He could not have prevented these eighty-three deaths by living longer. Think of the price he paid for living even as briefly and quietly as he did. Asthma attack they said sudden death they said and what was I to know of the many possible horrors? A mercy indeed and not a very small one: my dark imaginings were blurry.

But I am no longer the boy I was then. Even as time chipped away at the edges of my nightmares all the tales I heard over the years polished them to a diamond brilliance. The lacerations all over this dead prisoner's body, the nails strangely missing from the toes of that other one who supposedly committed suicide in custody, the nosy parkers pushed off balconies, the whistleblowers bound and gagged and stuffed into drumfuls of cement. All the methods our old government had for digging its claws into the shrivelled remnants of power and holding on.

So *if only* what, Kannu, if only *what* exactly? They would have destroyed your father anyway sooner or later. They would have found a way. He alone could not have changed them and as for the rest of us we did not care enough to risk anything that mattered. It was all a pleasant enough experiment but in the end our cari makan priorities would have prevailed. We would still be sitting under the ceiling fan studying these eighty-three faces in the newspaper while eating our roti canai roti telur roti bawang roti sardin roti tisu roti planta roti pisang and yes even roti bom because if ever there has been a people who would not flinch at ordering roti bom the morning after a bom that would be us.

The monster was already being handfed in its underground cave while my father was building his little utopia. How futile how desperate his attempt and he himself knew it. And then after his death all those years of pretending to fight that monster. An anti-terror raid here and there, while there and here a foreign-imported extremist preacher is presented with PR status on a silver platter. The fat cats purring on TV to soothe us after each close shave and then back to business as usual.

Maybe what I really mean by *if only* is exactly that. If only we'd cared more. If only we'd been more desperate. If only we'd all dared to dream a different dream.

Aftershock

We are watching yet another rehash of the Terrorist Attack on TV when Ani says (barely loudly enough for me to decipher her words), "No place is safe anymore I suppose. Anything could happen anywhere."

One cannot expect to feel otherwise after a daily diet of Terrorist Attack Replay and Analysis. I reach for the remote and switch off the TV.

"I know it feels like that," I say. "But these incidents are still so rare. We're still more likely to die in a car crash than a suicide bombing."

"All this time," she says as though I haven't spoken, "we Indonesians always thought Malaysia was safer. We thought this type of thing could happen in Jakarta but never KL."

"The way they're cracking down on every fool who's ever admired ISIS on Facebook, I don't think it'll happen again anytime soon in KL. I wouldn't worry."

Then as though she can no longer bear to hold the words in her mouth she spits them out: "I've been thinking about going back, tuan."

"Going back?"

"I'm not getting any younger. My parents are so old now and I don't even know my own nieces and nephews. So many were born after I left."

"But Nenek depends on you, Ani! How can we get a new maid now when she's so old and so used to you? Can't you go and see them and then come back as usual?"

She turns her face away from me. Her chest rises and falls like she's struggling to hold in some intense emotion.

"I know," she says at last. "I know Nenek depends on me. But it's not just me. I thought ... I think I should take Hana back. She's just not herself. I'm not sure if you've noticed, but she's been so scared since the bombings. So scared of everything."

"The bombings? Is she scared of bombs, or is she just sad her boyfriend played her out?"

Ani looks at me reproachfully. "Maybe you just won't be able to understand, tuan. In a way I suppose it's everything. First the boyfriend, then ..." She shakes her head. "Anyway," she says. "It doesn't matter. She's falling apart, she's not doing well at all, and I think I should take her back. If ... if anything happened, her parents would never forgive me."

"Even if you have to take her back, why would you have to stay? You can take her there and then come back, can't you?"

She nods slowly. "Yes," she says. "Yes, I suppose I could. I'll talk to her about it. Start making the necessary arrangements."

Before my eyes the future shapeshifts again. Just as easily as Hana came into our lives she will leave it. Let me not pretend I won't be mourning her. But really what I will mourn is not Hana as she is—I will mourn Hana as she could have been. As *we* could have been. A close-knit if unusual family beating our own path to happily-ever-after. Grandmother Father Daughter Auntie. All that disappeared with the arrival of the Bangladeshi boyfriend but it seems his departure could not bring it back. One might be mesmerized by the reflection of the moon in a still, glassy lake when suddenly some large object falls into the water and shatters the picture. One might say to oneself: *Never mind. When the water settles, the moon will be there again.* But lo and behold the clouds move in and smother the moon and the water remains dark. All you have left is the moon in your head. Hana came and now she must go. Yet our lives will not be what they were before. It's true nothing lasts forever but just because a thing doesn't last forever doesn't mean it has no value. I'm not going to waste the rest of my days chasing after false forevers. Let me instead be thankful for the beautiful things that have passed through my life. The pleasures that are all the more precious because they are fleeting.

Reconnaissance

Some of us are outside for gardening duty when the steel-blue car appears down below making its slowly narrowing circle up the hill.

"Must be going to the Catholic Priests' House," Mrs Arasu says.

But the car glides past Father Dubois pacing with his missal to continue up the hill. By the time it is crunching our gravel, someone has gone to get Cyril Dragon from his office. A Malay lady climbs out of the car. Despite our conditioning to disregard status symbols we can all tell that she is dressed expensively. She is wearing a baju kurung of shiny-but-not-too-shiny fabric. Plum-coloured with tiny white polka dots. Around her neck a silk scarf to illustrate the power of the air-conditioning in her car. Great monuments of the Western world are printed on this scarf: the Eiffel Tower, the Leaning Tower of Pisa, Westminster Abbey and the Houses of Parliament, an impressive domed building I do not recognize. On the lady's forehead is perched a pair of sunglasses in a heavy tortoiseshell frame.

The lady turns to Mrs Arasu with a not-quite-apologetic simper.

"I am looking for my cousin," she says. "Salmah? Salmah binti Majid? If I'm not mistaken she stays here?"

Mrs Arasu repeats flatly, "Your cousin." It is not a question.

"Correct. May I please see her?"

In an attempt to invest herself with authority Mrs Arasu

pulls herself up to her full five foot two and says, "And you are?"

"I thought I told you already. I am Salmah's cousin. I would like to see her."

Mrs Arasu sinks an inch. Her bosom deflates a tiny bit. "I believe someone has already gone to call Salmah."

But of course it is not Mama who comes. It is Papa—neither smiling nor unsmiling and already holding out his ready-to-shake hand like a politician. The lady does not take it.

"I am Salmah binti Majid's first cousin," she says. "I would like to see her in person. I believe she is one of your ... I was told she is here."

"Of course," my father says. "Of course you can see her. We have no problem whatsoever with that. Did she invite you to visit her?"

The lady narrows her eyes.

"No. No, she did not *invite* me. I am here because I am concerned about her and most of all about her children. There are two children, am I right?"

Mrs Arasu's hand is suddenly on my back. "You just keep quiet," she hisses. "Don't say anything." As though I had any intention of doing otherwise.

"You are concerned?" Cyril Dragon says. "What exactly are your concerns?"

Like a traffic policeman the lady holds up one hand. "Please," she says. "I don't want to discuss this with you. I want to see my cousin."

My father looks past her shoulder to the group of us standing with Mrs Arasu. He makes no eye contact with me.

"Kiranjit," he says. "Please go and fetch Salmah. She might be in the Recreation Lounge or otherwise in the Library."

Kiranjit plods off obediently. My father turns back to the lady and says, "I'm sure she'll be here shortly. Now if you don't mind my asking while we wait, what are your concerns?"

The lady leans forward and folds her arms. "My cousin is Muslim. As you know."

"We have no religious restrictions. Our people were raised in many different faiths."

"*You* have no religious restrictions! I am not asking you what restrictions *you* have. It is against *our* religion for my cousin to be here. And you might like to know that it is against the law as well. But why am I discussing this with you? I want to see my cousin."

But there is still no sign of my mother. My father turns around, squints at the house and says, "I'm sure she will be here shortly."

"In that case can I see the children? Can I see my nephew? Nephews? Is it two boys?"

Nephews! We are her nephews. I turn the word around in my head. I am wary of this woman. I am not sure I like her at all. And yet: *nephews.* I am a boy with blood ties beyond the Centre. The Muhibbah Centre was a bubble out of space and time and now suddenly it is not: I am a nephew. I study this woman for signs of resemblance. Not the nasal voice. Not the broad face. But who can tell what her features are like under all that makeup?

My father draws his breath in. "Two boys. Yes. But they are children. They are minors. You would need parental consent to talk to them."

"Parental consent! So all this time you're just pretending! I knew it anyway, I knew it! Just give me some polite bullshit and hope to get rid of me quickly. But I want to see those children, and I want to see my cousin today. I am warning you. What you are doing is illegal and I am warning you: you may not know but Salmah is from a powerful family. We have connections. Just like that I can get this place shut down and get the lot of you hauled off to jail. Just like that. You do what you like, that's your business, but you leave Muslims out of it. That's the law in this country. You know that anyway. I think you know that very well."

Mrs Arasu begins to shepherd us back into the house. In the corridor she mutters to Hilda Boey, "I told you isn't it? See how fast the news travels? These Malays just *loooove* to mind each other's business. From the beginning itself I said, we're just asking for trouble. Of course now how can Cyril Dragon turn back? She is not just a member of the community, she is his wife. She is the mother of his son. Now how?"

Hilda Boey shakes and shakes her head. "I myself don't know," she says. "I myself don't know."

Through the window on the landing I can see my father reasoning with the Malay lady as my mother continues to fail to appear. And then—after what seems like hours—she steps out onto the porch. She does not rush towards the lady. She does not greet her with open arms. Her arms hang limply at her sides. I cannot hear what they say but I can see my mother stiffen and fold her arms, hunch her shoulders to turn her back into a turtle shell. I can see her shrug and thrust her stubborn chin out as she speaks. I can see the other lady wag her finger at my mother like a soothsayer out of a folk tale. Then even this becomes insufficient: she pitches forward onto the balls of her high-heeled feet and jabs that finger at my mother's chest. My mother refuses to back away. There she stands solid as a small tree. Impossible to see from my angle if this self-proclaimed cousin has actually touched her or not.

Here is what I must confess: it is not the interaction between my mother and the lady that consumes me. To anyone else the main action of the piece is unfolding between those two women. One dark one fair. One shouty one sullen. But my whole body is tuned in to what is (or isn't) going on between my parents. They have not drawn closer together like the allies one might expect them to be in this situation. My father has not put a protective arm around my mother. They exchange no glances of solidarity or understanding. As my father begins to intervene my mother folds her arms and moves deliberately away from him as though he might be carrying some foul disease. The more he talks the further she edges away from him until two full feet of frozen air stretch between them. As my father reaches the climax of his impassioned monologue my mother finally darts him a single furtive look. Now that he is so wrapped up in the moment she can be sure he will not happen to catch the expression in her eyes. I myself do not actually catch it. But I do not have to see this look at all to recognize it from the twitching of her shoulders. It is a look of ... perhaps not hatred not yet at least but something very like disgust. A fed-up sick-of-you please-shut-up look.

And in that moment I cease to fear the visitor. She is no longer the danger. Whatever Mrs Arasu might say to me (*You keep quiet you don't say anything you go inside now*) or to Hilda Boey (*See how fast the news travels!*) or to Gurmeet Gill (*You know lah these Naatukaran! Once they get hold of you, finish man. We're finished!*), I know that the true danger is among us. Within us. We are finishing. We might even already be finished. In the end the lady turns on her disgusted heels and slams the car door to be borne off at high speed by her trusty chauffeur. But what does that matter when my father and mother can do her work without her? My mother's long murderous glance slides into my father's chest like a stiletto blade. *How the bloody hell* did *I end up here?* she is thinking. *For what am I defending all this?* And long after she has gone back into the house he stands there on the porch. Doubt spreading like an oil slick and him a sad sea bird with soaked feathers. Shivering in the cold with nothing to say and nowhere to go.

Distraction

MAY 1987

We are one body Papa always says. If one part is sullied the whole is contaminated. *A dot of indigo in a pot of milk*: and how proud he is to cite the idiom in translation. How pleased to be able to celebrate Malay culture to demonstrate his all-embracing principles. Only long afterwards will I learn that he either misunderstood or misrepresented this expression which is in fact all about reputation. The pot of milk is not what you are but what people say about you. Whereas what Papa believes is that one person's unclean thought or act could truly ruin all of us. All the drops of ink he does not see! One day his eyes will snap open to find the milk bright blue.

And so I bear these small offerings to him between my teeth like a cat leaving decapitated mice on its master's doormat:

Estelle Foo slaps Annabelle sometimes.

Mrs Arasu uses race words.

"Race words?" he says. And I say "Yes. Naatukaran. Chinaman. Like that."

"Oh dear," he mumbles. "How distressing." And then in a less mumbly fashion, "Thank you, Kannu. It is good to see that you care so much about our movement. About our principles and our vision. Yes, yes, very good."

Of course I do not expect the impressive effects of the very first accusation. Estelle Foo and Mrs Arasu are not expelled from Eden but pulled aside for quiet talks. Afterwards they may or may not be a wee bit subdued. How to tell?

With Annabelle Foo I play it cool. "I also got eyes lah," I tell her. "What you know I've already known for years."

Yet a new desperation is taking hold of me. Though I could become his favourite son if I wanted. Slowly-slowly I could manage it. The prize is within my reach. It's just that an urgent new mission has presented itself. Actually it has been there all the while staring me in the face. Mama's hidden fashion magazines. The lingering smell of smoke in the toilets. Her rolling eyes and sharp tongue. Except before, I observed these things and that was that. I did not consider it my business to fix what was breaking. It is only now—after the scene on the porch with the cousin—that I have understood what this new mission is. I cannot fix anything that is happening to Mama, I can only distract Papa from it.

So I may yawn and scoff at Annabelle Foo but I wait eagerly for her titbits. She is a carrion feeder dropping her morsels at my feet but so what? How is my father to know and why would he care that I did not kill the mice myself?

One day she tells me, "That Neela. She is the worst one. Other people at least came here for good reasons. Maybe bit by bit they got lazy or they forgot but at least in the beginning they had those grand dreams. Not Neela. She just came here to take advantage. To have an easy life for herself and her stupid son. Free room and board. If not she'll have to be washing dishes somewhere or scrubbing toilets isn't it?"

I wait for her to work her way in to the soft centre of her prey. The liver and kidneys and spleen.

"I've seen the type of person she is," Annabelle says. "Do you know she keeps aside the best parts of everything for her own son?"

"The best parts of what?"

"She *steals*. She steals from the kitchen. Just watch her and see if you don't believe me. She'll hide-hide and give her son extra portions. I've seen her do it for Deepavali, I've seen her do it for Hari Raya. And even on normal days. She takes out the ripest mango and the sweetest papaya and she hides it just for him. Can you believe it? She's just the *cook* here. She's supposed to be working for *us*. But she thinks she and her son are better than us."

The thought of it—the image of those thin quick hands flicking a mango here spiriting away a papaya slice there—twists its blade into me. But it isn't indignation that has left me gasping. It's the deepest saddest longing in the history of the world. How is it that I recognize it immediately—as though it were an old friend—although I do not know its name? What is it I'm longing for? Someone to squirrel away treats for me? A mother desperate enough to flee everything except me, the way Neela ran with Leo and Mama ran with Reza? Someone who picked me and only me as the other half of their team.

I shrug and roll my eyes at Annabelle but day by day her words worm their way up through the chambers of my heart secreting an urge to provoke my father to anger. To win. But here dear reader is where you are mistaken: you think it is the old jealousy. Sibling rivalry. Reza might be titillating entertaining intriguing but I am *useful*. Papa *needs* me. The rivalry is not gone of course, deep inside me it circles and swirls, circles and swirls quietly. But the darkest clouds are not those anymore: at some point Leo became the principal object of my jealousy.

So that now I see so clearly what I did not see before: Leo it is who has everything I want and do not have. A mother so fiercely on his side that she is willing to break all the laws of the universe for him; a life free of shame and guilt despite all these sins committed in his name; and my brother. Leo has my brother.

Spurned

I'm sitting on my hands in the chair across from my father in his office.

"It's not ... something about Mama, is it?" my father asks. His throat is dry, the fine lines on his face as clear as pen-and-ink strokes.

About Mama! He thinks I have come all the way up to his office to tell him about the glossy magazines and the toilet cigarettes.

"It's not about Mama. It's about Neela."

All at once his eyes dull. A transformation as visible and inarguable as the membrane drawn across the eye of a cat.

"She steals from the kitchen," I press on. "She takes things and puts them aside for Leo. I just thought maybe I better tell somebody just in case ..."

When he looks at me his eyes are clear again. Clearer in fact than I have seen them in many months. Like a skewer his gaze pierces my fumbling.

"It's okay, Kannu. No need to worry about Neela. You see ..." He shakes his head and starts over. "We have so much and Neela has—had—so very little. We have all been so fortunate compared to her. She has had a hard life, you know. A very difficult and ... uncertain ... life. We cannot talk about changing the world if right in front of us we have people like Neela and we count every penny and every grain of rice."

Shame blazes in my ears. Hopelessly I begin, "I know, I wasn't trying to ... I just—"

"No, no, I am not scolding you, Kannu. When you help me to help others I am grateful. But there are some things that cannot possibly be wrong in God's eyes when a person has had so little. Even if ... even if they seem to be against our small human rules. You mustn't ..."

The words seem to dissolve in his mouth. He turns away to gather his thoughts. Then he looks back at me and says very quietly, "You're a good boy. But please, please, Kannu, leave Neela alone. You see—she suffered a lot, and in the beginning, people ... we all made a lot of mistakes. She wasn't accepted here. Let her have some peace now. If she's not perfect, that's all right. Don't go after her like that."

My hands are trembling and I am already standing up. I do not want my father to see my burning ears or my shaking hands. I do not want him to hear my voice sagging with the weight of my tears. I have to speak quickly and briefly, "Okay. Okay, Papa. Good night."

In the corridor the lump in my throat swells and swells and there in the dark it bursts and spills its salty cargo down my hot cheeks. I am ashamed to have chosen wrong. To have misstepped—overstepped—presumed myself to be wiser than I am—but all that does not explain the furious mournful beating of my heart. Like a Chinese funeral drum in my ribcage and nothing I do will quiet it now. What have I done? What did I say? Why do I feel like a fallen angel? *Please leave Neela alone. Don't go after her like that.* Like as though I was a hunting hound and Neela a terrified fox too tired to run any further. And his voice! His quiet cracking voice! All of a sudden and without meaning to I have flipped and I am the master holding all the strings in my hand and he ... well no. He is not even the servant. He is the beggar. He is the supplicant. And I am not just the master but the Cruel King. *No, I should have said, No, please, Papa, that is not who I am! I am not cruel! I am not evil! I am a good boy, I am, I am!* But I did not dare to say it. I am a good boy but I am a coward. And now ... and now it is too late. When my father looks at me he will see the Cruel King in training.

Salmah Unleashed

As doddering and liver-spotted as Father Vincent Dubois is his visit that July unleashes something in my mother. Where before she might have muttered a *my great husband* or dropped a subtle eyeroll-and-sigh here and there she now lets loose at full volume as and when she pleases. One day in the middle of her lunch she wipes her fingertips over and over again on her serviette and launches into her new favourite subject with unprecedented vigour.

"You know what my husband. The great hero. Not frightened of Mahathir, not frightened of the army, not frightened of anything."

What I have been thinking and feeling she has said out loud but no sooner has she said it than my ache to protect my father comes back sharper than ever. It falls to me to witness Papa's visible confusion now because nobody else is going to be brave enough to do so. I must bear the bulk of the burden. Father Dubois's prognostications were nothing to him but this—this public denouncing by a woman he still loves despite everything—has stung him.

"Well," says Mrs Arasu with her voice on full blast like she is selling something, "well, if Cyril is forced to take a last stand it will be because of you, Salmah, so you should be thankful isn't it? It is for you he has taken such a risk."

Under the graveyard stillness of her face something gleams like gold coins. She thinks she has scored the big one. That now finally Cyril Dragon has seen what she is really made of compared to his shallow fickle wife. Now he knows who will defend him and who will simply kick him and laugh at him when he is down.

Except that even now he has not seen. Even now he says like a fool, "It is not just for one person I take—we all take—the risks we take. What we are risking we are risking for our convictions. At least I should hope so. Nobody needs to feel indebted to me for anything."

But his lips are thin and pale and he and my mother do not look at each other. His tongue darts out to lick those lips before he goes on. "I have always said that anybody is welcome here regardless of religion or of ... of race. Anybody can come and by the same token anybody can go. Anybody who is not happy here, anybody who does not like the way we as a community choose to run the house, anybody who does not agree with our decisions, you know you are not being forced to stay here. Because if even one person is here unhappily and against their will it is bad for all of us."

You would be forgiven for imagining that whatever acrimony a peace-loving high-minded soul like my father could muster is directed in that moment to my big-mouthed mother. But it is Mrs Arasu's gaze he makes sure to catch as he speaks.

Family privacy was not what anyone had in mind when the house had been converted into the Muhibbah Centre. Whatever internal business the families of the Centre chose to conduct therefore had to be conducted in semi-public. On the day of this painful lunch my mother must go up to my father's office to continue the attack afterwards because there is nowhere else. My parents even have a small advantage over the other couples because at least the office is all the way at the top of the stairs and removed from the rest of the house. Only the committed snoops hear my mother's song circling around and back to its refrain: "Oh you and your pride so much pride but pretending to be so humble! You and your pride even one word against you makes you look like you got shit in your mouth! You and your holier-than-thou talk, you expect everybody to fall for it but the minute anybody starts to see through it, oh you and your pride!"

The committed snoops deliver their commentary in the same light casual tones they use for disappointing weather and unsatisfying meals. Rice overcooked not enough salt in the dhal potatoes half-raw tsk tsk tsk and by the way did you hear that she called him an arrogant son of a bitch? It's because she's worried isn't it? What if he finally sees through her? What if he finally opens his eyes and sees what type of person she is?

In the attic Mama cackles and says to Papa, "Wah they talk like as if you are God's gift to mankind and I am a streetwalker you rescued from the gutter! Any one of these days you will realize that I am just some stupid kampung girl with a face like a monkey. Please lah! Make my day. Send me packing like what they think you are going to do."

That evening at the dining table I catch my father's haunted eye. To be more precise I should say: I catch his eye but he does not catch mine. He looks at me but sees nothing and no one. He trains those empty golden eyes at one thing after another all the while seeing none of it. As the evening draws on those eyes seem to grow larger and emptier until there is nothing at all in them but the reflections of the figures around him which themselves seem to feed upon his emptiness and grow ever more grotesque: the scarlet lips the ravenous mouths the mad darting eyes the arms and legs whose shadows dance their menace across the walls. But in the middle of them all—surrounded on all sides by these hideous whirling dwarves—stands the one perfectly still figure who occupies more space in my father's eyes than all the others put together: my mother. She speaks little and moves even less. When she looks at my father it is no longer boredom or irritation that colours her gaze but bafflement. She has transcended all those states to reach this one. There she sits wearing her burnished skin and her straight spine like the pelt and bones of an animal she has just killed. Screened by her blackened curled lashes she studies my father as though he were a new species of monkey demonstrating its coprophagic tendencies.

When the meal is over my father does not leave the table. Long after everyone else has gone upstairs he sits there lost in thought. He closes his eyes but does not sleep. Again and again his eyelids spring open to reveal those same empty staring eyes.

No doubt about it now: at one end of my parents' story is that perfect May morning with the birdsong and the hydrangeas and the playful breezes; at the other end—for some mysterious reason—is Father Dubois's visit a month ago. In between are all those tiny twitches and shifts I have buried deep inside my brain each time I noticed them. The smuggled magazines the cigarette smell the new perfume. One minute humming like the miller's happy wife in a fairy tale, the next minute stabbing bystanders with her dagger eyes. And the long solitary walks she takes nowadays. Coming home spattered with mud and singing pop songs under her smoky breath so that the other women exchange meaningful glances.

"What did I tell you?" Mrs Arasu says to Hilda Boey. "I told you isn't it?"

Under different circumstances their gossiping could have been a comedy routine: Mrs Arasu small and hard and tightly contained, Hilda Boey softly spreading. Yet Hilda Boey for all the physical space she occupies is nothing more than a sponge and Mrs Arasu, as unobtrusive as her little body might be, is a syringe. Straight into the sponge Mrs Arasu delivers her poison until the sponge is saturated.

"Ya," says Hilda Boey lolling on the Recreation Lounge sofa. No resistance in her body or her mind. "Cannot say lah." You might wonder what kind of sneaky dishonest boy I am to be standing somewhere hiding listening to this exchange. Let me assure you: I did not want to hear any of it. With every sentence I am moving further and further away but I cannot escape them. Into my unwilling ears Mrs Arasu pours her unceasing words.

"Very funny she is behaving all of a sudden. Singing and humming nonstop. Every day acting like she struck lottery number. Going for a walk it seems! Like as if she sudah mabuk but you know what I mean lah. Not from beer or wine, the other kind of mabuk. We all know what kind of woman she is. That's why she came here in the first place."

"Ya, true."

"Anyway you know lah. A leopard cannot change its spots."

"No doubt."

I am ten years old and I know this much: they are circling my parents like vultures.

The Secretest Secret

SEPTEMBER 1987

I am alone in the boys' dormitory, reading:

*Whosoever desires (by his deeds) the reward of the
Hereafter, We give him increase in his reward, and
whosoever desires the reward of this world (by his deeds),
We give him thereof (what is decreed for him), and he
has no portion in the Hereafter—*

Those familiar footsteps. Light but confident. Measured
but nonchalant. Fifteen-sixteen-seventeen steps and she
stands at the doorway.

"Wah so hardworking you. Sitting here all by yourself
doing homework while everybody else is wasting time.
Model student. Model son. Model everything."

"It's not homework. I'm just reading. I like to read."

"You like to read or you like to fool people into thinking
you don't notice anything because your nose is always in a
book?"

I slam the Quran shut. I stand up as though to bring
myself to her height.

She sits on the edge of my bed. Folds her arms. Crosses
her legs. Looking up at the ceiling she says, "I'm sure you
can see what I see."

Just to provoke her I look at the ceiling too. And right on
cue she snaps, "Okay you want to make this difficult means
go ahead. I'll spell it out for you: you know what is going on
between your mother and my father."

Her face triumphant. Glowing. She is still talking but I am no longer listening. I am thinking about Mrs Arasu's *I told you isn't it?* and *a leopard cannot change its spots*. I am wondering what is wrong with all these women that they let their imaginations run wild like this and all to shoot down someone who has done them no harm. Is it boredom? Jealousy?

Your mother and my father. My father and your mother. Again and again the words come out of Annabelle's mouth. I cannot stem the flow of her glee. So pleased with herself she is that she has put two and two together and managed to come up with five. Slowly I tune my ears back to the frequency of her chatter.

"You saw how they locked themselves away for days to write that leaflet. And after that? In the printing room for even more days. Cyclostyling it seems. First time we all knew it takes two people to cyclostyle. And then? Went off in the van from morning until night. In front of everybody they could do it. They don't even care lah. Just watch the way they look at each other. Winking winking. Hiding here and there. Before, your mother used to go alone to the toolshed to smoke her cigarettes but now your mother and my father go in and come out of the toolshed together and wah nowadays it takes sooooo long to smoke one cigarette man, I wonder why? You pass any empty room and suddenly those two will come out. The faces so guilty some more."

What comes out of her mouth is what she wants for herself. *She's* the leopard who can't change its spots. She thinks I don't know her nonsense. If I wanted to I could reach out my hand quick as a flash and slap her hard on that blabbing mouth of hers. But I fling only my words in her face.

"So? People are allowed to go inside any room they want. Doesn't mean just because they are in a room together they are doing something wrong. You only see filth everywhere because you have a dirty mind."

"Oh? I have a dirty mind is it?"

"You must have, to simply make up rubbish like this with no ... no *proof*."

She tilts her head and kicks out her top leg. "What if I got proof?"

"You can't frighten me lah. What proof? How can you have proof of such a thing? You can't ... What, you mean you took photos? You put a tape recorder in the toolshed?"

"Wah, you got so many ideas man! You yourself are the master spy, what for you asking me for proof? You should already have plenty of proof."

She's making fun of me and she's enjoying it. If I'm not careful she will corner me. She will make me say what she wants and I won't be able to take it back I won't I can't oh God if only I could scratch her eyes out but thinking of scratching out her eyes I close my own instead and press my fists into them.

"Go away!" I say. "Why can't you just go away and leave me alone?"

A long silence forces me to open my eyes and see her smiling that cat smile of hers. Then in a low lush whisper she says, "What are you frightened of actually? Only a person who is frightened will pretend not to see things he can see."

"What are you talking about? I can't see anything. All these things are only in your own head so how do you expect other people to see them?"

"Hahaha! What for all this pretending? Your father is the only one who doesn't know about it. Don't you think he will feel like a fool when suddenly he realizes everybody knew the whole time? At least if you tell him quietly it's not so embarrassing."

"If everybody knows then why wouldn't my father know?"

"Don't tell me you're going to ask me that question again lah, stupid. Same reason your father doesn't know about anything else."

Tears prick my eyes. (Do not think for a moment that

they are tears of sadness.) I speak quickly to still the shaking of my voice.

"Last time I told you already. I'm not going to carry your tales to Cyril Dragon anymore. No way. Not in a million years am I going to bring your stupid fantasy to him. You imagine everybody having dirty thoughts and doing dirty things. Well you can imagine it all by yourself. You don't have one bit of proof. You got no shame, I tell you."

"You don't have to carry any tales to him. You don't have to do anything. I can tell him myself, don't worry. You don't need to see my proof. I just have to produce it for your father only."

"Okay fine. Then what for you came here? What you want me to say?"

Her smile turns sickly sweet. "Oh! I don't want you to say anything! But"—she looks down at her skirt and smooths it pleat by pleat—"I think so you don't want me to tell him isn't it?"

"That's up to you," I lie.

Only now I become aware that my hand has found its way to the stack of holy books on my bedside table and opened the one on top. Up and down up and down along the smooth onionskin page my fingers run like a blind man's.

"Yah. It's up to me. I also agree. But I know you're shitting bricks. Your father will just drop dead straightaway if he finds out. So I'll give you another chance. I tell you what: I don't need to go in the van anymore. This time I make it much easier for you, okay? You just tell your brother to go down to the river alone on Saturday. Ask him to wait at the waterfall. Where he and Leo go to beg for cigarettes from the kampung boys. Saturday afternoon three o'clock. You tell him to be there without Leo, or you figure out how to get Leo out of the way yourself."

At the very thought of it big-big goosepimples pop up all along my arms. Annabelle Foo lounging on the rocks in her wet T-shirt and short shorts trying to get her claws into Reza—

"I already told you before, you can't make somebody like you with all this nonsense. Secret letters and secret meetings and what not. If they don't like you, they don't like you."

"I'm not asking you to make your brother like me lah. I'm just asking you to make sure he is at the waterfall at three o'clock on Saturday. He doesn't need to know it's anything to do with me. Understand? The rest you don't worry about. The rest I can manage."

She flashes her dimples at me and then adds, "You got five days from today. Do your best for your darling Papa's sake."

I think about all the words Reza and Leo use to describe Annabelle Foo. *Itchy. Hum sup. Bimbo.* Words they bring back from town with the meat and the cigarettes. I think about what my brother will say after I trick him into meeting her at the river. The way one corner of his mouth will curl up and the filthy talk that will come out of that mouth. And then I think: *All bullshit lah her proof. Just talking big to scare me. She'll never dare to go to Papa because there's nothing actually going on between Mama and Selwyn Foo.* I repeat it to myself like a mantra. *She'll never dare she'll never dare she'll never dare.* But it won't sink in. It floats on the surface of what I know about the world like scum on a pond.

Satay

The two of them lounging in the toolshed eating stick after stick of it, forty wrapped in a plastic-lined newspaper with the whole works: peanut sauce and cucumbers and raw red onions to bring out whatever base instincts are left unaroused by the meat. They line up the empty skewers like trophies.

Right in front of me they boast and compare.

"I ate twelve pieces already. You still struggling with number five?"

"Yah but I'm enjoying them properly! I'm savouring them! You? Just swallowing labaku-labaku-labaku like a dog. Cannot get the taste also."

"Don't worry, I get the taste all right. Dogs' tongues just taste faster, that's all. More efficient."

With their mouths full of half-chewed meat they guffaw.

What comes out when I open my mouth to speak is not at all what I have come to say today: "Don't you feel shy? Just because everyone knows you think you can just do whatever you want now?"

(Let no one be forced to name unpleasant things let alone discuss them: the unspoken commandment of the Muhibbah Centre and the unwritten principle of our Rukunegara.)

"First of all," says Leo, "who the hell comes in here? Mrs Arasu for her fertilizer and her pruning shears. Actually *she* is scared of *us*. Does her best to avoid us because otherwise she'll be in a very embarrassing position isn't it? Either she'll have to report us and be the one who upsets your father or she'll be guilty too. And your mother, of course. But you know your mother what. As long as we don't tell about her she won't tell about us. She doesn't give a damn. Anyway, so what if everybody can see? There's nothing wrong with doing what you feel is right. Why should one fler make rules for another fler? Does your father have God sitting right inside his ear, that he knows God doesn't want us eating animals even though we have been doing it since caveman times?"

"At least we're not hypocrites," Reza says. "If you are going to do something you should be able to do it without hiding isn't it?"

"Not everything lah," says Leo and once again Reza is falling over, the shoulders shaking the laughter bubbling from his lips. "If you want to shit or if you want to rub-rub-rub your thing you should hide and do that. Or at least close the bathroom door."

They beat the ground with their palms and laugh like two baboons.

"How did you get that meat anyway?" I say. "From where you get money to buy all these things? Just tell me once and for all."

"Somebody bought for us," says Reza.

"Somebody? Somebody who?"

"Friend of mine," says Leo.

As if I cannot see him nudging Reza's knee with his.

"But the vegetable lorry didn't even come today," I say. "How did you go to town?"

"Vegetable lorry, vegetable lorry, vegetable lorry. Tsk tsk everything also this jackass must make it his own business I tell you. Reza how come your brother is such a busy-body?"

"I also don't know. We didn't go to town today lah Kannu. Satisfied? We brought this back yesterday."

"Yesterday? Ee yer! Then you kept it in the dorm until

today? You are going to get some funny disease. Not only eating meat you are eating rotten meat!"

"Who said we kept it in the dorm?" Reza says. "You think we got no other place to keep it ah?"

But Leo cannot contain his boast. "We kept it in the fridge in the kitchen lah. Okay? Satisfied?"

"You kept it in the fridge in the kitchen and your mother did not see?"

He blinks at me incredulously. "Stupid ah you? Of course my mother saw. She is the one who hid it there for us lah bodoh. Some years back she herself decided if she can't stop us she better just help us."

Just like that in my face. Neela's mutinous resentment of the rest of us a point of pride for her son. I picture it now: Neela shrugging and saying *Okayfine if you're going to eat meat then at least hide properly and eat it.* Helping them to hide it in nondescript newspaper bundles at the back of the fridge, suggesting the toolshed as a good hideout, giving them meat money out of her own meagre wages.

Even I had not guessed that she was going this far! And Leo waving it at me like a red flag. My hand shoots out and shoves his shoulder, taking us both by surprise and sending him sprawling backwards. I hear myself shouting. "You're ... you're a devil! You just want to drag others down with you! Not enough that you started all this, you had to get your mother to help you also? Because of you and your mother, my brother is going to go to Hell!"

Leo props himself up on his elbows and regards me with dispassionate amusement. "You're a real clown lah you," he says. "If only I had a tape recorder right now, I would tape you and play it back for you in ten years and you'll dig your own grave and crawl into it and beg us to bury you alive."

But this time Reza doesn't laugh. He doesn't even take his eyes off me.

"What the bloody hell is wrong with you?" he says.

"There's nothing wrong with me. It's Leo and his mother

who don't belong here. My father gave them a place here out of the kindness of his heart and this is how they repay him?"

"Out of the kindness of his heart it seems," Leo says.

I note the sudden bitterness in his voice with satisfaction: I too know how to aim my arrows at sensitive spots. I know I've contravened my father's teachings with what I've said. But I said what I said because Leo deserves it and so does his mother.

"Just shut up, Kannu," Reza says. "Just go away. Go away, once and for all. Stop hanging around us. Go and say your prayers or do your chanting or memorize your bhajans or whatever it is you do for fun."

It is only when Reza waves me away that I realize I've forfeited my chance to get him to meet Annabelle alone. There is nothing I can do to salvage this moment now.

There's only one remaining option and that is to come clean to Reza. To reason to plead to beg. And so for two days I shadow him waiting for my opening. I have to catch him alone. Even if it is thirty seconds while Leo is pissing behind the hydrangeas on the evening of the second day.

"It's a stupid thing," I tell Reza. "I don't know what she's trying to achieve, but she's made up some stupid story about Mama and Selwyn Foo and if you don't go and meet her she's going to go and tell Cyril Dragon. And he probably won't believe her but all the same …"

But all the same what? The way Reza is looking at me has stolen whatever words I prepared right out of my mouth. And now Leo is standing next to him still zipping up his shorts and grinning like a bloody donkey. He's about to spout some nonsense, but then in such a quiet voice that he and I both catch our breath Reza says, "Do you want to hear a story?"

I don't say yes I don't say no but Leo of course cannot keep his own mouth shut.

"Your anneh going to tell you one nice bedtime story.

Come come. Pull up the blanket and snuggle up."

Even Reza ignores him. He turns away and grits his jaw. Suddenly he looks smallboy nervous. His voice when he speaks again is not resonant with his usual bravado. He won't look at Leo but he won't look at me either.

"One time when I was small, Mama tried to swallow some pills to kill herself. I'm the one who saw her and knocked them out of her hand. They rolled under the bed and she fell to her knees and cried and said *sorry sorry sorry*. After that we never talked about it. Not once. But you know what?"

He doesn't wait for us to ask what.

"We never talked about it but I never stopped thinking about it. So many times since coming here I've thought about it—she made me think about it. And you know what I wish? I wish I'd let her take the bloody pills. I wish I'd just let her die."

Even Leo's not breathing now. We stand there feeling the small lapping waves of each other's discomfort against our skin. He stiffens his shoulders like a big cat waiting to pounce but there's nothing to pounce on.

"I swear to god I wish I'd just let her die," Reza says again as though we might have missed it. "Because if I had, she wouldn't have dragged me to this godforsaken madhouse where I've had to miss my whole childhood, my whole *life*. If she'd just died, somebody would've plucked me out of the mess and sent me to school, at least. And I wouldn't have had to spend twelve years—twelve years and still counting!—watching her make a bloody fool of herself. Nobody knows her foolishness like I know it, because I've been watching it all my life. First-first she'll be so lovey-dovey with whoever the latest fler is, so excited and giggly and starry-eyed. And the worst example was with Cyril Dragon, wah anything also can come out of his mouth she will simply repeat like a parrot in the beginning, you remember or not Leo?"

Faced with Reza's eagle gaze Leo only shrugs. Draws in his breath like the first part of a sigh he can't let out. Doesn't matter because Reza doesn't need an answer to keep going. "Oh, you remember all right. We used to laugh about it. How she'll fall at his feet and say yesyesyes like as if he was the biggest genius in the universe. And now? Now what? Now she's bored just like every other time. Of course lah. Who can blame her? How long can a person fall for all this bullshit? She's just more honest than all the others. And because of that you want me to do what? Service Annabelle Foo so that nothing will disturb or interrupt Cyril Dragon's lifelong stroking of his own ego?"

"What?" Leo says. "What's this about Annabelle Foo?"

"I didn't say ... That's not what she ... She only said to meet her there, it's not what—"

"I don't care," Reza says. "I don't care what you said or she said or anybody in the world said. I don't give two hoots about what is happening between Mama and Selwyn Foo, and I don't care what people are thinking or saying or who carries which stories to whom. And if you weren't so busy trying to carry your father's balls, you wouldn't care either. Why shouldn't Annabelle Foo tell him if he's too stupid to see it himself? As far as I'm concerned it would be better for everybody."

After all I'm not asking much of him. All he has to do is to go and meet Annabelle Foo. What could she do to him at the waterfall? It's a public place. A bit of playacting—a few mysterious and suggestive smiles, some feigned interest in her fantasies and melodramas—and she'll be satisfied. She's not going to ask him to marry her. In all likelihood she herself will know he's just playing the game but that will be good enough for her. How much unpleasantness and pain could be avoided just by this tiny compromise! But I can see already from his expression that nothing will convince him to do it. The sickening cruel grin that slowly fills his face until, just at the moment when it can grow no wider, he says, "In fact, if Annabelle Foo doesn't manage to tell him, maybe I should tell him myself."

"Hahaha!" Leo says. "Don't bluff around lah you. As if you'll dare to go and tell him such a thing."

Reza swings round and when his eyes meet Leo's something unfurls in them that I cannot identify. What is it? Menace? Desperation? Bravado? Whatever it is I know that Reza will do anything to show Leo what he's made of. He's not a pussyfooting shrinking violet sissy boy. He doesn't care what happens.

Suddenly the truth comes into focus: I will have to choose. Which would break my father's heart more: learning that Reza and Leo have been filthifying our holy house with flesh foods or seeing that his true love has betrayed him once and for all? Because I know my father after all. I know him backwards forwards inside out through my many years of close observation: when he finds out about the fishballs and the chicken and the satay he will find a way to spin some forgiving fantasy for himself. It might take him a bit of time but eventually he will get there: "Boys will be boys," he will say. "They are only having a bit of fun. Testing the limits." Between his fingers he will knead it and knead it into a nothing-at-all just like he did when I told him about Neela. After all, he has been explaining away Reza's insults to man and God for more than ten years. Compared to the questions Reza will ask to anyone's face this is after all easily set right in my father's universe. Our house our community our we-are-one-body may have been defiled but he will undefile them with prayer and blessings with offerings dedications ceremonies. Reza and Leo may have stained their souls with the blood of innocent beasts but they are young; the stain will fade just as it has for all of us who once ate flesh foods (which is to say: all of us except I myself Clarence Kannan Cheng-Ho Muhammad Yusuf Dragon).

But what fairy tale would he be able to tell himself about

the wife who is cheating on him? Even Cyril Dragon cannot conjure that away. Nothing to be done: I will have to sacrifice one of my father's illusions in order to preserve the other.

A small voice in my head whispers, *But what if you tell him about Reza and Leo and the news of Mama and Selwyn still reaches his ears? Any of them could tell him. Reza or Leo or Annabelle Foo. And then he would have two disappointments to bear.*

And then look what happens to that small voice. Its eyes turn white and glow like devil eyes in the dark. Its tongue forks. It licks my ear and hisses. *Maybe Reza should have just let her die, isn't it? At least then she would have had some chance to go to heaven. Now look at what she is doing.*

I pull that small voice up out of me by its roots and hurl it into the darkness.

They're laughing now. As usual. Like two bloody jackasses. Half of me wants to hear what they are saying but the other half of me says *Don't waste your time with them just do what you're going to do.* Look at what type of person Reza is! His own mother—and he is the one who was always the soft centre of her heart, her real kannu (I am only Kannu by name)—his own mother is going astray and he is gloating because it's all a big game for him.

My father might end up with two cracks in his heart instead of just one but the risk is still worth it. At best the distraction will work just like it did when I (mis)informed on George Cubinar: in the excitement Reza will back off from his threat just like Annabelle shelved hers. Of course this will be an altogether different spectacle: Reza and Leo will not play victim like Annabelle Foo did. They will gloat and luxuriate and strut as they always do. But even if Reza and Leo don't give two hoots what all is being said about them Annabelle Foo will delight in the free-flowing judgement of Mrs Arasu et al. She will know exactly who ratted on Reza and Leo and whether or not she congratulates me for it she will accept it as a temporary peace offering. If she cannot pocket Reza whole then she will settle for seeing him lose a bit of his lustre.

And at worst—if Papa is to find out about Mama and Selwyn anyway—I will at least have exacted some revenge upon Reza and Leo. For their years of showoffing and swaggering and laughing at me behind my back and to my face. For insulting my father and my mother both. Even if Papa gives them nothing more than a stern warning they will still know I was the one who told. I will have shown them at last what I am really made of. Won't I?

It is not joy I feel at this prospect. Not even pleasure. Why would I take pleasure in betraying my brother? It is not that kind of victory I seek. You see, one day a long time from now when Reza is no longer so sure of himself I will not stand there and laugh at him. I will kneel by his side and show him the way.

Turned Tables

I'm on the jungle trail one afternoon when I look up to see my father coming the other way. It's early afternoon: not a time at which he normally takes walks. Something in his expression frightens me a little even before he speaks but it's what he says that makes the blood drain from my face.

"I was looking for you, Kannan. I was thinking, after all our conversations—oh dear, I wonder how to explain what I mean. I suppose I just wanted to ask you—if there were … if you knew that someone was lying about something very important, you would tell me, wouldn't you?"

I'm trying to keep breathing but the air is thinner than ever.

"You care very much about the Muhibbah Centre, but you also care about people, don't you? About your mother, about me?"

"Yes," I say. Only the hiss of the *s* is audible.

"If anything happened—don't look so scared, Kannu, I don't mean people dying, but if anything … What I mean is, maybe the Muhibbah Centre would survive whether or not I were able to lead it. There are good, capable people here. But I feel a responsibility for it, you know, I started it, I should … I should *nurture* it for as long as I can. I don't want … I wouldn't want any foolish drama to destroy everything behind my back."

How long can a ten-year-old boy go without breathing? I'm growing dizzy.

"You must never feel guilty about telling me anything.

You are not the sinner, you are only the messenger. Do you understand what I mean, Kannu?"

I nod then: because it is what he wants and I am desperate to give him whatever he wants so that I can escape. But *No no no* is what I am thinking. *Please no. Please get me out of here.*

"Ah, good," Papa says. "You do understand then. And you do care about me and your mother?"

I stop nodding. I hold stiller than a mouse under the shadow of a hawk.

"I know it's difficult, it's awkward for a boy your age to express these things. I know you care. I know you would do the right thing." He half-smiles at a point somewhere over my head. There is an almost imperceptible old-man tremble to his chin that reminds me of Father Dubois. Before my brain understands what I'm doing my mouth is blurting out a string of words.

"There *is* something, Papa. There is actually something. It's about Reza and Leo."

He frowns and smiles at the same time. Faintly shakes his head. But before he can stop me or divert me I go on.

"They eat meat. All kinds of meat. Fish, fowl, pig, cow. They eat outside when they go in the lorry but ... but the worst part is they bring it back here also. They bring meat into the house. They've been doing it for a long time."

My father is drawing in his breath but I'm not going to slow down.

"Everybody knows about it. They do it openly. Everybody knows except you, Papa. They eat meat on the front porch, on the back porch, everywhere. Sometimes they even keep it in the fridge in the kitchen and Neela helps them hide it. Cow meat, pig meat, next to our clean food in the fridge, can you believe it, Papa, can you believe it?"

He's shaking his head more firmly now. Disbelief? Denial? Regret? Whatever it is I must seize my advantage.

"They've been doing it for years. They don't feel shame. They don't feel guilty."

"Okay," he says quietly. "Okay, okay."

Almost as though he's trying to comfort himself. *Shush, shush, Cyril Dragon. Everything will be okay.*

Then he stands up and puts his hands together. A small part of me expects him to launch into prayer. But instead of closing his eyes he goes on.

"Don't worry, don't worry. Yes, it is bad to bring such things into the house, but in the end our God is a reasonable and loving God. We must remember that. We must hold on to it. Unclean it may be but in the end each of us is only responsible for our own body and our own soul. We cannot control what other people put into their bodies. God will not punish the many for the actions of a few."

In that moment I gather up everything I have left and begin afresh. If the unvarnished truth will not work then I must varnish it.

"I know you said Neela has so little and we all have so much but ... but they eat satay in the kitchen even. *Beef* satay. I think ... I think she herself makes it for them, Papa. With our knives and our cutting boards and our pots and pans. They eat it on our plates. I was only saying it wasn't her fault because I think they *make* her do it. They bully her."

"Hmm," he says. He nods deep and slow as though trying to grasp some unfamiliar concept. Then he says, "You know, Kannu, everybody makes mistakes. No life is free of mistakes. Even Gandhi, do you know—"

Like a drowning man I gulp and shout. "But you always say eating meat is allowing violence into your body! You always tell us that our karma—"

"Yes, yes, I know," he sighs. "But people cannot be perfect. What to do? We all have our struggles. Each person has their own past, their own memories. Your brother used to eat meat before coming here, whereas you were born here so you never knew anything else. Naturally it is a little bit more difficult for his body, his tastebuds, you see?"

"But *Leo* was brought up here."

"That, yes. What to do?"

"And his own *mother* is helping him to sin instead of—"

"Kannu! No. In the end it is not for us to judge other people's sins. We must each of us do what is right, and then we must ... sometimes we must leave the rest to God. Small-small things we have to let go."

"Small-small things! But you always said—"

"No, no, we have to let go of all that. I realize now—whatever I said then I don't know, Kannu—I realize most things are not so important. You don't have to be scared. Nothing bad will happen to you because of what they are doing. I know, Kannu, everything you've told me you've told me because you care about what we are trying to build here. And it is true, once there was something serious enough for me to have to ask someone to leave. But mostly these are all small lies people tell, you know, excuses we make for ourselves because we are weak and sometimes—well, sometimes it is so hard to do the right thing. Isn't it? So very hard that we feel we deserve some respite. So we give in to temptation and then we find a way to justify it. Everyone does this. Even me." A sad smile crinkles the corners of his eyes. "All the same," he says, "if and when there is something big you must not hesitate to come to me. But I won't keep harassing you now, you want to get on with your day, don't you?

"You are a good boy," my father says. "You are a very good boy."

Then he walks on past me and leaves me standing there. Tears prick the backs of my eyes. I am the Good Boy. Other people can be clever but I have always been the good boy. But that I am used to by now; what has my life been but a series of consolation prizes? It's the thought that even the consolation prize might come at a higher price than I am willing to pay. What do I have to give to remain the Good Boy?

Confrontation

Saturday afternoon four o'clock. Annabelle Foo and I are by the goat pen behind the house. I've had a few days to calm down and prepare myself to face Annabelle.

"Bloody useless lah you," she says. "I should have known from the beginning. As though anybody will want to listen to you. You're a joke."

My father has trained me well: I am master of my violent urges. I smile and say to her, "Don't simply talk without knowing what I did."

"What? What great thing did you do? Washed your brother's backside is it? Licked his balls?"

With a pugnacious flourish I produce my shocker.

"I told my father what my brother and Leo are doing," I say.

Something briefly clouds her eyes. For a moment she looks at me as though I've said something she can barely understand. Then the clouds clear and she says, "Oh. You mean that they eat *flesh foods?*"

"Yes! Yes, I told him. You thought I would be too scared to tell him but I wasn't."

But her momentary confusion has not left behind even a trace of awe. It's as though she went from not believing I could have told my father straight back to despising me for my cowardice.

"Ha!" she says. "So what? You want me to give you a trophy now? You want me to clap and cheer for you?"

"You thought I would be too scared to tell him, but I wasn't."

"Great. Good for you. So tell me, what is your father going to do?"

How does she do it? How does she manage every time to cut right through all the layers to the heart I've tried to hide?

"What is he going to do?" I repeat stupidly. Why did I not formulate an answer to this predictable question while I had the time?

"Yes. What is he going to do about it? Is he going to make an announcement in front of all of us who already knew what they were doing for donkey's years? Is he going to find some uncle to come and pick them up and take them away?"

"How should I know?" I snap. "That is up to him isn't it?"

She sniggers and gives a funny little sniff. "Up to him! Ha! Nice try, boy-boy. You know just as well as I do. Your father won't do anything. He's … You know what? I was going to say Reza is his pet but it's not even that. He's scared of Reza. He's scared of what will happen if he ever says anything."

Dread churns my stomach. Uselessly I protest, "No. You're stupid. My father is not scared of anybody."

"Really? Okay, let's see. Let's wait and see what he does then. If he dares to say anything to your brother then …" She stops and presses her lips together as though she's trying to stifle a smile. "Then," she says, "I will give you a special prize."

But of course we both know she won't even have to think up a special prize.

Toolshed

Of course Papa says nothing to Reza. He says nothing to Leo and nothing to Neela. The smells of satay and sotong bakar and barbecued chicken wings mingle and like a meaty mantle envelop all those who enter the toolshed.

Annabelle becomes bolder and bolder with Reza. Jostles him with her elbow. Bumps her bony hip into his bony hip. Straightens the collars of his shirts when they are askew.

"One of these days," Leo jokes, "she's going to lose her patience and pull off your trousers. Just like that in public."

And they laugh the way they always laugh at each other's jokes. Like each one is the funniest joke in the world since the last one.

All the time at the back of my mind is the fear that any one of these days Annabelle is indeed going to lose her patience. But she's not going to pull off Reza's trousers in public. She's going to unleash the drama of dramas upon all of us. She's going to unveil the mad concoctions of her fanciful mind for my father and then—however little truth there is in them, even though it all boils down to a few suggestive smiles and shoulder-rubbings—it will all be over. I knew I was only buying time anyway telling my father about the satay but what I did not guess was how very little time I was buying.

The toolshed holds my and Annabelle's attention like a magnet now. At any given moment either one of us would be able to tell you who is in it and for how long. We watch the door and check the clock. Even when our backs are turned to it we are conscious of its solid squatting presence.

That day Harbans Singh is admitted to hospital for a false-alarm heart attack. An ambulance cruises up the hill at a leisurely Sunday-drive speed. The ambulance men dart rat-sniffing looks around the Centre and ask wary questions of us: "All of you live here together? Really? What religion again? Is this ... legal?"

They take Harbans Singh away (to diagnose his chest pains as nothing more than fulminating gas). Someone else will need to lead the Nature Walk. Others volunteer—Thomas Mak Rupert Boey even Mrs Arasu—but in the end my father decides to do it himself. "I ought to be spending more time with our young people," he says. "How fast they are growing up!"

We hang around on the porch waiting for everyone to be ready as usual. In the milling about I cannot say for sure who was on the porch when. I can only speak for myself and my own two eyes: I see my mother and Selwyn Foo come out of the toolshed. My mother with a still-lit cigarette in her hand blowing a glamorous stream of smoke out of the side of her mouth and then putting out the cigarette by pressing it to one of the stone boulders on the path. And then I see Reza and Leo go into the shed. In each of their four hands a plastic bag heaving with newspaper bundles.

My father appears with a bright God's-in-His-heaven smile on his face. Rubbing his hands and beaming at each of us in turn. "Off we go," he says more than once.

Annabelle clears her throat and says, "Shouldn't we wait for Reza and Leo?"

My father looks at her while gathering his thoughts. His eyes rake her face piteously.

"You know," he says at last, "those of you who are past school-leaving age are not obliged to come for these Nature Walks."

"Past school-leaving age," Annabelle repeats thoughtfully. "So that means ... we can just do whatever we like?"

"If you don't want to come don't come lah Annabelle," Kiranjit says quietly. "Stop wasting our time."

"Or if you want to call Reza and Leo, just go and call them," says Irene Mak. "Ask them if they want to come and if they don't it's fine isn't it?"

Annabelle's whole face lifts.

"But that's the thing," she says. "I can't go and call them. They're not even here. They went to town isn't it? They walked down to the road and hitchhiked. They don't even wait for the vegetable lorry anymore. They do whatever they like."

I've opened my mouth to correct her when something holds me back. Why should I get involved? Let her say what she wants to say. My father doesn't care anyway. He knows what Reza and Leo are doing and he doesn't care.

"Come, come," my father says and claps his hands. "No point arguing about all this. Who wants to come, come. Who wants to stay, stay. Annabelle?"

She chews on her lower lip for a moment then says, "I'll come."

We are directly across from the toolshed—not ten yards from it—when suddenly with no warning whatsoever Annabelle turns off the path like she's sleepwalking.

"Wait!" she says. "I just want to check something."

I catch only the smallest glimpse of her smile as she turns but it's enough to tell me what she is thinking. Today is the day. Everything that came before must have been an elaborate red herring to throw me off the scent of what she is about to do. This is the moment when she has had enough. *All right Cyril Dragon*, she is thinking. *Okay. Reza can do no wrong as far as you're concerned. Fine. But let's see what you think about this!* And she will throw open the toolshed door with a magician's dramatic flourish and stand back to watch our faces as we witness the perfidy of our two resident adulterers.

She holds her head high like a mediaeval warrior princess leading an army of peasants. And of course they all follow her. Kiranjit and the Mak twins and even my father stretching out his hand and opening his mouth into an *O!* like a tragic character in a play. In that moment I see what he is thinking and I see that he knows, he knows what she wants to show him and he doesn't want to see it. He doesn't want her to be the one showing him and most of all he does not want the whole crowd of children to be witnesses to the spectacle: not because he fears for their sensitive impressionable souls but because of the shame in it. That everyone—if the children then soon their parents too—will have to admit that they have all known what was going on behind his back. What they have thought of it—where their sympathies lie—hardly matters. You can stand up for the cuckold you can be outraged on his behalf you can pity him but whatever your choice he is still the cuckold.

Cyril's feet drag themselves behind Annabelle as though they are shackled and weighted but he has to go on he cannot give up now he has to stop her he has to do something even though his whole body is crying *Oh! No not this not this I beg you!*

He forces himself to speak.

"You yourself said, Annabelle, they've gone to town. They're not here. It doesn't matter. Please don't waste your time looking for them."

I'm the only one who knows they've come back from town. It's just them in the toolshed eating their dead pigs and cows, not my mother and her paramour. So when I shove Annabelle aside and step forward you must believe that I do it—I did it—only to pull the rug out from under her feet. In those few moments I too fully imagined my own triumph: the shock in her eyes when I threw open the door faster than she could, the small gasp, the dull thud of her revelation hitting the floor when before us we saw only Reza and Leo after all. Only Reza and Leo sitting amongst the ruins of their meaty feast.

You must believe me. How could I have known? It is easy to sit where you are—on the high horse of your hindsight—and say, a boy like you, a sneak, a sly cunning shit-eating schemer, of course you knew. Of course you knew everything.

But I have hidden nothing. Though it has broken my heart to go back—to force myself down that deep well, to relive these moments—I have given you the whole truth. Untouched. No—I did not know. I only thought that with the opening of that door I would trip her up. I pictured her sucking her teeth and stammering "But, but!" while my father sighed gently and anticlimactically. Then I would stand unmoved in her path watching her wheels turn to come up with a Plan B.

But how can *you* believe or disbelieve me, you who I most want to reach? You, Reza and Leo, are not here to read this and revise your opinions of me. You made up your minds there and then. In that split second when my sweaty hand pulled open the door and our eyes met—first yours then his—you made up your minds.

"Look!" I am crowing. "Look! Just look for yourselves! It's no big revelation for most of you, is it?"

Both hands tugging at that heavy door—which I know has a broken latch but is so warped it closes tightly—because the movement must be quick to pull the rug out from under Annabelle Foo's feet and so yes one big heave and it bursts open and I am thrown back all eighty pounds of me losing my balance and falling backwards as though struck to the ground by some divine vision. And at the very moment my bottom hits the muddy ground my brain takes in the sight before us: my brother lying on the filthy floor of that shed with his head in Leo's lap. Leo's five fingers in my brother's hair. Leo's five other fingers entwined with the five fingers of my brother's right hand. For the first time since I have known him Leo looks terrified. For the first time in Reza's life he looks lost. And I? Like a fallen soldier

I lie there in the mud. Like a fallen angel. Annabelle towering over me with folded arms and narrowed eyes. The wind in her hair making her look like a warrior princess. It's then that I realize: she *knew*. She was never going to expose my mother and her father. Just like me she saw them come out of the toolshed but unlike me she knew what she'd find instead. A tiny smile flickers across her face. In her mind's eye she is taking a bow.

The Lost Boys

You see I could stop now couldn't I? There is no reason I should keep going till the end. I could stop now and you would not know the difference. Only a handful of people on this earth know the rest of my story and they are not reading this. But now it is no longer a choice; it is a compulsion. I began for all the reasons one begins stories: to know myself. Then to explain myself. Then to wheedle forgiveness out of those in fact unqualified to give it. Also: to see old things with new eyes, to repair in the retelling what I broke in the original, to go back to go back to go back. Always this desire not merely to return to my unfinished business like a ghost, but to reinhabit that world as my living breathing bleeding self. To redo. All the minuscule moments when we could have chosen differently by intention or accident. Every narrow crack that leads to some other life unlived. Those parallel universes. What if what if what if. I turn my life around and around in my hands I cannot stop looking I cannot stop poking and prodding and yet there will be no answers. I know that now. There will be no answers.

So come with me. Get up and follow me. You don't want to but you must. If I am going to go there I cannot go alone. And let's face it: you avert your eyes but you also want to know. Your curiosity is insatiable.

By evening on the day we found them everybody had heard. But it wasn't Annabelle Foo who spread the news. No sooner had we come back to the house than the sweetness seemed to drain out of her triumph. She'd won the game. She'd exposed them once and for all for the bloody pondans they were. She'd always known that no red-blooded male would have been able to resist her charms and she'd been right. But what was her prize for being right? Not Reza. It was as though she hadn't realized that he still wouldn't be hers after she'd had her revenge. She went up to the girls' dormitory and sat on her bed and there she stayed as the news began to eddy and swirl around her. She felt as though she'd taken her boat out on familiar waters and nevertheless managed to lose her way. She was marooned and it was getting dark. But no one came up to coax her downstairs. No one begged her to eat. "Very upsetting lah, what to do?" they said to each other as they relished the drama.

To save face my father had no choice but to call Reza and Leo into his office. Everyone was waiting for it. It was not the time to let himself look like a fool. Or rather: he already looked like a fool for other reasons so he could not risk a whole new foolhood. *Look what they are doing right under his nose and he cannot do anything!* Mrs Arasu would have said and she would have made it clear to all present that she did not just mean Reza and Leo.

Mrs Arasu seethes. "Cannot believe it," she says. "Disgusting. Cannot believe it!"

The women cover their mouths as though holding back vomit. The men put their heads in their hands. All of them in a row: Thomas Mak Rupert Boey Selwyn Foo Harbans Singh. Identical sculptures of dejection and despair.

Rupert Boey says, "This is what happens when boys grow up without the father figure. Broken marriages means all this type of thing will definitely happen."

"But Reza had a father figure what," Rupert Boey said. "From day one Cyril Dragon treated him like his own son. Ungrateful, that's all there is to it!"

"Aaah, Cyril Dragon was too busy," says Harbans Singh. "Too busy with his dream, too busy with his cause. Cyril

Dragon could never properly belong to anybody. Don't you know Gandhi was also a terrible husband and father? Prophets and revolutionaries cannot be family men lah."

Mrs Arasu says, "Don't simply blame Cyril Dragon lah. Look at the mother. From the beginning she just wanted to have her own fun instead of paying attention to the boy isn't it? Simply dragged him up here because she wanted to meet Cyril in person. For her he was just like a pop star. She didn't come for anything she believed in. She didn't come for a better life for her child. She was only thinking of herself. So? See lah. See what she has done to her son."

"This type of thing is in the blood lah," says Bee Bee. "Nobody can do anything. The mother itchy the son also itchy." No one seems to recall that Bee Bee herself once stole Thomas away from his wife.

"Itchy is one thing," says Estelle Foo. "But this! Aiyo! How to say also I don't know." She puts her hand on her mouth and presses her knees together.

What my father says to Reza and Leo nobody knows. Nobody knew then and nobody will ever know. He would have spoken perhaps of the natural order of things. Of sins against nature. Against God-who-goes-by-many-names-but-is-always-the-same-God. For make no mistake: my father was ahead of his time in many ways but his imagination had its limits. And what did any of us know then of Pride and rainbow flags? To expect him to have said to those boys *Love is never wrong so do not be ashamed*—it is asking too much of my father. Is it not enough that he transcended history and convention and his education and upbringing in so many other ways? In this way he could not.

While Reza and Leo are in his office my mother is upstairs in her bedroom puffing and puffing. Cigarette after cigarette until one whole pack is gone and the smoke even by just seeping out through the crack under the door has filled the whole corridor. Let it waft through the house then.

Who cared about such things anymore?

Neela is perched on a three-legged stool in the kitchen. Her eyes are bright red but her face is dry. She who has never truly belonged. She who feared for her son from the beginning. That he would not belong. That he would not be loved. That he would be displaced by That Boy. That That Boy would drag him into mischief and then the minute they got caught say *It was all his idea not mine.* But her imagination too had its limits. Never could she have suspected this. Never could her mind even at the greatest heights of its paranoia have cooked up such a thing. She sits alone and knows that she has no friends in this whole godforsaken mildew-eaten house. No one who will come to her and say, *Never mind. Everything will be okay.* Not even That Boy's mother because while you might think they are in the same boat they are not. Oh no. That woman is in a very different boat indeed. Her boat will carry her safely to shore. Men will fall over themselves to wait upon her. Money and fortune will welcome her back into the Outside with open arms.

My father calls a General Meeting. Absent: Mama and Neela. Reza and Leo. Exempted once again. Special treatment. Funny thing is nobody complains about it this time. My father talks about counselling and therapy and about how there is always Hope. *Human beings are always capable of change*, he says. With God's help. Inshallah.

They would be prepared to keep Reza and Leo away from each other by force or by trickery if they had to, but thank goodness there is no need: Leo goes off for a walk by himself.

Here is Leo striding down the track. Overhead the trees meet but the track is a tunnel of light through the dense green. Here are Leo's footprints in the mud. All the way down to the river. Once, long ago, when I was scared of the current Leo said with that big sparkling grin of his: *Once you know how to swim you can never drown.* The sun on his shoulders and in his hair. The water glinting like mosaic tiles in front of him. But look more closely at the cocksure grin. Look how it is ever so slightly ever so heartbreakingly lopsided. Look how fragile it really is. The secret crack running through the centre of it. The darting of the eyes to Reza then away from Reza then back again as though an invisible thread stretches taut between them. Anything to get a laugh or a *Good one!* out of Reza.

Were they just two friends horsing around in a river back then? Or was that invisible thread more than even I could have imagined?

Only when Leo does not return that night do they realize Reza is upstairs in his bed. Lying wide awake with his eyes closed. That it is not another Moonlight Bungalow adventure updated to include deviant activities. That they have not run away together. Because it is Reza who goes knocking on doors to tell them Leo is missing. "Where did he go?" they ask him. "Where do you think he went? Surely you must have some idea." But for once he has no clever answer. He shakes his head at them like a lost traveller surrounded by people giving him directions in a foreign language. He looks around with unblinking glassy eyes.

"Gone," he says. "Just gone."

The men go out with torchlights. Leo has made no effort to hide his footprints in the mud. In that cool black river they find him quickly. Right there at the base of the waterfall. Snagged like a twig among the rocks. The frayed hems of his trousers pulled by the current.

The house falls silent except for Neela's howling. Neela who never threw a tantrum in her life who took what life doled out and made the best of it whose judgments and warnings were all delivered out of earshot of the others: now she explodes. She goes mad. Like an animal she snarls and spits. Nobody can hold her. Nobody can even touch her. She has no friends under that roof and she does not want to pretend otherwise. She will not let anyone forget it just to make themselves feel better: she is all alone here. Only Cyril Dragon makes no attempt to console her. After some time he says quietly, "We have to call the police now."

The silence thickens around Neela. Selwyn Foo speaks first.

"At a time like this you want to bring the police in?"

"If not at a time like this, then at what sort of time would you bring in the police?" my father says. "A boy has died."

"I mean, given what is going on in the rest of the country. And what do the police have to do with anything that has happened here? We know what happened. There was no foul play. We can pray for him and we can have him cremated or buried or whatever. It's not something for the police."

"I'm afraid we must," my father says. "It was an unexpected death. We cannot even be sure there was no foul play."

"But we know what happened! And we know why it happened!"

"We may have our guesses, but we cannot try to hush this up. People will find out a boy has died, whether we like it or not. And the more we try to hide, the worse the stories will be that they will cook up. They will say we killed him. They will say we sacrificed him. People are always willing to believe anything they hear about those they don't understand."

From the roots of his hair to the point of his chin Selwyn Foo's whole head is red.

"That's it then," he says. "This is it. This is the end of this community. We might as well pack our bags."

My father covers his face with his hands and shakes his head. From behind his hands he says, "It is the end. You are right. It is the end of many things."

Then he lowers his hands and looking at no one he goes on. "But it isn't the end for the reasons you give. It is the end because we let a boy die. It is the end because we drove him

... we drove them ... we never paid attention. We closed our eyes. I closed my eyes. I thought everything would work out for the best. I thought ... I thought he would be all right. I thought he would find his way, that he was tough, that boys like him—people like him—would always find their way. But I ..."

He stops. When he speaks again his voice is even quieter than it has been. So quiet that the other men have to lean right into his face to hear his words.

"I was wrong. I made a terrible mistake. I failed the boy. I failed him. I failed my son. My own son."

Even Neela falls silent. Like a blind woman she turns her bright blank eyes towards the sound of Cyril's voice. Her face tells us nothing.

In fifteen minutes the grandfather clock will kick off the hourly ten minutes of staggered clock-striking. This time those ten minutes during which all those diverse chimes will echo through the house will seem endless. We will stand there waiting for them to end. Barely breathing like as if the action of our lungs is compromised by the loudness of the clocks. Ten minutes here ten minutes there: of course it matters. In three seconds—in the time it took to speak a short sentence—I have gained a brother. Except I've gained him too late. He is no longer with us or with me. To be precise: two half-brothers were what I had. Two halves equal a whole. In three seconds I gained a half and lost it. For three seconds I had a whole but now I am once again left with a half. The additions and subtractions swim around inside my head. All these numbers. I cannot make sense of it. Who is whose father whose mother whose brother whose son? In the classroom we are sometimes given those logic puzzles that require the drawing of charts and family trees:

X is Y's brother and Z is X's grandfather but Y is not Z's grandson. Who is Y?

In the waiting room, there is a mother, a father, a son, a daughter, a brother, a sister, an auntie, an uncle, a niece, a nephew, and 2 cousins. However, there are only 4 people in the waiting room and none of them have other relatives. What is the explanation?

What indeed is the explanation? *At the Centre there is 1 father, 2 mothers, and 3 sons. The father has 2 sons; Mother A has 2 sons; Mother B has 1 son. One of the sons has no father. One of the sons is drowned in a pond.* Solve the riddle. Solve it now. Do not shy away.

"Cyril," offers Rupert Boey, "I think you just need more rest. Maybe you are having a migraine and it is … it is muddling your thinking. It is not Reza who drowned, you know. It is Leo."

"Of course it is not Reza," my father says. "I said it was my son, and Reza is not my son."

They shut their mouths and look at him remembering all his formal and informal speeches about how all the children of the Centre were his children. About how in our house all the children belonged to all the adults. How the adults would not differentiate between mine and not-mine. How they would raise us together as one tribe—lift us up and show us the way and protect us from all the cruelties and stupidities of Outside—because this was the way of the wisest peoples of the world.

But now—caught unawares by grief and stripped of all his defences—he says: *that boy was my son and this boy is not.* And it is when a man has been stripped of all his defences that you know he is telling the truth.

How and when and where? we ask ourselves. What we thought was Reality whips off her mask and says, *That was a fairy tale. Actually this is the real me.* We are familiarizing ourselves with the newly revealed contours of her face when Cyril Dragon says, "Neela and I knew each other before … before all this. She was … she worked in my father's house. My father's sisters—my aunties—brought her in from the estate when she was—How old were you, Neela? How old were you when you came to the house on Ipoh Road?"

Neela does not answer. She sits perfectly still. Not one bit of her stirring or stirred. Those bright eyes unblinking. As far as we can see she is not even breathing.

"She was twelve or thirteen maybe," Cyril Dragon says. "My aunties trained her up to do the cooking and cleaning and all that. She worked and worked like a horse but in that house we were both slowly dying of loneliness. We saw it in each other. We recognized it and drew closer to each other for comfort. Who can blame us? When I left she was ... If I had known—I would not have left if I had known. If I had found out just a bit sooner. But I did not know. I did not know she was going to have a baby. Maybe even she ... You yourself did not know, did you, Neela?"

Neela presses her fingertips to her lips as though to stop something from falling out of her mouth. Cyril goes on:

"My aunties threw her out of that house when they found out. She went back to her mother and he—the baby—was born, but then ... even her mother threw her out. She came here because she had nowhere else to go. Nowhere else to go! No home, no money, no family. Who can understand that? Which of you can understand such a thing? I should have ... I could have ... I made a mistake for which no God will ever forgive me. I thought what I was building was more important. I thought I could not devote myself to the cause if I became a normal family man. I could not belong to mankind and also to a wife and a child."

No one says what all of them are thinking in one way or another: *Until someone sexy enough came along. Then you found a way to balance service to mankind with servicing your wife.*

"I did try to do right by the boy," he says as though he might have heard what they were thinking. "I thought, even if he could not know, even if I could not tell him, I could lift him up, I could help him along, I could give him something he would not get Outside, without me. I used to buy him books, I used to teach him just by himself at one time, before I asked George Cubinar to take over, yes or not Neela? And such a bright boy he was, such a joy to teach."

She smiles a wise and trembling smile with half her face. But her smile is not for him nor even for the rest of us. It is a private smile for herself. An inside joke for only the joker.

No one says, *And then just like that you replaced him. With a snap of the fingers and a click of the heels.*

"I ask myself what I should have done differently. You see, once, once there were two of them—two boys like that—everything changed."

I will tell you what you could have done differently, Cyril Dragon. From my safe and comfortable spot thirty years in the future I will tell you.

"They were always ... well of course Leo wanted to impress the new arrival and then they were always competing for something, who knows for what, in that way in which boys always compete. So of course Leo had no use for me anymore. I thought ... I suppose it made everything easier. Just as well, I thought. Just as well they can be friends with each other instead. More natural anyway for children to be with other children. I took the easy way out."

As though a few more private poetry and astronomy lessons might have saved Leo from buggery and shame and suicide.

"But now the time for taking the easy way out is over." His voice is shaking. He's holding himself together just enough to form words. "Now I must face what I did. I must call the police and I must tell them that my son has ended his own life. And when they come I must let them see what they want to see."

No one asks him what he means by that. Each of us has our own ideas of what the police will want to see: the Arabic calligraphy of Allah's name next to the Lord Ganesha painting on the wall. The Bhagavad Gita and the King James Bible and the Talmud and the Quran all lined up on the bookshelf. And of course the lady who answers to Salmah in this house of lunatics.

We cannot consider all the ramifications at this moment because for the first time in our shared lives we are faced with the sight of Cyril Dragon's naked emotions. He is not dripping silent tears onto his shirt; he is not even sobbing. He is howling. He is keening like King David learning of Absalom's death. He has done all his explaining and now his grief is pouring out of him as unmediated sound.

Unpardonable

After the police have gone I go upstairs to stand by Reza's bed. You might think *Look at the foolish bastard of a boy thinking he's going to be forgiven so easily after what he did.* But forgiveness was not my first goal. Before anything else I needed to know. I needed to find the missing piece of the puzzle and pocket it along with all the other pieces. In this way I could own everything that had happened and my suffering would be whole. This is what I cannot locate among the fragments of yesterday: Reza's eyes when I push open the door of the toolshed. I cannot see them. If I do not remedy this then in my memory of that moment my brother's eyes will forever remain as blank as the no-iris whites of Roman sculptures. If you cannot remember the sin then for what do you ask to be forgiven?

A barely perceptible shift in the pattern of Reza's breathing tells me he knows I am here. Yet he does not open his eyes. His eyelids are smooth and pale and so thin I can almost see him looking at me through them.

"Reza," I say.

Not a flicker.

"What did you think?" I say. "When I opened the door like that? Did you think I … I came to punish you on purpose? Did you think I knew?"

Downstairs—almost directly under my feet—Leo's body is slowly seeping river water into the lining of his casket. Beneath the heavy wooden lid he is debloating himself. Those are pearls that were his eyes. These are sausages that were his fingers. Red patches on his hands and feet show where the fish were already starting to nibble. Had they had a bit more time they would have gnawed his eyelids into lace. Even in death Leo would then have been unable to shield his eyes from the inquisitive.

"Reza," I say. "It wasn't my fault. I thought I was only going to show everybody what they all already knew. It was Annabelle Foo's idea to open the door. I only thought I would teach her a lesson. I thought she'd planned this big shocker for Cyril Dragon and I could spoil her glory." *But she knew. That's what I can't bear to tell him. She knew about you and Leo. I can't do it to him: I can't tell him it wasn't an acci-dent.*

His eyelids spring open to show his fever-bright eyes.

"You—you've always been so ... so ... *proud* of yourself, so satisfied with your snooping and spying and carrying tales. You think it makes you so great. But you're nothing but a pathetic little piece of shit."

I will my feet to step backwards slowly one foot at a time *come on now just one step one small step please come on* but no. I've turned to stone. I cannot escape. Now Reza is hoisting himself into a sitting position but not for one second do his eyes leave my face.

"You can try to blame Annabelle Foo now but it's always been you with all your godliness, you minding everybody else's business, you trying to climb straight up to heaven on other people's backs. You think you are sitting at the right hand of not just your wonderful father but God him-self. You always wanted to cause trouble for us. You were always jealous because we knew how to have fun and you didn't. Well now you've caused the biggest trouble of all so I hope you're happy. Are you? Are you happy? Because for sure if this is the kind of thing that pleases your God then you will go straight to heaven when you die. You have offered up a human sacrifice after all. What could be better? Straight to heaven you'll go, Kannu. Straight to heaven. But until you die you can spend the rest of your life thinking about what you did and I hope it will torture you and make you sweat at night. I wish I believed in ghosts because then I could say I hope Leo will come back to haunt you. But failing that I hope your own guilty conscience will poison the rest of your life. Just don't call me your brother anymore. Don't ever call me your brother again."

He slides back down. Turns over onto his stomach and buries his face in his pillow. I am dismissed.

In one day I have now lost two brothers. I will have my whole life to mourn them. My whole life to mourn and to puzzle over God who was supposed to show me Right and Wrong and guide my hand and act through me. And now at last it comes to me: the truth of what Reza has been saying for years. God already knew what would happen at the end. He had not only seen the scene in the toolshed the footprints in the mud the body pulled from the water; he had decreed it. Nothing after all happens without His will. So I must puzzle. I am not Reza, I cannot dust faith off my skin with a chuckle. Somewhere out there is the explanation. With God all things are possible isn't it? X is Y's brother and Y is Z's brother but X and Z are not brothers. In the Scottish tea planter's house there is a boy with two brothers. One of his brothers is dead and the other has disowned him but he can still—with God's help—have two brothers. God can change the future and the past. He can raise the dead, He can make the blind see, He can make the unforgiving forgive. Can't He?

Flower-Name Baby

2024

Returning home one morning from a charitable bolstering visit to Dawood and his dazed women and his now-subdued son, I see police vans and an ambulance clustered outside our building. Afterwards I cannot believe I did not at once guess why they were there, had not seen the evidence in front of my eyes, did I not know what had been unfolding for months and had now reached its culmination. Or maybe *did not know* is an obfuscation of the truth. Because afterwards it occurs to me what everybody else must have been thinking when they saw the commotion and the police vans and the ambulance: *terrorists terrorists terrorists.* That my mind did not go in that direction even for one second just goes to show how much I must have known without ever having admitted it to myself. Maybe there are more ways of knowing than what we are taught in school. There is the kind of knowing where you raise your hand and jump up with the one hot-hot ready-made answer that is the Right answer. But there is also—I now realize—a deep stomach-knowing that does not say its name. That has no one name but twists and turns and slithers along your corridors so that one minute it is a glinting silver coil and then it is a thin black line.

Before the next day's newspaper report the whole apartment building knows who it was. Turns out everybody had been nudging each other and whispering and pointing for months. Wondering why we weren't doing anything. When we were going to send her back to her family. And of course that's what Ani had been trying to say herself. *We've got to send her back.* Only thing is I'd been too stupid to extrapolate the whole truth from her insinuations. And she herself had miscalculated. Got the timing wrong or perhaps been misled by Hana.

A dumped baby in an apartment complex like this one is not an everyday occurrence. Sure, nice girls from good families get into trouble too but the solutions are usually more discreet. A baby wrapped in a cursory tea towel and stuffed in a cheap duffel bag (the zip considerately left half-open) and the whole package dropped off by the dustbins: this scenario understandably leads people to different and more accurate conclusions.

Ani does a brave job of pretending she didn't know. Pacing in the kitchen growling "How could you how could you after everything they've done for you? Blindly we trusted you and this is how you repay us?" Whether it's because Ani bribed her or threatened her or simply because she's too exhausted from giving birth, Hana plays along. Covers her face and weeps and weeps. I don't have the heart to seize Ani by the shoulders and say *Stop this bullshit.* Leave my half-senile mother aside, but there is no way on earth two adult human beings could have failed to notice.

When Ani reaches the end of her dramatic monologue I plant myself in front of them and say, "The question is, what are we going to do now?"

They stare at me like two baby owls in their nest.

"What are we going to do now?" repeats Ani. "What do you mean?"

"For one thing, surely we need to take Hana to hospital to get checked up. I don't even know how—where—she ... where the baby was born. Thank God everything went all right and you are okay, Hana, but we should ... I don't know much about these things but I think we should take you to a doctor just in case."

Hana is shaking her head violently *no no no no* but I force myself to go on before I lose my momentum.

"The other question is: here we are in this house and there in the hospital is that small baby. They are asking people with information to come forward. Surely one of the many neighbours who've been watching Hana all this time is going to very proudly ring up the number they gave. You know what Malaysians are like. So why should we wait for them to turn you in? Shouldn't we go to them ourselves?"

Again that owlish stare.

"But tuan," Ani says, "they will find the baby a good Muslim home. A beautiful newborn baby like that with those big Bangladeshi eyes, there won't be any problem."

Fifteen years Ani has been in this house and now for the first time I look at her and my heart turns to a block of ice.

"A good home?" I say. "You are okay with this, Hana?"

Hana will not look at me of course but I am not going to play the game this time. I am not going to save face.

"This beautiful newborn baby with the big Bangladeshi eyes is *your* baby, Hana! You wrapped her in a dirty cloth and stuffed her in a bag and threw her away. They'll find a home or they'll put her in an orphanage. You're okay with that?"

"Tuan!" Ani says in her gravelly crying-all-night voice. "Please, we beg you, this is not the time."

My feet take a step back without my permission: that is how horrified I am.

"You're right," I say. "You're right, this is not the time. Maybe there never will be a good time. You're right. It's not my business."

I go to my room like a child sent to bed without supper. But I don't go to sleep. How could I? I am still recoiling from their words. *A good Muslim home.* A good Muslim home we won't know a thing about. My mind—my whole body—is on fire as it hasn't been since the night after I learned my father was dead. I sit on the edge of the bed knuckles white blood gurgling loud enough to drown out all the sounds of the world. When I close my eyes the earth tilts and pitches like I've drunk a bottle of whisky in one gulp. *Calm down calm down. Think think think!*

But in the end this is not about thinking. This is about feeling.

You must be telling yourselves—now that you have heard nearly my whole story—that I've never been good at feeling the correct feelings. Or even that I am incapable. That I'm having to close my eyes and say *Calm down calm down. Feel feel feel!* and that in fact feeling is a taller order and far less realistic a goal for me than thinking at such a time. *Bastard has no heart at all, so with what is he supposed to feel?* you must be thinking. And maybe there is some truth to that. Maybe I have lived a cold and unfeeling life up to this point. But tonight I feel and feel and feel until I might burst and my blood blooms across the wide skies like a giant African daisy. I cannot stop feeling. I can do nothing else.

In the morning I get up and brush my teeth and leave the house before anyone else is stirring. I take a taxi all the way for maximum speed. Never mind the expense. Some occasions demand it. I've got the newspaper cutting in my wallet. I know exactly whom to ask for at the hospital and where to go.

I can hear Mama's voice in my ear whispering *Mad, mad, who's the mad one now? Gone bonkers, poor Kannu.*

I haven't gone mad Mama. I'm about to make the sanest decision of my whole life. I am teetering on the brink of sanity and let me tell you it is so perfect and so utterly redeeming that every icy breath I manage to gulp down up here is a shock to my grimy old lungs. Oh feel it feel feel feel the great gusty wind of it whipping about my face and knocking me senseful: couldn't we all use this kick in the pants at some point in our lives? To get up and *do* something instead of drooling comatose before the babies starving and drowning and getting bombed and gassed on our TV screens: tell me now which of us is mad and which sane?

The baby is in the nursery with all the other babies as though she too is a baby born to a normal family who loves her more than life itself. As though she too will soon go home to one-hundred-per-cent-cotton singlets and oil massages and tiny mittens to stop her from scratching her own face bloody. What to say about a one-day-old baby? The unearthly ancient face still suspended between this world and that other world. The unseeing all-seeing eyes. (Are they big Bangladeshi eyes or amygdaloid Indonesian ones? Time will tell.) The fierce damning frown the indignant fists. The sadness of the whole crumpled mass: how can a person enter the world already so used and exhausted? And yet on the other hand the bright newness. The downy skin. The will to survive, that nothing—not the smelly tea towel or the hours at the foot of the dustbins—could extinguish. I take a picture of her on my phone. I run a little finger down a cheek and she opens her mouth. Her skin like water: close your eyes and you're not sure you're touching anything at all.

Someone—a doctor or a nurse?—is saying close to my ear, "We cannot simply release the baby like that today. We would need ... You say you know the mother? Normally we would ask ..."

And so on and on in an aeroplane drone. What does it matter? What needs to be done will be done. We have no choice in the matter. This innocent barely begun life demands it. Look at the force of it and tell me that it is not more powerful than the very revolutions of our planet in space. And then I realize that even Ani and Hana have no say in this matter. Let them wash their hands of her if they want to. Who am I to impose my decisions on them? What will be will be with or without them. All Hana has to do is to come forward and claim the baby. After that her life is hers. Let her go back to Indonesia. Once she signs on the dotted line I will need nothing else from her.

Ani considers my offer and makes a decision on Hana's behalf. She will adopt the baby as Hana's auntie. She will take Hana home and come back to us. Mama will tell us we are all mad. And she does.

"Ya Allah, what do you know about taking care of a small baby, Kannu? What does any of us know? I'm the only one who's done it and I hardly remember it myself!"

At one time I might have said or at least thought, *How can you remember what you only pretended to do? Reza was taking care of you by the time he could crawl and me you left to my own devices.* And so on and so forth but that was then and this is now.

"You don't have to remember anything, Mama," I say.

Both of us know I am not just talking about the care and feeding of small babies. She blinks at me like some trusting beast. Blind. Uncomprehending. I go on.

"It must be quite common, people who've never taken care of babies doing it for the first time I mean. It's not as though every new mother and every new father in the world has had extensive practice with other people's babies."

"But I'm seventy-five years old!" she cries. "I can't even help you!"

"It's true, I'm embarking on this adventure late in life. But better late than never isn't it, Mama? To love now or never to love at all: is there even a choice to be made?"

"Kannu, Kannu, it's such a big responsibility, you're not thinking straight! I don't know what's happening to you!"

I don't know what's happening to me either, Mama. Any more than a caterpillar knows what's happening to it inside the chrysalis or a tadpole understands the sprouting of its arms and legs. But it doesn't matter what you think. It doesn't matter what anyone thinks. Because this baby this jewel frog this bruised rose apple this wobbly velvet fawn will crack open my hard heartshell and will sweep me up into the sea of life rather than out of it yes she will drown me alive. I will fall into the water and find my lungs have turned into gills. I will grow webbed skin between my fingers and toes. I will discover the workings of organs I did not know my body contained.

I will have my happily-ever-after at last. Nothing else is possible now. *Off his rocker* you're thinking. *Poor chap is in for a terrible letdown a seeping sinking sagging as the years pass a slow but sure disappointment or somewhere down the road a broken heart with a bang.*

No. Those are your lives—tarnished with all the small mistakes you are too lazy and complacent to avoid because you have only ever known the relative contentment of lives that bob along inoffensively—and this one is mine. Bright as a sea of new pennies. Bursting with potential like a bed of freshly ploughed earth. I will make no mistakes. My baby—for she is mine in every real sense—will be cosseted in the softest cleanest nappies and fed the best milk money can buy. She will be burped and bedded without the faintest hint of a tear. Her first teeth her first words her first steps will all be celebrated in unrestrained wholehearted joy as though she were the only baby in the history of the world. Which in a way she will be. The baby of babies. Baby Jesus himself will not have embodied such newness such purity such clean-slatery nor will he have known such adulation. She will be applauded and cheered on and held up every step of the way. She will never be unseen or unheard. She will never feel second best. From the day she enters my house to the day she leaves it she will know only Love perfect Love. It will cushion her when she falls. It will sing in her ear when she skins her knee. When she lays herself down to sleep she will feel it under her like the downiest of pillows and over her like the finest of blankets. She will see it in the dark last thing at night before her eyelids droop. All night it will fill her head leaving no space for a single nightmare throughout her childhood. First thing in the morning when those eyelids spring open she will see it again: Love so perfect the air itself is shot through with it. A colour for which we have no word because no one else can see it. She will have to name it herself. One day we'll ask her. "Tell us," we'll say and she will open her mouth and release the word—clear and round as a single bubble between a baby's Cupid lips—as though it has waited all those years on her tongue.

But how can I begin to capture all this for Mama now? To her I can only say, "I don't know what's happening to me either, but should I let that stop me? Sometimes it's precisely when we don't know what's happening to us that we should let it happen."

"Ya Allah, ya Allah," Mama groans. Turns away closes her eyes covers her face with one hand but so what? She has the rest of her life to get used to what's happening to me.

"Why don't you help me choose a name, Mama?"

I sink down to my haunches before her as though I am asking for her blessing. I bend my head and feel that slow blind blinking over me in the silence. Without looking up I continue.

"What about a flower name? A nice old-fashioned Malay flower name. A name like girls used to have those days when you were small. Mawar. Melur. Melati. What do you think?"

Above me Mama exhales long and slow. I can feel her close her eyes again but this time it is different.

That same evening I pull out Reza's twenty-year-old email address. You must believe me when I tell you that my intention is not to shock him or to crow: *Look! Finally I have something you don't. My life is going to be Meaningful in ways you cannot fathom.* A year a month even a week ago I would not have put such small-mindedness past myself. But I am not that person now. And besides Reza might have a brood of his own already: who knows? Probably people in hippy vegan co-ops spawn joyfully and frequently. All that free loving, natural living etc. Is this even his email address anymore? Maybe. Maybe not. But at the very least someone will remember Reza. And they will tell me try here or here or here. And I will follow the trail. Follow it until I can say to him: I have come to right my wrongs at last. A star has burst open in my chest and I have more light than I could ever need. I am reaching inside myself and filling my fists with light and holding it out to you Reza in a bouquet: Come. Here is my sorry. Not a please-forgive-me-because-I-am-afraid-and-I-need-you sorry. A pure and clear sorry that wants nothing in return: hold it up to the light and you will see no speck or cloud in it. I am sorry because I hurt you. I am sorry because I was wrong. And here too is love at last. Not jealousy. Not a painful for-your-own-good love. Not a lying-vying competitive love. I mean real love. Not the perfect Love I can only give my daughter oh no no I have to save that up for her but this other love is still real in its own right. Unselfish and true. Because we are brothers. Because once we were babies and look, look at what a baby is! Is it possible not to love anyone who was once a baby? Now—at this late stage in life—I finally understand: when you are truly happy you are generous with your love. You don't keep a ledger. You don't keep a list of who's naughty and who's nice. You don't keep account of who is receiving more than you. You want only to give. So take, take. Don't hold back. Take as much as you want. I am not afraid of running out. There is always more. After today there is tomorrow. The rest of our lives a wide golden road unspooling before us. We are only young after all. Look at this tiny baby. I am attaching a picture. Look at her and see: we are beginning again. All things are beginning again. The world is new. Touch a finger to its thin silky skin. Feel the life pulsing just beneath. Twitching muscles. Blood beating in a million hairline vessels. Close your eyes and breathe it in: this infinite delicate invincible brand-new world.

POLITICAL BACKGROUND

This is a work of fiction, but the lives of its central characters are shaped by two watershed real-life events in the history of modern Malaysia.

The first of these is the race riots that began on May 13th, 1969, and laid the foundation of the deeply unequal political and economic system still in place today.

Under the British, immigration and the importation of indentured labour had created large ethnic Chinese and Indian minorities in Malaya. At the time of independence in 1957, the appointed leaders of these minority communities agreed to accept Article 153 of the Malayan Constitution, guaranteeing the special position and privileges of the country's ethnic Malay majority in exchange for citizenship for minorities. (Malaysia would not exist until 1963, when Sabah, Sarawak, and Singapore joined the Federation, from which Singapore seceded in 1965.) Tensions between the largely urban Chinese minority, perceived to be in control of the country's economy, and the largely rural Malay majority erupted regularly: in 1957, 1959, 1964 (leading to the secession of Singapore), and 1967. In the 1969 general election, opposition parties made significant gains against the ruling Alliance coalition. Within the United Malays National Organisation (UMNO)—the party representing Malay interests in that coalition—a chauvinist faction cast the opposition's victory parades and celebrations as a provocation and an attack on Malay political power. Evidence suggests that this faction orchestrated the riots, whipping up fear and resentment and bringing rural Malays into Kuala Lumpur, in order to be able to oust then Prime Minister Tunku Abdul Rahman, whom they perceived as being too friendly with the Chinese and insufficiently committed to Malay interests. Estimates of the death toll range from 196 (according to official police figures) to more than ten times that number (according to foreign diplomatic sources). In the aftermath of the riots, Tunku Abdul Rahman stepped down and an overtly Malay nationalist government took over, putting into place the New Economic Policy (NEP). Sometimes described as an "affirmative action" programme, the NEP aggressively favours the Malay majority (and in theory, but less so in practice, the country's indigenous peoples) in public-sector employment, higher education, home ownership, land access, banking/wealth acquisition, and many other areas. Among the first and strongest voices to call for such a policy was Mahathir Mohamad, who, in his book *The Malay Dilemma* (1970), argued for the government to concentrate economic and political power in the hands of the Malay to prevent a takeover by other races, in particular the Chinese. Rising quickly through the UMNO ranks in the 1970s, Mahathir became Prime Minister of Malaysia for the first time in 1981.

For the twenty-two years of his first term (he was Prime Minister again from 2018 through 2020), Mahathir was an authoritarian leader, quashing dissent, profoundly undermining the independence of the judiciary and the police, and putting into place agencies to police the practice of Islam and secure its place in society. The separation of religion and state, which had never been complete, was effectively abrogated. In 1985, a siege on the compound of an Islamic sect in the northern town of Memali resulted in fourteen deaths. On the 27th of October, 1987, Mahathir launched Operation Lalang, claiming that the failure to take such drastic action would result in another May 13th.

A total of 119 people—opposition politicians, activists, journalists, religious leaders, and others—were arrested under the Internal Security Act over the course of the following month. Newspapers were shut down and police powers increased. Some have argued that press freedom, freedom of expression, and freedom of conscience in Malaysia never fully recovered from this assault.

GLOSSARY

(BM = Bahasa Malaysia; C = Cantonese; T = Tamil)

ANAK HARAM (BM): an illegitimate child

ASTAGHFIRULLAH (Arabic): literally "I seek forgiveness from Allah"; used as an expression of shame or disapproval

BALIK KAMPUNG (BM): to return to the village (*balik*: to return; *kampung*: village). The phrase is not only derogatory; urban dwellers "balik kampung" before holidays and festivals.

BUMIPUTERA (BM, derived from Sanskrit): literally "sons of the soil"; a Malaysian term for ethnic Malays and (in theory) other indigenous peoples

CINCAU (BM, derived from Standard Chinese): Chinese grass jelly, usually consumed in a sweet beverage

CINTA PANDANGAN PERTAMA (BM): love at first sight

FLER: Malaysian English colloquial spelling/ pronunciation of "fellow"

FREEHAIR: contemporary term for a Muslim woman who does not cover her hair

GORENG PISANG, UBI, CEMPEDAK (BM): banana, tapioca/yam/cassava, and cempedak (a fruit related to breadfruit) fritters, a popular teatime snack

HUM SUP (C): literally "salty and wet"; perverted, dirty-minded, lustful, or sexually aroused

IKAN BILIS (BM): dried salted anchovies

JAKIM: acronym for Jabatan Kemajuan Islam Malaysia, the Malaysian Department of Islamic Development

JAMBAN (BM): colloquial word for toilet

KACANG PUTEH (BM): literally "white nuts"; assorted savoury snacks including (but not limited to) deep-fried spiced chickpea dough; roasted peanuts, broad beans, green peas, and lentils; tapioca chips

KELING (BM): a derogatory term for an ethnic Indian (especially South Indian) person

KERIS (BM): a traditional dagger indigenous to the Malay Archipelago and several other Southeast Asian countries, now largely used for ceremonial purposes and as a symbol of Malay nationalism

MAHRAM (Arabic): in Islamic law, unmarriageable kin, i.e. family members with whom one is not permitted to have sexual relations. Women are allowed to uncover their hair in the company of those with whom they have a mahram relationship.

MAKCIK (BM): auntie, used to refer to or address any woman older than the speaker

MAMAK (BM) or **THULKAN** (T): a Muslim of South Indian descent

MAT SALLEH (BM): colloquial term of uncertain etymology for a white person

MATA SEPET (BM): slit-eyed

NAATUKARAN (T): literally "man of the land," a native, a local, a Malay

NASI LEMAK (BM): coconut rice, commonly served with deep-fried ikan bilis and sambal

ORANG PUTEH (BM), frequently shortened to *omputeh* in colloquial speech: white person

PAAVAM (T): a loser, a pathetic figure

PENGLIPUR LARA (BM): a teller of (often comic) folk tales interspersed with traditional Malay forms of poetry

PERKIM (BM): Pertubuhan Kebajikan Islam Malaysia, the Malaysian Islamic Charity Foundation, a nominally nongovernmental Muslim missionary organization

PONDAN (BM): a derogatory term used to refer to trans-sexuals, transvestites, and effeminate men

SAMBAL (BM): a pungent condiment/sauce made from chilis, spices, herbs, and aromatics

TANDAS (BM): standard word for toilet

TOK DALANG (BM): the master puppeteer and storyteller in a wayang kulit (shadow-puppet play)

TUDUNG (BM): a hijab, a head covering worn in public by some Muslim women

TUKANG KARUT (BM): a group leader in a competitive form of Malay singing and storytelling. The tukang karut is expected to incorporate socially relevant themes and traditional poetry in an artful way into his performance.

UMNO: the United Malays National Organisation, the Malay nationalist party of the Barisan Nasional coalition (known as the Alliance Party before 1973) that has governed Malaysia for all but three years since the country's independence from the British in 1957. UMNO is the dominant member of this coalition; its goals are to protect the interests and the special position of ethnic Malays and to uphold, defend, and expand the power of Islam in Malaysia.

WAYANG KULIT (BM): shadow-puppet play

1MALAYSIA: a national campaign launched by Prime Minister Najib Razak in 2010 to promote inter-ethnic harmony and national unity. The campaign is much mocked by Malaysians, who perceive it as yet another example of smooth talk over substance.

Acknowledgments

Thank you to the many people who believed in this novel during the long years that preceded its publication. To Jérôme Bouchaud, for his relentless support for my work and for his commitment to bringing our many Asian stories to readers beyond Asia. To everyone else at Agence Astier-Pécher. To Judith Uyterlinde for getting it; to Robin Shimanto Reza and Lydia Unsworth for their attention, rigour, and enthusiasm. To the friends who read earlier drafts with so much generosity and imagination: Tash Aw, Amrita Narayanan, Gareth Richards, Marc de Faoite, YZ Chin. To V. V. Ganeshananthan, for being the other half of what was the world's best Tamil Lady writing group while it lasted. To Nawaaz Ahmed, for the solidarity and the long conversations about art and beauty; race and publishing; life and love and memory. To Ayesha Pande, who championed this book for so long against all odds. And, of course, to Rob, Rumika, and Juniali, for the considerable patience that living with a writer requires.

Book Club Discussion Guides are available on our website.

On the Design

As book design is an integral part of the reading experience, we would like to acknowledge the work of those who shaped the form in which the story is housed.

Tessa van der Waals (Netherlands) is responsible for the cover design, cover typography, and art direction of all World Editions books. She works in the internationally renowned tradition of Dutch Design. Her bright and powerful visual aesthetic maintains a harmony between image and typography and captures the unique atmosphere of each book. She works closely with internationally celebrated photographers, artists, and letter designers. Her work has frequently been awarded prizes for Best Dutch Book Design.

The author's name on the cover allows Espoir to put its beautiful lowercase *a* on display. Wahyu Hadi Yuana's versatile and elegant Espoir fonts were inspired by late-nineteenth-century engravings. The colors of the writing on the cover complement the image of *Host and Vector*, a large contemporary oil painting by artist Alexis Rockman, which he made inspired by and based on a trip to Guyana. There is a naturalist aspect to it, but Rockman's meticulous representations and saturated colors also conjure the hyperreal spectacle of science-fiction films, portending a world on the brink of possible destruction.

The cover has been edited by lithographer Bert van der Horst of BFC Graphics (Netherlands).

Suzan Beijer (Netherlands) is responsible for the typography and careful interior book design of all World Editions titles.

The text on the inside covers and the press quotes are set in Circular, designed by Laurenz Brunner (Switzerland) and published by Swiss type foundry Lineto.

All World Editions books are set in the typeface Dolly, specifically designed for book typography. Dolly creates a warm page image perfect for an enjoyable reading experience. This typeface is designed by Underware, a European collective formed by Bas Jacobs (Netherlands), Akiem Helmling (Germany), and Sami Kortemäki (Finland). Underware are also the creators of the World Editions logo, which meets the design requirement that 'a strong shape can always be drawn with a toe in the sand.'